'*The Lost Detective* employs many of the conventions of a detective novel but, in Latimer's hands, the genre is elevated to that very rare beast - a literary page-turner. The novel is so beautifully written - measured, reflective, elegiac. It is as much a meditation on grief and loss as a gripping detective story, and Latimer skilfully manages to make the two work side by side, without detracting from either one. I can't wait to see what she does next.'

Bridget Walsh, author of *The Tumbling Girl*

'*The Lost Detective* is a novel of confluences, a beautifully written and finely poised story of loss and longing but also of redemption. Its setting, in the enigmatic and endangered East Anglian landscape of the Brecks, perfectly underscores the human mysteries the novel explores. A notable debut and a very good read.'

Sarah Bower, author of *Lines and Shadows*

'Luminous, haunting, humane. Set across the fields and rivers of Norfolk and Suffolk, it's a mystery with a beating heart: forensic in its detail, propulsive in its plotting, and tender in the way it watches people try, fail, and try again to love and to tell the truth. The writing is effortlessly vivid and the tension tightens with every page as past and present collide. A beautifully crafted, deeply affecting story about loss, obsession, and the small, stubborn ember of hope that refuses to die.'

Ashley Hickson-Lovence, author of *The 392*

'*The Lost Detective* is not only an impressive crime novel with a great sense of place but a beautifully-written evocation of loss, grief and, ultimately, hope.'

Trevor Wood, author of *The Silent Killer*

The Lost Detective

Elspeth Latimer

The Lost Detective
Copyright © Elspeth Latimer, 2025

Cover design: © Natty Peterkin
Typesetting: Natty Peterkin

ISBN 978-1-912665-52-5

First published 25th September 2025 by Story Machine.

Folly House,
Harts Lane,
Bawburgh,
NR9 3LS

www.storymachines.co.uk

Set in Garamond; used under licence.

Printed and bound in the UK by 4Edge

**Story
Mach\ne**

Dedicated to my family
and the landscape of the Brecks

4th July 2001

Alice shifted in the armchair, felt a prickle of velvet through her thin summer dress. The scent of lilies hung in the air. A tracery of plasterwork arched across the high ceiling. She watched the two women sip gin martinis from glasses with gilded stems. They were debating wallpaper, which colour to choose, but Alice barely listened. The room was awash with brightness, sunlight flooding through the tall windows. This had been a chapel, centuries ago. Gothic? Words escaped her these days. Fear, on the other hand, never went away.

Her gaze strayed outside. 'Maybe I should just check on...'

'Relax,' Lydia said, 'the pram's right there. Trust me, children are indestructible.'

Catherine smiled, saying, 'They always survive, unlike the mothers. My Emily is such a tyrant.'

Yelling from the garden, and raucous laughter. Alice hoped their games would not wake Felix. On the table was a glass of mineral water. It tasted of salt and did not quench her thirst. Fabrics were discussed, then Lydia complained about her son Jack. A clock chimed, in the depths of the house. A door slammed, somewhere upstairs.

The wind? Or those noisy children. Alice peered out the windows, blinking at the glare. She had been obliged, earlier, to shake hands with Jack and Emily. Mud on the boy's knees, twigs in his hair. The girl had stared at her, blank-faced. They were ambassadors from a race of small beings who harboured secrets. And Jack had seemed so solid, everything done with force.

Her own son would be different. Alice pictured Felix all grown up, and it took her breath away. Tall, a casual grace, a shy smile. Then he was gone, leaving her bereft. 'I have to—'

'Ali, do sit down,' Lydia said. 'I want your opinion on these.'

A large book of wallpaper samples was thrust into her lap. As she laid a hand on the burgundy flock pattern, Alice felt her mouth go dry.

Urgent footsteps in the hall. The door burst open and the boy stopped on the carpet. Jack frowned at Alice, rubbed his nose with a fist. Then he turned to his mother, saying, 'It's hungry.'

'What are you talking about?' Lydia said.

'The baby.'

The book thudded to the floor as Alice leapt up. 'Did you give him anything?' She ran into the hall, heading for the back door.

Lydia was behind her, calling, 'Of course not. Jack knows better than that.'

Alice raced toward the pram and pulled Emily away.

'Ouch,' the girl said. 'You hurt me. She hurt me.'

Felix was awake, arms and legs waving like he was learning to swim. Alice picked him up, heart pounding.

'Sorry,' she said, glaring at Jack and Emily, 'but you mustn't touch babies.'

'I'm sure the children weren't doing any harm,' Lydia said. 'Emily was just tickling him, weren't you.'

The girl chewed the end of her ponytail, then she and Jack ran off down the garden.

Alice watched them go, feeling weak with panic. Felix was restless, sucking his fingers.

'I assume you brought a bottle,' Lydia said.

'I'm feeding him myself.'

'How admirably Mother Earth. Bring the baby, we've abandoned poor Catherine long enough.'

'I was hoping—' Alice glanced at the house. 'Is there somewhere quiet I might use?'

Felix in her arms, she followed Lydia to a room off the hall. A single chair, piles of boxes. A metal rail, crammed with garments in zipped plastic bags. The woman left, shutting the door.

8

Alice stood there, still shaken. She looked at her son, the curve of his cheek, the glimmer of tiny fingernails. This was so new to her, the responsibility. Alice held him tight. No one warned her it was possible to feel so much love.

More shouting from outside, but further away. Were Jack and Emily playing by the river? Alice pictured them knee-deep in water. It was not safe. Should she say something to Lydia and Catherine? They would laugh, then tell her again, *children are indestructible. They always survive.*

The years go by, but that day never ends. So many awful moments. This one kills her every time.

Alice stands in the garden. There is a sharp smell and warm liquid fills her shoe. Faces staring, all of them worried. This is not real. Children survive.

Someone touches her arm. His clothes are black. His mouth is making noises.

Alice shakes her head.

The words come again.

Missing. Gone. No trace.

She looks at her hands.

21 years later

Chapter 1

Dan parked in the cul-de-sac and stared through the windscreen. The sky was an empty blue. A rush of sound startled him – swifts shrieking as they swooped past – then silence once more. He often brought flowers for Beth, irises, gladioli, but at the shops earlier there were none she would like. Dan got out of the car and walked up the path, went inside. Closed the door, hand trembling. From the cupboard under the stair, he retrieved the green canister. Then he placed it in the bare room and sat nearby, his heart beating.

The house accused him, as it did every visit. *What are you doing here?*

There was no answer. Dan glanced at the white walls, the chipboard floor, the fake fireplace, the narrow stair, the front door without a lobby. All corners cut to make this miniature home. Everything new but showing signs of neglect. A few cracks in the plasterboard, a small blot of damp. Paid for by the monthly mortgage and still waiting to be lived in.

Their hopes had met with devastation. Eyes closed, he saw the litany of her life in the days leading up. The pages in Beth's diary, a shopping list in her bag, the emails that spoke with her voice. Text and Facebook messages to a host of friends. None of these explained what she was doing on Magdalen Street.

Then, in the aftermath, the protocols of tragedy. They kept hold of her for two weeks, on a steel trolley inside a chilled cabinet. An enquiry was initiated into her death, documents signed and authorised by people he knew. No longer his colleagues, not since he left the police service.

His gaze rested on the canister of ashes.

Beth died. He lost her. With each waking moment, he lost her. Some nights she came back to him, fully alive and unaware, as if no one had told her she was dead. Dan would join the pretence, but even in his dreaming state he knew it was a lie, and he hated himself for deceiving Beth. For not telling her she was gone. Did he not owe her that one truth?

Dan returned to the car and made himself breathe. So easy to forget how. Cassie would call this a panic attack. She had been his partner, back when he was a DI. They still met for Wednesday drinks and sometimes talked about grief. Seven months on, he knew she was edging toward the word *closure*.

He shook his head and started the engine. Driving soothed him, it filled the countless moments. No requirement to feel and always well within the speed limit. The town became wide fields of wheat, then onto the A11 for a coffee from the petrol station. Back via a narrow lane through woods, trees arching overhead. Dan drained his cup while waiting for the barrier to lift on the level crossing.

At Summerlands he found a space in the car park. Bulky caravans squatted on the slopes, either side of winding tracks. Not yet peak season, the site was full of young families and older couples. A thin veil of smoke drifted from a BBQ. Two small boys were dropping stones into a tin can. People chatting, dogs racing about. The bustle and activity were a comfort, but Dan was aware of watching from afar. A spectator.

Taking the outer path, he headed for Mrs Faulkner's bungalow. Why had she summoned him to her home? Their conversations usually happened in the reception area, surrounded by a barrage of notices about Calor gas cylinders, cycle routes in Breckland, day trips to the Broads, a walking tour of Peddars Way, phone numbers for doctors, vets, hairdressers and Silverline Taxis, Hari's firm.

Dan paused at the gate, thinking of the difference between provisional and permanent. Mrs Faulkner never asked how long he planned on being here. He liked this about her, the lack of questions. When Dan was not driving for Hari, he did odd jobs at Summerlands and handled security, in exchange for rental on a caravan that had seen better days.

Heat radiated from the gravel and he blinked. All this came about through a series of make-do measures. After the accident. Dan had so many words for what happened to Beth, none of them adequate. There was an antiseptic distance to the term accident, something clinical that was nobody's fault. But it was someone's fault. Cassie had no right to tell him he should stop obsessing and *let go*.

The door opened with a loud, 'What's got into you today?' Mrs Faulkner frowned. 'I could see you muttering to yourself.'

Dan smiled, apologetic.

Mrs Faulkner was mid-forties, a decade older than him but it seemed more. She was pointing at his boots now. 'Those stay outside.'

'The Norfolk welcome.'

With a laugh, she ushered him inside. Dan followed her to the living room, the low ceilings a reminder of his height. He sat on a green sofa, felt the hardness of unforgiving foam.

'Working last night?' she said.

'Got back at two. Airport run.'

'Easy money. Maybe you can start paying rent.'

Mrs Faulkner was teasing him, but Dan was too tired for this game. 'You wanted to see me.'

'No time for chit-chat?'

'You don't do chit-chat.'

She laughed. 'I worry about you, Daniel Hennessy.'

'And I worry about you too.' *As if.* Dan had long ago realised that the future belonged to the Mrs Faulkners. They had been waiting in the wings for millennia, these ruthlessly capable women.

The room was warm and his mind drifted.

'Daniel. Daniel. I'm talking to you.'

Another coffee was needed. 'Sorry.'

'I was telling you about a resident on Primrose Drive. Unit 16. Arrived end of April.'

Dan frowned. 'Single guy. Bit of an oddball.'

'His name's John Strang. He seems to have disappeared.'

'Gone missing?'

'More like done a runner, owing two weeks' rent. Story was, he was waiting to be paid for a job. Kept saying he'd bring the money.'

'When did you last see him?' Dan said.

'Fortnight ago. In the shop? I never actually spoke to the man. No doubt he avoided me because he knew I wouldn't cut him any slack. Samantha is a soft target. When she told me Strang was late on his payments, I went to have a word with him. Never there during the day so I tried evenings. Light on, but no reply. And for the past week not even that. As in, he appears to have left Summerlands.'

'I didn't know you were having trouble.'

'I'm a big girl, Daniel. I managed well enough before you came along. On Monday I put an invoice under his door, itemising what he owed plus a surcharge. Yesterday was the deadline.'

'Did Strang leave any of his stuff behind?'

Mrs Faulkner picked at a seam on her denim skirt. 'How should I know?'

Dan felt he was being told a lie.

'Anyway,' she said, 'your job is to recover the debt. Maybe you'll find a handy bank statement or letter. Everything else goes to the dump.'

'Understood.'

Mrs Faulkner peered out the window. 'I imagine the place is less than sanitary, if his clothes are anything to go by.'

'Did Strang have a car?' Dan said.

'No vehicle registration in my records, no proper address either. Told Samantha he wasn't sure how long he'd be staying. Offered to pay fortnightly in cash. Yes, I know what you're thinking.'

'I'm not thinking anything.'

'Well I certainly am.' She sighed. 'Samantha was supposed to be helping me expand the business. My hope is she'll learn from her mistakes.' Mrs Faulkner stared at the mantlepiece.

Dan waited, unsure if his presence was still needed.

After a minute, she turned to him with a half-smile. 'This funny thing happened when I was at the hospital.'

'Oh?' He wondered why she was telling him, as they rarely spoke of their private lives.

'I'm in the waiting room and my name gets called, so I go over to the nurse. But then this other woman starts saying *she's* Mrs Faulkner and the appointment is for her. I thought for some ghastly moment this was my ex-husband's second wife. My ex was a livestock auctioneer. Probably still is, for all I know. I had this sudden vision of how cheated he'd feel. Furious at having married women who were not from a good line. A couple of heifers always needing the vet.'

'Is that how you see yourself?' Dan said.

'I was aiming for comic effect. Apparently this other woman was Falconer spelt like the bird of prey. Not the second wife after all. But a weird experience, wouldn't you say?'

'You kept your married name,' he said.

'What?'

'After the divorce. You decided not to change your surname.'

Her body stiffened. 'I had my reasons.'

Mrs Faulkner gave Dan a look that caught him by surprise. Not bitterness over the marriage, but an aching sadness.

She reached something off the table and threw it at him.

Dan snatched it from the air. A small key.

Mrs Faulkner stood up. 'Glad to see you aren't totally comatose.'

'This Strang, were there complaints from other residents?'

'None.'

'Why didn't you mention him before?'

'What exactly would I have said to you? That he gave Samantha the creeps? Empty his caravan and bring me the missing rent. And if you see Strang, escort him to the gate. Use force if you have to. There's something not—' She glared at Dan, breathing hard. *'Just get rid of him.'*

Chapter 2

Dan had always lived in the Brecks, a hinterland that reached from south Norfolk across the border into Suffolk. Rural, made up of fields, forest, heath and fen. A place of shallow undulation and long dry summers, of grass singed yellow by drought, with sandy soil full of sharp flints. A seasonal land of foggy autumns, reluctant winters, and blackthorn-scented springs. Farm after farm, villages and towns, but no cities. Breadth and distance and sky and stacked clouds and five-mile vistas that measured the curvature of the earth. Time wandered in and got lost, last century or the one before. Outdated attitudes too, which Dan fought against. Timber-frame houses, pink, cream or white, low-slung cottages, thatched roofs, red pantiles. Handwritten notices, *Pullets for sale*. Vintage petrol stations, old corner shops, A-roads and no motorways. Vast blackened barns, subsiding under corrugated iron. Short rows of red-brick houses, next to dog-leg turnings in the middle of nowhere. Hectares of wheat, barley, sugar beet and asparagus. Fields divided by long lines of Scots pines on a slow march, their twisted limbs etched against the sky. Narrow lanes with deep ditches either side, meandering rivers, flint-stone churches, overgrown graveyards. Reed beds and hedgerows and huddled woods. Foxgloves and rusty bracken, gnarled trees shrouded in ivy. Dragonflies, swallows, swifts, buzzards. Muntjac, badgers, pheasants, hares. Fritillaries, brimstone butterflies.

An unhurried landscape of small mercies and unobvious beauty. Dan loved the Brecks. This was home, more so than any building he had lived in. Was that why he said yes to the caravan at Summerlands? Close to the land, close to where he grew up.

Far enough away from Norwich and the street where Beth was killed.

With a start, Dan woke up. Peering round, he recognised the laundry room at Summerlands. Two residents had arrived while he slept, both elderly, sitting well apart on the row of red plastic chairs. The machines were churning, making a background hum. Soporific, and he blinked, still struggling to rouse himself. The air smelled of washing powder. Dan massaged his right shoulder, which ached, after six hours of driving with no break. His mind went back to this morning's conversation. So far, Dan's duties for Mrs Faulkner had been minimal, and 'Security Adviser' was a title on the website rather than anything involving much input.

A beep came from the vast tumble drier, announcing that the cycle was complete. Dan was placing his basket on the floor when Cassie called. With the phone in one hand, he listened to her while pulling warm clothes out of the drum. She was apologising for the short notice, saying the regular babysitter had let her down. A Saturday evening, and Dan had no place else to be.

'There's free food in it for you,' she said with a laugh. 'I don't imagine you want to partake of Archie's chicken nuggets, but there's a ready meal in the fridge – Prawn Bhuna, Sainsbury's Taste the Difference. Tempting, huh? You okay to come straight round?'

Supper took a while, as Archie was a great talker for someone so small. After, Dan helped him clean his teeth, then they played a game where the boy ranked his dinosaurs in order of preference. It was nearly eight-thirty by the time Dan tucked him into bed and came downstairs. He turned on the television, blinked at the screen, then switched it off. Cassie was always recommending Netflix shows for him to 'binge', but he could not tolerate the onslaught of images or the unreality. Dan sat on the sofa, unsure what to do with himself. His gaze went to the coffee table. Stacks of magazines, including *Scientific*

American, a legacy from when Archie's father was still on the scene.

Dan got out his phone, opened Classic FM, but the music was too plaintive and he closed the app. He glanced at the toys heaped in the corner, next to Cassie's kettlebells. She had been in a strange mood when he arrived, earlier. Dark eyes darting about. Slightly wired. His friend would never take drugs. Both of them had dealt with too many broken lives and dead bodies to think narcotics were the answer. But something was definitely up with Cassie. A nervousness unsuited to a night out with 'the girls', a long story about whose birthday it was. And too much enthusiasm in her explanation of Archie's bedtime rituals, all of which he knew. 'Don't forget socks or he'll do his banshee act screaming about cold feet.'

Clearly, Cassie had been trying to stop other words escaping. Dan picked a *Scientific American* off the pile, and leafed through it. Maybe she was going on a date but did not want to say, because of his own 'situation'. He skimmed the photographs, the columns of earnest text, then shook his head. No, pity was not Cassie's thing. Dan had always been grateful for her no-nonsense approach. Turning the pages, an article near the end caught his eye, 'Covid-19 Quiets the Earth'. Lockdown caused a drop in seismic readings across the globe. Scientists had not anticipated that human activity could penetrate to those depths. Dan swallowed. Laid the magazine aside. Felt the light dimming.

Beth, the day of the accident, a tremor passing through the earth's crust. 4.06 p.m.

Did a needle flicker deep underground?

They told him *death was instant*. Meant as a kindness but nothing softened the brutality. It was Cassie who came to him with the news. He had been in the Control Room at HQ. He could remember falling over. Part of him was still there, trapped in that moment.

Face to the carpet, weeping.

Dan carried a list of such memories, abject in their awfulness, some he had not even lived through. Those last seconds in the air before her head struck the kerb. Tuesday 30th November. No adverse weather conditions. Clear visibility.

PC Lomax was driving the RPU, with PC Duke in the passenger seat. Dan did not ask to view the footage from their dashcam, but he had read the transcript. *6H32, siren and blue lights deployed, travelling at 53mph in close pursuit of subject vehicle, red Ford Fiesta. Pedestrians on adjacent pavements, including adult female later confirmed as Bethany Davenport. Red Ford Fiesta passes Davenport. With no prior warning, Davenport runs into road. 6H32 brakes, swerves right, strikes—*

Dan fled to the bathroom, his body doubled over as he clutched the sink. From upstairs came the thin wail of a child crying.

Sunday, and Dan had no bookings, as Hari insisted he take at least one day off a week. 'Everyone needs a rest, mate, especially you.' Dan would promise to relax, but he could not bear inactivity, that twitchy tension in his muscles. He had to be doing *something*.

Armed with a roll of bin bags, Dan knocked on the door of Unit 16. No reply, so he let himself in with the key. The smell hit him first, but it was not cadaver. Unfettered mess, junk stacked on every surface and across the carpet. Dan stepped into the living area, past cartons of half-eaten takeout food, covered in mould. As a police officer, he had seen places like this far too often, the indicators of a life out of control. Mrs Faulkner wanted Strang 'evicted'. *Use force if you have to*, but that was not Dan's way. The man was missing and clearly in some sort of trouble. Suicide risk?

Dan weighed the phone in his hand, then he called Cassie, asking a favour.

'Sure,' she said, 'but seems like a case of rent absconder.'

In the background he could hear murmured voices, buzzing fluorescents, keyboard clatter. It had not occurred to him that she would be working on the weekend.

Taking a breath, Dan said, 'I feel there's more to it. And I'm hoping you'll be inclined to help after my babysitting stint. How's your head?'

'Still on my shoulders, last time I looked.'

Cassie promised to check if a John Strang had been reported missing, and whether a hospital admission or body in the morgue matched his description. Late thirties, medium height, medium build, brown hair. A forgettable face.

'Oh, and I'll run him through the PNC for priors. Bye, Danny Boy.'

He put his phone away, relieved the call was over. Contact with MIT, even remotely, was best avoided. Dan picked his way through to the bedroom. Muddy clothes on the floor, a plastic bowl. Dirty sheets twisted on the mattress and a barricade of newspapers around the bed. He thought about the half-dozen times he had encountered Strang. The man was always going somewhere in a hurry, hands in the pockets of a greasy padded jacket. Shoulders hunched, eyes evading contact. Strang had winced on the one occasion Dan tried saying hello.

Haunted, that had been the main impression. With a sigh, Dan directed himself to the task ahead. It would take at least a day to clear the place. He bagged up the newspapers in the bedroom. Next came the rotting food and stacks of empty cans and boxes from meals that had comprised baked beans, tinned peaches, cornflakes, fish and chips, curry. In the fridge there was a bloated carton of curdled milk. After filling eight bin bags, he went to strip the bed. The mattress, duvet and pillows were jaundiced and stank of sweat.

In search of fresh air, Dan sat on the caravan steps. Yawning, he rubbed a hand through his hair, black, straight, always in his eyes these days. It could do with a cut and his beard needed trimming. People barely recognised him but that was good. He had no desire to speak to ex-colleagues or friends. Except for

Cassie. And Hari. He peered at the ground, the dry grass. Hard to believe he was still thirty-five. He had aged so much in the past seven months.

Heaving himself off the steps, Dan opened the boot of his car. Flattened down the seats and loaded up the bin bags. So far he had turned up nothing with Strang's address, or any means of recouping the missing rent. Back inside the caravan, he stared at a bulky footstool. Not part of the regular furnishing at Summerlands, it must belong to Strang.

When he picked up the footstool, the padded lid came loose. There was a storage area containing baby clothes. Dan blinked, felt the off-kilter thud of his heart. The items were clean, neatly folded. So different to the mess and filth elsewhere. His gaze swept across the interior of the caravan. Had Strang been keeping a child here? But there were no nappies or remains of baby food.

Dan reached inside the footstool and his throat went dry as he checked the clothing. All of it soft and well washed. White knitted bonnet, pale blue cardigan with tortoiseshell buttons, yellow knitted bootees with silk ribbons. White towelling sleepsuit, poppers up the front, from Mothercare, age 0 to 3 months.

Underneath there was a blue plastic dummy. The rubber teat was dark brown and cracked. Maybe this had all been in the past, and Strang had lost contact with his child. Perhaps the baby died. Dan shook his head at the thought of another explanation. During his time in the police, he had liaised with the sex offender unit.

Again, Dan scanned the caravan for answers, then his gaze dropped to the baby clothes. These items had been cherished. It seemed only right to keep hold of them for now. Dan placed the blue dummy and tiny clothes in a white carrier bag. Then he sat back, frowning.

Where was Strang?

And what happened to the baby?

Chapter 3

Wrenched from a dream, Dan did not recognise the dim contours, and then it came to him. This was the caravan. His phone was ringing. He grabbed it from the side table, nearly knocking off a glass of water.

'Where are you right now?' Cassie said, excitement in her voice.

'Bed.'

'Jesus, Dan, it's noon. You missed the full fleet plus SOCOs heading for that solar farm near Summerlands. I've got a vic you might be interested in. Male. One metre eighty, at a guess.'

His breathing faltered.

'Can you be up and dressed in fifteen minutes? I'm not going to sit in your skanky caravan with you in your underpants.'

'You think it's Strang.'

'I'll come by and show you photos on my phone. Don't have breakfast.'

'I need to see him,' Dan said.

'You will, soon as—'

'If you want my help, I can't do it off a photograph.'

'You know that's against protocol.'

'You're the one that rang me.'

'Fine. Mazur's still examining the scene, but the remains should be bagged in about half an hour. I'll give you a look before they stick him in the van.'

Thirty minutes later, Dan was heading west in his Volvo. As he came over the shallow rise he blinked at the glare. On the far slope were sleek black panels that made diagonal stripes across a large field. In the centre Dan could see SOCOs in protective clothing, plus a few officers in uniform. Along the southern edge was a line of police vehicles. He parked behind them and got out.

Cassie was waiting nearby, in her usual black trouser suit and white shirt. A version of office wear, but Dan knew the trainer-style shoes were capable of a fast sprint, and the jacket was a loose cut with pockets for the necessary kit. She loved jewellery, large earrings, but not on duty, nothing a suspect could grab or tear or yank.

'Better make this quick,' she said, glancing round.

Dan followed her toward the ME's van, which was by the entrance to the solar farm. Piotr Mazur was writing on a clipboard. He stood next to a wheeled stretcher. On it was a long bulky bag with a snaking zip. Dan was struck as ever by the unsettling resemblance to a garment bag for storing clothes, something you would find lurking in a wardrobe. The black plastic gave off an oily gleam. The zip was not fully closed, and he found himself staring at the one-inch gap.

Mazur frowned. 'I'd say good to see you, Hennessy, but you shouldn't be here. I know what you're up to, DI Fisher.'

'He lives a mile down the road,' Cassie said.

'He's a civilian,' Mazur said.

'He's a potential witness who may recognise the deceased. There's no phone or wallet on the vic. The lab will take a week to ID him from DNA or teeth. If we're lucky. You want this sitting in your fridge for months on end while we scratch around in the dark?'

Mazur scowled, then turned to address Dan. 'If word reaches me you've told anyone about this visit, I'll swear I had nothing to do with it. And just to be clear,' he said, pointing at Cassie, 'I'm not happy about this, Fisher. I want you in gloves and suit, and Hennessy at arm's length. Understood? No contamination and no contact.'

As the man walked off, Cassie muttered, 'Prick.'

'Don't,' Dan said. In the past, he and Mazur had worked a number of cases and their dealings had always been cordial and professional. It was Mazur who carried out the autopsy on

Beth. That memory was a jolt to the heart, bringing on a flush of grief. Dan had been required to identify her first. He had gone to the morgue in a state of mute shock. But he could still remember the tenderness with which Mazur guided him through each step.

'Don't call him that,' Dan said quietly.

'Sure,' Cassie said, 'whatever.' She ran a hand over her close crop hair, then tapped her chin. Gestures he was familiar with – Cassie annoyed but trying to contain her vitriol.

While she went in search of protective gear, Dan stared at the bag on the stretcher. Maybe this had been a bad idea. Cassie reappeared in a white suit and latex gloves, complaining that she did not need to be told the operational procedures at a crime scene.

'You better *stand back*,' she said, still irked about Mazur. With a flourish, she unzipped the body bag, releasing the smell of decay.

Dan averted his gaze. This used to be routine work. He steadied himself, then looked at the remains on the trolley.

'The vic was lying on his front,' Cassie said. 'Cheek pressed into the metal leg of a solar panel. Seems to have protected some of the features. An electrician found him. Noticed the stink when she was checking the transformer. No info yet on how the body wound up here – under his own steam or this was the dump site – but the electrician says the gates were locked when she arrived.'

Dan's vision shrank, as if he was seeing everything from afar. Even Cassie's voice sounded distant. A nudge to the ribs startled him.

'Wakey, wakey, is this your guy?'

'No.' He shook his head. 'It's not John Strang. But there's something... Cass, I think I know him. I think I recognise the victim.'

'So who is he?'

There were crustings of dark red where vermin had eaten one of the man's eyes and part of his cheek, exposing some teeth. Dan made himself focus on the other half of the face. Small chin and a long nose. Curved eyebrows, darker in colour than his hair.

Dan shrugged. 'All I have is this vague feeling I've seen him somewhere.'

'Great. Really worth a royal ticking off from Mazur, bringing you here, then.'

'Stop it.'

'Sorry,' Cassie said, 'but I need an ID. I neglected to mention he's missing both hands.'

'Nasty.'

'Current estimate is time of death was three weeks ago. The local wildlife have had a go, but the hands were definitely chopped rather than chewed off. Post- not pre-mortem, Mazur reckons. His prelim conclusion is an axe.'

'Cause of death?'

'Blunt force trauma. Base of the skull was crushed.' Cassie zipped up the bag, taking care to avoid contact with the body. 'I need a name, Dan. Sooner rather than later.'

They were heading back when an officer stopped them, with a lengthy question for Cassie about securing the scene. Dan went to find Mazur again. The man was still writing on his clipboard.

'I'm not sure I ever thanked you properly,' Dan said. 'For how you treated Beth. And me. I don't know how you do it.'

The two of them stood for a moment, in silence, then Mazur said, 'This is my way of honouring the dead. It is a heavy privilege.' He rubbed his brow. 'I am sorry for what you are going through. If talking to me would help, you know where I am.'

'Thanks,' Dan said. 'I do appreciate the offer.'

Cassie was waiting next to his Volvo, not pleased. 'Did Mazur say anything about the vic that I need to know?'

'We weren't discussing the case,' Dan said. 'I'll give you a call if I remember why he seems familiar. By the way, his hair looked freshly cut. You could check the local barbers, not that I—'

'It's okay, I'll ignore you mansplaining my job. That suggestion is actually pretty good. It merits a non-sarcastic *thank you for your service*.'

He laughed, and the sound felt foreign in his chest.

'Christ,' Cassie said, 'I should try platitudes more often. Oh, and you'll no doubt see some plods at your caravan site, making enquiries. Promise me you'll be nice to them, Danny Boy.'

Heading back, Dan spotted an IRV in his rear-view mirror. The road was narrow and the two officers were driving at speed, nearly upon him now. Dan pulled into a lay-by, then closed his eyes, gripping the steering wheel as they raced past. It was another five minutes before his journey resumed.

At the entrance to Summerlands, Samantha was smoking a vape next to the garish signboard. Thankfully she was peering at her phone. Dan had no wish to be interrogated about events at the solar farm. Had local media got hold of the story already? He parked in the usual spot, then took the lower path to his caravan. There were two families with children in pushchairs, then he caught sight of Mrs Faulkner.

She stopped to say hello. Dark shadows under her eyes, like she was underslept.

'DIY?' Dan said.

Mrs Faulkner glanced at the screwdriver in her hand, as if surprised to see it. 'I knew I was in the middle of something. Thomas texted, wanting me to return this – he's currently wedged under a leaking sink.'

'The man never lets me borrow his tools.'

'I pay his wages. You, on the other hand, are not much use to him.' Then she frowned. 'Speaking of usefulness, any idea what the police are doing at the solar farm?'

'You saw the vehicles? Me too.' Dan hesitated, formulating a response. 'Must be serious. I messaged my friend but was politely reminded I'm Joe Public these days. She said they'd be by later to question everyone.'

'Dead body?'

Dan shrugged.

'Such a boon,' she said, 'having an ex-cop in my employ.'

'You don't pay me. Unlike Thomas.'

'I pay you in kind,' she said. 'More like in kindness, thanks to your sob story.'

Mrs Faulkner had never offered sympathy for Beth and it was one of the reasons he liked her.

'You do realise,' she said, 'you're occupying a viable unit free of charge.'

He gave her a look. 'Next to the septic tank.'

'Yes, but demand is outstripping supply. Lashings of nostalgia and ice cream available here. Without having to renew your passport or risk feeling European. By the way, how's it going on Unit 16?'

'Place is a mess. Strang left a lot of stuff, most of which can be binned. Some of it seems more personal. I'm storing a few things in the west barn, on the off chance he reappears with the money he owes. The guy's clearly going through a rough patch.' Dan considered whether to mention the baby clothes but decided against. He felt a pain in his chest.

'Does Strang remind you of yourself?' she said.

Dan blinked. 'No, not at all. I'm just not happy getting rid of his belongings when we don't really know what's happened.'

'Did you ask your detective friend about him, or is that forbidden?' It was voiced as a challenge.

'No one has reported Strang missing. But my friend has his details and she'll let me know if anyone turns up. Adults are allowed to walk away from their lives and disappear. Unlike children.'

Mrs Faulkner flinched.

'You okay?' he said.

'Yes, Daniel,' she said, glaring at him. 'Why wouldn't I be?'

'Sorry. I just thought...'

'That's not Strang at the solar farm, is it?'

Dan could not discuss his unofficial visit to the crime scene. 'We'll know more later,' he said. 'I better leave his caravan for now, in case there's a connection.'

Mrs Faulkner shook her head. 'I didn't like having him at Summerlands. Hardly the sort we try to attract. Not that I wished him dead.'

'The police will be here soon,' Dan said. 'Sorry I can't be more help.'

He walked back to his caravan. It was a warm afternoon and there were people in deckchairs, drinking coffee or smoking, reading a book or a newspaper. A few looked up and nodded as he went past. The caravan park was for holidaymakers. Strang had been working while he was here, a job in the grey economy by the sound of it, given he paid his rent in cash. The man had indeed been the 'wrong fit' for Summerlands.

Dan boiled the kettle, put toast on, and a poached egg. Sustenance after that visit to the solar farm. But once the egg was ready, wet and glistening, he dropped it in the bin.

He sat at the table, recalling the moment when Cassie showed him the body.

Why did he recognise the victim? Where had Dan seen him before?

Chapter 4

Jay rubbed a hand through her hair and examined the cottage. A month or so since she was last here, but everything looked much the same. Yellow walls, wincingly bright in the sunlight. Domino runs of red pantiles, and a zigzag of dormer windows that pushed upward through the eaves. To her left, tacked on the end, was the double garage with wide blue door.

There was a smell of manure. Norfolk was always more rural than she remembered, and further away. Her body was stiff from the ride. The Yamaha made a ticking sound as the engine cooled. Jay laid her helmet on the fuel tank, then she crossed the gravel toward the porch. Her childhood home, but she felt like an intruder. The doorbell gave a muffled chime, and she waited for a shape to appear through the frosted glass. No reply, so she headed for the side passage.

Empty plant pots were stacked alongside the wooden fence. Jay stopped at the corner and unzipped her leather jacket. Shielding her eyes, she stared across the back garden. Beneath the beech tree, her father was on his knees, digging a hole with a trowel. His forearm thrust at the ground in a steady rhythm. Gardening. The image was reassuring, a reminder that there had been nothing of concern in her recent Sunday phonecalls. Jay watched as he pulled a handkerchief from his pocket, then dabbed at his nose, obscuring the prow of flesh and bone.

'Jacqueline. It's you.' His voice was warm and he waved, still clutching the handkerchief.

A white flag, like a surrender.

Colin had wanted her to catch him unawares. *Don't tell the old bastard you're coming*.

Her father levered himself off the ground. He had the wide stature of a big man, overlaid by gauntness. They walked toward each other, his footsteps gathering pace. He was wearing his all-seasons Tattersall shirt and cords. Jay studied his face for signs of change but could see only the familiar.

'Sorry,' she said, 'I should have called.'

He smiled, a hand raking back his fine dark hair. 'You're here now.'

Jay hugged him, noticing he had lost weight. She frowned, recalling that her last visit was Easter.

'You've been busy,' she said, her gaze exploring the lawn. It had always been one of her father's obsessions. Feeding, mowing, applying weedkiller, scarifying, watering with a sprinkler, levelling with a roller. Now, toward the back, the smooth surface was disrupted by a grid of small mounds – maybe a dozen in total. Next to where he had been digging there was a sheet of newspaper.

'Daffodils?' Jay said.

Then her eyes deciphered what she was seeing. On the newspaper were the remains of a dead pheasant. The body had been crushed flat.

'What's going on, Dad?'

After supper, Jay cleared the table. Her father was washing dishes, his bony feet on the splashed linoleum. At some point in the past three months, the Formica doors had been removed from the upper and lower cupboards. Pans, plates, tins and jams stared at her from open shelves. The curtains had gone from the window, and next to the cooker there was a clean square on the yellowed wallpaper where the spice rack had once lived. Her father was down to two chairs, and she wondered if the others had been used for firewood.

When her phone rang, Jay knew it would be her brother.

'Well?' Colin said.

Her gaze darted toward her father, who was still at the sink.

'You sound a bit faint,' she said, talking across Colin in a loud voice. 'The signal's stronger outside.'

Jay stepped into the back garden and kept going, past the scent that leaked from a honeysuckle.

So?' Colin said. 'What d'you reckon?'

'I see what you meant in your email.'

'The living room's okay, but the kitchen's like an encampment.'

She glanced around. 'How was the garden, last time you were here?'

'Seemed fine,' Colin said. 'He's still managing the upkeep. Why?'

'Only, Dad's started burying things. As in, roadkill.'

'What—you mean dead animals?'

'A pheasant. Other things too.' This felt like a betrayal.

Her brother laughed. 'Told you he was going downhill, but I hadn't realised he was nuts.'

'That's unfair.'

'Oh and you know for a fact he didn't wring its neck with his bare hands?'

Jay wondered if Sandra was in the room with him – he liked an audience.

'Definitely roadkill.' She pictured the flattened body, iridescent blue and brown, raw edges that had dried. Claws curled, its tail feathers jutting at the sky.

'Tell him to get his eyes tested,' Colin said.

'Dad's not the one who drove into them all. I asked.' She stopped beneath the beech tree. 'How long has he been like this?'

'So I'm his keeper now? I do have a life, you know.'

Jay passed a foot across the shallow mound of earth, the last in the row. While she had been to the local shop, her father must have finished interring the dead bird.

'Colin. When did you spot he'd started behaving oddly?' She glanced back at the figure in the kitchen window.

'Gaga, you mean?'

She could hear the clack of ice cubes – Colin was on the whisky.

'Want to talk about it or not?' she said.

'Honestly? I've had a shitty day and could do without this.'

'I'm the one in Norfolk.' The calmness of her voice told her she was not angry.

'I rang, didn't I? I haven't noticed you going out of your way to look after the old sod. I've had it up to—'

She tapped the screen and slid her phone into a pocket. Why did Col always have to be such a dick? Walking back, she saw her father at the window, a dark silhouette. Next moment he dried his hands and left the room.

Jay went inside, her gaze flicking to the clean square on the wallpaper. At supper she had asked about the spice rack. 'Oh that never got used,' had been her father's reply, and she even followed his argument that cupboard doors hid what he was looking for. The adaptations made a kind of sense, but Jay could not reach or find a reason for the scattering of small mounds under the beech tree. What had her father said earlier? Something about sadness, and how he had passed those poor creatures for years without stopping. But they were already dead.

A graveyard in the garden dedicated to roadkill. Was her father losing his mind?

The question scared her. Peering into the living room, Jay wondered what had become of the brown three-seater. Her father lay on a bulky armchair, marooned in the middle of the room, his body twisted to one side, his long legs resting on a low table. Directly in front of him was a large new flat-screen TV. His feet were daubed with splatters of light, out of sync with the studio laughter. The effect made her dizzy.

'Tea?' she offered, not expecting to be heard.

'No thanks, love.'

Jay lingered in the doorway. 'It's no trouble.'

'You go on up,' he said, eyes fixed on the TV.

The noise of the game show hounded her into the kitchen. Jay turned the tap on, water thrashing the steel sink while she drank a glassful, followed by another. She tightened the tap until the dripping stopped, then watched her fingers slide the bolt on the back door. It had always been her father's job to lock up.

Jay climbed the stair past school photos of her and Colin in dated frames, skewed by passing shoulders. In her old room she hoped to find bare boards and ghosted shapes on the wallpaper, but the contents remained, all the debris from childhood.

Her phone rang. Jay blinked at the screen, relieved to see Ruben's name.

'Got a spare few hours?' she said. The phone felt heavy in her palm.

'Why?' Music was playing in the background of wherever he was, a track she did not know.

'Any chance of a rescue mission?'

'That bad, is it?' he said. 'I got your message.'

Crossing the room, Jay slipped a hand through the curtains and opened the window. 'Pretty bad. Dad's started doing odd stuff in the garden. I'm trying to figure out why.'

'But you'll be back Friday.'

She sat on the narrow bed and smoothed a hand across the quilt. 'Glad to hear you're wearing your work hat.'

His hurt was measured by the pause that followed. 'You're forgetting the sequence of events, Jay.'

'Sorry,' she said, 'I know you don't like to...'

The band was the only topic they were allowed these days. How to improve the intro to this or that track, whether there was a sound limiter at the venue.

'Friday's gig,' he said, 'you'll be there.'

Hearing a hiss, Jay glanced at the Artex ceiling. The tank in the loft was refilling. Her father slept on a camp bed in the dining room and kept his toothbrush by the kitchen sink. More changes.

'Not sure yet,' she said.

'You kidding?'

'I'll text Gary. He knows the set list. And maybe he can get along to Wednesday's practice.'

'Yeah but Theo hates the guy.'

'That's his problem. I need to stay here a bit.'

'Your dad's in Norfolk, right? Send me the address. I'll happily give you a lift Friday and drive you back after. Please say you'll do it.'

'I can't promise. Bye, Ruben.'

Jay put her phone away. Stared at the carpet, worrying about her father. After a while she went to stand by the door, listening for movement downstairs.

All she could hear was the pounding of her heart.

Dad's started doing odd stuff in the garden.

Chapter 5

Dan hurried through the door, as the shop was due to close. Vanessa was sweeping the floor and he apologised as he skirted past, heading for the first aisle. They had a brief chat about the weather, no rain for weeks, as Dan paid for a tin of beans. He thrust it in his jacket pocket and stepped outside.

'Daniel, do you have a moment?'

It was Mrs Faulkner. She looked worse than earlier, almost ill with fatigue.

'I'm afraid,' he said, 'I've nothing to report.'

She blinked. Wrapped a cardigan tighter round her body.

'About the incident at the solar farm?' he said. 'You were asking this morning if I'd any information. But nobody has— what's happened, are you alright?'

'I'm...' Mrs Faulkner was swaying slightly. 'I was wondering if I might have a word. There's something I've been meaning to... is now okay?'

Dan peered at her. 'Now's fine.'

'Let's...' Mrs Faulkner gestured toward her bungalow.

He followed, with a sense of foreboding. Was she going to ask him to leave Summerlands? His caravan was all he had.

Once they were seated in her living room, silence fell. Dan waited for the decree to be issued. His eyes darted around, taking in details of a place he might not see again. There were pieces of ceramic on the mantlepiece, a pair of figures and a row of small blue bowls.

Mrs Faulkner rubbed the knuckles of her right hand. 'Anything to drink?'

'No, I'm good,' Dan said.

She nodded. Glanced at the mantlepiece, then down at her hands. 'I want to tell you about something that happened. A long time ago. Something personal. Would you be okay with that?'

Dan blinked, adjusting. 'Of course. I'm fine with that. But we don't...'

'Know each other very well? True. But we have something in common. I got the impression you might have...'

'Might have what?' he said.

'First I need to establish some ground rules. I don't want you to look at me when I'm talking. And Daniel, please don't offer sympathy. When someone says *I'm sorry*, there's this moment where you feel better. But it's a lie because better is not possible. On the 4th of July 2001 my son Felix went missing from his pram when he was six weeks and three days old. He was never found.'

A baby son. Never found. *Christ*. Dan shook his head, heard himself moaning. 'Forgive me,' he said, wiping a hand across his face.

'You want me to stop,' Mrs Faulkner said.

'No, it just came as a shock. I didn't know... your history.'

'We are not here to talk about feelings. I will tell you the facts of my son's disappearance, and once I'm done we will bid each other goodnight. And when I see you tomorrow, we will behave as if this conversation didn't happen. I don't want to see it in your eyes. Do you think you can stick to these terms?'

Dan managed to say *yes*. That sorrow he had glimpsed in Mrs Faulkner, it was unspeakably real. He stared at the floor. 'I hope I'm the right person for this.'

'You told me about your fiancée. I didn't say how sorry I was, because it wouldn't change anything. I just nodded. And you looked thankful. That's when I decided.'

'To ask for my help?'

'Yes,' she said.

'You want me to try and find your son.'

'I am not expecting a miracle. I just...'

'It's been twenty-one years,' he said.

'That sounds like an accusation.'

'I didn't mean it that way.'

Dan could see her on the edge of his vision. Shaking her head.

'Time becomes amorphous,' she said. 'Twenty-one years ago but still here and now. I live that day every day of my life. I have never given up on my son. *Never*. And nor have the police. Or so they tell me. But then I...'

He heard her breathing in and out.

'I decided,' she said, 'with this being...'

Dan sensed Mrs Faulkner looking at him, but he kept his eyes on the floor. Then it came to him, today's date. The anniversary of her son's disappearance.

'What I'm hoping,' she said, 'is that you can give me the answers I've never had.'

'I'll try my best,' Dan said. 'That may not be enough.'

'I understand. But I can't let this go. I can't let Felix go.'

'Tell me what you remember about the incident. If you feel able.'

There was a pause, then Mrs Faulkner spoke. 'It happened in Beccles. Back when I was still married. Robert and I had only recently moved there. Everyone thought, my in-laws especially, that I needed to get out more. Make friends in the area.' She coughed, then swallowed. 'Lydia was the wife of Robert's work colleague. I was shopping with my husband one day and we bumped into her in the street. A couple of weeks later, I was invited to spend the afternoon at her house. It should have just been a forgettable thing. A few hours of awkward chit-chat, which neither of us was obliged to repeat. Lydia was a ghastly woman. I sensed it even during that first encounter on the street. If I'd said no to her invite, Felix would still be here.'

Mrs Faulkner stopped speaking. Dan heard fingernails scraping across upholstery.

After a minute, she said, 'So I went round for afternoon tea. Only it wasn't tea. It was cocktails with another awful woman called Catherine. They didn't want Felix in the lounge as it would upset the party atmosphere. The children were outdoors taking advantage of all that *lovely fresh air*.'

Dan could hear the voices of Lydia and Catherine coming through in her words.

'How old were the other children?' he said.

'Lydia's son Jack was nine and Catherine's daughter Emily was eight. The house was huge with a long back garden, which sloped down to the river. Felix was in his pram on the upper terrace, next to one of the windows. Only Lydia could see him. She made me sit at the other end of the room. I could hear Jack and Emily in the garden, yelling and laughing. I was worried they would wake Felix.'

'He was still in his pram at this point,' Dan said.

'Yes. Felix never cried much, even when he was hungry, but at three o'clock he was due a feed. Lydia put us in a room off the hall. It was a warm afternoon, but that room was freezing. I wrapped a blanket round Felix. Once he'd finished feeding, he was drowsy and I tucked him into his pram. On the terrace. That was...' She paused. 'That was the last time I saw Felix. He was sleeping, and I remember looking at his eyelashes, the way they brushed his cheeks. And I remember thinking he was perfect. And feeling amazed that this was my son. Then I...'

Dan had the impression she was shaking her head. He waited, then said, 'Can I fetch you some water?'

'No, no thanks. I need to keep going with this. When I got back to the lounge, Lydia and Catherine were still talking about her plans to redecorate. I wanted to leave, but it was all arranged that Robert would collect me and Felix at six o'clock. So I just had to wait. My son was... Felix was asleep on the terrace. Jack and Emily were playing nearby. They left him alone at one point and went down to the river. They weren't supposed to. It was fenced off and there was a gate that rang a bell. But Lydia's son must have worked out how to bypass the alarm. Perhaps they climbed the fence. Children climb, don't they? A witness saw Jack and Emily next to the water. This was before Felix went missing. There's a report from him, the witness, I forget his name. The police put out an appeal, but nobody came forward. Apart from the man on the riverbank. They interviewed lots of people and you can have those too, the statements. Not that they'll help much. There's a high wall round the garden and lots of trees. You can't see in. And the house is on a side street. Nobody walked past at the time Felix went missing. Why am I even using that word? Felix was *stolen* from his pram. And yet nobody saw a thing. It's all in the file.'

'You hired a private investigator,' Dan said.

'No. My ex-husband didn't want the... Everyone kept telling me the police were doing an excellent job. I put my faith in the detective in charge. Alec Drummond. You know of him?'

'Before my time.'

'He used to visit me. After. After they closed the investigation. Officially the case was still open but...'

Dan frowned. 'They weren't allocating any more resources.'

'Alec said he'd never stop trying to find my son. I begged him to keep looking. But I asked him not to visit me unless... it was too painful to hear, time and again, that he had made no further progress. Then I got a delivery in the post. It was the police file from Felix's disappearance. Alec Drummond had died. Apparently he kept copies of the files for a few of his cases. Those that remained on his conscience. His widow explained this in her letter. Her husband had asked that after his death she should give those files to what he called *the survivors*. I need you to know, Daniel. Because I'm trying to be honest about this. The file was sent to me in December. A few days later, Hari Nijjar rang asking if I'd a caravan available and could a friend of his come stay for a bit.'

'He told you I used to be a DI.'

'I took it as a sign.'

Dan stared at his hands. 'Are police aware you have the case file?'

'No, according to the widow.'

'Have you read it?'

'I looked at it once. Quickly. It was too upsetting to read in detail. But there were post-it notes stuck to some of the pages. In Alec's handwriting. The one that stays in my mind is where he expresses concerns' – she cleared her throat – 'about the way things were handled in the first few hours. After Felix went missing. Alec always told me the police were doing everything they possibly could. No stone unturned. Not once did he refer to mistakes in the investigation.'

There had been tears in her voice.

Dan said, 'Do you want to tell me what his concerns were?'

'He wasn't very... I prepared myself for this. I've waited months for the right moment to talk to you. Summoning the courage. I'm still not sure I want to know what happened to Felix. I've imagined all these terrible things and then for someone – for *you* – to name the terrible thing. And for it to no longer be an imagined possibility but a horrific fact. Do I want that?'

Dan waited, then said, 'Do you?'

'Yes. But please don't speak to me about this. Until you have the answer. Do not give me false hopes.'

'No updates. I understand.'

'He was my son. My beautiful son. I know I haven't told you everything but I'm hoping the rest will be in the file. I'll fetch it now. Then you should leave. As I think I'm about to be sick. Don't thank me for the file or say any other meaningless thing. Just say goodbye and go.'

Chapter 6

Exhausted, Dan had barely slept. Hour after hour awake with Mrs Faulkner's voice in his head, those searing sentences his memory had retained and which kept repeating. He switched on the kettle and reached for a mug, almost dropping it. Should he have said no to her? Dan was not capable of refusing someone so desperately in need.

Light slanted across the table, landing on the buff-coloured file. He thrust it in a drawer, then frowned at his phone. Zero charge, and the cable was broken. Dan went to fetch a spare from the Volvo, choosing a route to the car park that avoided her bungalow. Walking back, Samantha spotted him.

'Speak of the devil,' she said, smirking. 'Her highness wants a word. She's in reception. Good luck.'

'Thanks,' Dan said as he turned on his heels and headed that way.

Mrs Faulkner stood behind the desk, no traces of sorrow. Instead, that look of being infinitely capable and a certain impatience that everyone else was less so. Her hair was scraped into a harsh ponytail.

'Tell me, Daniel, when will your people be done snooping around my caravan park? It's upsetting the residents having the police here. Like we've something to do with that *horrid* business at the solar farm.'

Dan breathed in and out, to steady himself. 'The incident happened a mile away. Everyone in the local area will be getting this level of scrutiny.'

'Maybe your detective friend can tell you how long they'll be.'

'I'm not police anymore.'

'So you keep saying.'

Did Mrs Faulkner regret talking about her son? She had shown Dan the fault line that ran through her life. He hoped she was not going to be angry with him from now on.

'It's a murder investigation,' he said. 'These take time.' Dan was unsure if he was referring to the body at the solar farm or his enquiries into Felix's disappearance.

'And when will you be finished in Unit 16? I have someone wanting it this Saturday. If you need help, you can borrow one of the cleaners. Speak to Vanessa and say you have my permission.'

Dan felt heavy as he returned to his own caravan. The mention of Unit 16 was a reminder of those baby clothes in the footstool. Obviously they had nothing to do with Felix Faulkner, but it was an odd coincidence.

Around him, Summerlands was waking up, residents emerging, sitting on camp chairs, another fine day, smiles on faces. They looked alien to him, a different species. Dan put his phone to charge and checked the roster. No Hari bookings until late morning. He made a coffee, then retrieved the file from the drawer and laid it on the table. A failed investigation, fully documented. A young baby that was never found. Dan tried to imagine what that would be like for the mother. Tried to imagine what it must have done to Mrs Faulkner. Year after year of not knowing, of fearing what had happened to her son.

'I'm sorry. Deeply sorry.' She had forbidden those words, but Dan understood her reasons. For seven months he had mourned Beth. Mrs Faulkner had borne her loss for over two decades. He recalled what she said to him yesterday as he left the room. 'Everyone says it's good to talk. *Not* talking is the only thing keeping me alive.'

Alec Drummond had arranged for the file to be sent to Mrs Faulkner. It took a lot for a serving officer to copy a file and hang on to it during retirement. And then to break further regulations by giving it to the victim's mother. A cold case, unsolved for twenty-one years. A child that was perpetually missing. Such a small body, so much easier to hide than adult remains.

Dan shook his head. He needed to believe Felix was not dead, that there was still hope.

He opened the file and began to read.

Jay had been attempting to reach Colin all evening, but texts and voicemails were being ignored. Up in her room, she switched on the light, igniting a synthetic sparkle in the carpet, the curtains, her old dressing gown. Jay got out her phone again and tried Colin's landline. As the dial tone droned in her ear, she glanced round. The clutter had become unbearable – was this her father's influence? On the wardrobe door was a patchwork of photos, crowded with faces. Jay studied them, struggling to remember everyone's names.

Then a voice barked, '*What now, Father?*'

'It's Jay.'

'Oh. Trouble at the ranch? Is he interring a herd of bison?'

She could tell that her brother was on the whisky again.

'Dad's been home all day,' she said. 'No road trips. I tried talking to him about the dead animals. I'll keep trying, but I'm actually calling about something else.'

'Money?' Colin said.

'Why would it be money?'

'Times are tight for me and Sandy too, with the kids and everything.'

'Tell Sandra she needn't worry. I'm not emptying Dad's coffers while your back is turned.'

'I never said you were.'

'Col, I didn't ring up to have this conversation. I wanted to ask you about someone who came by this afternoon. To speak to Dad. His name's Dan Hennessy. An ex-cop who seems to be working as a private investigator.'

'What the hell has Father done?'

'Nothing. Just listen, will you? Did he ever say anything to you about being a witness in a child's disappearance?'

'No. Never. A witness? When was this?'

'July 2001. A six-week-old baby went missing from a garden in Beccles. There's a river at the bottom of the garden and a public footpath on the opposite bank. Dad was walking along that path—'

'Christ, are you kidding?'

'He walked past, at around the time the baby disappeared. There's a statement by him in the police file. It's quite brief, apparently. Which is why this detective guy wants to speak to Dad.'

'And you let him?'

'No, Colin. I didn't allow a stranger to browbeat Dad about something that happened years ago. Not until I knew more of the facts, but you've heard nothing about this either.'

'Not a word.'

'The guy said Dad was on his own. It was a Wednesday so we'd have been at school, then the childminder's.'

'Why the hell was Father taking random walks through Beccles?'

'I've no idea,' Jay said. 'Feels strange he never told us what happened.'

'We were kids. You said 2001, which makes me twelve and you ten.'

'I'm talking about when we were older. Odd for it not to come up, given the sad fact that missing children are in the news fairly often. So I'm just surprised Dad didn't mention being a witness. The baby's name was Felix Faulkner. He was never found.'

'You think Father had something to do with it.'

'Why would you say that?'

'It seemed to be what you were inferring.'

'Well it wasn't,' Jay said.

'Doesn't mean this private dick isn't thinking along those lines. Otherwise why bother to question Father again. And on whose authority? Who's employing him? And why does he have access to police files?'

'Col, you're making this much more cloak and dagger than it was. The guy was actually quite nice. I didn't get the impression he's targeting Dad. I think he's just trying to find out what happened. He seems to be working for the baby's parents.'

'I don't want him putting words in Father's mouth.'

'Me neither. I haven't spoken to Dad about this yet, but I'm planning to over the next few days. If the parents of the missing baby are paying for a detective, they could be looking to put pressure on the police.'

'To reopen the investigation?'

'I don't know. I just want to speak to Dad before it all gets official. I don't like that he never said anything. That we're only finding out about this now.'

Chapter 7

Dan's day started at 7 a.m. but the sun had been up for hours. He ferried passengers across the Brecks, through woods and heath, fields and villages, crossing the Waveney on narrow bridges that took him over the border into Suffolk. Classic FM playing on the radio, conversations were kept to a minimum.

He focused on driving, on hazard perception, complying with road signs and traffic signals, observing speed limits, but every time Dan waited outside an address, his thoughts fell apart. So much had happened. The resident disappearing from Summerlands. The dead body at the solar farm. The trauma in Mrs Faulkner's past. And beneath them all, his own loss, weighing on his chest. How could emptiness be so heavy?

By late morning Dan was in his caravan, sitting at the table with the buff-coloured file. He could not solve his own life, but maybe he could find answers for Mrs Faulkner. It anchored him, analysing a case – there was method in its procedures and processes. DI Drummond had copied multiple documents from the Suffolk Constabulary investigation, and the file was over an inch thick. Inside the cover, on a plain sheet of A4, there was a handwritten index of the contents.

Dan glanced at the words *Witness Statements*, in blue biro. It had been an impulse decision yesterday to visit the footpath witness, Peter Olsen, and a stroke of luck that the man was still at the same address. His daughter, however, had been extremely wary. Jay Olsen had stood in the doorway of the acid yellow cottage. Glaring at him. He had felt a moment of attraction, which made no sense. His emotions were not reliable these days.

With a frown, Dan checked the notes he had begun yesterday, a summary of the initial steps taken by police after Felix Faulkner was reported missing. According to the two child witnesses, a man 'stole' the baby. Jack and Emily were in the garden and they saw the abduction. When Mrs Faulkner spoke to Dan the other evening, she mentioned the children but said nothing about them being key witnesses.

During questioning, Jack Ingleby and Emily Nash were accompanied by their mothers, the interviews being conducted by DI Drummond and a female DS, in the dining room of Chapel House. Vital testimony was also gathered from Alice Faulkner, Lydia Ingleby and Catherine Nash. Clearly Mrs Faulkner had been in a state of extreme distress, as it was noted in the file that a doctor was summoned to assess her wellbeing.

While these interviews were underway, a group of uniform officers did a search of the premises and garden, the riverbank, and meanwhile a team was dispatched to carry out house-to-house in the vicinity and beyond.

Taking a fresh sheet of paper, Dan began to draw up a timeline, using the witness statements. There was some uncertainty, due to the conflicting accounts of the three women, but it appeared that Jack and Emily first reported the abduction at around 4.15 p.m. According to Alice Faulkner, the children ran into the living room, and it was Jack who said, 'A man stole the baby.' A further ten minutes elapsed while they looked for Felix in the house and garden. The owner, Lydia Ingleby, said she had been reluctant to contact police until she was certain. She seemed to think Catherine Nash's daughter Emily had hidden the baby to play a trick on Jack. But they were unable to find Felix and at 4.27 p.m. Lydia called 999, with officers from Beccles Police Station first on the scene.

A county-wide alert was issued, and relayed to police services across England, for a 'male with dark hair and dark clothing'. A description was also circulated of Felix and what he was wearing. Mrs Faulkner did not own a camera phone – this was 2001 – so it was not possible to share a picture of Felix until several hours later, after one had been retrieved from their home. But babies have few distinguishing features. A photo was never likely to yield a response from the public, unless the adult with the baby was behaving in a manner that drew attention.

Dan fetched a glass of water and sat down again. On Monday, Mrs Faulkner had referred to a post-it note in which Drummond expressed concerns. He glanced at the curl of yellow paper. It was stuck to the inside of the file's buff cover, and not attached to any particular section. He therefore had no way of knowing what issue or failing had worried Drummond. And the post-it note was vague. *Mistakes were made in first two hours.*

Closing the file, Dan pushed it away. Paper and words could only tell him so much. He grabbed his keys, wallet, and headed for the car.

From the opposite pavement, Dan studied Chapel House. Georgian, red brick, tall windows with white-painted mullions, and dormers visible above a parapet. He recalled the photographs in the file. Not much had altered in twenty-one years, different curtains, a change of colour on the front door. Dan thought about Mrs Faulkner arriving here as a young woman, a new mother with a six-week-old baby. During his time in the police, he never worked a cold case. But colleagues had talked of how hard it was to investigate matters that had lain dormant. Witnesses fresh from an incident could barely offer an accurate account, so there was little chance of them providing useful testimony decades later.

Dan was staring at the front door – picturing Mrs Faulkner on the threshold of that terrible afternoon – when it opened and a woman stepped onto the pavement. She was late fifties, her hair brushed back from a high forehead.

'You're early,' she said, frowning. 'We agreed three-thirty.'

'Sorry,' Dan said, 'you may be mistaking me for someone else.'

'You aren't from the estate agents.'

'No.'

'Ah,' she said, 'it's just I saw you staring at my house.'

'It's for sale?'

'Interested? I can give you the agent's number.'

'I should probably explain myself. I'm not sure how to put this. But I'm making enquiries into something that happened here in 2001.'

A look of fright, or was it horror, passed across the woman's face. Then she blinked, touched a hand to her neck.

'You know what I'm referring to,' Dan said.

'I didn't speak to the press back then. And I have no intention of doing so now.' This had to be Lydia Ingleby, the original owner.

'I'm not a reporter. I used to be in the police. A friend has asked me to see if I can turn up any new leads on the disappearance of Felix Faulkner.'

'You're a private investigator.'

'Sort of,' Dan said.

'Do you have a licence?'

'It's not a requirement in the UK. And as I said, I'm hoping to find out if the police missed anything.'

'Who sent you?' the woman said.

'I'm afraid I can't say. But they have a connection to the victim.'

'I bet you're some nasty little blogger that read about Felix on the internet.'

'Fair comment. You have no way of knowing if I'm genuine. I wasn't planning to speak to you today. I just came to look round Beccles. See where it happened.'

'Does it give you a thrill? Poking around in other people's misery?'

'It gives me no pleasure,' Dan said. 'But I made a promise.'

'If Alice sent you, please tell her I wish... No, I'm not using you as messenger boy when I've no idea who you are. I *am* prepared to talk about that day. But you need to bring proof of who you are and who you're working for.'

'I'll do that. And I'm sorry for springing this on you. I didn't even know you were still living at Chapel House. Please accept my apologies.'

The woman glared at him. Then she went back inside, without another word.

The door banged shut, the noise echoing like gunfire in the narrow street.

Dan's enquiries had touched a raw nerve.

The woman was prepared to talk about 'that day', but why the anger?

Chapter 8

Jay climbed into the Nissan, banging both knees. Her father always drove with his chest up against the steering wheel. She slid back the seat, adjusted the mirrors. On the road to Diss, she wound down the window, letting in fresh air, a scent of pollen. There was less chance of her father getting into trouble if he was marooned at home. Jay smiled. Weaving through the fields, wind in her hair, she began to relax, shedding the tension of the past two days.

At Tesco, the car park was busy and she manoeuvred the Nissan into a narrow bay. Jay walked to the entrance across hot tarmac. It felt good to be in a dress and sandals, not the heavy garb of her leathers and boots. At the corner she waited as a rusty pickup drove by. Pacing inside the open truckbed was a large Alsatian, tongue lolling, tail wagging. So Norfolk, it made her laugh.

When she reached the lobby, Jay was confronted by people, pushchairs, trolleys, bins, cardboard megaliths with special offers. Her anxiety came crowding back, all the worries about her father. Burying roadkill was bad enough, but then to learn he had been a witness in an unsolved case. She could not stop herself seeing a link between the missing baby and those pitiful graves in the garden.

'Jay, is that you?'

The bloke had fair hair and a keen gaze. She had no idea who he was.

'It's Sean,' he said.

Someone from her school days, the name seemed familiar. 'Hi there.'

'Good to see you,' he said, smiling.

'Yeah, you too.' A trolley nudged her foot.

'How about we...?' He pointed to a free corner.

A bloated Noddy stared at them from a pound-a-ride car. Jay wanted to flee, but Sean was behaving like they were mates. Maybe they had been close.

'Back for long?' he said.

'Not sure.'

'You look great.'

'You look tired.' She smiled. 'Sorry, that was unkind.'

'Not really.' He laughed, then gestured to his ear. 'I like your piercings.'

Jay gave him a slow blink.

'They're really cool. Jeez, what am I saying?'

She remembered him now, his awkward honesty. For a while they had hung out.

'You still in the band?' Sean said.

'Still in the band.' To her left, framed on the brick wall, there was an advertising hoarding that revolved on a loop.

'You'll make it,' he said. 'I know you will.'

'Got a few things on the go, but it's a Doors tribute act that pays my bills.' Jay laughed. 'Who knows. We'll see.'

'You're busy by the sound of it. That's great.'

A memory, her and him on a roundabout, spinning in the dark. Talking for hours. About how to create a better world?

'Sean,' she said, 'I'm sorry but I need to head off.'

'Call me, yeah?' He handed her an orange business card. 'I'm there most days.'

'Rehearsal studios,' Jay said, reading the details. 'Nice. When d'you get into music?'

'I'll give you a tour. Four rooms and a coffee machine.' He seemed embarrassed, but also proud.

'I'm not sure I'll have time. What with my dad and everything.' Jay looked at the floor. Spots of chewing gum were welded to the tiles.

'I remember your dad.'

'You do?'

'He loaned me a shirt when I was sick into a hedge. At that party you had? I always liked him. We used to talk football and politics. Man to man, even though I was just some annoying kid.' Sean laughed. 'Tell him I said hi.'

'Thank you,' Jay said, resisting the impulse to give Sean a hug. 'You've no idea how grateful I am to hear something normal about Dad.'

'Glad to be of help.' He smiled.

'I should...' Jay gestured at the supermarket.

'Of course. Me too.' He raised his bag of shopping. 'We're like those figures on a clock.'

'Huh?'

'You're going in, just as I'm coming out. Those clocks they have on town squares – like in Austria and places?'

'Oh yeah,' she said.

'Jay, it's so good to see you. You got my card. Drop by if you're bored.'

She watched him walk away. He dodged round the trolley store and stepped onto the tarmac. His gait was uneven, like he had a sore ankle. Jay lost sight of him behind a large van.

Smoky kisses and the stars in a slow swirl. Was that Sean?

Jay had been sorting her old bedroom for the past hour. Rubbing her knees, she found an imprint from the carpet, a Braille message telling her *this is taking too long*. And what was that smell? Stale adolescent angst. Or cabbages, a lingering odour from the cardboard boxes. These were now filled with gaudy books, posters, knickknacks, school folders, clotted makeup. Even the dust was sticky. On the dressing table there was a stack of photos. Jay picked one up, peered at it. Six grinning teenagers squeezed onto a couch. Balancing on the armrest was a fair-haired boy, mid movement, his face blurred.

The photo was added to the 'keep' pile, then she went downstairs. The door to the passageway was open, and she could hear the murmur of Radio 4, overlaid by the tink-tink of something metal. Her father, busy in the garage. Jay stepped into the garden, feeling lighter. She breathed the summer air, enjoying the forgotten intimacy of grass on bare feet.

The blue sky unspooled a ribbon of childhood days, memories of where she used to play, hide, make dens. Jay wandered to the end and leaned on the wooden gate, looking at the path that parted expanses of wheat, leading to woods. Perfect for a dog. Age nine or ten she had begged for a puppy. Her father's response had been, 'Your mother didn't like dogs.'

Jay was eleven months old when the woman left. He had tried to mix traces of her into their lives, behaving as if she would be back soon. At some point the references ceased, but Jay could not put a date to her father's silence. A shimmer brushed the beech tree. Not once had Jay asked if he was lonely, and now the things they never talked about had become harder to say.

Walking back, she stopped by the hedge. Remembering what Sean had said about being ill at her birthday party. He wanted Jay to give him a call.

Her arm jerked.

'Sorry,' a voice said. 'Didn't mean to startle you.'

For a moment Jay did not recognise this man with middle-management hair and face. Only the long upper lip and small nose belonged to her brother. Colin had been so thin as a boy. A pink gingham shirt now hung over his khaki shorts.

'You okay, Jacks?'

'You're early.'

'Something came up. We'll have to head off before three.' Colin smoothed his hair.

'Thought you took a personal day to see Dad. He was hoping you'd stay for tea.'

'Is that where he's stashing the roadkill?' Colin nodded at the hedge.

'No,' Jay said, pointing, 'they're over there.'

His eyes flicked in that direction. 'I'll warn Sandra not to let the girls out. Don't want them finding any stray corpses.' Colin snorted. 'I never thought he'd lose his marbles.'

'You've made up your mind, then.'

'I see you've added to your graphic novel.' He was staring at her left arm. 'What's with the fish scales?'

Not this again. 'It's a dragon.'

'My sister the slayer. You always were into fantasy stuff.'

'Bollocks.'

Her brother grinned. 'You're right. What do I know?' His foot scuffed a clump of weeds. 'So what's the plan with the old man?'

Her teeth ached. 'Colin—'

'Father's letting things slide. Even you can see that. If we ever want to sell the cottage, it's going to take a major spend to get it on the market.'

'You're talking like he's already dead,' Jay said.

'That's unfair' – the words fanned by a laugh – 'I'm just saying maybe this place is too much for him.'

'Pay for a cleaner if you're so concerned.'

'Wrong side of bed?' He nudged her. 'Or was papa dearest up at dawn, digging a grave for poor Peter Rabbit.'

Jay sucked back a smile. 'It's not funny.'

'Bloody right, it's not. You aren't the only one having sleepless nights.'

'About Dad?'

'He's on the list.'

'Next to global finance?'

'Ha, ha, sis. You and I need to pull together on this.'

'It's not our job to tell him how to live his life.'

'You serious?' He jabbed a thumb toward the beech tree.

'People bury pets in their gardens.' Jay cringed – had she really just said that?

Colin looked at her in disbelief.

'Okay,' she said, throwing her hands up. 'Different league. But is he doing any harm?'

'Where does he park the car when he's scraping up entrails? Middle of the A11?'

'I'll have a word.'

'Good luck with that,' Colin said.

'Why is Dad doing this?'

'God knows. Does there have to be a reason?'

'Something's bothering him,' she said, 'I can tell.'

'It's dementia if you ask me.' Colin sighed. 'Any chance of a coffee?'

They headed for the back door, not speaking. Jay needed to rewind to Monday and those last seconds of ignorance when she greeted her father across the lawn. She craved that emptiness, before it became filled with dead animals and a missing baby.

The kitchen was quiet. Jay flicked on the kettle, then propped a hip against the worktop. 'Where are Sandra and the girls?'

'They've gone to the swings.' He unscrewed the coffee jar. 'Want one?'

She shook her head.

Colin was staring out the window.

Into the stillness came a litany of those moments and hours she and her brother had spent in this room. Eating mince on Mondays, fish on Fridays, a weekly rotation of alliterative meals, or doing homework, Colin helping unravel the maths and physics, or the wet weekends when they had built competing pyramids from playing cards. Birthday parties with flushed school friends, and a small turkey at Christmas. She glanced at the flakes of paint uncurling from the ceiling, the halo of dirt around the light switch. Their family history.

Jay was about to say, *Remember that time we*, when Colin turned from the window.

'What is it?' she said, seeing the look on his face. 'You're not plotting something, are you?'

'The detective guy – has he contacted you again?'

'Why?'

'You need to be very careful what you say to him.'

Jay felt a jolt of fear. 'What d'you mean, Col?'

Noises from the front of the cottage, a crying child and Sandra's impatient tones. Colin frowned, business-like, and Jay knew their 'meeting' was at an end.

'Why do I need to be careful?' she said, following him out of the kitchen. Her brother gave a few muttered responses, grabbing up a stuffed giraffe on his way to the front door.

A minute later, they were all gathered next to the BMW, which was sleek and alien on the unkempt gravel. Her father was offering Sandra the biscuits.

'Take them with you,' he said.

Jay closed her eyes at the plea in his voice.

'We're all right for biscuits,' Colin said.

'We try not to give the girls too many sweet things,' Sandra said, jiggling Chloe in her arms.

'Come on, Dad,' Jay said. 'They need to go.'

Sandra instructed Hannah to climb in, then she strapped both girls into car seats.

Jay glanced at her father, who was now plucking up weeds. She hugged Colin, whispering, 'I won't let you stick him in some cruddy care home.'

His smile was tight. 'Good to see you, little sis.' He turned, saying in a louder voice, 'I'm sure Father really appreciates you finding the time to pay a visit. Don't you?'

Her father seemed upset. About the biscuits?

'Must dash,' Sandra said. 'Lovely to see you all.' She blew a single kiss.

Colin stared at his wife's back as she climbed into the passenger seat.

'Less risk of germs,' Jay said quietly.

He sighed. 'Tell me about it.'

They smiled at each other.

'Jacks,' he said. 'Don't make me the enemy on this.'

'I'm not. There's clearly something going on with Dad. I'm just trying to give him the chance to talk about it.'

'Sure. As long as he keeps it to you and me. Who knows what's lurking in that head of his. We all have things that are better off left in the dark.'

Dan walked to the caravan on a slow meander, loosening his muscles after a day spent in the Volvo. The evening sunlight was warm and yellow, lending Summerlands a vintage charm. He could smell cooking. People were sitting at open doors, or on rugs outside. Between two units there was a table with a large gathering, different ages, maybe an extended family, beer bottles and wine, a birthday cake.

On Primrose Drive, his thoughts turned to the missing resident. Dan needed to finish clearing Strang's stuff, see if there were any clues to the man's whereabouts. Glancing at Unit 16, he paused. The door to the caravan had been damaged. There was a scuffed area on the white paint, with ridges of bare metal around the edge. Then his gaze went to the windows. The curtains were open. He could remember closing them to hide the mess when he was here on Sunday. Someone had been back since. Strang?

Dan peered inside. The place was unrecognisable.

He tracked down Mrs Faulkner in the shop, where she was rearranging the shelves.

'Unit 16 is looking spick and span,' he said.

She rotated a tin of soup, until the label was at the front. 'You here to thank me, Daniel?'

'I was a bit surprised, that's all.'

'Didn't take us long. Vanessa had a free hour so we teamed up, finished the job. I knocked on your door, but you weren't around.'

In the distance, Dan could hear children laughing. Mrs Faulkner stared at him intently. He had the sudden feeling she knew about his visit to Beccles. And what a failure it had been, turning up unprepared, antagonising a witness. Dan needed a letter from Mrs Faulkner to show his enquires were legitimate, but the words died in his throat.

Instead, he said, 'Hari keeps me pretty busy.'

'I was tired of waiting,' she said, lining up the small bags of rice. 'It's been four days since I asked you to sort 16. I did say I had people arriving Saturday.'

'What happened to the door?'

'I take it you're referring to the dent in the lower half. Thankfully Thomas was able to do a reasonable job of flattening it out.'

Dan frowned. 'Someone tried to kick the door down.'

'So it would seem. My instincts were right about John Strang. We've never had vandalism at Summerlands, not until he came along.'

'But I thought he still had a key?'

'I don't care who took a boot to that door,' Mrs Faulkner said, 'so long as it doesn't happen again.'

'I'll keep an eye out,' Dan said.

'There's something else you can do for me. *If* you have time, of course. Perhaps you have room in that car of yours for the old mattress. It's unsalvageable. And a padded footstool? I've no idea where it's from, but that also needs to go.'

'I'll take them both to the dump, first thing.' He felt a flush creeping up his neck.

'Apologies,' Mrs Faulkner said. 'I think I may have offended you.'

'You're fine, I don't bruise easily.'

'By the way, there was a hundred and twenty in cash, under the mattress.'

'That's odd,' Dan said, 'him leaving money behind.'

Mrs Faulkner frowned. 'Not enough to cover the missing rent, but it's better than nothing.'

'You want me to—?'

'I think we're done with Mr Strang, don't you?' The words were sharply spoken.

'Sure,' he said, feeling the flush deepen on his neck. 'Message received.'

Later, Dan took a walk to the west barn. He did not switch on the overhead fluorescents, but used a torch to find his way to the corner. The beam of light picked out the white carrier bag. The baby clothes were still there. As far as Mrs Faulkner was concerned, the matter was now closed. He shook his head, recalling the state of the man's caravan. A life in freefall. Dan should have done more to help him.

Chapter 9

Jay played Scrabble with her father after supper, having found the battered box under her bed. A board game was preferable to being stranded in the glow of the flat-screen TV. Her father broke open the Jammie Dodgers, dishing out two stacks with a smile and a 'glad we got to keep these'. Then he sliced up apples, cutting out the pips, and it touched her that he remembered. He won both games, of course, producing seven-letter words with a smooth brow and a casual hand. It felt like old times.

During the night, Jay was woken by an owl, the wheep-wheep of its cry circling the darkness. Twelve storeys up was too high. Then she understood. Norfolk not London. She drifted back to sleep, lulled by the ease of that evening. The plink of plastic letters, her father's gentle teasing, and a table covered in crumbs and apple cores. Everything was going to be okay. Dad was fine.

The caravan was stifling and Dan opened a window, but the morning air made little impact. After a strong cup of coffee, he wrote a note to Mrs Faulkner, requesting the letter *to show I have been appointed to investigate your son's disappearance*. Dan sealed his note in an envelope, then set off for the bungalow, feeling the sun's heat on his back. He pushed the envelope through the letterbox. It landed softly and the letterbox snapped shut.

Dan collected his car and parked on the grass near Unit 16. Opening the door to Strang's old caravan, he was met by the fake citrus scent of cleaning fluids. Every surface gleamed. Mrs Faulkner and Vanessa had even managed to remove the stains from the carpet. Dan dragged the mattress outside and folded it into the back of his Volvo. Then he went to retrieve the footstool. Lifting the lid, Dan peered inside, needing reassurance it was empty. There was an odd feeling in his chest, something murky. He did not like that a missing baby seemed to figure in Strang's life as well as Mrs Faulkner's.

At Snetterton Recycling Centre, Dan heaved the mattress into the giant metal container for non-recyclables. He fetched the footstool and threw it into the same trough. The attendant activated the mechanism. A large blade like a snow plough travelled across, compressing the contents. The footstool had fallen awkwardly and its sturdy construction resisted the compressor. The creaking timber and grating metal emitted a screeching wail. Dan felt nauseous, wishing it would end.

From Snetterton he drove to Great Hockham for his first pickup, a total of six on this morning's roster. Dan was having lunch at the caravan when he got a text from Cassie, confirming the arrangements for later. Not their usual evening but she had asked to switch to Thursday. Tacked onto her message was the question *Any luck with the vic??* Cassie would have cancelled this week's drink if there had been no prospect of him being useful. An uncharitable thought, and Dan felt guilty. She had sat through Wednesday after Wednesday of him in his grief-stricken state. Cajoled and joked, told stories about his ex-colleagues, entertained him with mishaps and 'stupid arrests'. He regularly thanked her for being a good friend, but for the first time he sensed how difficult it must have been for her.

If Cassie needed help with the murder investigation, it was the least he could do. That afternoon, Dan set off on foot. Maybe a return visit would loosen a memory about the victim. The road went due west from Summerlands on a gradual ascent. Norfolk was known for its flatness, but having lived here all his life, Dan was attuned to how the ground rose and fell in slow-motion waves. From the shallow summit, the solar farm was visible in the distance. Black panels on metal legs, in regimented rows that sliced across the landscape, at an angle which bore no relation to the field pattern. Renewable energy was 'a good thing', but he was always struck by the crudeness of the technology.

The road took him down into a dip, and as it climbed again, Dan reached the solar farm, which occupied a large tract that slowly rose from east to west. On his last visit he had not paid much attention to the perimeter, as vehicles had obscured it. Next to the tarmac there was a grass strip, then a thin hedgerow of hawthorn and beech, and behind that a two-metre metal fence topped by razor wire. There were CCTV cameras mounted on posts at intervals, and small Tannoys.

As Dan approached the fence, a message was broadcast. *Stand back. Trespassers and vandals will be prosecuted.* A recording activated by proximity sensors. He studied the verge, wondering if anyone had taken photographs before police parked on the grass. There may have been evidence of a vehicle used by the perpetrator to transport the body. Or maybe the victim had walked here with his killer. These questions were not Dan's job anymore but it was hard to switch off. No doubt Cassie had conducted a thorough examination of the scene.

The turn-in for vehicles was midway along the road, and from here Dan had a good view inside the solar farm. It sloped upward, south to north, and the body had been about forty metres in. Not directly opposite the entrance, but if someone set off from this point, up the gap between two diagonal rows of panels, they would arrive there. Provided they had a key for the gates. Again, none of his business. What Cassie wanted was help with identification.

Closing his eyes, Dan took himself back to the morning three days ago when he had stood here. His mind was a black void, and as he pictured the dead man's face, Dan allowed that darkness to spread across the damaged flesh. Leaving him the unmarked side. Not a living face but discoloured and slack from decomposition. He felt, once more, that sense of recognition – it brought back no memory of where and when he might have encountered the man.

Dan continued on the road, until the end of the solar farm. From there, he scanned the surroundings. Unpopulated, given to agriculture, with limited public access. Many of the old rights of way had fallen out of use or been ploughed over. There were large acreages with very few through routes other than tracks that led to remote farmsteads. Field after field, hedgerows, ditches. Lots of places where remains could be left, such as the foul-smelling pools of brackish water, so prevalent in the Brecks, that stayed wet even in summer, hidden by stunted trees.

The solar farm had equal merits, a fenced area where access was forbidden. Perfect for disposing of a body, but was the location also a message? Not everyone agreed with renewable energy. Fields planted with wind turbines, rapeseed grown for biodiesel, maize destined for anaerobic digesters, to produce biogas for generating electricity. Land use was changing. Food was no longer the sole purpose. Dan noted the sharp difference between the solar farm and the fields around it. For those owners able to get planning permission for such a facility, it pulled in grants and steady profits. This could create rifts among neighbours. In the post-Brexit rural economy, margins were tight.

The motive for the murder was not yet determined. Nor did Dan know how the body came to be inside the solar farm, behind locked gates. He stepped off the road and walked north, up the side of a wheatfield. To his right were the hedgerow and fencing that enclosed the solar farm. Dan kept glancing at the metal mesh but could see no obvious breaks. At the corner, he turned onto the far boundary, continuing his examination. Here, small trees were planted among the hedging. No Tannoys and the CCTV posts were further apart.

Halfway along, a sapling had been blown against the fence. The tree was still growing, even in its uprooted state. Dan could make out a CCTV camera hidden among the leaves. The sapling would block the view of anyone approaching. Under the fallen tree, obscured by hedging, Dan could see where someone had cut through the fence to create a small door. The mesh was now back in place. He noted the dusting of fingerprint powder, thinking *good work*. Pleased but also surprised the entry point had been spotted.

Dan grimaced. His grand gesture to leave the police because they killed Beth. Had that been the sole reason? Or had part of him wanted to prove that MIT would fall to pieces without him? Nothing very noble in that, and the thought left him hollowed out. Dan stared across the fields, acres of wheat to the north. No commitments between now and 8.30 p.m. when he was meeting Cassie. He could stay here for hours and not be missed. Again, dropping like a shroud, that sense of being old beyond his years, and so very tired. Dan stretched out on the ground, next to the solar farm. Sunlight flickered on his face where it shone through the thin hedging.

Time drifted, like the push and pull of the breeze. He heard waves washing over the small pebbles of a shoreline. Felt Beth's hand in his, as they lay on a beach in the sun. Covehithe, the summer before last. Beth had woken early, saying, *Let's go*. An hour's drive, then a beautiful walk along the edge of a ploughed field that fell away to the shore below. From that crumbling cliff, they had looked at the wide blue sparkle of the sea, the wind blowing Beth's hair across her face. The path dipped down, brought them to the beach. No one around. Husks and limbs of ancient trees, sun bleached and sea scoured, were strewn across the sand. It was prehistoric. Dan curled his hand, wanting to tighten his grip on Beth, but she had gone. He was no longer in the memory, but seeing it from afar. Dan sat up, blinked at the field of wheat not sea. That lurch of travelling from then to now, that moment of registering how much he had lost in the chasm between.

Taking deep breaths, Dan tried to steady his heart. There were tears on his face and he wiped them with a sleeve. He stood up slowly, deciding to return to Summerlands across the fields. No path, but if he headed east, roughly parallel with the road, then he would reach the caravan park. Walking was good.

Soothing. Dan knew to follow the hedges and ditches, not stride through the crops. A large wedge-shaped field sent him northward, then it cut south. Ahead was a small woodland on a mound, which he recognised as the old icehouse. This meant Summerlands was about twenty minutes away. Some evenings he would take a walk, on a route that skirted the icehouse, but Dan was surprised to come upon it now, never having approached from the back.

This had all been the grounds of Gazeby Palace, which burnt down in the 1910s, its foundations visible at the east end of the caravan park. Here and there, in the middle of fields, were specimen trees from when the area had been a country estate. Some of the land was owned by Mrs Faulkner, though she leased it to local farmers, as her main focus was Summerlands. The icehouse was another legacy of the Gazeby days, and it too belonged to her. Roughly conical in shape, its sloping sides were covered in shrubs and Scots pines, and on the north face there was a door with a brick surround.

Dan had thought it was a burial mound, until Mrs Faulkner told him its purpose, how there were steps leading to an underground chamber. In winters long past, staff would carve blocks of ice from the mere, a small lake, and these would be transported here and carried down into the chill depths. Dan had never been inside, the door was locked, but the idea of this sunken void intrigued him, with its capacity to preserve winter through the height of summer.

His footsteps slowed as he approached the icehouse entrance. Dan peered at the padlock. The metal loop had been carefully sawn through, then put back in place. Only on close inspection was it possible to see that the padlock had been tampered with. He used a stick to lift it off and slide back the bolt, avoiding fingerprints. The door opened, scraping across the threshold, and a dark tunnel was revealed, descending beneath the mound. As he stood in the dappled light of late afternoon, Dan was engulfed by rising air that smelled of mildew and rot.

The steps were slippery, the walls of the tunnel were damp brick, with a shallow vault above, and Dan had to stoop as he went down, one hand aiming the torch on his phone. He arrived at a low-ceilinged area, hexagonal in shape, with an arched doorway on each face, five in all, the sixth taken up by the stair. The doors had all been removed and he flashed his torch into the opening on the left, curious to see how the ice had been stored. There was a small room, narrow near the door then widening out, like a triangle in plan, the walls made from red brick, stained by salts and minerals. At the foot of these walls were stone troughs, the size of sarcophagi. Dan checked the other cellars. At the entrance to the fourth one he stopped.

The light from his phone illuminated an eerily domestic tableau. In the middle of the floor Dan could see a metal chair and table, with a mug, plates, a glass, some cutlery. A candle on a saucer. The stone trough on the left contained a sleeping bag and pillow. The trough on the right had a pile of clothes. The one at the back was full of water.

'Hello,' Dan called. 'Anybody here?'

His words echoed. He stared at the black water in the trough, which had been carved from a single block of sandstone. Then he looked at the clothing, all of it old and worn. Belonging to a man, but no sign of a wallet or ID. Everything in the cellar was cold to the touch and damp. No fresh food, but a few tins stacked in the corner and a carton of UHT milk. Unopened.

Hard to tell if the habitation was recent or not. Dan frowned. It was less than a mile from here to the solar farm. Where the body of an unknown male was found. Beaten to death and both hands cut off.

Chapter 10

Jay had last seen her father twenty minutes ago, when he disappeared beyond the conifers. She put down the tea towel and headed in that direction. He was upright on a chair, asleep, his chest rising and falling. The chair was a renegade from the kitchen. Judging by the faded paintwork, it now lived under this lilac tree, along with a cluster of mugs, in a corner of the back garden that caught the late sun.

When Jay was growing up, there had always been four seats around the kitchen table, one of them empty. Her father had maintained the illusion of being part of a couple, sleeping in a double bed and having enough furniture to accommodate visitors. Even after Colin left home, then Jay, those customs had continued. But now they were being reassessed and dismantled. Finally, it seemed, her father had accepted his solitary status.

Conscious of trespassing, Jay studied his features. Not the face of a madman, but someone she recognised. His bluish eyelids were smooth, and below them were the puckers of skin which she and Colin had inherited, though hers only showed when she was tired. Like today. A full bottom lip was another shared trait, but the rudder nose was sole property of her father.

Loosely clasped on one knee was a spanner. Jay pictured his Sunday hands from her childhood, dark mazes on the fingertips, whorls blackened by all those hours fixing a dynasty of vehicles. Or if he was not under a bonnet, he was chopping and mowing and pruning. Never at rest.

His eyes opened.

'Sorry, didn't mean to wake you.'

'No, no,' he said, smiling, 'I wasn't asleep.'

The shadow of a cloud moved across them both, dimming the colours and chilling the back of her neck.

'Dad.'

'Hmm?'

'I was thinking it might be a good idea to see your GP.'

'Went last month for an MOT. Birthday treat. Doctor said my blood pressure was remarkable for a man my age.'

Jay glanced at his feet. Red socks, but no sandals or shoes. 'Did the GP ask about anything else?'

Confusion crossed her father's face, then he laughed. 'Everything's in working order.' He tapped his head. 'Have you forgotten who beat you at Scrabble?'

Jay tried to feel reassured.

Dan arrived a few minutes before eight-thirty. The pub was quiet, two elderly men on bar stools, chatting to the landlord. Cassie was in their usual spot, a corner table. There was an empty glass in front of her.

'Am I late?' he said.

'Babysitter was early so I decided to jump ship.'

Dan noticed she was still giving off an odd energy – a tremor below the surface of things unspoken.

'Same again?' he said.

'Better make it a Coke. I've maxed my units.'

Drinking on her own. This was not the Cassie he knew.

Dan returned from the bar with a pint of Coke and a pint of Guinness.

'My bladder won't thank you,' she said, raising her glass. 'Cheers.'

'How are things?'

Cassie frowned. 'Fine. Why wouldn't they be?'

'No reason. Just wondering how you're doing. Archie okay?'

'Being a little shit if you must know, but he's three and it goes with the territory. But tell me, Daniel, how are you?'

The words were mocking and she flashed him a look.

'Sorry,' he said. 'Didn't mean to wind you up. Shall we start again?'

She shrugged, then had a sip of Coke. 'When Cassandra Fisher rules the world, one of the decrees will be to outlaw serving half a pint of ice with a drink.'

Dan swallowed some Guinness and put the glass down, wiped the froth off his upper lip. 'Did you want crisps? Forgot to ask.'

Cassie shook her head, and her large red earrings swung side to side.

After a pause, she said, 'I see the PM finally fell on his sword.'

'Haven't been paying much attention.' Dan tried to remember how their evenings usually began. Not with politics. Maybe with 'hello' or 'what can I get you?'

Cassie was staring into her glass, so he took the opportunity to check the clock above the bar. Less than five minutes had passed. Dan knew he would have to stick it out until nine-thirty at the earliest. Had they somehow swapped roles, Cassie becoming the mute unresponsive one. Which left him to fuel the conversation and provide entertainment. Once again, Dan was reminded of what it must have cost her to turn up week after week and sit opposite him.

'You were asking,' he said, 'if I'd remembered where I might have seen your victim from the solar farm.'

'Was I?'

'In your text.'

She pulled a face. 'Oh yeah. That's right.'

Cassie often became defensive if he showed interest in the cases she had taken on since he left the service. Even when praising her detective skills, Dan knew he managed to be patronising. He decided not to mention his walk to the solar farm. She would assume he was checking up on her. No lies. He had been checking up on her.

'I still can't remember where I might have seen him,' Dan said.

'Forget I asked, it's not your concern. Another half?' She gestured at his glass, which was nearly empty.

'No, I'm fine. But thanks.'

They both turned as a noisy crowd entered the bar, some of them underage. Dan noticed Cassie giving the landlord a look. The man nodded. Dan and Cassie had been regulars here for several years, and it had not taken the landlord long to establish they were police. Dan knew, even without the uniform, that police was something he emitted like a signal. They all did, current and former officers. The watchful gaze was a giveaway. Along with the stance, weight forward on the balls of the feet, and the tendency to eye up the exits.

'By the way,' Dan said, 'I'm still on the hunt for John Strang.'

'The resident who scarpered without paying rent?'

'Mrs Faulkner found some cash in his caravan, under the mattress.'

'Problem solved,' Cassie said.

'It's just he seemed kind of troubled.'

'Social work your next vocation?' Again, the mocking tone.

'Anyway,' Dan said, 'if he does cross your radar... well, it would be great if you could let me know.'

Cassie laughed. 'You're turning into a right little private dick.'

'Hard to shake the habit of a lifetime,' he said with a wry smile.

'You aren't all bad. A whopping saviour complex, but you do have some merits.'

'Cheers,' Dan said, clinking his glass against hers. 'That almost sounded like a compliment. Speaking of being a private dick, I noticed something a bit odd when I was out walking this afternoon.'

'You could ask for your old job back if you're that desperate.'

Ignoring this, he said, 'Remember me telling you about Summerlands being on the site of Gazeby Palace?'

'Yeah, you gave me a whole history lesson.'

'There's an underground icehouse north of the caravan park. The padlock on the door has been sawn through, then put back on as if it was still locked. I was curious to see inside.

Turns out someone's been sleeping in one of the cellars. Maybe it's being used as a hideout.'

Cassie nodded. 'Interesting. I'd like to take a look.'

'Thought you might,' Dan said. 'The icehouse could be linked to the solar-farm murder.'

'Still the detective,' she said, raising her eyebrows.

'There's clothing, bedding, dishes, some tins of food. Oh, and a table and chair from Summerlands. Mrs Faulkner revamped the cafe a few months ago – the old furniture was left behind the west barn. Everything was supposed to go to the dump, but the van's been in for repairs.'

'And now this table and chair find their way to your icehouse. A cosy little home, by the sound of it. I'd like you to give me a tour. I'll check if it's worth summoning the CSI cavalry.' Cassie glanced at her watch. 'Sorry, need to get back. Would tomorrow suit for visiting the icehouse? If you're busy I can go on my own. Someone at the caravan site can point me in the right direction.'

'I'm free in the afternoon.'

'I'll message you.' She downed the rest of her drink. 'What I said about Archie being a little shit, I didn't mean it.'

'I know,' he said, reminded once again that they had forgotten how to talk to each other.

'And don't go back inside the icehouse,' Cassie said. 'Not unless I'm with you.'

'Of course.' Another thing that went without saying.

Dan found himself thinking what had seemed unthinkable. Now that he was no longer police, they might drift apart. Stop being friends.

Driving back, Dan had only seen darkness beyond his headlights. But as he stepped out of the car, he noticed a soft brightness from the moon, all across the caravan park. It was late. After Cassie left the pub, it had taken him a long time to summon the will to go. The landlord had asked if he was okay, and Dan wondered if he knew about Beth, if Cassie had told him at some point.

There was not much activity at Summerlands. A few windows glowed, and Dan heard a muted burst of laughter from inside a caravan. The route to his own took him past the bungalow. Glancing across the garden, he noticed a figure at the far end, silhouetted against the moonlit field beyond. It was Mrs Faulkner. A breeze rippled the pale fingertips of wheat. Was she talking to her son?

Dan hoped that one day he would feel able to speak to Beth. For the past seven months, the words crowding his lips had been accusations. *Why did you have to die? Why didn't you look when you crossed the road?*

Safer to say nothing. Less painful.

But what was Beth doing on Magdalen Street? She worked at the University of East Anglia, and its campus was on the other side of Norwich. Had Beth been meeting someone? All these questions made it seem like he blamed her for what happened. Dan dragged a hand across his face. There would be little chance of sleep tonight. He collected a dark jacket and black cap from his caravan, then he set off for the icehouse. Cassie had told him not to go in, but he could watch the entrance. The icehouse belonged to Mrs Faulkner – checking for intruders was part of his job.

The land was so quiet, spectral under the moonlight. Dan followed the path, taking it slow. There was something magical about walking at night, no one around. It felt like stolen time. Once, when he was driving somewhere, on a dark winding lane near Blo Norton, his headlights picked up a pale shape and he had stopped the car. The narrow road had flooded. A small deer, the colour of snow, was drinking from the black pool, its image reflected in the surface. The moment had been uncanny. This was the white hart from folklore. The creature raised its head, met his gaze, then it darted through a hedge. The encounter had cast a spell and on a night like this, making his way between hushed fields, Dan felt again the presence of that white deer.

In the distance, the wooded mound seemed blacker and more looming than in daylight. The trees were taller and through them, in what registered as a change of texture, he could see the sloping sides of the icehouse. Dan approached from the right, using a hedgerow as cover. Then he skirted the mound until he had a slant view of the entrance to the icehouse. The door was shut. Dan crept nearer. The padlock was in place, which meant nobody was inside. For now.

Closing his eyes, he pictured the underground chamber. Tomorrow, Cassie would decide whether to call in forensics. But Dan wanted time alone with his own thoughts, his own deductions. The table and chair came from Summerlands – Strang could be the one living here. No money, no options, and so he had set up home in the icehouse. But anyone could have removed that furniture from behind the west barn, when it was dark. Anyone looking to create a hideout.

Did the murder victim take refuge here?

Or was the killer using the icehouse and sleeping in that dank cell?

The man might return any moment. The thought held no fear for Dan.

He withdrew, back among the trees. Found a hollow at the base of a Scots pine, the ground covered in soft brown needles. Warmth lingered in the night air, but he did not know how long this vigil would last.

Silence, stillness, just the shallow rise and fall of his soundless breathing.

Dan leaned against the tree. Waiting for the icehouse sleeper.

Chapter 11

In the morning, Dan found a white envelope lying on the carpet in his caravan. There had been no sign of it when he got back in the early hours, so the envelope must have been pushed under his door while he slept. It contained a handwritten letter, along with colour copies of a driving licence and newspaper article. Dan examined the letter first.

To whom it may concern,

The bearer of these documents is Daniel Hennessy. He is a former Detective Inspector with Norfolk Constabulary. He now works as security advisor at the caravan park which I own and manage, Summerlands, near Candlesham.

On 4th July 2001 my son Felix went missing while I was visiting a house in Beccles belonging to a colleague of my ex-husband. My son was six weeks old. His disappearance has never been solved.

I have commissioned Mr Hennessy to make enquiries in order to turn up new leads. Please do not contact me direct but relay any information or questions via him. So that you can be assured this letter is genuine, I enclose copies of my driving licence and a newspaper article. I hope these bona fides are enough to satisfy you.

I need to know what happened to my son Felix.

Please help me.

Alice Faulkner

The letter was in black ink on white paper. Her handwriting was elegant, laid out in neatly parallel lines, with an inch margin round the edges and a date at the top. Not a mistake or hesitation anywhere. Dan put the letter down and rubbed his face. He wondered how many attempts it had taken Mrs Faulkner to produce such a clear and concise missive. When he saw her staring across the moonlit field, had she been composing this letter?

Mrs Faulkner had let her guard down, the other evening, when she talked to him about Felix. The rest of the time she maintained strict control. He could envisage her walking back up the garden and writing that letter in one go. Ruthlessly efficient even in her state of suspended mourning. Dan had to keep reminding himself of the small chance that Felix did not die.

He glanced at the date on the driving licence. Mrs Faulkner was forty-two. Younger than he thought, but maybe sadness had aged her. She would have been twenty-one when she gave birth to her son. Not as young as some mothers, but young all the same. Dan recalled who he had been at that age, and 'still a kid' seemed the best description. He had done a lot of growing up in his twenties.

Dan picked up the newspaper article, published the day after Felix went missing.

Mum Makes Desperate Plea was the headline. Below was a colour photograph of Alice Faulkner standing beside an older man in a tweed jacket. This was the husband Robert. Behind them was a hedge but no other details showing location. Alice Faulkner held a small framed picture in front of her chest. The newsprint was grainy, but Dan could make out what appeared to be an image of a baby. Proof that Felix existed, and which his mother was gripping tightly.

Alice Faulkner stared out of the newspaper. Pain dragged at her mouth, clawed at her eyes. The husband was looking to the side, gaze directed at the ground. Robert seemed to be in his early thirties. Youngish face but receding hairline. An age difference between the couple. Dan read the short article that gave the main details of Felix's disappearance. Nothing in there he did not already know.

Why was the headline not *Parents Make Desperate Plea*, given they were both in the photograph? The newspaper editor had gone with *Mum*. There was something diffident about the husband's posture. He had an arm around Alice Faulkner, but that sideways glance made it seem as if he was distancing himself. Not everyone chose to feed the media's appetite for suffering. After Beth was killed, a number of journalists rang and left messages, saying they wanted him to 'share his love story' and tell the public 'how Bethany touched so many people's lives'. He never returned their calls. Dan peered at the photocopy of the article, angling it to the light from the window. In the grainy colour photograph on cheap newsprint, he could detect two explanations for Robert Faulkner's diffidence. The man did not wish to speak to the media. Or he had something to hide.

Dan pulled out the case file and checked the references to Robert. He had arrived at Chapel House at 5.15 p.m., the afternoon of the disappearance, having been contacted by Lydia Ingleby. The police questioned him regarding the possibility of a kidnap, and whether there had been any issues that might have triggered a vendetta, such as a serious dispute with a client or acquaintance. Or perhaps the Faulkners had recently come into an inheritance, with someone looking to capitalise on this via a ransom demand. Just as Dan was doing now, the police had tried to find a motive for abducting a six-week-old baby.

That interview at Chapel House had been transcribed in the diplomatic language of police statements, but clearly things became heated. Robert Faulkner responded with anger to the notion that he or Alice were 'to blame' for their son's disappearance. Robert was further angered by questions about Felix's parentage, and the possibility that the baby had been taken by his biological father. The interview was suspended for half an hour, with Robert requesting the presence of his solicitor. DI Drummond had then apologised for insinuating that Robert Faulkner was not the real father.

Dan switched his attention to the newspaper article, rereading the quote from Mrs Faulkner. 'I just want my baby back.' Not *we* or *our*. She did not include her husband in the statement. Robert Faulkner was on the list of potential suspects, but Dan's first step was to visit Chapel House and the garden where Felix was last seen. Begin at the beginning.

With a frown, he folded up Mrs Faulkner's letter, the copies of the article and driving licence. These were no guarantee that Lydia Ingleby would allow him through the door.

After Dan dropped a passenger in Besthorpe, a notification came, cancelling his next booking. No others currently on his roster, so he headed for Wymondham railway station in the hope of some passing trade. But as he neared the town's southern outskirts, his resolve went. It had been a rough week and only Beth could help.

At the roundabout, Dan turned left and drove the familiar route. He parked on the brick paved area assigned to their house and three others. The smaller properties did not come with a garage or forecourt. Nor was there room to park in front, as the road was deliberately narrow. The whole estate had been designed to minimise the impact of vehicles, but to his eyes it did the opposite. Everywhere he looked there were garages the size of bungalows, along with clustered parking bays that reminded him of a town centre.

Dan reached the keys from the glove box and walked up the path. The grass needed trimming. A fortnight since he last did the lawn, using a strimmer borrowed from Summerlands. No rain and the grass still managed to grow. Dan stopped by the front door. Someone had removed both lavender plants from the pots either side of the entrance. He came here most weeks and always watered them. Now the pots were empty.

'Hi,' a voice said.

So far Dan had avoided contact with any residents.

The man was smiling at him over a low fence, which separated their two gardens. 'Are you our new neighbour? My wife was just saying she was wondering when the house might be occupied.'

'Pleased to meet you. But I'm not... I'm looking after the place for a friend.'

'Any idea when they're moving in?'

'No. Sorry.' Dan went in and shut the door, leaned against it.

He swallowed. Sadness came in many forms. Wet, raw, numb, a wrench of the heart, or slow, blunt, like a toothache, a gut ache, sometimes piercing, a migraine, an itch on his skin, scalding, a rush of the blood, a punch to the chest, shivering with cold, a leaden weight in his feet, a clamp squeezing his skull. The sadness of this moment was parched. Sore and dry. They had been due to move in when she died. He and Beth were on a countdown, packing boxes, arranging wifi, utilities, less than a week until the move. And then she died. 30th November. Last day of the month. Last day of her life. They never got to live here. The house was furnished with dreams not memories. And ever since, Dan had been visiting, allowing himself to hide behind these walls. Escape the world for a few hours in this quiet mausoleum. Today, with the inquisitive neighbour, the stealing of the lavender, he was exposed.

Dan sat on the floor but left Beth's ashes in the cupboard. He did not want to bring her out on a day when the house seemed different. There was a tremor in his body so fast he could not know if it was real. Like a sound higher than the threshold of audibility. Dan stretched out his hands. The fingers twitched, making tiny movements of their own accord. It was a deception to imagine the 'I' inside had control. Was this what madness felt like? He crossed his arms, and silenced his fingers, pressing them against his ribs.

An email had come yesterday afternoon – there was a limit to how long he could ignore it. Beth's parents had only contacted him a few times since the funeral. They were dealing with their grief just as he was dealing with his. Dan had always found them odd. Their tendency to dwell on the fact he was two years younger than Beth. Their barely disguised disappointment that she was planning to marry a police officer. Beth and he used to joke about this. Her mother and father had seen too many cop dramas about detectives with drink problems and broken marriages. Dan also knew that when they looked at him, in the aftermath, all they saw was police and it was police who killed their daughter.

The day Beth was cremated, her parents had been holding hands, silent as they left the chapel, when they both stared at him. With such loathing. Ready to mow him down in the street if it could have saved her.

The email was from Beth's father. Its awkward politeness had brought a wave of nausea, and Dan felt it again as he recalled the wording. They were asking when he would take sole possession of the house. *We know how difficult this must be for you, but Janet and I are keen to finalise matters.*

The house was joint owned by Dan and Beth. The payments came out of a shared account and he made sure, after her death, that there was enough money each month for the mortgage. The two of them had put down a deposit of thirty thousand. Dan had covered his half with savings and an inheritance. Beth's fifteen thousand had been a gift from her parents.

They were asking for it back. Her father had suggested, in his email, that Dan should either sell the house or rent it out if he did not want to live there. *Janet and I have discussed a timeframe of two months, at the end of which we would appreciate it if you could arrange to transfer the £15,000.*

Dan was not ready to let go the home that he and Beth chose. How could he? It was meant to be their future. His heart lurched, and he felt that kick of adrenalin, his skin flushing with sweat, fear, panic. Dan tried to breathe it away, but a memory had been triggered. Too late to stop the replay. He closed his eyes, expecting a flashback to the funeral, but smelling woodland instead.

Heart still racing, Dan is seeing nighttime, black shadows, the greyness of moonlight. He begins to recognise where he is. Sitting under a tree, near the icehouse. Waiting. Then he feels his inner self loosen and rise, unpeeling. Dan walks over the soft ground, slides the bolt across, grasps the handle, pulls back the door, crosses the threshold, and slowly descends the steps. The stone sarcophagus is calling him, the dark water beckoning. He lies down in its cold embrace, his breath slowing as minerals seep into his lungs.

'*No.*' The word burst from his mouth as his eyes flew open.

Chapter 12

Dan stood up, shook the stiffness from his limbs. Eyes blinking, he registered the stark familiarity of the room. So white, so bare. What time was it? On the way out, his fingers brushed across the small cupboard door. *Bye, love.*

Inside the car, he checked his phone. 11:51. A message had come from Cassie, saying she was heading to the caravan park. They had talked of going in the afternoon, so she must have changed her plans. He texted back *With you ASAP x*

As soon as Dan arrived at Summerlands, Mrs Faulkner accosted him, saying, 'What's this about a break-in at the icehouse?'

'DI Fisher here?'

'Apparently the tip-off came from you. May I remind you, Daniel, you're supposed to be my head of security. Why didn't you speak to me first?'

Dan muttered an apology, then went to grab a coat from his caravan. No real memory of the walk, he found himself at the icehouse. Even in daylight it seemed to retain some of last night's shadows. The wooden door was open.

'Is that you, Cassie?' he called.

Silence, then a flicker of light at the bottom of the stair.

Dan joined her, saying, 'Not worried about cross-contamination?'

'Ha ha. Just don't touch stuff, okay?'

Cassie had already put on latex gloves and she was holding an LED torch.

'I'm not convinced,' she said, 'that this is anything other than some vagrant finding a place to kip.'

Dan weighed up whether to tell her the vagrant could be John Strang, the misper from the caravan park. Then he decided against. Cassie would dismiss it as pure speculation.

'Hello, by the way,' she said.

'Yes, hi. Great to see you last night.' The words sounded false even to his own ears.

'You came prepared.' She nodded at his coat.

'Want me to do the chivalrous thing?'

'Apparently women don't perish from the cold. It's remarkable what feminism has taught us.'

Dan smiled. 'Seen much of interest?'

'Haven't been here long. Your landlady didn't seem keen to allow me access. Tricky customer.'

'Sorry if Mrs Faulkner gave you a hard time.'

He and Cassie stood in the doorway of the fourth cellar. Their torch beams scythed across the floor, walls and ceiling, then lingered on the items that furnished this incongruous home.

'Creepy,' she said. 'It's a bit Mary Celeste, everything sitting here in the dark. And this is how it was yesterday?'

'Yeah.'

'You're certain nothing's been disturbed since?'

'Don't think so.' Dan had no intention of saying that last night he kept the icehouse under surveillance. It would ruin her mood.

'You said the table and chair are from the caravan site. Recognise anything else?'

'No, nothing.'

'What d'you make of that?' Cassie aimed her torch at the trough of water. 'Not the usual place for a garden pond.'

'Washing and drinking?'

'Yeah. Probs. Weird all the same.'

Cassie then examined the clothes in the trough on the right. Dan watched, angling his phone torch to help. Her hands slid between layers, she was nearly at the bottom of the pile.

'Wait,' he said, 'that blanket, the brown fleece one. They have them at Summerlands.' There had been one in the caravan when Dan first moved in. It had smelled of cigarettes and he replaced it with a new duvet.

'Your Mrs Faulkner will not be pleased someone's been raiding her caravans.'

'Looks like it's a bloke,' Dan said, 'if the clothes are anything to go by.'

Cassie felt the pocket of a jacket, then she pulled out a small object. Dan aimed his torch, making it gleam. A ceramic figure, glazed pale blue, conical in shape, semi-abstract. Arms reaching. The surfaces were smooth, with very little detail. He had seen it before, somewhere.

The ornament sat in Cassie's hand. She eyed it. 'Bit naff, if you ask me.'

'Odd thing to have in a pocket,' Dan said.

'Pretty odd to sleep in an icehouse.' Cassie shivered. 'Not sure how much longer I can last.' She put the ceramic back in the jacket pocket, then reassembled the pile, pulling into place the blankets and clothing.

Dan frowned, recalling his visit to Mrs Faulkner's bungalow. On her mantelpiece there had been a pair of figures. A mother and child embracing. 'I need to check,' he said, 'but Mrs Faulkner has a ceramic very like that in her living room.'

'You think it came from there?'

'Possibly. I'll ask.'

'Spending a lot of time in Mrs Faulkner's private quarters?' Cassie nudged him.

'It's not like that. Are we done?'

'Reckon so.'

After a last look round, they climbed the stair toward daylight. Dan was about to close the door when Cassie stopped him. 'I've got gloves,' she said, pushing the door and replacing the broken padlock.

'So you're going to call in the techs,' he said.

'Can we find some sun? I need to defrost.'

Dan followed Cassie through the trees and sat next to her on the ground. She tilted her face up, eyes shut. Her head was impenetrable. Hard and round. He wondered what she was thinking right now. Not about the icehouse. Dan could feel the barrier she had erected. Cassie was hiding something. Why did he not just ask? Fear prevented him. *Sticks and stones may break my bones but words will always hurt me*.

'Whoever it is,' Dan said, 'he's trespassing.'

Cassie's eyes snapped open. 'What do you mean by that?'

'I'm talking about the person sleeping here.'

'Oh,' she said. 'Him'

'Who else would I be talking about?'

'Forget it.'

He glanced at her, but she was now staring into the distance. Dan waited a moment, then said, 'So this trespasser, he must have broken in during the past six months. I remember examining the padlock in December, and it was fine.'

Cassie blew out a breath. 'This sun makes me long for a holiday. A proper one. Going on holiday with Archie is basically looking after a toddler in a less convenient location and with food he won't eat.'

'I could take care of him, give you a break,' Dan said. 'I'm sure me and Archie could manage a long weekend. Allow you a chance to get away.'

'Stop being so goddam nice.' Cassie smiled at him, but something flickered across the back of her eyes. The thing she was keeping secret?

Chapter 13

Jay texted Gary about the change of plans, then went to find her father. He was seated at the kitchen table, slicing a peeled potato.

'Can I borrow the car later?' It was like being eighteen again. 'The starter on my bike's misbehaving and I need to go to London.'

His knife wavered.

'We've got a booking.'

Her father nodded. 'Safer in the Nissan.'

'Plus I want to collect some stuff.' True, but she also wanted to restrict his movements.

'I haven't seen you perform in a while.'

'I'll fix up a Norwich gig,' she said, knowing the band would never agree.

Jay remembered her father's trip to that pub in Hackney, three or four years ago, to hear Life Class. Him balanced on a high stool, blinking at the glorious din from the speakers. A man trying to enjoy a wind tunnel, that was the image which stayed with her.

'Jacqueline?'

She smiled. He was the one person who could use that name without making her wince.

'Want me to take a look?' he said.

'Huh?'

'Sounds like your ignition switch.'

'Let's do it when I'm back. Probably just needs a good clean.' She glanced at his shirt. 'It's not the only thing.'

Her father grinned. 'This isn't my visitor shirt.'

'How often does that get an outing?'

'Pension day.'

He raised the chopping board and nudged the pale slivers into a pan of water. His mashed potato had plagued her childhood, puddles of white on the plate. She and Colin still laughed about it. Jay wanted her brother here, right now, seeing this – Dad doing normal stuff. He poked a finger in the pan and stirred it about, releasing eddies of starch.

After lunch, Jay carried their dishes to the sink but her father said, 'You should be off.'

She reversed the car out of the garage, wheels grinding the gravel while her father gave signals suited to a Boeing 747.

'Might rain later,' Jay said, peering at the sky as she climbed out of the car. 'Okay if I stick my bike under cover?'

In the space of four days, the Yamaha had stiffened into a solid mass. Her father offered to help and they steered it over the apron of concrete. The sinews on his forearms stood out like bungee cords.

'Hope the concert goes well,' he said, as they headed back to the car.

'It's more of a gig.' She yanked her earring. Why correct him? 'I've got a key, don't wait up. It'll be two at the earliest.'

Jay hugged him, then sat in the driver's seat. Her father gripped the door and leaned in. Beaky nose and a warm smile. He was a pop-up figure in those picture books she had piled into boxes, now destined for a charity shop.

'You'll have things to do in London,' he said. 'There's no hurry on the Nissan. Keep it until next week.'

'Thanks, but I'll see you tomorrow. I want to finish sorting my room.'

'Up to you, love.'

Her father stepped back and slammed the door. He walked alongside as she steered down the drive. Pulling into the lane, Jay braked at the sound of two sharp slaps. What had been forgotten? Then she smiled. Just her father's country habit, slapping the car's flank like it was livestock.

Ten minutes later, she was on the A11, that odd airless sensation of driving at high speed with no wind. Her hands gripped the wheel, thoughts moving ahead. Tonight's booking was for their tribute act, Riders. Money from those gigs allowed them to keep going with Life Class, their real band. What had Sean said the other day? *You'll make it.* Jay used to think so too. She switched her mind to the Doors set list, beginning with 'Light My Fire'. Krieger's chords and solos in her fingers, she stared at the road, seeing but not registering the onrush of sounds and shapes that sped toward her, leaving blurred trails across the windscreen.

Then, off to the left, Jay glimpsed a jagged colour that cut through the thin margin of trees. The music vacated her fingers and a buzzing silence filled her head. She glanced at the figures in fluorescent jackets and hard hats, grouped round a theodolite. This had been her father's world. Before retiring, he was a civil engineer. Trade magazines had lain around her childhood home but she had never picked one up.

The forest closed in once more, the taller trees held back by lines of Scots pines. The long dual carriageway funnelled the perspective into wedges of green, and for a moment Jay was breathing in the leather tang of Thomson's and being fitted for new school shoes. There had been a heavy curtain that led to a wall of boxes, and to the left of it a framed advert for Start-Rite. The poster must have been vintage even then. The image of two lone children on an empty road had always disturbed her.

Jay spotted a motorbike in the rear-view mirror, weaving in and out of traffic a long way back. It was catching up fast and she felt her breath quicken, sharing the adrenalin of the anonymous rider, her hand twisting an absent throttle. Driving a car might be safer, but when had 'safer' ever defined her actions? And like a sudden scalding burn, she remembered what that attitude had cost her.

Frowning, Jay wondered if she had come to the wrong pub, as the place seemed dead, no lights in the windows. The entrance was a pair of doors with peeling varnish. They were locked, no bell or knocker, so she banged a fist. Half a minute later, a key rattled on the inside. The right leaf opened a few inches, then came to a grating halt.

'Fucking thing,' muttered a familiar voice.

Damn. She had been hoping for Ruben.

The wood screeched as the door was wrenched back. Theo glared at her. 'What're you doing here? Where's Gary?'

His T-shirt was too tight, and the smell of aftershave unwrapped a memory. Not now.

Jay blinked and said, 'Change of plans.'

Theo scowled, then rubbed his nipple with the flat of his hand. 'Get a move on, you're late.'

Next second he was gone. The inner doors swung back and forth, like a fading heartbeat. Her gaze dropped to a mosaic of worn tiles on the lobby floor. The White Horse. A handy getaway. Why had she bothered coming.

Jay glanced along the street, noticing a newsagents. Her mouth felt hollow. Theo. Ruben. What a mess. And now she did not even have the shabby, momentary respite of a cigarette. She rubbed her face then entered the pub. In the semi-darkness, bottles and optics gave off a dusty coloured glow. No one to be seen. An amp screeched somewhere to the left and she followed the bar round to a large windowless space with lights shining on a stage.

Ruben was crouched down, making adjustments to the whining amp. Jay glanced at his narrow hips and the flare of his broad back. Then she forced herself to look away.

Nick was behind the drums, talking to someone she did not know.

'Hi. Sorry I'm late.' Her mouth was dry.

Ruben stood up. His smile was almost a flinch.

Nick gave a salute, then carried on chatting to the guy in the plaid shirt.

'How was the journey?' Ruben said.

'Slow.' She put her guitar down. 'And I had to go via the flat.'

'Why didn't you call?'

She thought about the warm slide of space beneath his shirt. 'Wasn't sure I was coming.'

Ruben frowned. 'Well, you're here. I'll send you the set list.'

A few taps on his phone, then he said, 'What did you do to Theo?'

Jay swallowed. It took her a moment to realise he meant now, not the night in May when she screwed everything up with a capital F.

'Nothing,' she said. 'You know what he's like.'

A door burst open and Theo appeared, along with a girl and two hipster guys, carrying guitar cases. This must be the support act. Theo was laughing and talking, his foul mood gone. No doubt he was spinning some fable from his rock 'n roll past.

At the corner of the stage, Theo stopped and pointed at Jay. 'See? Told you the prodigal bitch had returned.'

Ruben tensed. 'Shut it, Theo.'

'Remind me to slaughter a fatted calf.' Theo surveyed his audience, then he looked at Jay. 'Though maybe a doner kebab's more your thing. Quick and easy, huh?'

She made a grab for Ruben's arm. 'Don't. My problem not yours.'

The three newcomers seemed ready to leave. Jay smiled at them, saying, 'Sorry, guys. Theo gets very uptight before a gig. Don't you, *sweetie*?'

Her eyes locked on Theo. He was a bastard, but Jay knew he would not jeopardise tonight's performance with an all-out fight.

Then Nick cut in, saying, 'Anyone seen my stick bag?'

Jay left them searching the stage. She followed the sign for *Ladies* through two sets of doors. Hands gripping the cold sink, she breathed out. The face in the mirror was small and tired. Four days with her father and already she had lost the habit of wearing make-up. Jay dug out a kohl pencil from her bag and drew thick lines round her eyes. She still looked like shit.

With a sigh, Jay read the message on her phone, forwarded by Ruben. She could see from the time stamp that Theo had changed the set list ten minutes ago. Just after she arrived. Tonight they would be opening with 'People Are Strange'. Not good. They were in for a bumpy ride.

Jay sniffed her armpits. Not good either. She stripped off the vest, her flesh seeming alien under the fluorescents. None of the sinks had plugs, so she wetted some paper towels and wiped her armpits. Rinsing them with water, Jay shivered as it slid down her ribs. She dabbed herself dry and yanked the vest back on.

This pretence that things were 'okay'. That the band could carry on as before. That the needle of her life had not scraped across the vinyl and landed on a different track, where childhood and adulthood were being rewritten, and the music was warped.

People Are Strange.

Her own father, a stranger to her. Someone she barely knew.

Chapter 14

Dan peered at the morning outside. Hands cradling a mug of coffee, he tried to remember what day it was. Friday? He fetched his phone, laid it on the table. 07:43 Saturday 9 July. Dan had slept worse than usual, his mind fixating on a particular memory, and it was still with him. Most of the time he and Beth had got along great, but they did argue now and then. Those disagreements would often return if he was struggling to sleep. Like a punishment.

For hours, Dan had lain awake, reliving when he and Beth went for a drink at The Boars, in Spooner Row. Early summer, last year. They had sat in a garden at the rear. The two of them laughing, as Beth recounted a funny story from her childhood. Then the mood soured. Dan had made a throwaway remark, to do with her being adopted. Beth had always seemed 'cool' about this fact, but that evening Dan touched a nerve. The look on her face. *You've no idea what it feels like to never know where you came from.*

He had said some things he regretted.

The phone buzzed, making his body jump.

It was a text from Cassie, coming through in rapid bursts.

Rubbing his eyes, he tried to lose that difficult memory about Beth.

Then he read Cassie's message.

CSIs on way to icehouse

Act like you don't know

Not supposed to be keeping you in the loop

Someone's told Walsh you're living at Summerlands

She reminded me you're no longer one of us... x

Yesterday afternoon, as they were walking back, Cassie had said she would have to speak to the SIO before calling in forensics. Budgetary concerns were always foremost in Elaine

Walsh's mind. Somehow Cassie had persuaded her to spend resources on checking the icehouse.

Dan finished his coffee and went in search of Mrs Faulkner. She was in reception, next to the noticeboard, removing posters and adverts that were now out of date. Riffling through them, she said, 'Did your detective friend find anything at the icehouse?'

'Someone has clearly been staying there. The police will be back to follow it up. This may or may not be connected to that murder at the solar farm.'

'I sincerely hope it's not.' Mrs Faulkner threw a sheaf of papers in the bin.

'I wanted to ask—' Dan stopped. It meant referring to when he sat in her bungalow and she told him about Felix. Mrs Faulkner had insisted they were to behave as if that never happened. He respected her reasons, knew what it was like to live a life governed by avoidance.

Dan began again, saying, 'There was clothing at the icehouse. We discovered an item in a jacket pocket. A small ceramic figure with reaching arms. Pale blue. About so big.' He indicated with finger and thumb.

Mrs Faulkner blinked and then she laughed, a fierce sound. 'Daniel, why are you telling me all this?'

'I thought I saw something similar on your mantlepiece. It's not been stolen, has it?'

'I can't help you,' she said, turning back to the noticeboard.

Dan watched as she prised out a drawing pin with her fingernails. He was about to say, *Are you sure?* when Samantha burst through the double doors.

Her face took on an avid gleam as she looked at him and Mrs Faulkner. 'Sorry, am I interrupting? You guys seem kinda tense.'

Dan had asked the dispatcher if there were any bookings in the direction of Beccles. At lunchtime, he was allocated a drop-off in Lowestoft, and once the job was completed, Dan headed back along the A147.

'You again,' the woman said as she opened the front door to Chapel House.

He stood on the pavement while she read the letter from Mrs Faulkner. Her attention shifted to the driving licence and newspaper report, several minutes passing as she rechecked the documents. Dan kept a neutral expression on his face.

The woman was wearing a yellow blouse and pale pink skirt. Gold necklace. Finally, she gave him back the envelope, saying, 'I suppose you'd better come in.' Dan was led through a square lobby into a kitchen. 'I'm not Lydia, by the way. Last week you may have got the wrong impression.'

He frowned. 'Is this some kind of trick?'

'Hardly. Can I offer you a coffee? You assumed I was Lydia Ingelby and it wasn't my business to correct you. Especially given I thought you were some low-life journalist. I'm Catherine Nash. I was also there that day. Along with Alice and Lydia, of course. So I imagine you want to speak to me too.'

'But is this not Lydia Ingleby's house?'

'It was. Apologies for the confusion but you were a stranger on my doorstep. I didn't know if you were genuine. Did you say yes to coffee?'

'Thanks. Black, no sugar.' He felt the sudden vertigo of how it must have been the day Felix disappeared. Dan anchored his hand on the worktop while Catherine busied herself with a shiny kettle. The kitchen seemed ordinary enough, cluttered with cookbooks and utensils, two Georgian windows overlooking the street, a dresser crowded with plates and novelty mugs. A teapot shaped like a strawberry. On the table there was a stack of A4 brochures for something called *Young Minds*. A photo of saccharine-faced teenagers on the cover. All of them white, Dan noticed.

It was the kitchen of an upper-middle-class person who had lived here a decade at least. Being a police officer had trained his observations and Dan wondered if the habit would ever leave him – assessing a room's history and socioeconomic signals. In this case, they showed a financially secure life running on predictable tracks toward a comfortable retirement. But Dan was on guard. Catherine had pretended to be somebody else, and although she offered an explanation, the ease of her deception rang a high-pitched warning in his ears.

The woman thrust a mug of coffee at him. It was burning hot, and he transferred his grip to the handle. She was not having one herself, and Dan wished he had said no.

'This way. We'll take a seat in the drawing room.' They went along a corridor, Catherine saying, 'I mentioned the house was on the market?' She paused in a large hallway with oil portraits, shafts of light from an oculus two storeys above. 'You can spot the serious buyers,' she continued. 'They don't speak much, just walk about looking in cupboards and corners. Very different to what I call the day trippers. People who see it as a nice outing to come and view someone's home. No intention of buying but very enthusiastic, you know?'

Dan nodded, feigning interest.

Catherine then led him to a tall oak door. She opened it, announcing, 'Now for the *pièce de résistance*.'

The drawing room was intended to impress. Dan said, 'Oh, wow,' aware that if he wanted information from this woman, he had to comply with the charade.

'It's a former chapel,' she said, 'thought to be as early as 1630. Listed by English Heritage, of course, because of the historical significance.'

Dan was reminded of an underused lounge in a provincial hotel. The space was vast, decorated in a burgundy flock wallpaper, and it had an ornate ceiling, cream-painted vaulting, from which hung a huge crystal chandelier. A plush Persian-style carpet on the floor. The end of the room was curved, like an apse, with gothic alcoves full of ornaments. Against the right-hand wall was an antique sideboard sporting a bronze statue of a stag. The left-hand wall was dominated by three tall windows with pointed arches. The curtains were burgundy, with swags and gold tassels. Stepping near, Dan peered outside. The garden at the rear fell toward the River Waveney, a screen of trees on the far bank and fields beyond.

'Please.' Catherine gestured to a small velvet armchair.

When Dan sat down, his knees were by his elbows. No table nearby, so he had to hold the scalding mug of coffee.

Catherine was on a chintz sofa with her back to the light. 'I've always loved our chapel. It's why we bought the house off Lydia. Because of this room, you know?'

Clearly the woman had decided he was a philistine.

'It's certainly unique,' Dan said.

'I wish I could take it with me.' She laughed.

'Was this where you and Lydia and Alice were? The day her son was abducted?'

Catherine blinked as if he had said something vulgar. 'That poor baby, such a tragedy. But lots of other things have happened here – the room has so much history. That little niche was where the priest used to wash his hands.' She pointed to the left. 'A chapel makes the perfect party space. Family Christmases, my husband's sixtieth. Our daughter had her eighteenth here. It was stunning.' Then her gaze dropped and she frowned at her coffee.

'This is a happy place for you,' Dan said, 'but Alice Faulkner only remembers the day her baby vanished from his pram. I want to establish the circumstances. See if I can uncover any additional details. Will you help me, Catherine?'

'Whyever not?' she said, her response almost angry. 'I'll do my best, but it was a long time ago. So sad. I try not to think about it. Affected all of us, you know? Not just Alice. And Robert, of course. We mustn't forget Robert. Alice wasn't very nice to him. Afterward. She wasn't very nice to any of us.'

'The woman lost her son.'

'I know that.' She glared at Dan. 'It was truly awful, but Alice acted like it was *our fault*. Like we stole him from her.' Catherine gave a strangled laugh. 'It was verging on ridiculous. And don't give me that look. You've no idea how horrendous it was being blamed for something we had absolutely nothing to do with.'

Her words reverberated in the room. The crystal chandelier made a ringing sound.

Dan waited until it was quiet, then he said, 'Tell me how you came to own Chapel House.'

He sipped his cooling coffee while Catherine recounted that she and her husband took on the house about six months after Felix disappeared. Dan learned that Lydia Ingleby's marriage had been rocky and that the tragedy 'widened the cracks'. Alice Faulkner told everyone that Catherine and Lydia were drunk that afternoon. That they bullied her. That Lydia promised she would keep an eye on Felix but was too inebriated to spot an intruder stealing him from his pram. These accusations created tensions in their social circle. Dan found it hard to feel any pity for Catherine and Lydia.

'We bought the house via a private sale,' she said. 'Lydia and Magnus were going through a divorce by that point. And putting the place on the market would only have attracted the wrong sort of crowd, because of...'

'Did Lydia get custody of Jack?'

'No. She always referred to him as her son, but he was Magnus's from a previous marriage. Jack went with his father. After the divorce.'

Dan was surprised this had not been noted in the case file. Were the police unaware that Jack was Lydia's stepson? As a DI, he had always sought to equip himself with every aspect. Even those with no direct bearing could still contribute to an overall sense of the situation and relationships.

'Are you still in touch with Lydia?' he said. 'I'd like to speak to her if possible. Also Jack – he witnessed the abduction. Maybe you have a way of reaching Magnus, so I can get Jack's details?'

'I can't help you with Magnus or Jack. A divorce means choosing sides. I voted for Lydia.'

'Do you have an address for her?'

Catherine bristled. 'I'm not sure she'll appreciate you turning up uninvited.'

'Let me give you my number.' Dan could feel her disapproval as he put his coffee mug on the carpet. Taking a page from his notebook, he wrote his number and handed it across. 'Perhaps you could do me a favour and have a word with Lydia. See if she's prepared to speak to me. Over the phone or we can meet somewhere.'

'I'll tell Lydia you're asking questions about that day. But I can't promise she'll ring you. Like I said, Alice wasn't the only one affected by what happened.'

'Your daughter Emily, I'd like to talk to her too. Could you give her my number?'

Catherine smiled like she was on narcotics. Disturbingly radiant. 'Emily's no longer with us.'

Dan hesitated. Surely the woman would not be smiling if her daughter had died.

'No longer living here?' he prompted.

'Emily passed.' Then the smile faltered. 'During her first year at Cambridge. An accident.'

He felt his heart thudding. 'I'd no idea. Alice Faulkner never said. Forgive me, I wouldn't have...'

The smile had regained its unsettling glow. 'Darling Emily. Such an inspiration. Did I mention I run a charity? We help so many young people to reach their full potential.'

'That's great.' Dan did not know what else to say.

'More coffee?'

'No thanks, I'm fine. I have a few more questions. If you're sure you're okay to...'

She blinked and smiled. 'Of course.'

Dan nodded, resisting the urge to flee from the room. Now that he knew about Emily, it seemed like an assault to ask about Mrs Faulkner's son. Then he heard musical chimes. A carriage clock struck the hour, its brass mechanism catching the light as it span inside the bevelled glass case.

'Right,' Dan said. 'So. If you could possibly tell me the location of Felix's pram. When he was abducted.'

Catherine twisted round and pointed through the far window. 'The pram was on the terrace. Lydia was keeping an eye on it. She was on a sofa near that window.'

'Could you see the pram too?'

'No, I was sitting about here. Alice was on your side, maybe nearer the door. The pram wasn't visible from there.'

'None of you noticed the intruder,' Dan said. 'The person who took Felix.'

She smiled. 'I had my back to the window. How could I? Lydia clearly didn't spot him either or she'd have said. We all wanted Felix found. Lydia and I did everything we could to help.'

Dan needed to get out of here and away from Catherine. 'Would it be alright if I look round the garden?'

'Of course,' she said. 'I'll change my shoes.'

'Please, I've taken up too much of your time as it is. I'm sure you have things to be getting on with.'

'Yes. Indeed.' The woman frowned. 'It's very marshy by the river, just to warn you. All the neighbours have been allowed to reinforce the bank. Proper edging with steel piling and what have you. But because our property is Listed – I think I said that, didn't I? – English Heritage would not permit flood defences. Our gardener has given up trying to plant anything decent down the bottom.' She gestured through the windows. 'Sometimes it's *completely* underwater. Far from ideal, and my husband wrote many a letter, but the authorities are not remotely interested in us little people, don't you find?'

Dan made an appropriate noise, though he did not like being put in the same category as Mr and Mrs Nash. When it suited them, the wealthy were adept at pretending to be one of the masses, forgetting how privilege set them apart.

Catherine rose from the chintz sofa and he followed her back into the hall. She then directed him along a narrow passage, a glazed door visible at the end. 'I'll be in the kitchen,' she said.

'Once you're ready to leave, head that way' – she pointed to the right – 'and you can tap on the side door. I suspect your boots won't be fit to come inside, and I never like seeing a man in stocking soles.' She laughed. 'So demeaning, don't you think?'

From the terrace, Dan took in the view of the garden. Beyond the stone paving was a lawn that descended via two tiers to the marshy section referred to by Catherine, next to the Waveney. The different levels were linked by a paved path and sets of steps that rippled down through the middle. There were high walls flanking the garden, which also dropped in stages.

Up here on the terrace were tubs of plants, a metal table and chairs. To his left, the wall abutted the house. To his right, where Catherine had mentioned a side door, the garden wall joined a row of brick sheds and Dan glimpsed a small yard, next to the gable end of the house. He would explore it on his way out. Police had concluded that the intruder must have entered from that direction. The pram had been positioned near there, on the terrace.

Dan went down the stone steps to the first area of lawn. The garden felt like a wide avenue leading to the water, as there were mature oaks and beeches in the adjacent properties, their dense green canopies massed above the brick walls. At the foot of these walls were flower beds, with tall perennials growing against the crumbling red brick. He continued down to the second area of lawn. According to the file, this was where Jack and Emily were when they saw the intruder. Dan crouched to their approximate height, testing the angles from different positions. A child of eight or nine would have been able to see the pram on the upper terrace, provided they were near the outer edge of the grass.

It was important to corroborate these details, to ascertain the reliability of the children. Dan went down the last set of steps, where he stopped to survey the lowest section of garden. A shallow slope began as lawn but became coarse grass, followed by reeds. The high walls continued into the water, creating a bay, almost, where the current barely moved. Substantial brick pillars, each with a large stone globe on top, marked the ends of the walls. Beyond was the Waveney proper, about thirty metres wide, but this inlet added another fifteen or so.

On the far bank there were no boats moored on that stretch, and Dan had a clear view of the path which the witness, Peter Olsen, must have walked along on 4th July 2001. In his statement Olsen described seeing the children near the river, though they were supposedly not allowed down here. He referred to them 'having a picnic'. Dan made his way over the coarse grass, which became increasingly wet and muddy. He was heading for a boardwalk that extended into the reeds.

The timber posts and planks were rotten in places. Dan walked out carefully. He heard an engine chugging and then a small cruiser appeared on his left, past the tall brick pillar. A middle-aged couple waved at him and Dan waved back. Once the cruiser had gone, he noticed how private it felt. Chapel House was near the centre of Beccles but the garden was long enough to leave the town behind. The garden also seemed secluded from the Waveney. Even here on the boardwalk, it was only possible to see a short way up and down river, because of the projecting brick walls.

Dan glanced again at the path on the opposite bank, and found himself thinking about Olsen's daughter. The day he visited the man's home, Jay stood there barring entry. Dan had tried to make conversation, asking if she lived with her father. The reply had been curt. *I'm a musician in London*. Dan recalled her face, the directness of her gaze, the fullness of her bottom lip. Wanting to know what Jay's smile was like. He shook his head, caught by an obscure feeling of guilt. Then he turned away, retracing his steps across the rotten boardwalk.

Mrs Faulkner had mentioned that in 2001 there was a fence, with a gate and an alarm, intended to keep the children safe from the water. The fence had gone but when Dan examined the brick wall, he noticed rusty metal brackets. His gaze went back up the garden. The house was an unhappy union of Gothic and Georgian, the pieces mismatched. He saw movement in a window. Catherine? Whoever it was then stepped away from the light. Behind, Dan heard another cruiser pass by. Had there been much river traffic the Wednesday of the abduction? He would check the file. It was an obvious line of enquiry that had no doubt been covered. As he stood with his back to the water, the wake of the boat was still audible, pushing and fretting at the reeds.

Dan returned to the upper terrace. The chapel was built of stone and the three gothic windows were set at intervals. He paced to and fro, peering through the glass. The wall was deep, meaning the windows were recessed, and this restricted the views in as well as out. Dan confirmed which sections of the drawing room were visible from the terrace, and whether this tallied with Catherine's description of where the three women had been seated. He called to mind the photographs from the file and went to stand in the location of the pram. Only someone at the apse end of the room would have been able to see it. Again, Dan had the feeling of being watched, but when he glanced at the other windows there was no one.

Beyond the chapel was the small yard, and Dan headed in that direction. On his right was the house, on his left the row of brick sheds, which joined a short stretch of wall, with a door that led to a lane. The afternoon Felix went missing, the door had not been locked. In her statement, Lydia Ingleby blamed the gardener for forgetting to secure it after his visit the previous day. The gardener had been interviewed. An elderly man who could not remember categorically whether he had locked the door, but who kept insisting, 'I always do.'

Dan studied the door. Solid wood, painted green, set into a wall that was a mix of brick and flint, over two metres tall.

'That's how the kidnapper got in,' a voice said.

He swung round. How long had Catherine been standing there?

'Thanks,' he said, 'for showing me everything. And for answering my questions. You've been a big help.'

'I wanted to block it up. Afterward. But my husband said we might regret this. The door's useful for when tradesmen come. They don't have to traipse through the house.'

'Tell me,' Dan said, 'which is the window to the toilet?'

'That's the downstairs cloakroom.' Catherine gestured to a small window. 'It was Lydia who saw the kidnapper, not me. She was washing her hands when someone went past. She thought it was Jack. The glass is frosted – you can't see out much?'

'Yes, it's mentioned in the file.'

Catherine frowned. 'The police file?'

Dan realised his error. 'Just a file I put together with notes on the case. Based on what Alice Faulkner told me. And newspaper reports.'

From the depths of the house came the sound of a washing machine churning.

Catherine looked at the ground, then composed her face with a smile. 'I often think about her and Felix. Please send Alice my kind wishes.'

'Please accept mine as well. I'm really sorry about your daughter.'

The smile became a rictus. 'Emily never liked it here. She said it was too big to be a home. Another reason to sell.' Catherine raised her chin and met his gaze. 'The upkeep is endless on a place this size, you've no idea.'

'I hope...' Dan paused. 'I hope the sale and everything goes well. You have my number in case you remember anything else. And if you can put me in touch with Lydia, I'd be very grateful.'

'It's open,' Catherine said, pointing at the door to the lane. 'I usually keep it locked, but I knew you were heading out.' She seemed to be telling him that if the property had been hers the day Felix disappeared, the tragedy might never have happened.

'Thanks again,' he said.

With a nod, the woman ushered him through the door, then closed it firmly. Dan heard a key grating in the lock.

At the top of the lane, he turned left. His mind was full of impressions, questions, doubts, but nothing conclusive. A ten-minute walk, not registering much, heading down a gradual slope, through the familiar texture of a Suffolk town, with houses, cottages, terraces, brick and daub, Georgian and earlier, which pressed their frontages to the pavement edge. Dan then reached the Waveney and a hump-backed metal bridge, with a lower footpath attached to one side. Wanting a clear view, he walked across in the road and stopped midway.

A car drove past, and Dan stood by the parapet. To the north, further down the river, was Beccles Quay. A sunny weekend, and he could see lots of boats, trees, activity, family groups, children running about on the grass. To the south, up the river, more of the town was evident, but not many people and it seemed less busy. He rested his hands on the warm metal parapet, stippled with bolts, and stared in that direction. A faint wind on his face.

The Waveney cleaved through the land, a mass of moving water, thirty to forty metres wide on this stretch, marking the west boundary of Beccles. On his left were small jetties, boathouses, gardens, walls, gables, an impression of red brick and pantile, the town rising to a ridge, and at the summit, like a castle keep – grey, forbidding – was the bell tower of St Michael's. The river swung away from Dan on a gradual bend, such that Chapel House was hidden from view. Over to the right, flanking the water, were moored boats, reeds, then a grassy bank, trees at intervals, substantial willows, and in the distance a large flood plain of yellow grass. In the foreground near the bridge was a boatyard, cruisers propped up on makeshift trestles and oil drums. That boatyard led to the path which the witness had walked along. Dan needed to return here with Peter Olsen. Find out what the man remembered, prompt his memory by retaking the same route. Maybe Jay would come too.

Leaning over the parapet, Dan's gaze was drawn to the water, its opaque surface sliding slowly beneath him. There were so few details in Olsen's statement from 2001. Did he get to Beccles by car or bus or train? None of this was recorded, and nothing about the direction he had been walking, north or south, when he passed the end of the garden.

Did an inexperienced officer question him? Or had Olsen been unwilling to talk.

Chapter 15

Jay stood at the far end of the garden and stared across the fields. Breathing in, her bra felt tight, constricting her ribs. The air was hot and dry, like a London summer. She frowned, remembering what greeted her on the balcony, yesterday, when she went by the flat. Her tomato plants had all died in the heatwave. The vines were brittle and brown, the leaves yellow, the tomatoes soft and decayed, leaking. Jay had only been gone four days. It did not take long to create a rupture. Stepping through her front door, the place had seemed like it belonged to someone else. Were those really her books, her records, her stereo? That rug, those floor cushions?

Trying to restake her claim, Jay wished herself there right now. Curled on the couch with her acoustic, sounding the music that strayed through her head, her hands. Jay swallowed. Who was she kidding? She had produced nothing new in months. And her life was a mess. People wanted emotion in songs, but did it have to be her most painful wounds? Jay had no intention of writing about the breakup with Ruben. It really was over, and it was her fault. She pressed a thumbnail into the flesh above her jeans, then she turned and walked toward the cottage.

Her father was standing by the back door. With his white teeth and a wash of shade on his face, he was the boy scout in that sepia photograph. Jay smiled. It had been a while since the two of them had looked at the leather album. Ten years could pass in a single page.

A cat slipped out from under a hedge. It locked eyes with Jay, then headed for the far corner, a smear of black travelling across the lawn.

Her father watched it go. 'Timid bugger, that one.'

Dan slowly focused. Through the windscreen he could see a car park. Tesco in Diss. There was a bag on the passenger seat. Then it came to him – he had gone in to buy supplies. On his way round the aisles, Dan had spotted a shampoo Beth always used. He had opened the lid, inhaled its scent, and she was with him, for just a moment.

He slapped his face. It was not safe to drive in this state. Dan got out of the car, paced around, went back to the store for a bottle of lemonade. Twenty minutes later, he felt able to resume his journey. Inside the caravan, he unloaded the shopping and stared at the mushrooms, an onion, mince. Cooking was something he did with Beth. As Dan sliced the vegetables, he wondered what became of their old cookbooks. When Beth died, the rental flat was full of boxes, in readiness for the move. Throughout November she had been elated. Unaware it was all about to end.

Grieving, distraught, alone, Dan had to empty the flat. Most of it went to a charity shop. One box he kept with photographs of him and Beth, mementoes, the champagne cork from when they got engaged. Another box had memories of her life before they met, her degree certificate, old report cards from school. *Bethany shows great aptitude in physics and is ideally suited to a career in science*. Five days prior to the funeral, he took that box round to her parents. They had been pitifully grateful.

Dan adjusted the flame on the gas and added mince to the pan, followed by a tin of tomatoes. Somehow, for no reason, this was one of those brief instances, with the smell of food and the steam on his face, where it seemed maybe he could survive. A broken life that he was stitching back together – through his friendships with Cassie and Hari, and the routine of working as a taxi driver. Through the simple rituals he enacted each day of waking up, showering, dressing, no longer forgetting to eat. As Dan put on a pan of water, he pictured Mrs Faulkner. How did she spend her evenings – looking at photographs of her baby son? Sometimes he saw her drive off at dusk. Going to the cinema or a pottery class? Dan hoped there were moments when she remembered what happiness felt like.

He switched on the radio, but his mind kept returning to the day Felix Faulkner went missing. Jack Ingleby was, sadly, the only key witness now available. But when Dan used Safari on his phone, the name brought up nobody who seemed to match what would be Jack's current age. Nor were there any profiles for him on social media. And when Dan then searched for the father, Magnus, the material was related to his profession as an auctioneer, and the man must have retired, as the references were from several years ago.

Putting his phone aside, Dan pulled out the case file, recalling the idea that came to him earlier, about checking the river traffic. There was a sheaf of reports on various day-hire boats, sailing boats, and cruisers, which had passed along the Waveney that afternoon. Brief interviews were conducted with the occupants, some of them using it as a chance to complain about the waterways not being adequately policed. A particular gripe seemed to be cruisers not giving way to sailboats.

None of those interviewed could remember noticing anything unusual when they went past Chapel House. This did not surprise Dan. Having visited the location, he now knew that the projecting walls meant there was only a short period when someone on a boat would be able to look up the garden. Nobody saw the intruder or the children. One person did refer to a lone male in his forties, walking on the path next to the bank, about a mile upriver from Chapel House. Dan wondered if this was Peter Olsen.

Along with vessels that travelled the Waveney that Wednesday, there were a few which served as houseboats. Dan read statements by the occupants of two cruisers with permanent moorings, located near Chapel House but on the opposite side. A young couple had been trying to repair their bilge pump and had been below deck the whole time. The resident of the cruiser next to them had also seen and heard nothing. His name was Adam Wright and he had been ill in bed with flu. Appended to his statement was a note about Operation Hyacinth. Two years prior, Wright had been a confidential informant and would have earned himself a reward. On being questioned about Felix Faulkner, the man had expressed 'deep regret' that he was unable to help on this occasion.

Opening Safari again, Dan took a brief look at news reports about Operation Hyacinth. It had been a joint initiative in 1999, by Suffolk and Norfolk Constabularies and the Broads Authority, to clamp down on drugs. Three cannabis farms in agricultural sheds had been supplying Lowestoft, Great Yarmouth and Norwich, with the 'goods' transported on small boats via the Waveney and the Yare. Arrests were made and a substantial haul was seized.

Dan pushed his phone away. This was reminding him of a conference he attended at Wymondham. Back in 2017? Officers from Norfolk, Suffolk, and Essex, including marine units, had met with their equivalents from Belgium and the Netherlands. Brexit was looming, and the awareness that collaborations would be harder in future. The conference title had sounded like a PhD – 'A Hanseatic Model for Reconceptualising Criminality in the Twenty-First Century'. The use of small vessels for drugs trafficking had been the topic of several presentations, in this case plying their trade across the North Sea. A Dutch delegate ended up staying the night with Dan and Beth after a last-minute problem with the hotel bookings. A fun evening, happier times.

Smell of burning. Dan leapt up and switched off the gas on both hobs. The sauce had survived, but the water in the other pan had been boiling for a while and the caravan was full of steam. He opened the door, to clear the air, then returned to the case file. Now that Dan had been to Chapel House, the investigation was coming alive. Those first few hours were where his focus went next, as he turned the pages.

Officers were deployed at the scene, but there were also checks happening via databases at Suffolk's HQ in Martlesham

Heath. Many different scenarios were considered by the incident team. Ports and airports were notified, in case Felix was trafficked abroad. Kidnapping remained a possibility, and an officer was stationed in the Faulkners' home, ready to intercept any ransom demands. There was a list compiled of registered child sex offenders, with visits made that evening to those resident within thirty miles of Beccles, two men and one woman, each of whom carried previous convictions for indecent images offences. All three were brought in for questioning, but upon their alibis being checked, they were released.

The horror rose inside, as Dan allowed himself to feel, rather than analyse, what could have happened to Felix. Abducted by someone who knew the baby would be there. Or taken by a complete stranger. But why risk entering the garden? From the lane there was no view in. Had it been an impulse decision to open the door, see if there was anything worth stealing? And then the thing worth stealing turned out to be a baby. A crime of opportunity.

Dan frowned. Suffolk police had traced and interviewed known sex offenders, but no one, it seemed, had considered the abduction as 'a robbery gone wrong'. Very badly wrong.

At 9.20 p.m. Dan got a call from Hari, asking him to do a job. Three drivers were off sick and there was nobody to pick up a repeat booking, a couple who went to the theatre once a month and needed a ride back to Mulbarton. Forty minutes later, Dan was parked above the Market Place, not far from the Theatre Royal. The streets nearby were empty, the performance not over yet. He hardly ever visited Norwich these days. Not since Beth died. The two of them used to come here for nights out – theatre, ballet, restaurants, readings at Dragon Hall, salsa at Voodoo Daddy's, films at Cinema City. On those trips he had always been surprised how quiet it was around the Market Place. This was the hub of Norwich during daytime, but at night all the action shifted north into the Lanes or east toward Riverside, location of the chain restaurants and bars.

Dan tapped the steering wheel. Still no sign of his passengers, though he only had a vague description – women in their sixties. Hari had given them details of his Volvo, where he would be parked, and visible on his windscreen was the Silverline logo. Well after ten now, and Dan scanned his surroundings, in search of movement. There was a narrow passage, overshadowed by trees, next to the graveyard of St Peter Mancroft. At the far end, he spotted a young couple heading up the slope. The woman stopped and pulled the man into a kiss. Dan wondered if they had been at the Sir Garnet, one of the few pubs that defied the lack of nightlife in the centre. The couple carried on walking. Light caught their faces and he felt his heart drop through his chest.

Cassie and Lomax.

Dan stared at them, barely able to process what he was seeing. Cassie was dating the man who killed Beth. At that moment someone knocked on the window, and his body jerked.

He turned, saw a woman with long grey hair. Behind her a second woman was smiling and waving.

Dan pressed the button, lowering his window.

'Taxi for Marshall?' the woman said.

'Are you okay?' her partner said, peering at him. 'You look like you've seen a ghost.'

Chapter 16

Jay frowned, hearing the crunch of wheels on gravel. Dad's car coming up the drive? She switched on the kettle, cross with herself for not noticing he was out when she got up. It was barely nine. He must have gone to the shops for a Sunday paper. She reached another mug from the cupboard, then spotted a figure outside.

Her father was in the back garden. Jay felt like a spy as she watched him through the window. He strode across the grass, collected a wheelbarrow, and headed for the side gate. Had he been to the garden centre? During her 'regular' life in London, Jay had little knowledge of what he did with his days. But now that she was staying here, it was hard not to monitor him.

A few minutes later, her father reappeared with the wheelbarrow. In it was the upside-down carcass of a deer. Bloated and stiff. Jay found the solemn answer to why she felt compelled to chronicle his actions. The birds in their small graves had invoked a quiet pity. A reminder of the fragility of wildlife. But the dead deer frightened Jay because of the escalation. This was no longer a problem that could be held in two hands. It took a wheelbarrow to move the body.

Should she tell her brother? His reaction would be delivered with the usual sarcasm. *It'll be a dead horse next. Have you rung the GP? Father's mental capacity needs to be assessed.* Jay could imagine the conversation with Colin, but these were her thoughts too.

The wheelbarrow was now parked on the left side of the garden. Four legs stuck up from the barrow and she could see the deer's swollen belly. It appeared to be a muntjac. Her father examined the grass near a magnolia tree, then he fetched a spade, rolled up his sleeves, and began digging.

Jay made two mugs of tea. Before going out to the garden, she splashed cold water on her face. It was too early in the day to be debating the burial of roadkill deer. But no circumstance would ever make that a sane conversation.

When Jay offered her father the tea, he smiled and put down his spade.

'Where was it?' she said, keeping her tone neutral.

'On the back road to Diss.'

'Been there a while,' Jay said.

The stench was overpowering but her father seemed oblivious. He finished his tea in a few gulps.

'A farmer would have got rid of it,' she said.

'I don't like them being in the open. I told you.'

'Were you out buying a paper?'

Jay caught a fleeting expression on his face – a mix of guilt and deceit.

'I'm never usually up this early,' she said. 'Were the shops busy?'

He shrugged.

Jay could sense the conversation closing down. She started telling him about meeting Sean the other day. 'He was in my form class at high school.'

Her father did not remember him, not until she said it had been Sean who was sick at her party.

'The lad carried a torch for you,' he said.

'What d'you mean?'

'He was sweet on you.'

'Oh!' Jay laughed. Her father had a store of phrases only his generation used. 'Me and Sean were mates. That's all.'

'Thanks for the tea.' He thrust his spade into the ground.

'You'll need to make it a deep hole,' she said, walking away. 'Otherwise the whole garden's going to stink.'

Yesterday, the two of them had gone to Diss. Her father must have spotted the deer by the road, then returned for it this morning. Jay sat at the table, under attack from the noise outside, the spade hacking and slicing. It went on and on and she felt paralysed. Then the digging stopped. Jay approached the window and peered out. Her father was pushing the wheelbarrow toward the hole. The muntjac lurched side to side, like a drunkard. She heard herself laugh, a throttled squeal. Her father tipped up the barrow, but the carcass remained where it was. He tipped it further and jerked the handles. The muntjac tumbled into the hole.

Jay blinked, the awareness forming. Her father had always hidden things. His thoughts. His feelings. Telling her only so much, then closing down the conversation by making a statement. *It's the right thing to do*. What else had he kept from her? There would always be secrets in a relationship. Omissions. Such as the baby that went missing in Beccles and her father's role as witness. A significant event and yet he never referred to it. A six-week-old baby who was abducted. If Jay had been the only person to pass that garden, it would have tormented her for years. The possibility that she could have prevented the kidnapping.

Her mind returned to Wednesday and the conversation with Colin. His insistence that he was trying to protect their father when he told Jay to be careful about speaking to the detective. Colin was two years older than her – there were parts of the past that only he recalled. Details she was too young to notice. A queasy lump was now lodged in her stomach. The conviction that Colin knew much more than he was letting on. When Jay told him about Felix Faulkner, did he remember something from that summer in 2001? Her brother was keeping secrets, as well as her father. She swallowed, afraid of what they were both concealing.

Her gaze darted outside. The burial had moved to stage three. Hands gripping the spade, her father was covering the muntjac with soil, filling up the hole. The graves would reach the back door in a few months. The front garden would be next, and then her childhood home would be surrounded by sadness and putrefaction.

Jay fled upstairs. Her bedroom did not overlook the rear – she could pretend none of this was real. But as she scrolled through Instagram on her phone, pressing likes and adding comments, her anxiety dug deeper. What happened to the baby, why did her father never talk about this? How much did Colin know? Opening Chrome, Jay resumed her searches. She tracked down an article published the day after the abduction, which said Felix Faulkner was 'snatched' at around 4.15 p.m. No information on when her father passed the garden – his name was not mentioned, all emphasis being on the two child witnesses. A vague description was issued of the intruder.

A week later, news reports began to play up the idea that the baby had 'vanished'. That was the story which dominated the coverage in the following month. Felix Faulkner had 'disappeared into thin air'. She frowned. Journalists were interested in selling papers not finding missing children.

Jay rang the number in her contacts list, but her sense of resolve was rapidly fading. She was about to press the end-call icon when Dan Hennessy picked up.

'Hello?' he said.

His voice sounded odd. Then she heard him swallow.

'Who's this?' he said.

'It's Jay. Jay Olsen. You came by on Tuesday.'

'Sorry?'

'You were hoping to speak to my father. He was on the riverbank – the afternoon that baby was abducted?'

'Thanks for getting in touch. I'm sorry, but could I call you back?'

Jay heard him swallow again. And she wondered why she had chosen to phone Dan Hennessy rather than her own brother. But the question Jay wanted to ask could only be put to a stranger.

'Maybe this evening?' he said. 'Or tomorrow. Right now is a bit difficult.'

Jay laid a palm on her bedroom wall and felt the encroaching bodies in the back garden.

'Do you think my dad kidnapped that baby?'

There was a pause, then the detective said, 'I'm still trying to establish what happened. I promise to keep you informed if there seems to be anything implicating your father. Let me call you back tomorrow. I' – he cleared his throat – 'have to go now.'

The connection was cut. Jay stared at her phone. He had been crying, that was why his voice sounded odd. She could not match this weeping man to the Dan Hennessy who turned up on her father's doorstep. He had looked like Keanu Reeves, but a shabby, knackered version. A smile on his face, nice eyes. An impression of kindness.

Jay had wanted the detective to declare her father innocent. He had carefully avoided doing so.

Chapter 17

Dan felt bruised when he woke. Hungover, but he had drunk nothing. It was the start of a new week. Sunday had passed him by, hour upon hour of misshapen sorrow. Beth was killed on a road for no reason. They had all been left with consequences. He slammed shut the cupboard door. Cassie. Lomax. When did the two of them hook up?

His teeth ached. Dan sat at the table, opened the lace curtain, and peered outside. There was a triangle of grass between his caravan and the ones opposite. A man was reading a newspaper while throwing a ball to his dog. A woman was plaiting a young girl's hair. A toddler was walking and falling over, walking and falling over, a parent in pursuit, arms wide like two wings.

Staring at the dirt under his fingernails, Dan thought about Lomax. Maybe Cassie felt the need to comfort the man after the accident. Or maybe their relationship started before then. How long had Cassie been lying to Dan? Making up stories about Tinder and disastrous first dates. Knowing that sleeping with another officer would be something he disapproved of. As somehow incestuous. And for it to be Lomax – how could she do that to him?

Surely friendship involved honesty. He had always been truthful with Cassie. A truthfulness which became an open wound, after Beth died. Dan had let her see how bad things were. She had knelt next to him in the Control Room, stroked his hair while he lay weeping. When they went to buy a black suit for the funeral, she kept him upright, passed a handkerchief. Cassie had offered the sofabed in her house for as long as needed. She had brought meals to the caravan and talked to him, making sure he ate. She had invited Dan to spend

Christmas with her and Archie, refusing to take no for an answer.

But at some point, Cassie had begun sleeping with Lomax. *Sex is just sex,* was one of her phrases. *A functional requirement of the human body.* A transaction. If it meant so little to her, why not do it with someone else? Anyone but Lomax. He shook his head. Why didn't she tell him? All it would have taken was, *Dan, I've got something to say that you're not going to like.*

At 10 a.m. Dan was due to collect one of his regulars, Mrs Bailey. Her son had a mental health condition and lived in residential care. She visited him most Mondays and was always slow leaving her house. Either the cat had disappeared or she could not find her purse. Dan parked the Volvo by the kerb. The street ran south from the centre of Attleborough, bungalows on both sides, with driveways, garages. His was one of the few vehicles sitting in the roadway. He let his gaze wander up and down. At the far end, newspapers were being delivered. A man in his sixties was wheeling a bright orange trolley. A woman was with him, similar age.

Dan registered, without giving it much thought, that the couple were new. He did not always see the paper delivery when he was waiting for Mrs Bailey. But every so often the timing coincided, and Dan would notice that orange trolley making its way toward him. Only it had never been with an old couple.

The recognition came like a sudden thrill, reminding him of when he was police. The body at the solar farm. This was where Dan had seen the dead man before. Here on Hargham Road, delivering papers.

The old couple were drawing near with their trolley. Dan glanced at Mrs Bailey's door. No sign of her yet, so he got out of the car and approached the man and woman.

'Excuse me,' Dan said. 'Do you mind if I ask a few questions? To do with the paper round.'

'Why?' the man said. 'What's this about?'

The couple eyed him warily.

'We just deliver them,' the woman said. 'You need to speak to the distribution people if you've got a complaint.'

'No complaint, it's fine,' Dan said. 'I'm trying to get in touch with the person that used to do this route.'

'We don't know anything about them,' the man said.

'When did you take over?' Dan said.

The couple looked at each other, then the man said, 'Three weeks ago. We did Tacolneston before, but this came free and it's nearer home.'

The woman frowned. Clearly her husband had revealed too much.

'Thanks,' Dan said, 'I won't trouble you anymore.'

He walked back to the car. Mrs Bailey emerged onto the pavement just as the old couple arrived. Dan smiled at them, then he helped Mrs Bailey into the rear of the Volvo. As they drove off, she said, 'Friends of yours?'

'No. They're new. Someone else used to deliver the papers. A youngish bloke. You ever see him?'

'Never.'

After dropping Mrs Bailey at the care facility, Dan headed north. Then he pulled over, by the entrance to a field. How certain was he about identifying the man? It had been a month or so since Dan last saw him. All the same, he should tell Cassie that he might have a lead on the body at the solar farm. Dan squeezed the phone in his hand.

Her and Lomax. How could she.

Cassie had lied to him. He did not owe her anything.

Can't do pub this week. Got an airport run x

Dan sent the text, then threw his phone onto the passenger seat. He programmed his satnav for the next pickup – he had a busy morning ahead. Blanking his mind, Dan tried to focus on the A to B, the C to D, but the payment systems were bothering him more than usual. The network coverage seemed to vanish every time someone wanted to use a card or phone, which meant driving them to a high point just to find a signal. And who carried cash these days? Nobody under the age of seventy.

By 2 p.m. Dan was exhausted. The shift was over and he returned to Summerlands for a few hours' rest. He was locking his car when Mrs Faulkner marched up.

'The police were back,' she said.

'Checking the icehouse?'

'This is not good for business. Daniel, I need to know if my caravan park has anything to do with that murder.'

'Can't help you, sorry.' He looked at her face. Maybe she regretted asking him to investigate her son's disappearance. And what progress had he made?

'It's *my* land,' Mrs Faulkner said, 'but apparently the police have no obligation to keep me informed. Although they did deign to tell me they're now finished with the icehouse. Find Thomas and see what he has in the way of padlocks. Go with him, make sure he does a proper job. And check the police left the place in a reasonable state.'

'Permission to eat first?'

'*Please* have lunch and *please* could you supervise Thomas. Will that do?'

Dan tugged an imaginary forelock. 'Yes, ma'am.'

She laughed. 'Feudalism was so much easier.'

As Mrs Faulkner walked away, he recalled the woman who had wept silently in her living room, mourning her missing son.

After lunch, Dan went in search of Thomas. There was not enough work at Summerlands for a full-time handyman, but Mrs Faulkner was adept at arrangements. Thomas did a few hours each day, in exchange for somewhere to stay. The man's wife had died of cancer. Dan never mentioned his own loss but someone must have. On the one occasion they skirted close to discussing this, Thomas had said, 'Time is a great healer.' Dan tried to avoid such platitudes.

The man's workshop was on the west side of Summerlands. Dan found him round the back, in a deckchair, nursing a chipped cup.

'Tea?' Thomas said, looking up.

'No thanks, I'm fine.'

Thomas pointed to a wooden crate and he sat down.

'We've been issued orders by the boss,' Dan said with a smile.

'Likes to keep us busy.' The man put down his cup. 'In case we have too much time for moping.'

They sat in silence. Dan could feel himself being scrutinised.

Thomas then reached across, saying, 'This is your grief.' He placed an imaginary object in Dan's left hand and pressed down hard.

Dan blinked. He was not used to being touched. Beth's funeral was probably the last time anyone embraced him.

Thomas dropped another imaginary weight into Dan's right hand and wrapped his fingers round it. 'This is your love for Beth. That's her name, isn't it?'

Dan nodded.

The man folded Dan's fist toward his chest. 'Keep that love next to your heart. Loving won't do you any harm. But grief?' He frowned at Dan's left hand. 'Grief is a monster. Carry it around if you must. But remember, grief and love are not the same. You can let go the grief and still keep hold of Beth.'

Dan felt his heart beating. His vision blurred. Thomas was passing him a handkerchief.

He shook the tension from his left hand, then wiped his face, saying, 'You caught me off guard.'

'I've had eleven years to think about losing my wife. Don't let grief destroy you and Beth. Otherwise she dies twice.'

Dan could hear the man's laboured breathing as they walked up the edge of the field. Thomas had always played the part of affable OAP, equipped to discuss the weather, football scores, the septic tank at the caravan park. Someone to share a sly joke with, about Mrs Faulkner. Dan was uncertain what to do, now that Thomas had told him those searing truths about grief and love. He felt dazed and slightly sick.

'Slow down,' Thomas said. 'Some of us aren't so young.'

'Sorry. Bad habit.' Dan glanced at him. 'Did you ever notice anyone heading to the icehouse?'

'Maybe a few weeks ago, but it was getting dark. Could have been a deer. Could have been yourself? I've seen you out and about at all hours.'

Dan said nothing.

Once they reached the icehouse, he left Thomas examining the door. As Dan descended the damp stair, he could feel the chill. At the bottom, he flashed his phone torch around the brickwork of the hexagonal lobby, then he checked the cellars. The one on the right had been stripped bare – the small table and metal chair, the sleeping bag, blankets, clothing, crockery, food, all removed. He wondered where everything was. At the forensics lab? Nothing had been said to Mrs Faulkner about further enquiries. Dan glanced at the shadowy trough on the left, where the bedding had been. The icehouse sleeper had lain there, in that stone sarcophagus. Arms crossed on his chest like a corpse?

His gaze went to the trough full of water, unfathomable in the torchlight. On the surface, dust particles had joined to make small islands. Drifting across, slowly colliding. Pale grey, oddly shaped, so thin they were barely there. Dan stared at the fragile archipelago for several minutes, then he climbed the stair.

'Well?' Thomas said.

'They took everything away.'

'No chance of a vermin problem.'

'None.'

'The ironmongery is sturdy enough,' Thomas said, nodding at the door. 'But I've replaced the screws with something longer. I'll leave you to set the code. Mrs Faulkner will want a note of the numbers and I'm bound to forget.'

Earlier, in Thomas's workshop, it had been Dan's idea to use a padlock requiring a number not a key. He now felt guilty. Thomas had offered a moment of intimacy, an insight on his sadness. And yet Dan was still ready to manipulate the man. He had told Thomas a padlock with a code would be easier, but in truth, this was for his own benefit.

Dan could visit the icehouse whenever he wanted. Day or night.

Chapter 18

Dusk was falling. Dan packed a small rucksack with a torch, a flask. As soon as it was dark, he set off. On reaching the icehouse he removed the padlock, then found a sheltered spot, half hidden by a fallen tree. Dan thought about the man he was here to watch. A vagrant who had lost his bearings on the world.

There was a self-destructive satisfaction in knowing this was his own trajectory. Dan groaned, aware how upset Beth would be. He rubbed his face, and turned to peer across the fields. No sign of anyone, just the distant cry of a fox. Dan poured himself a coffee from the flask. Maybe he would come through this, somehow survive. But he no longer had Cassie to help him back up when he stumbled.

The phone buzzed in his pocket. Two messages from Jay Olsen. Dan had forgotten to ring her, after yesterday's conversation. She was worried her father was involved in Felix's disappearance, and he could see why. There were gaps in the man's testimony – his statement contained that short description of the boy and girl having a picnic, but that was all. Dan texted Jay, promising to call. Again, he found himself remembering the moment, last Tuesday, when he first set eyes on her.

A metallic *click* brought him to his senses. Dan looked up. Someone was at the entrance to the icehouse. A man in a hooded jacket. John Strang? He heard a faint scraping as the door opened then closed. It would take the man less than a minute to confirm his belongings had been removed. Dan had no legal right to apprehend the intruder – all he could do was try and speak to him. But this was someone who prowled the land at night and who slept in an icehouse. His first impulse would be to run.

The door grated across the threshold. The man emerged, then moved off at speed. Dan grabbed his bag and hurried through the trees, gaze fixed on his target. There was sweat on his palms, the thrust of blood in his body. Cassie talked about sex being a basic need, but stalking a person, exposing their secrets, this too was a sensual act, and Dan craved it.

The icehouse sleeper was now tracking north next to a hedge. The clouds had cleared, and faint moonlight was sifted across the fields. The man did not glance behind or pause to recce the way ahead. Instead, there was the unwavering aim of someone who knew where he was going. Dan watched him slip through a line of trees. He ran to catch up, finding himself on a narrow lane, deserted in both directions. On the far side was a ditch and beyond it a Christmas tree plantation. Norway spruce, seven-foot high, in regular rows, tightly packed. He stood and listened. Silence. Then he heard a pheasant take off, among the conifers, wings thrashing and its cry of alarm.

Dan jumped across the ditch and thrust his way into the plantation, torso twisted, moving quickly between the trees. The conifers reached above him, a dark mesh of branches. He peered in front but could see nobody, only trees pressing. The ground was ascending on a shallow slope, then it levelled off, and now he was heading down one of those marginal differences of gradient that acquired significance in Norfolk. The plantation ended and Dan scanned the terrain.

Ahead was a low spread of fields, some with sugar beet but mostly cereal crops, lines of dark hedging. Clumps of trees stood like islands amid the wide expanses of wheat. Over to the left was a belt of Scots pines. Stillness, no movement. So many places where the icehouse sleeper could hide. Dan kept watch for several minutes, hoping to catch sight of him in the pale grey landscape, or hear the cries of wildlife disturbed by his presence.

Time appeared to thicken, and the beat of his heart slowed, as if matching the long inhalation and exhalation of the land. In and out. In and out. Dan felt immersed, losing the skin boundaries of his being, letting the sense of himself reach out and claim affinity with the air that touched him, the ground beneath his feet, the distant vistas that his eyes saw and yet he was everywhere in the same moment, in every moment. Here on the margin of this plantation, but also way across there, next to those trees, smelling the dampness of a hidden pond, or far to the right, hearing the rapeseeds crackle in their desiccated pods as the night cooled.

Could this be peace? A huge burden was lifted off the land when humans closed their eyes. Dan felt that same burden lift from his own shoulders. Beth's death had subjected him to so much scrutiny. The nocturnal landscape did not ask anything of him. No expectations beyond the tacit offer that being here was enough. He was no longer cold or needy or hungry or aching. Dan was calm and fulfilled, sensations that were new and which he had only fleetingly experienced in his past.

Then he heard a splash. Far away to the left, the unmistakable boom of something or someone plunging into deep water. Dan set off toward the sound, back in his own skin, and yet a legacy remained of that fuller connection, and he moved with ease, as if his body had already been along these paths and ditches and knew what to expect. And yet he was mistaken.

A trick of perspective had lured Dan into thinking the field was flat. The land ahead now tipped toward him, a steep grassy slope ending in a horizontal ridge. A reservoir? He had seen a number in the local area, built by famers in response to the dry summers. This one took advantage of a natural rise to the right, with trees and the ruins of a church. Dan was fairly certain it was St Cecilia's – he had come across the name on an old map. The other sides of the reservoir were constructed from banked earth.

There was a fence with wooden posts. Dan clambered over, avoiding the barbed wire, then made his way up the incline. Near the summit he lay on his stomach, crawling forward until he was peering through grass at a vast rectangle of water, glinting darkly. No sign of the icehouse sleeper or any indication of what had caused that loud splash, but Dan was convinced it came from here.

The basin sloped back down from him, making an inverse pyramid. The recent drought had affected the water level, which was two metres below, exposing the black rubber material that lined the reservoir. The water might be lower, but it was still a huge volume. In the middle was a metal structure, with a horizontal gantry for pumping and aerating.

Silence, apart from the hum of the night sky and the rustling of the grass as Dan changed position. The reservoir seemed unwelcome in the landscape. No creature would ever spawn in it, no plants could soften its geometry. Where the grass stopped and the rubber began, there was a line of rough rocks. Granite from a far-flung quarry, nowhere near Norfolk.

A gust of wind scudded across the basin. His eyes studied the blackness of the water, angular, like carved glass chopping at the moonlight. In his head he recalled the heavy liquid sound of something – someone? – launching in. Dan was reading the surface for signs. Convinced of a presence, lurking beneath. But why go night-swimming in a reservoir? It was deep. Dangerous.

On the opposite shore, he noticed the fluid dark begin to coalesce, taking form. A figure was crawling from the water. Light glinted on a wet head and shoulders as the man stood up. This had to be the icehouse sleeper. The man walked up the slope, silhouetted against the more infinite black of the sky. Then, swiftly, purposefully, he disappeared over the far edge.

Dan leapt up and sprinted to the right, skirting the reservoir. The ruined church loomed above him, shrouded in trees, and then he reached the other side, where the land fell away. The icehouse sleeper had vanished. No movement in the fields below or next to the tracery of hedges. Dan hurried to where the man had climbed out of the water. Wet footprints glistened on black rubber. Dan took a photograph with his phone, to prove this was real.

From the top of the embankment, a faint track was discernible, descending at an angle, parting the grass. There was a wooded area in the distance. That could be where the man was sleeping, now that police had found the icehouse. Dan half ran, half slid down the slope, and aimed for the trees on a route that stayed close to the field boundaries. The moon was casting a bright blue-grey light, bringing every detail into stark proximity. Dan hid next to a thicket of hawthorn that edged the woodland. There was a secretive silence, held and contained by the trees. He sniffed the air, not yet at ease with the feral habits his night-time roaming seemed to waken.

Somebody was in there, he felt certain. Dan heard a sigh, but it could have been the wind. His view into the woods was an array of pale grey stripes painted on a black backdrop. Then the depth returned and he saw trees receding into darkness. No flickers of movement or flashes of light. Maybe the man had headed in a different direction, but Dan's instincts told him this was his new hideout.

Briefly, Dan surfaced, then the dream claimed him once more. He was in the ballroom of a mansion. Loud, crowded, hot. Too many people, breathing into his face, and he felt fearful. His chest was tight, all those bodies jostling and pushing him. He closed his eyes, opened them, saw the heavy brightness of a chandelier, searing his vision, and sensed the pressure of all those people squeezing his lungs. He closed his eyes again, opened them, saw a dark figure, a man, peering down at him. Dan tried to say *help* but failed. His eyes shut. When he opened them, the man was gone.

Low shafts of pale orange sun slid through the trees, and in his ears the insistent cacophony of the dawn chorus. Dan sat up slowly. Shivering, he reached for his backpack. The flask of coffee was cold but he drank some, grateful for wetness. He had woken up frozen, disoriented, and yet he had slept well. Today felt like a possibility. Then Dan remembered. *She's dead.* Each morning and in the waking hours of every night, that knowledge needing to be relearned, his mind and body unable to accept. *She died*.

For five years, two months and seventeen days, Beth had been his life. And Dan gasped, for in that moment she came to him, vivid in sunlight, her smile loving, and with love in her eyes. Beth stroked his cheek and pressed a finger to his lips. *Hush*.

Then she was gone, like a vanishing. Did Beth turn away at the last second? A noise distracting her, someone calling. It had happened too fast.

Love you, Dan said quietly, clasping the empty place she left behind. *So much*. He touched his cheek, his mouth, trying to hold on to her caress.

But the sadness returned, weighing on his arms, the memory of the many times he had lifted her canister of ashes. The memory of carrying her belongings in all those boxes. The one he gave her parents, report cards, their promise of a bright and hard-working girl with a whole future ahead. The crumbling rose corsage from a school prom. Then Dan thought about the rites of passage that would no longer happen. His marriage to Beth. The birth of their children. The new house had been part of their plan. The ordinary life that most people followed but that became something special when it was him and Beth.

Dan pushed a hand through the dry leaves. Two months before she was killed, they had stopped using contraception. If Beth had been pregnant when she died, Mazur had spared him that detail. There would be no more memories for her and Dan. The fact that Beth could end in a single shattering collision, he was still bound up with disbelief. Still remembering the moment Cassie took his hand and said, *Something really terrible has happened*. Language did a poor job of relaying the devastation.

A shiver convulsed him and he rubbed his arms. The sky had lightened. The dawn chorus was over and Dan could hear individual birds, in the nearby woods. His limbs were cold and stiff. Cassie kept trying to steer him back to who he once was.

But Dan could never be that person again, and now his friendship with her was broken too.

He swallowed another mouthful of coffee. Cassie knew how much he hated Lomax. The man killed Beth. He *killed* her. The IOPC were conducting an investigation, but Dan had no faith they would rule against Lomax or Duke. The pursuit had been authorised. Duke maintained radio contact, Lomax had enhanced driver training, siren and lights were deployed, and Beth stepped into the road without looking. Dan learned these details within hours of it happening. Everyone tried to convince him it was a tragic accident.

With a trembling hand, he put his cup on the ground. The pursuit had been authorised because Lomax recognised the driver as a perp wanted for violent assault on an OAP. Dan heard, the next day, it was not Jacob Reed driving, but a sixteen-year-old who stole the Fiesta as a dare. Would Control have instructed the chase for the sake of a stolen vehicle? It had been down to Dan to remind everyone of Lomax's reputation. A hothead who leapt to conclusions, misidentifying the perp. Lomax was also a hothead behind the wheel. There had been previous incidents, though this was the first fatality. Dan made sure everyone knew Lomax was to blame.

Maybe Lomax had approached Cassie precisely because of their friendship. He could not confront Dan – colleagues would shun him for attacking a grieving man – but Lomax could have sought her support. Dan did not wish to know how the relationship started. A sour taste leaked into his mouth. Cassie was no longer his friend. Nor did he care.

Nothing could change that he now lived in a world without Beth. She left Dan behind. Here he was, sitting on weeds and muck, miles from nowhere and so alone. A heavy shunt of grief dropped through him, gathering in his legs. Another piece of sadness, weighing him down. The latest email from the IOPC had identified 'a possible contributory factor'. There had been a broken silencer on the exhaust of the stolen Ford Fiesta. This noise could have masked the police siren. Beth had stepped into the road, totally unaware that a second vehicle was bearing down on her.

Dan stared at the trees, a mute and motionless crowd, marking out the space. He channelled his thoughts toward the icehouse sleeper, anything was better than reliving the moment when Beth – on an impulse that died with her – ran across that road. His sight sank deeper into the woods. He tried to conjure up that feeling of liberation from the night before, when his being had seemed to travel the land ahead, when looking had been enough to ferry him to the far reaches of his gaze. But that loose freedom had gone.

He glanced at his phone. 05:40. Dan collected his small rucksack, brushed some leaves off his clothes, and aimed for Summerlands. Already there was work going on in the fields. A tractor pulled a long rig, irrigating or spraying crops, and in the distance he saw a minibus heading along a track, transporting pickers. Further away, he glimpsed intermittent cars on the Candlesham road.

The walk took thirty-five minutes. Only as he neared his caravan did Dan remember about the dark figure looming over him, when he first woke by the woods. Dan went inside and set his alarm for nine. As he lay in bed, he tried to recall more details, but his memory was hazy. Dan could not be certain if that man was John Strang. Or if he was a dream.

Chapter 19

Panicked, Dan sat bolt upright, but it was just his phone ringing. Day or night, he had no idea. Day, he decided, it would be Hari asking him to fit in an extra job. But Dan did not recognise the voice on the other end. The woman introduced herself as DC Sullivan, and he knew instantly from her tone that this was Cassie's new partner. Cassie had only ever referred to her as Ms Shiny Shoes. Sullivan wanted Dan to come in for 'a chat' at ten.

'Is it urgent?' he said. 'I'm working this morning but I'm free in the afternoon.'

'Perhaps,' Sullivan said, 'you can arrange someone to cover for you.'

A command not a request. Sullivan was now saying she had booked a room at Earlham. 'DI Fisher felt you might prefer it to HQ.'

Not only had Cassie lied about Lomax, she was not even bothering to do the interview, relegating it to a DC and a station on the outskirts of Norwich.

'What's this about?' Dan said.

'Easier if we do it face to face.'

'Easier if I know what I'm being called in for. Parking ticket?'

She laughed, but he could tell his sarcasm had not been appreciated.

When Dan arrived at Earlham, Sullivan was waiting outside, as if guarding the entrance. She was in her early twenties, wearing a grey trouser suit.

'Good to meet you,' she said, the greeting perfunctory, with no offer of a handshake. 'I've heard a lot about you.'

'Likewise,' he said, though in truth Cassie had said very little. Sullivan was a product of the Degree Holder Entry Programme, and Cassie had always been suspicious of anyone who joined via that route. It had secretly pleased Dan that her new partner was unlikely to become a friend. Dan glanced down. The woman's shoes were indeed shiny. He laughed.

Sullivan pursed her lips, then said, 'Perhaps we should get started.'

As they crossed the lobby, the desk sergeant stared at him in half recognition. Since leaving the police, Dan had grown a beard and taken his work clothes to a charity shop. Sullivan led him along a carpeted corridor to an interview room. It was windowless with lino on the floor, a table and two plastic chairs. The walls were pale green.

The DC told Dan to take a seat, then settled herself opposite. There was recording equipment on the table, but Sullivan left it off. She gave him a bland smile and picked up a file, glanced through it, occasionally frowning. Dan shook his head. This was meant to unsettle him. Why? He was not a suspect. Sullivan seemed to be practising techniques she had learned on the job rather than via PowerPoint. Dan went through the things he wanted to do this afternoon. First off, ring the estate agent about selling the house. He needed to get the money to Beth's parents, putting an end to further communication.

'You must be wondering,' Sullivan said, 'why I've asked you here.'

'I'm sure you'll tell me in good time.' He gave her his own bland smile.

She fiddled with the file again, pulling out a sheet of paper.

Dan considered what price he should put on the house. To secure a fast sale he was happy to lose a few thousand. Calling the estate agent was the easy part. The next item on his list was the one that wrenched his heart. What to do with Beth's ashes.

Into the silence of the room came a very quiet sound. Sullivan's hand rested on the table – with her thumb she was twisting a ring on her little finger, and the silver tapped a rhythm. Dan felt a moment of self-loathing. Here he was, a big

Jackass prepared to bully a young female officer who was just trying to do her job.

'Sorry,' he said. 'I was in a bad mood and you got the brunt of it. I'm genuinely happy to help. Fire away.'

'Great. That's great.' Sullivan flashed him a smile, then put down the document. 'Cassie's your friend, right?'

Dan nodded. No point in mentioning the current state of their relationship.

'That's what makes this a bit awkward,' Sullivan said. 'It was you that drew her attention to someone sleeping in the icehouse. None of us thought it likely to be connected to the enquiry, but with so few leads...' She shrugged. 'The thing is, your DNA is still on the database.'

'For elimination purposes,' he said. 'What exactly are you trying to say, DC Sullivan?'

'You told Cassie, you told DI Fisher, that when you first saw the broken padlock at the icehouse, you went down for a look?'

'Correct,' Dan said. 'The owner of the caravan park has put me in charge of security. I wasn't planning to contaminate a crime scene. I was just checking what had been going on down there. It was only afterward that I wondered about a link to the solar-farm murder.'

'This has put DI Fisher in a difficult position. Because of your friendship. As you know, the lab are very thorough. Nothing escapes their notice.'

'So? I touched a few things. I was trying to work out who the trespasser was.'

Sullivan blinked rapidly. 'You direct police attention to the icehouse. Resources are spent on examining and photographing and logging and processing the scene. Then the results come back.' She tapped the document.

Dan frowned. Maybe Sullivan's nervousness had been an act. This was a technique Cassie often used – on arrogant IC1 males. Allow them to feel superior and they reveal more than intended. Cassie had either taught this to Sullivan, or the young officer had observed her during interviews.

He glanced up and met Sullivan's gaze. She was in full control and he was an idiot. 'I take it there's a problem with the DNA results.'

Sullivan nodded slowly. 'Cassie did think about handling this herself. But we agreed it would be best if I took over. You and I have no prior connection. We're not friends or ex-colleagues. I can only imagine that leaving Norfolk Constabulary must have been very difficult for you.'

Dan could sense it was his turn to be patronised.

'Police,' she said, 'is a mindset. A lot of former officers get jobs in security. Like you have, at the caravan site. It's hard to switch off being a detective. I know DI Fisher showed you the murder victim at the solar farm. She feels she may have encouraged you to get involved.'

'Cassie should be telling me this. Not you.'

Sullivan's face was grim. 'You're plain Mr Hennessy, not a detective inspector. You claim you made one short visit to the icehouse. And yet your DNA is *everywhere*. Proof you spent a considerable amount of time down there. I believe DI Fisher has suggested you get grief counselling and frankly I agree. To waste police resources, to point us toward that icehouse which is literally covered in your fingerprints...'

What was she talking about? He was down there five minutes at most. His mind retreated from the bright room, the harsh words, but then Dan felt his hand being patted. It was Sullivan.

'Sorry,' she said, 'but you need to listen. We had no choice but to make this semi-official. Cassie's told me what you've been through, and it sounds terrible and enough to destroy anyone. Inserting yourself into the solar-farm enquiry is obviously a cry for help. Dan, *we hear you*. You've got everyone's attention. But the last thing you want is to be charged with wasting police time. I know a good counsellor. She helped me with a problem I had, I really recommend her. Contact her today. Please.'

Sullivan reached in her pocket and passed him a small card.

Dan could barely comprehend what she had said. His mouth felt strange, jerking into a smile, and he covered it with a hand.

She scowled. 'You think this is funny?' There was real anger in her voice.

'I'm not—'

'Why did I bother? You've no intention of getting help. I couldn't care less, believe me. But I do care about Cassie. She only just escaped a formal warning about her conduct. You infiltrated a major investigation. You need to keep your nose *out* of police business. Have I made myself clear? Stop interfering. Stop dragging Cassie into your mess.'

'That wasn't—'

'We have a job to do. A murder to solve. We're not puppets in some twisted game you're playing. Stand up, please.'

Dan followed her out of the room. He felt like he was floating, as if none of this was real. His DNA all over the icehouse? Not possible. There must be a mistake.

When they reached the lobby, the desk sergeant gave them a curious look.

Sullivan was speaking again, in a professional tone that did not match her final words in the interview suite. 'Mr Hennessy, thank you for coming in, and for allowing us to eliminate you from our enquiries. I'll tell DI Fisher the issue has been resolved. Yes?'

Dan nodded. His mouth was dry. Police stations had always been a second home, but now it was alien territory. He sensed the unhappy people who had been brought here to answer questions about their unhappy lives, which had gone astray before they were even born. He smelled the sweat of all those who had been in the wrong place at the wrong time and were expected to explain why. Dan had joined the police believing he could make a difference. And maybe he had done some good during his sixteen years in the service. But today marked his final departure, and now, standing in the institutional, hard-walled, unwelcoming lobby, Dan realised that he did not belong here.

Sullivan waved a hand in his face, a gesture that annoyed him.

'You seem in a bit of a daze,' she said with a smirk.

Dan glanced round. Another officer had joined the desk sergeant, so three of them were now staring at him. The outsider. His conduct today would become canteen gossip, further proof of how far Hennessy had gone off the rails.

'Don't look so glum,' the desk sergeant said. Dan recalled that his name was Matt Forbes. The man gave him a warm smile. 'I think our young DC is done with you. Best clear off before she changes her mind.'

Out on the pavement, Dan blinked at the sky, still reeling at what Sullivan had told him. He tried to make sense of it all. Prior to CSIs removing the contents, there had been only two occasions when Dan was inside the icehouse, both of them brief. The day he first noticed the broken padlock and examined the fourth cellar, handling a few items. Then the visit with Cassie when – instructed by her – he did not lay a finger on anything. But evidence gathered by the techs said otherwise. *Proof you spent a considerable amount of time down there.* Enough to leave significant traces.

The strength went from him and he sank onto a low wall. Of course he knew that things had been bad, since the accident. Dan had lost whole hours and sometimes days, when his mind and body had been so bound up with grief that the world stopped. Then he would surface, finding himself in the aisle of a supermarket, or in a multi-storey car park, or sitting at the table in his caravan with a stone-cold cup of coffee and a list of missed calls on his phone. Never, during these trances, had Dan gone to the icehouse. But how could he be sure? How could he be certain of anything? The furniture, bedding, clothes, plates, food – did *he* put them in the cellar?

Dan stared at his trembling hands, feeling like a stranger inside his own skin. He stood up and started walking, not heeding the direction. On the roundabout ahead was a pub. He went in, saw four sets of eyes flick across him, along with a cautious look from the landlord. Dan ordered a drink and said, 'I'm not police.'

The landlord laughed awkwardly. 'Nobody's saying you are, mate. Malt or blend?'

'Jameson's, if you have it.'

'Here's to the luck of the Irish,' the man said, as he slid the glass over. 'Reckon you need it.'

Dan headed for a corner table. Behind him, the conversations resumed, barely audible, as there was now music playing, a loud pop tune. He raised the whiskey to his lips and swallowed a mouthful. Dan did not usually drink during the day but he was unclear whose rules he was keeping. Perhaps he should thank DC Sullivan for the categoric proof that grief had driven him mad.

His phone rang in his pocket. Dan pulled it out, glanced at the screen. Cassie. He had no intention of answering. She gave him zero warning of the ambush Sullivan had sprung. Cassie was clear where her loyalties lay. Dan had always admired her drive. Now it was him being sacrificed to that ambition, and who could blame her. He destroyed anyone that came near. Thomas said grief was a monster. Dan was the monster.

The phone rang again. He checked the screen, expecting Cassie, but the number was not on his contacts list. Dan was about to press the end-call icon when he remembered giving his number to Catherine Nash in Beccles. He answered, and put the phone to his ear.

'Hello,' a woman said. Not Catherine. This voice was deeper and less sibilant. 'Who am I speaking to?'

'Hi, I'm Dan Hennessy.'

'I believe you have some questions. My name is Lydia Armstrong.'

She had been Lydia Ingleby when she lived in Chapel House, but Catherine had referred to the marriage break-up.

'Thanks for getting in touch,' Dan said. 'Could we arrange to meet?'

'Certainly not. My only reason for making this call is to stop you poking about trying to find me. I have a life I'm perfectly happy with and I intend to keep it that way. I don't dwell on the past. I especially don't dwell on that ghastly day. It was a tragedy. What more can one say? Catherine Nash tells me you're a private detective – a grubby job that carries with it no legal authority. I am not in any way obliged to speak to you.'

'You're right.' Dan felt a moment of nausea, alcohol on an empty stomach. 'But maybe you owe it to Alice?'

'There's nothing I owe that woman, not after what she did.'

'Are you saying she had something to do with Felix's disappearance?'

'You misunderstand me. I'm referring to her behaviour afterward. She turned a tragedy into a nightmare. Poisoned everyone against me. How on earth was I to blame? Alice Faulkner spread all sorts of nasty rumours. My marriage fell apart, thanks to her. I lost a house, a husband, a son.'

'Your stepson Jack. Are you still in touch?'

'I have a new life now. That woman didn't leave me much choice after she destroyed the last one.'

Dan gripped the phone. 'Her baby went missing and was never found.'

'You're hoping to elicit some compassion. I felt sad at the time. I feel sad now, discussing this. But life goes on.'

'She just wants answers.'

'And I have none to give. Other than what I told police at the time. I really don't see why you would expect me to recall some crucial detail after two decades. I suggest you read the reports in the file. Catherine tells me you have it, which I find surprising. Maybe I should contact the police myself and let them know you have access to documents that I understood were not for public consumption.'

'My work is carried out discreetly.'

'And I'm supposed to take your word for that?' Her voice blared in his ear.

'All I'm aiming to do,' Dan said, 'is find out if anything was missed. A stray detail that could open up new lines of enquiry. Maybe something occurred to you later. Is there really nothing you can add?'

Lydia Armstrong huffed out a breath, angry and impatient. 'Nothing I say will make a difference to what happened.'

'You mentioned you lost your stepson when the marriage broke up. That must have been hard. Did you try and stay in touch with him?'

'Poor boy took the divorce very badly. I decided to cut all ties. Painful at the time but better in the long run, seeing as he was Magnus's not mine.'

'So no further contact with Jack or your ex-husband.'

'I've no idea what they're up to these days. I take it you haven't spoken to them.'

'Not yet,' Dan said.

'If you do, keep me out of it. I wouldn't want my ex thinking I've mellowed in my old age and am ready to bury the hatchet. I do so hate the idea of making amends. We both behaved abysmally in the divorce, but that was how I felt at the time and I'm sticking with it. I'm not going to pretend now that it's water under the bridge because—'

Lydia Armstrong stopped talking and Dan waited for her to continue.

'Goodness,' she said, 'I knew speaking to you would be a mistake. I tend to get very hot under the collar when I stray onto the topic of my ex. I cut all ties for a reason. We all have a duty to preserve some form of sanity.'

'But you kept in touch with Catherine.'

'Her? Oh no. Did she give you the impression we were still friends? I've always found her slightly creepy. She was forever borrowing my clothes and laughing at what I said. And then she tried to be *helpful* by buying my house when the marriage ended. Stalker material. It was a relief to leave Catherine Nash behind in *charming* Beccles. But then I bumped into her, or rather she bumped into me, at a university open day.'

'Can I—?' Dan's throat felt tight. 'I'm making a mess of this conversation. Could we do it face to face?'

'No. Not under any circumstances.'

'All this happened a long time ago and I know you're trying to put it behind you but Alice—'

'I have put it behind me,' Lydia said. 'Very successfully. I will not have my life contaminated *again* by that woman. I don't know what her motives are in employing you. Now, after all these years. Menopause? Maybe she's looking back at her life and feels bitter. Maybe she resents that some of us managed to make a go of things. The hatred she directed at me and Catherine was verging on obscene. And don't you dare remind me that poor Alice lost a baby. She isn't the only one to experience tragedy. Did Catherine tell you about her daughter?'

Dan stared into his empty glass. 'She mentioned that Emily sadly died.'

'Like I said, we've all had to go through terrible times, but that's life. The police investigated Felix's disappearance. They weren't able to find the intruder who stole him from my garden. I will not be held accountable by Alice Faulkner.'

'The only witnesses who saw the intruder were Catherine's daughter Emily and your stepson Jack. They were children.'

'Children aged eight and nine. Not *toddlers*. They described the man who took him. The police had ample information and yet they still managed to botch the enquiry. Alice Faulkner is an unhappy woman looking for someone to blame for her unhappy life. And as for what she did to Robert.'

'What do you mean?'

'Not much of a detective, are you. Robert Faulkner died of a heart attack in March this year.'

'Dead?' Dan felt the shock. Mrs Faulkner clearly did not know.

'He was fifty-three. I read it in *The Telegraph*. The way Alice tormented him over their son – I swear she drove the poor man to an early grave. If I were you, I'd tread with care. Don't let Alice Faulkner fool you. And above all, don't get on the wrong side of her. She's a thoroughly nasty piece of work. And now, Mr Hennessy, your time is up. Don't try and contact me again as this number will no longer function. Goodbye.'

The room seemed to pulse, music throbbing from the speaker above his head, lights winking on a fruit machine. Dan put his phone away. He felt exhausted. The interview at the police station had been bad enough, and then to have to speak to that woman. All her venom, and the unexpected news about Robert Faulkner. When Dan touched his mouth, he noticed his hand was shaking. And he recalled what Sullivan had said about his mental state. The evidence of him sleeping at the icehouse.

Dan stood up, legs weak, and he staggered. As he passed the bar the landlord said, 'Need me to order a taxi?'

'I'm just tired,' Dan said.

The landlord raised his eyebrows. 'That's what they all say. How you getting home?'

Chapter 20

Dan crawled into bed with his clothes on. When he woke, late evening, it was like coming up for air. Staring at the darkness, he felt a stab of fear that this was the icehouse. Then the caravan window took shape, a grey glow with curved corners. Dan crept slowly through to the kitchen. Whatever matrix his thoughts had arrived at while he slept, it seemed vital not to bring this crashing down.

After finishing his meal, Dan eyed the spare rice in the pan, contemplating what it was like to be hungry and alone. He parcelled up the rice in silver foil, then fetched from the cupboard another tin of curry with a ring-pull lid. Half an hour later, Dan reached the woods and located where he woke this morning, the weeds still compressed. He left the food there, unsure if his offering would be found. He thought about the man who slept in the icehouse, who swam in the reservoir, and who now spent his nights in these woods. Dan had felt this before, but it acquired a bleak clarity. He knew the signs, as he experienced them daily. The dislocation.

This man was a victim of trauma.

What happened to him? What did he do or see?

As Dan walked back to Summerlands, the certainty grew. John Strang was the icehouse sleeper. And somehow, somewhere, he was tied to the recent murder. Mrs Faulkner said Strang left Summerlands around mid June. Mid June was also when the unknown male was killed, based on Mazur's estimate that the victim lay undiscovered for three weeks.

Was Strang the murderer? Dan stopped in his tracks. He could envisage a situation where Strang accidentally killed someone, but to chop off the hands and drag the body inside a solar farm, it seemed too calculated. There was no doubting, however, that the man knew something about the murder. Why else had he gone into hiding?

These questions played on Dan's mind as he neared Summerlands. He went down Primrose Drive, glancing at Unit 16. Mrs Faulkner had told him it was booked from Saturday, and sure enough, he could see movement inside. Dan carried on toward his own caravan, still plagued by the sense that he had got this all wrong.

Trauma. Strang had suffered, but when did it happen, the incident that 'damaged' him?

The man arrived in Summerlands at the end of April. Dan recalled his impressions, in the weeks that followed. Strang was agitated, disturbed, isolated. Already in a bad state when he turned up at the caravan park.

Those baby clothes, neatly folded and put away in the footstool. Dan, with a reflex that had become familiar, felt his mouth go dry. The pale blue knitted cardigan. The well washed towelling of the sleepsuit. The cracked brown rubber of the dummy.

Trauma, associated with a baby. Just like Mrs Faulkner. He burst into his caravan and grabbed the police file. Scanned the details of what Felix was wearing.

Not the same. The day Felix disappeared, he was in a pale yellow cardigan. And his sleepsuit was described by Alice Faulkner as cream with a thin yellow stripe.

Not the same clothes. Not the same baby.

But Dan was convinced of a link. He had made a promise to Mrs Faulkner, to find the truth about her son. Dan had no choice but to keep asking questions, spiralling into dead ends and back out again. He had to get to the truth.

He was lost without it.

Next morning, Dan forced himself to complete each stage of his routine. He showered, dressed in clean clothes, and did not skip breakfast. Washed the dishes, did not leave them in the sink. Put his dirty clothes in the laundry bag and straightened his bed. These small acts calmed him. Once he was ready, Dan texted Jay Olsen, asking if she and her father were free that afternoon to meet him in Beccles. A reply came moments later, fixing a time.

Felix's disappearance was the trigger, the catalyst, the ground zero. Mrs Faulkner, her son, Strang, the nameless body at the solar farm – they were all connected. Was this more madness?

No. Dan clenched his jaw, recalling the trip to Earlham. He had been singled out as one of those mentally unstable people who contact the police with fabricated clues. Dan was not that person. But his DNA was all over the icehouse. Had Strang been to Dan's caravan and taken some of his things? This had to be the explanation. Dan could not accept that he had lost all grip on reality. It was not him who furnished that dank cellar and started sleeping there. He silenced the voice that said, *Of course it's you, it's been you all along.*

Dan shook his head. He was mad with grief not *mad*. And he had information which was crucial to the solar-farm enquiry. Police needed to know that the dead man used to deliver papers in Attleborough. But anything Dan said would be dismissed. He checked local news on his phone – no significant updates, and still no identity on the victim. However, police had issued a digital facial reconstruction. Dan stared at the image on his screen. The man's injuries had, of course, been removed. But the features were exaggerated, too heavyset, and the face did not seem to match the person Cassie showed him on the trolley. And it only vaguely resembled the man delivering papers. Dan frowned. It had been a month or more since he last saw him on Hargham Road. And it was not as if Dan had ever paid him much attention.

But should he speak to Cassie? Again, Dan felt the shame from Earlham coursing through him. He could not, would not, tell her about the possible ID, after the part she played in his public humiliation. Dan knew Cassie did not have the power to stop what had been heading his way – once the DNA was logged, interviewing him had been inevitable – but she should have rung him. Dan was no longer police, but he had still sensed that partner bond with her, always looking out for each other. Not anymore. Of the two betrayals, this almost felt worse than Cassie hiding her relationship with Lomax.

By noon, Dan had completed his roster and was only a short drive from Attleborough. He parked on Queen's Square and used Google on his phone to find a number for the *Anglia Herald*. A woman in distribution told him the address of a newsagents to the south, on a wedge of land by the A11. As Dan turned into the labyrinth of freshly built homes, he was reminded of the empty house in Wymondham. He stopped the car and rang the estate agents, agreed to drop off the keys at their office the following day. This gave him a deadline. Dan had to reach a decision about Beth's ashes.

His eyes went back to the satnav and he headed for a small roundabout. The newsagents doubled as a convenience store. The owner was heavy-set and balding. He was willing to answer questions once Dan mentioned he had been sent here by 'Hazel from the *Anglia Herald*'. Dan learned that, up until a month ago, the *Herald* was delivered by someone called Ryan Taylor. Aged thirty or so, according to the owner. Ryan had been paid in cash and had done the job for about six months.

'Did he move away from the area?' Dan said.

The owner shrugged. 'Monday came and he never showed. Had to do the deliveries myself. Bloody nuisance.'

'You tried contacting him?'

The owner shrugged again. 'Rang his mobile. Automated message saying not in service. So I found someone else to take the gig. Someone more reliable.'

'Any idea where he lives, this Ryan Taylor?'

The shrugging was beginning to irritate Dan.

'I think he does seasonal work,' the man said. 'Picking veg? Turned up one week looking like he'd been dragged through a ditch. I told him not to do that again if he wanted to keep his job with me.'

'So Ryan maybe stays somewhere rural?' Dan took care to refer to him in the present tense.

'There's this place they used to stick the Eastern Europeans. Before they fucked off home thanks to Brexit.'

'You mean the migrant workers who did all the menial jobs that aren't suitable for us Brits. Seeing as we're so highly qualified.'

The man scowled. 'I've got a shop to run. I haven't time to talk politics with the likes of you.'

'Soon as you say where Ryan Taylor lives, I'll leave you to your business. And I'll be certain to tell Hazel you're an excellent ambassador for the *Anglia Herald*.'

'You do that,' the owner said, glaring at him. 'Ryan's gaff is on the way to Watton. Take the first left in Mettlesham and you'll pass a house on the right has a walled off bit with chalets inside. Like a bunch of rabbit hutches. I was driving by one day when I saw him come out the gates. Some geezer with foreign plates was giving Ryan a lift. They were blocking the road.'

'When was this?' Dan said.

The man shrugged. 'Three or four months ago? And just you make sure and tell Hazel I gave you all the help you needed.'

On his way to Beccles, Dan kept an eye on the satnav, aware he might be late for his meeting. The traffic behaved and it was 2 p.m. exactly when he pulled into the car park near the bridge. His eyes were drawn to two figures by the river and he recognised Jay Olsen. She was wearing a polka dot skirt. Dan climbed out of the Volvo and felt a wave of dizziness. There had been no time for lunch, which was always a mistake.

The man next to her had to be the witness, Peter Olsen.

Jay turned and said, 'Hi.' No smile. She seemed uneasy. A text had come from her earlier, confirming where to meet. The message ended with *I need to know everything my dad remembers about that day*. Dan did not want her father to be guilty, but his only choice was to expose the facts, regardless of who got hurt. An investigation was a blunt instrument.

'I'm Daniel Hennessy,' he said, proffering a hand to Jay's father. 'Please call me Dan.'

The man blinked. He was wearing cord trousers and a frayed shirt, the sleeves rolled up. His forearms were sinewy and strong. A rough-hewn face. Dan saw little resemblance to his daughter. Maybe a similarity across the brow?

'Thanks,' Dan said, 'for taking the time to meet me. I really appreciate it.'

Olsen nudged Jay and said, 'Did you lock the Nissan?'

'Yes, Dad.'

There was vagueness in his eyes and he was stepping from side to side. Dan wondered if Olsen had some form of dementia.

Dan smiled at him, then switched his focus to Jay. 'Have you told your father why we're here?'

Frowning, she said, 'He does understand English, you know.'

'Apologies, that was clumsy of me. Mr Olsen, I'm grateful to you for agreeing to this. Your daughter has no doubt explained that I'm investigating the abduction of Felix Faulkner. In July 2001. Anything you can tell me would be a huge help.'

'Dad?' Jay touched his arm.

'The baby,' Olsen said. 'I never saw the baby. I just saw the children.'

'If we go look at where it happened,' Dan said, 'you could talk me through what you remember. You may be able to add new details. Sometimes that occurs when people revisit a place, even if it's years later. Would you be okay with us doing that? Taking a walk along the riverbank?'

Olsen nodded.

Jay glanced toward the path then back at Dan, saying, 'I wanted to ask how you're getting on. With the investigation. Have you made any progress?'

Dan swallowed. Her question was a reminder of how little he had achieved.

'I've been reading online,' she said, 'about the disappearance. There were others there that afternoon. Other witnesses, not just my father.'

'I'm hoping to speak to everyone. Provided I can trace them.'

'It was a long time ago,' Jay said.

'True, but things sometimes surface. New information. Shall we?' He pointed to the path.

Jay took hold of her father's arm, and Dan stayed in front as they headed along. He found himself thinking about her silver hoop earrings, how they caught the light. On his right was a screen of trees, mostly ancient willows with split limbs, and beyond them were glimpses of the grassy flood plain. On his left was a margin of reeds and then the Waveney, a slow surge of water. It was peaceful here, no traffic noise, but the sound of birds. At regular intervals there were short jetties that led to cabin cruisers, the low type suited to the Broads, and a few sailing boats, styled like a Norfolk wherry, with hinged masts to allow for passing under bridges. When Dan glanced back, Jay had a hand on her father's elbow, guiding him. The concrete path was narrow and uneven.

The man was old, bewildered. Guilty? Olsen had come forward as a witness when the police made a public appeal, the day after the abduction. Why do that if he had been involved in some way? It did not make sense, but Dan could not discount Olsen until he knew more of the facts.

He scanned ahead – no sign yet of Chapel House. The Waveney was wide on this stretch, and across the other side were houses with back gardens ending at the water, the riverbank shored up by timber and steel. Small rowing boats were moored to quays, and there was the occasional boathouse. Two people were feeding swans. Those lawns on the far bank were oddly perfect, luridly green and flat – a contrast to the reeds and ragged grass alongside the path where he walked with Jay and her father. The further south they went, Dan noticed, the steeper the gardens became on the other side. He had a vision of Beccles as a richly cluttered fabric of walls and buildings and greenery, thrown on top of the land with its hard humped back that slowly pushed upward from the flood plain. At one point he got a surprise glimpse of a double decker bus, in the gap between houses.

'Nearly there,' Dan said, turning to smile at Jay and her father, struck again by what she wore. Vintage 1950s. Her skirt was cinched at the waist. Jay had said she was a musician and he wondered if she played in a rock 'n roll band.

'Lovely weather,' he said, peering over his shoulder again.

Jay frowned and he realised it had been a crass thing to say. They were here about a missing baby.

The Waveney was taking a slow curve, the buildings massed closer together, rising toward St Michael's and the bell tower. Dan could see, beyond the next property, a high brick wall and a line of trees, stepping down the slope. Where the wall reached the bank, there was a brick pillar with a large stone globe on top.

'Here we are,' he said, stopping directly opposite. Up on the ridge, Chapel House caught the sunlight. It warmed the red brick of the Georgian part, but the grey stone chapel on the left still looked austere with its pointed windows. The formality of the terraced garden was very apparent from across the river, Dan noting how the stone path and steps were positioned on the centreline.

'Big place,' Jay said.

He smiled, uncertain why. They were standing in the shade, and yet Dan was sweating – acutely aware of the rip in his T-shirt, and how the thin fabric stuck to his skin. He stepped closer to the bank, focusing his attention on Chapel House and the lower part of the garden. Water infiltrated the land, the walls either side creating a square-shaped bay. Dan had noticed these details when he visited Catherine Nash. And yes, the garden was very cut off, and more private than all the others they had passed. When Olsen walked along here in 2001 and observed the children having a picnic, they would have been about forty metres away. But as Dan peered up the slope, he realised how unlikely it was that the man could have witnessed anything relating to the abduction. The paved terrace had to be at least a hundred metres away – could he have seen someone lurking by the house, ready to grab Felix?

Dan turned to Olsen, but at that moment Jay said, 'I think it's best if you leave us to it.'

'Oh,' he said. 'I'd hoped to ask questions.'

Olsen was frowning at the river.

Jay shook her head at Dan and whispered, 'It's too much for him.'

'Bye, then,' Dan said, loud enough for Olsen to hear. 'I'll wait for you in the car park. Take however long you need.'

Dan was not police. He could not insist on staying. On his way back, he took another look at the various boats next to the bank. A few shiny cruisers were accessed via metal jetties with locked gates. There were also wooden jetties leading to older cruisers and yachts, with algae giving a green hue to their hulls and even the sailcloth. A vintage barge caught his eye, different to the usual Broads cruiser. It appeared to be a holiday let, with fresh paintwork and a phone number for bookings. Further along was a long cruiser that sat unevenly in the water. Most of the jetty had rotted away, but stapled to a post was a laminated A4 notice from the Broads Authority, entitled 'Sunken Vessel', indicating it was due to be removed.

As he stared at the semi-submerged cruiser, Dan recalled Adam Wright. The informant who had assisted Operation Hyacinth back in 1999. A 'snitch' who seemed to have no concerns about being exposed. He was still living on the same cruiser when police questioned him about Felix Faulkner two years later. Dan tucked the thought away, not certain what to make of it.

Back at the car park, he sat on a bench by the water. A posse of ducks came to inspect him, in search of food. You were supposed to give them frozen peas. Some habits were like folklore, handed down through the generations and hard to break. Dan could remember feeding bread to the swans on Diss

Mere when he was little. He got out his phone and sent a text to his mother. *Hope you and Dad both well. I'm hoping to come visit for a weekend in August. Let me know what dates would suit xx D*

His relationship with them was 'good' but there were boundaries. Parenting had stopped when Dan was eighteen, and they avoided the complexities of his adult life. This was painfully apparent after Beth died. *You need space*, his father had said as they boarded the plane back to Spain, the day after the funeral. And maybe their lack of involvement brought freedom. No obligation to consult them about his choices. They were not castigating him for throwing away a career in the police service. When Dan told them he had moved to a caravan park, his mother had texted *That sounds fun!*

'Hi,' a voice said. It was Jay.

Dan stood up, saying, 'Welcome back.' The words awkward, he should have just said hello.

Peter Olsen was staring at the ground. Dan gave Jay a questioning look but she shook her head. The silence was broken by the klaxon tune of an ice-cream van.

'Would you like an ice cream?' Dan said. 'My treat.'

'No thanks,' Jay said. 'We should go.'

'I'd love a 99,' her father said.

'Apparently we're staying,' Jay said with a laugh.

Dan got a mint Cornetto for Jay and double scoop 99s for himself and Olsen. They sat in a row on the bench with Jay's father in the middle. It was like some weird family outing, and again he reminded himself of why they were here.

Olsen finished his cone then wiped his fingers with a handkerchief. 'Thank you, Daniel Hennessy. I haven't had one of those in years.'

'Glad you enjoyed it.' Dan glanced at Jay. She seemed exhausted. 'You were saying you have to get back?'

She stood up. 'Maybe we can talk later. If anything...'

'That would be great,' he said. 'Call me if, well, you know.'

Dan walked with them toward a blue Nissan. Olsen headed for the driver's side but Jay said, 'Let me, you must be tired.'

He watched them drive away. Dan got into his Volvo and sat behind the wheel. He had learned next to nothing. No new facts to add to his tally. Just the strong sense that an old man had answers that he either could not or would not share.

Chapter 21

Dan lowered his window and stared at the gravel car park. It seemed obvious now – Jay had agreed to this Beccles trip for her own purposes. Whatever she had uncovered would not be shared with him. *Do you think my dad kidnapped that baby?* Jay was worried about her father. Dan had become a threat, and this saddened him.

He could feel his thoughts congeal, that downward lurch. Dan slapped the steering wheel. Keep busy. There was still the issue of Ryan Taylor, and whether he was the victim at the solar farm. Dan needed to achieve something with his day. Take his mind off Jay. She was just the daughter of a witness.

Ignoring the satnav, Dan zig-zagged his way on a cross-country route, via Forncett End and back through Attleborough, where he picked up signs for Watton. In Mettlesham, he turned first left and passed a number of isolated dwellings, painted pink or cream, with sheds and barns around those that were still farms. Then he reached the place described by the newsagent, its frontage stretching along the road. Dan drove past and parked on the verge. Twisting in his seat, he took photographs on his phone.

The large bungalow was built of yellow brick, the colour of margarine. At the end nearest him there was a garden surrounded by railings, painted white, with a trampoline and children's climbing frame. At the other end of the bungalow was the enclosure referred to by the newsagent. Protected by walls in the same yellow brick, two metres high and topped by spikes. There were tall double gates onto the road, made of solid sheet metal, with no view inside.

Above the walls, Dan glimpsed the shallow-pitched roofs of small chalets, crammed close together. Rural locations were able to hide the sorts of living and working arrangements that most people would deem unacceptable. Dan was staying in a caravan, but his was not barricaded inside a compound. Brexit had affected migrant labour, and the owner of this farm must have looked for alternative tenants to maintain income from the chalets. Ryan Taylor did cash-in-hand jobs like newspaper deliveries. It made sense he wound up here.

Visitors were not welcome, a message broadcast by the high walls and railings. After his years as a police officer, Dan was used to being unwelcome. He walked past the garden and the front of the bungalow – *Valhalla*, its name inscribed in curlicued metal – and headed for the walled compound. There was no intercom or bell by the entrance, but a small hole had been drilled in the left-hand gate, at eye level, though the back of this hole was covered. Dan stood for a moment, listening to the sounds from inside, water draining into a gully, a low murmur of conversation. He knocked on the gate and the talking stopped. Dan heard the faint scrape of metal, as someone peered at him through the spy hole, then it was blocked again. He put a smile on his face, expecting the gates to open, but nothing happened.

'I'm looking for Ryan Taylor,' Dan called. 'I've been told he lives here. Any chance I could have a word?'

Silence.

'Are you in there, Ryan? My name's Dan. All I want is a quick chat. I'm not a debt collector or anything, and I'm not police, so there's no need to worry. You there, Ryan?'

He heard two people whispering, the intonation unfamiliar, possibly a language from Eastern Europe. It was difficult to tell through the gates, which remained shut.

There was movement along the road. A woman had emerged from the bungalow and was walking toward him. She was in her forties and wearing jeans and a pink T-shirt. Her hair was brown and shoulder length. She had hard eyes and was not smiling.

'Can I help?' she said.

'I'm looking for someone. I was told he lives here.' Dan nodded at the enclosure.

'We don't have anyone living here,' she said. 'It's holiday accommodation. For visitors. None of them are permanent residents. You with the council? I need to see your ID.'

'You're telling me those people are on holiday?' He stared at the woman.

'No ID? Then you've no reason to be here.' She waved her phone at him. 'My husband and his foreman are two minutes away.'

'Perhaps,' Dan said, 'your husband is more familiar with the names of your *visitors*. Maybe he knows if one of them is called Ryan Taylor.'

'I handle the bookings. There is no Ryan Taylor. Whoever gave you this address is mistaken. So clear off.'

'Most holiday accommodation doesn't involve a two-metre wall.'

'What's your name?'

'Daniel. What's yours?'

'Goodbye, Daniel.'

'Am I the first to come looking? Or have the police already been?'

The woman blinked. 'Police? What d'you mean?'

'Make sure and tell Ryan Taylor I need to speak to him. I'll give you my phone number.'

'Don't bother.'

Dan scribbled his number on a piece of paper and held it out. 'You don't want it, but Ryan might. Take it. I'm not leaving until you do.'

She snatched the piece of paper and crushed it in her fist. 'This is private property and you're trespassing.'

The woman watched him – Dan could feel it on the back of his neck – as he walked to the car. After a three-point turn, awkward with the Volvo on a narrow road, he drove past the bungalow and compound. She lifted her phone and seemed to film him, getting a record of his face and licence plate.

Dan headed toward Summerlands, weighing up that strange encounter. The woman and her husband were conducting a less than legal business. Inside that walled enclosure were frightened people. Seasonal EU workers with expired visas, evading deportation. Or breadline Brits like Ryan Taylor, with no money and not many options. Dan shook his head. There was still no certainty that Ryan was the body at the solar farm. He required actual proof.

Back at the caravan, he used the online land registry and found details of Valhalla, the incongruously named bungalow. The owner was listed as Mr Anthony Walker. A further online search established that a Mrs S Walker had planning permission for a static caravan to be located on agricultural land next to Valhalla. Just the one, but Dan had seen at least half a dozen chalets. It was clear that Mr and Mrs Walker were unlikely to answer any questions. That left the chalet residents as his only source. Dan could intercept someone leaving the compound, but Mrs Walker would be on the lookout for his Volvo.

Silverline had a spare taxi, kept in the yard, a Skoda with worn upholstery and no air conditioning. Dan was not about to start lying to Hari. He texted asking to borrow the Skoda so he could spy on someone. Hari texted back straightaway, saying it was available. *Tell me the juicy details next time you're in.* Dan thanked Hari, promising to give him the highlights and return the Skoda with a full tank of petrol. His reply beeped moments later. *A half tank will do. Wouldn't want the fuel to exceed the value of the vehicle.*

Smiling, Dan ended the exchange with a laughing face emoji and a thumbs-up. He glanced around the caravan. The place seemed less sad now that he was achieving things not treading water. Then a memory came to him of the reservoir and the wet figure rising from the surface, like a fluid black shadow. Was that really John Strang?

He cooked pasta, doubling up the quantities. While the penne boiled in the pan and the sauce simmered, Dan checked for messages, with the sudden thought that Jay Olsen was trying to contact him. The phone lay silent in his hand. A professional musician was bound to have a presence online. He opened Safari, then dismissed the idea. There was nothing going on between him and her.

Dan made himself eat a portion, and wrapped the rest in silver foil. It was Wednesday, but he had cancelled Cassie. Instead, he was taking food to a stranger. A narrow road skirted an area near the woods, and after parking at the entrance to a field, he set off on foot. The icehouse sleeper knew how to make himself invisible. Dan wanted to speak to the man, but if he pushed too hard, that chance would never come. He was pleased to see that yesterday's curry and rice were gone. The silver foil was there, neatly folded, and this felt like a thank you. He pocketed the silver foil and put in its place the parcel of warm pasta.

Dan stood up. 'Hello? I'm here to help.'

He waited five minutes, then left.

Jay was woken early by sunlight flickering on the thin curtains. It was 5.15 a.m. and she lay for a while, hoping to fall back asleep. Crows were calling in the sycamore of the neighbour's garden. The birds did not roost there overnight, but the tree was a stop-off on a route they took most mornings. She could remember that noise from her childhood. Angular, not melodic. Her father disliked crows and would chase them away. Another memory from years ago, him standing outside, clapping his hands with a sound like gunfire, then aiming a garden broom at the trees. 'They're clever,' he used to say. 'The only birds that respond to the shape of a shotgun.'

Had her father's opinion changed? Jay wondered whether crows had joined the legion of wild animals whose passing needed to be marked with proper ceremony. His behaviour in recent days had been fairly normal. She had ordered a workshop manual for her beloved Yamaha V-Twin, and her father had spent his time reading it. No more garden burials since Sunday's muntjac. Nor did he seem upset by yesterday's trip to Beccles with the detective.

After Dan Hennessy left them on the path, her father had said, 'That's where I saw the boy and girl. Next to the river.' Jay had looked across the water, anticipating some trace of tragedy, but all she felt was an emptiness. And maybe that absence was because of the baby. A small void in time and space that could never be filled.

While her father peered at the Waveney, Jay had studied Chapel House, recalling from news reports that Felix Faulkner had been in a pram on the upper terrace.

'Is it bringing back memories?' she had said, wondering if he would say more about the missing baby or the two children.

'I came here with your mother a few times,' he said. 'Before you and Colin were born. Before we were married. We used to walk along here.'

Jay frowned. 'What was she like?'

'Full of plans,' he said. 'Not very good at seeing them through.'

'Did that include being a parent?'

'We should go. Your man will be waiting.'

'He's not my man,' Jay said. 'His name is Dan Hennessy and he's investigating the baby who disappeared.'

Her father nodded slowly, then he turned to look down the path. 'Marion wanted a house by the river. We didn't have that sort of money.'

'I'm sorry she left you,' Jay said.

'I'm sorry I couldn't make her stay.'

'Dad, I was wondering. When you saw the two children that day – were you in Beccles because it was a special place for you and her? You and Marion. Was that why you came here?'

Moments after asking that, Jay had seen the lucidity fade from his face.

Sighing, she turned over in bed. Poor Dad. Walking along that path in 2001, all on his own, thinking about the past. Hiding his sadness from her and Colin and doing his best to be a single parent. The man was a bit of a hero. But maybe the strain was beginning to show.

Jay chewed her lip. Stu, who managed the band, wanted her to confirm availability for a list of upcoming gigs. Riders as well as Life Class. She felt reluctant to do so because of her father. Jay rolled onto her back, feeling the narrow confines of a single bed. Ruben was the other factor.

Rising from the kitchen came the sound of furniture being rearranged, the low thrum of wooden legs dragging across lino.

What was her father up to now?

Jay pulled on jeans and went downstairs.

'Morning,' her father said with a smile. 'Tea?'

'Thanks.'

The table had been pushed against one wall, and the chairs stacked on top. She decided not to comment.

'Sleep alright?' he said. 'You aren't usually up this early.'

'The crows woke me.'

He laughed. 'They do make a racket.'

Her father poured the tea, stirred sugar into his own. Then he strode toward her – the kitchen floor seemed vast without the table – and handed her a mug. Too hot, and she put it on the worktop.

'Thought I'd give the lino a mop,' he said, gesturing at where the furniture had been moved aside.

'Ah,' Jay said, feeling guilty for detecting madness in a domestic chore. 'Good idea. Want me to do it?'

'No, no,' he said. 'You're my guest.'

His tea was finished. Her father had always been able to drink liquids at near boiling point.

'What about breakfast?' she said. 'I could do toast.'

'I'll get something later,' he said, washing his mug at the sink.

Her father fetched a clean tea towel from a drawer. The gingham fabric was stiff with starch – maybe it was a new purchase. Her father was now shaking the tea towel to make it more pliable. Jay was reminded of a dog shaking its prey.

'Seems to be resisting arrest,' she said.

He raised his arms above his head, still gripping the tea towel by the corners. Her father then ran around the empty kitchen floor.

Jay stepped away to avoid a collision. The tea towel flew above him like a banner – what was he playing at? Jay felt sick. The moment was lasting too long but she was incapable of ending this. It would be like waking someone from a fit. Her father seemed possessed, still running in circles in the early morning kitchen, just the sound of the whipping fabric and the slap of his slippered feet.

Then he stopped with his back to her and wrapped the tea towel round his head. Her father released his grip and the cloth was now draped across his skull, resting on his shoulders. He turned toward her but his eyes were downcast. Jay swallowed, her mouth completely dry. Her father put his hands together in a gesture like some bizarre sign language, until she realised he was praying. Who was this man? Her father had never been religious.

His gaze was still directed at the floor. Jay's heart raced, in abject fear of the moment when he would look at her. And she would see the crazed gleam in his eyes. Mixed with her fear there was revulsion. His aping of a nun, hands in prayer, and the wings of fabric draped round his face.

'Dad,' she said, her voice descending to a whisper. 'Dad. Please.'

He glanced at her and smiled, then pulled the cloth from his head.

His eyes were not mad. But they peered at her from somewhere else, a place she did not know and had never been to.

'The children,' he said.

'Hannah and Chloe?'

He frowned, as if her words made no sense.

'Your granddaughters?' Jay said. 'You remember your granddaughters?'

'The children next to the river,' he said. 'They were playing a game.'

'In Beccles? The day that baby disappeared?'

He nodded, his hands still clasping the tea towel, which he had crumpled into a ball.

'Do you think you might feel able to speak to Dan? The detective guy? I could try and get him on the phone.'

'Daniel Hennessy bought me a 99.'

'Shall I call him? He was keen to know anything you remembered.'

Her father stared at the tea towel. 'I think I might go for a nap.'

'Okay, Dad,' she said. 'Have a good rest.'

He went into the dining room and shut the door behind him.

Jay sank to the floor. Put her head in her hands.

Chapter 22

Dan stood for a moment, looking at their house in Wymondham. This would be his last visit, and the morning light seemed mournful as it shone on the yellow bricks and red roof. Taking a deep breath, he unlocked the door, then went inside. Dan glanced at where he often sat, left of the fireplace, back to the wall. Not today. If he sat down, he might never leave. Or summon the strength to do what had to be done.

Berating himself, Dan opened the cupboard. This was not a respectful and loving place to keep Beth. He picked up the canister of ashes, now, as always, registering how heavy it was. Dan held it to his chest. This was not really Beth. She was gone. But her ashes were the shadow left behind. Traces from her feet as she walked away, a grey vestige of who she had been.

Beth's parents wanted half the ashes. Her father had pulled him aside, the day of the funeral, and asked him. It had made his stomach heave. Cassie noticed and she had grabbed Dan's arm and led him away, on some excuse. Outside she lit a cigarette, a real one not a vape, and Dan could remember commenting that he did not know she still smoked. 'I keep these for emergencies,' she had said. 'This qualifies.'

'Don't let the parents get to you,' she then said. 'They'll try and do that *my grief is bigger than yours* thing. I've seen it happen in families. The mum and dad want first dibs when their kid dies. It's understandable, given they raised them from a babe. But Beth was a grownup with her own life. She's not their property anymore. Or yours for that matter, but you're who she's been with the past five years. You get to make the decisions, not her parents.' She waved the cigarette at him. 'I know you're dying for a smoke.'

He had been staring at the tip of the cigarette. Ashes to ashes. Dust to dust.

A week after the funeral, an email came from Beth's father repeating the request to divide up her ashes. 'It's what our daughter would have wished, and it will mean a lot to her mother.'

Dan gripped the green canister. He would write and say he had scattered her ashes off the end of Cromer Pier. A lie, but one he was happy to tell. When Beth was a child, that was where the family went on day trips. Her parents could visit Cromer if they wanted to commune with memories of their daughter.

With his Beth cradled in his arms, Dan took a last walk through the house, into all the white-painted rooms, the bathroom with its marble-effect tiles, the oak veneer kitchen, then outside into the small back garden with its paved patio, its wooden fencing, and long grass waving at the sunlight. He and Beth made a silent farewell to the home that never happened. Then Dan locked the front door and headed for the car. Disembodied. Afloat. He placed Beth's ashes in the footwell behind his seat, wrapped in a blanket.

At the estate agents, he dropped off the keys and completed the necessary paperwork.

The agent was a young man in a navy suit, who said, 'Do you mind me asking your reason for selling? Some buyers like to know.'

Dan blinked, and managed to say, 'A change of plans.'

Back at the caravan, he put the canister of ashes in the wardrobe. Next to the bag of items given to him the day he went to the morgue. Beth's belongings, what she was wearing. All of it inside a thick plastic bag, semitransparent. Glimpses of her shoes, her winter coat. As he shut the flimsy door, Dan realised his hand was shaking. He had another decision to make, more actions to undertake. But there were limits to what he could endure. Dan dropped to his knees, pressed his palms into the gnarled nylon of the carpet.

After a few minutes the nausea passed. He clambered to his feet, washed his face at the kitchen sink, then drove to South Lopham for his 11 a.m. pickup.

Jay dipped her spoon into the bowl of tinned soup. It was red, which meant tomato. Both elbows were off the table, like this lunch was a formal occasion. Her father also seemed to be trying to prove himself. After the nap, he had tidied his appearance and wetted his hair – she could see the tracks left by his comb. A newish shirt had been put on, but above the collar there was dark stubble in the creases of his neck and chin.

The kitchen smelled strongly of Flash. Jay had mopped the floor, completing the task her father began. The lino gleamed, and she blinked, still in a turmoil over what she had witnessed. And here they both were, behaving like nothing happened.

'About earlier,' she said. 'We need to talk. Colin's worried. I am too.'

'He bought me a new TV.'

'I saw. He's very generous.'

Jay put her spoon down, no memory of having finished the soup. 'So will you speak to a doctor?'

'Everything's fine, Jacqueline. Really. It's like, it's like...'

Then her father shrugged and smiled, lifting his big hands and pushing them through each other, the fingers stiff but interlaced. 'It's like this,' he said, staring right at her and shaking that mesh of fingers as if the gesture had meaning. 'Do you follow?'

Jay looked at his earnest face. 'I'm trying, Dad. I am trying. But you need to tell me what's bothering you. What's causing all this.' Her gaze flicked toward the garden, the plantation of graves. 'The children in Beccles. Did something happen? Talk to me, Dad. You said they were playing a game by the river. Then what? Is there something you need to tell me?'

Dan was free by the early afternoon and had no further bookings. He parked his Volvo in the Silverline yard and headed to the office with his portable safe. A few passengers still paid in cash and Hari would bank the £217 and send him the usual percentage. His friend was out but Sheenagh logged the amount, then handed him a key for the Skoda.

On the outskirts of Great Ellingham, he pulled over. Dan had brought OS 144, and his finger checked the route past Valhalla. The Walkers would be suspicious of anyone parked near their property. Scanning the map, he analysed where to keep watch, and how to intercept a resident from the chalets. The place was isolated – those shopping for supplies would do so by car. To the east was Mettlesham, but prices were high in village stores. The chalet residents were likely to prefer Watton, which had a Lidl and a range of discount shops.

Dan picked a lookout point on the map. Ten minutes later, he reached the track next to woods, parked the Skoda, but the location was not as hoped. There was a tall hedge on the other side of the road, blocking his view of the compound. If a vehicle drove by, he would have no clue where it came from. Dan grabbed his binoculars and crossed the tarmac. Thrust his way through the hedge and walked along. The land here was on a slight rise, not enough for seeing inside the compound but the grid of roofs was visible. Eight chalets in total, tightly packed. Behind the enclosure there seemed to be parking – Dan glimpsed a few car bonnets.

The landscape was deserted, and a breeze moved through the treetops. Vehicles passed at intervals, but nobody had left the bungalow or the chalets. A DPD van arrived from the direction of Mettlesham, then pulled in next to Valhalla. Moments later, the van sped off.

It was 3.45p.m. when Dan noticed the first signs of activity at the entrance to the walled enclosure. One of the gates opened, and a woman came out. She disappeared past the far corner, then he heard an engine starting up. A small grey car, a Vauxhall Vectra, emerged from the track at the side of the compound and drove away toward Mettlesham. If Dan had been watching from his car, he might have been able to catch up. He shook his head. Watton was still the best bet.

A child came out of the bungalow and spent five minutes jumping on the trampoline.

At 4.10 p.m. a white minibus with tinted windows drove past Dan, and turned up the side of the compound. He waited for people to appear, but nobody did. It seemed there was a back entrance. More noise rose from the chalets, after the return of the minibus. Snatches of music, voices. Then movement in the rear parking area and he spotted a blue hatchback on the track next to the compound. Toyota? It signalled right, heading for Dan. He ran back, using the hedge as cover. The vehicle grew louder and he saw a flash of blue through the leaves. Dan waited until it was past the corner, then he sprinted across the road.

The Skoda would not start. A second attempt, jabbing his foot on the accelerator, and the engine roared to life. He raced after the blue hatchback, but bends in the road restricted his view ahead. There were several turnings the vehicle might have taken. Dan reached Watton without having glimpsed his target. Weighing the options, he headed for Lidl first. There was a blue Toyota Yaris, 2007 registration, at the end of the car park. He parked nearby and approached it. The engine was warm. He photographed the Yaris, including the number plate, then went to wait in his own car.

The store was busy, people streaming back and forth from the entrance. So far, they had all left in different vehicles. Dan checked the time, and as he glanced up, a couple went by with a full trolley. They were heading for the last row of parking. This had to be them. Dan took photographs, then got out of the car. Sure enough, the man and woman were next to the Yaris, loading bags into the boot, multipacks of supermarket basics. The couple seemed to be in their late thirties. The man was thin but muscular, in a T-shirt and jeans, a baseball cap. The woman had black hair and was wearing a skirt and sleeveless top. They both gave an impression of durability, of long hours working outdoors.

'Sorry to bother you,' Dan said.

They stopped, mid movement.

'I'm looking for a friend of mine. Ryan. Ryan Taylor.'

The woman put a bag of shopping in the car. The man held Dan's gaze for a moment, then switched his attention to the trolley.

'Don't know any Ryan Taylors,' the man said as he lifted out a carton of tins.

'I saw you coming out of that place next to Valhalla,' Dan said. 'The bungalow back there, with the chalets. My friend Ryan lives in one of them. He's not replying to messages. I tried visiting yesterday but was turned away – by Mrs Walker? Said she'd never heard of him. It seemed to give her some sort of kick, not helping me. Like she enjoys abusing people.'

The woman gave him a look. His words had hit home.

'I need to be sure Ryan's okay,' Dan said. 'I think this Mrs Walker knows what's happened to him and is deliberately not telling me.'

'She likes playing games,' the woman said.

'This is none of our business,' the man said, addressing her.

'Mrs Walker your landlady?' Dan said. 'She's a right piece of work. Hope the rent's reasonable. Ryan's always short of money. Borrowed thirty quid, promising to pay me back, but he never does.'

'Is that why you followed us here,' the man said, 'because he owes you money?'

'No,' Dan said. 'I'm genuinely worried. Sometimes he goes off radar for a few weeks, but never this long.'

The man and woman exchanged glances, then she said, 'He moved out about the middle of June. We didn't see him go. Both of us were full-time picking.'

'Strawberries,' the man said.

She nodded. 'I mean we hadn't seen him for a few days, but that happens, because everyone does different hours. We get back one evening and word is Ryan's moved on. Didn't take any of his things, though. Mrs Walker said to help ourselves. Keep what we wanted and she'd chuck the rest. We're supposed to give a fortnight's notice. The bitch also claimed he broke the shower.'

'And you've no idea where he went?' Dan said.

The man sneered. 'A right joker, you are. You mean like a forwarding address? He probably had no clue where he was going next. And personally, I wouldn't trust any of the others not to tell the Walkers in exchange for cash.'

'Needs must,' the woman said.

The man frowned at her, but she was busy lifting the last bag into the boot.

When she turned round, Dan said to her, 'You're absolutely sure you've no idea where Ryan went?'

Her partner was staring at her too.

'What?' she said. 'Why the inquisition? I haven't a clue. Lucky him managing to escape. Sooner we leave that dump, the better.'

'Maybe this will help,' Dan said, opening his wallet. He took out forty pounds and offered it to the woman.

'We're not a charity case,' the man said, grabbing her hand as she reached for the money.

'Yes we are,' the woman said, shaking him off. 'Sixty would be *nicer*, don't you think?' She eyed Dan. 'Seeing as we've given you so much information about your *friend* Ryan. What did you say your name was?'

'Dan Hennessy. What's yours?'

'Funny,' she said. 'Ryan never mentioned a Dan.'

'Just because he didn't mention me, doesn't mean I'm not concerned about him.'

'I'm still waiting,' she said, 'for the extra twenty.' She nodded at the money in Dan's hand.

'Tina, we're late enough as it is,' the man said. 'We need to go. Now.'

Dan fetched another note from his wallet. The woman snatched the money, but Dan held on tight, saying, 'When Ryan wasn't at the chalets, who did he hang out with? One of his other friends might know where he went. You'll get the full sixty if you give me a name.'

The woman scowled. 'He used to do occasional work at a stud farm. Somewhere near Elme Green? Mucking out stables for twelve quid an hour. Sounded a decent gig but they're fussy about who they hire. Ryan knows one of the blokes that works there. They were school mates.'

'Name?' Dan said.

'No idea,' she said, taking the money. 'Hope you find Ryan. We liked having him around. He's a good laugh.'

On his way back to Wymondham, Dan stopped in a picnic area set among trees. No real rush to return the Skoda, and he needed time to think. The man who ran the kiosk was packing up, but he served Dan a sandwich and lukewarm coffee, apologising for the temperature. Dan sat at an empty table. The sandwich was tuna on soft granary bread, not too much mayonnaise. As the man headed off in a 4x4, Dan gave him a thumbs-up and pointed at the sandwich. The man smiled and waved.

Alone now, Dan finished his coffee. Nearby was a large wooden structure for children to play on, shaped like a squirrel. Warm evening sunlight dipped through the trees. There was traffic on the road but somehow this place felt secluded. He stared into his empty cup. A month ago, Ryan Taylor vanished from the chalet compound leaving all his belongings behind. Similar to what happened with John Strang at Summerlands. Around that time, Ryan Taylor also stopped turning up for work at the newsagents. Nor was he reachable by phone.

Dan sighed and shook his head. No choice but to tell Cassie. There was definite evidence that the dead man at the solar farm could be Ryan Taylor. And his murder coincided with Strang's departure from the caravan park. But how did this connect with Felix Faulkner? Closing his eyes, Dan focused on what he knew. Not a complete picture, but the beginnings of one.

Ryan was linked to Strang. In his caravan Strang had baby items he had kept for a long time. The rubber dummy was cracked, the clothes seemed old-fashioned. Strang owned a small ceramic of a child, which he left at the icehouse. In Mrs Faulkner's living room, Dan had seen that figure or one very similar. Was Strang also mourning a missing child? These strange parallels to Mrs Faulkner and her son – Dan could not understand what they meant. She did not appear to know John Strang, other than as a resident who had left owing rent. But maybe she had crossed paths with Ryan Taylor?

Dan crushed the paper cup. It pained him to think of questioning Mrs Faulkner, not until he had more information. Any mention of a name would imply he was close to solving what happened to her son. *Do not give me false hopes.*

There was also Peter Olsen to consider. Did he come forward as a witness to 'explain' what he was doing in Beccles that Wednesday? Maybe Olsen had been concerned someone would report seeing him. Dan had to follow his investigation wherever it took him. Even if it hurt Jay. He threw the paper cup in the bin.

At Wymondham, he dropped off the Skoda and was met by Hari, who wanted to know all about his '007 exploits'. They sat in the small office, surrounded by battered filing cabinets. Dan told him about the chalet compound and his attempts to trace a missing person, but he did not mention any names. The chat shifted onto football and Norwich's chances, a favourite topic for Hari. Dan joined in with snippets he had heard on local radio. The conversation was winding down when Hari asked him to stay for dinner. 'Nothing fancy, just Kes and the kids. You've not been for months and he keeps saying to have you over.' Dan declined and his friend knew not to push it.

There was a fresh scent in the Volvo. For the past few hours, his car had been at the yard – someone had valeted the interior. Kindness brought tears to his eyes these days. He thought about the dinner invite. Another kindness, but Dan could not step into Hari and Kes's home without being painfully aware of his own isolation. He rubbed his face, then headed to Summerlands on the back roads. There was a sign for Flaxton, a long white plank of wood with a pointed end. Dan turned left and parked on the edge of the village, reminded of happier times.

He and Beth had visited the castle on two occasions. Smiling, Dan thought about the procedure with the key. A notice had said it could be collected from the nearby garage that sold and repaired Reliant Robins. The forecourt resembled a scrapyard. The keeper of the key wore an oily boiler suit and had unkempt greying hair. He had been keen to impart his detailed knowledge of Flaxton Castle. Facts and dates and boundaries and fluctuating fortunes.

As Dan and Beth walked to the castle, she had said with a grin, 'Does he do that to everyone? Or did we look particularly ill-informed?'

The following year they went again but decided to avoid another long-winded lecture. Dan and Beth had forged a route round the outside of the castle, weaving through trees. There was a moat, a narrow and dank wooded valley that encircled the ivy-choked walls of the castle. Together they slid down to the light-dappled bottom, then made their way, on steppingstones and rotten logs, across the mud and shallow dregs of water. Beth gave a squeal and the two of them laughed, staring in awe at the ground, alive with tiny frogs. What had been brown mud was in fact creatures, crawling over each other.

Even now, Dan could feel the joyful shock of the newly hatched frogs. He released his grip on the steering wheel. The evening was still light as he walked to the entrance. The tall cast-iron gates were shut, but there was no chain and padlock. The keeper of the key had gone, of course. A month or so after Dan and Beth made their illicit trip to the castle, they happened to drive through Flaxton. The carcasses of all those Reliant Robins were being cleared from the forecourt. The site was being 'developed' into new housing. The garage had seemed like a permanent fixture of the village, until one day the garrulous man and his wrecks were no more.

Dan pushed open the gates, the hinges rusty. But on crossing the threshold, the recent past fell away and he stepped into another era. Time no longer marked by years and decades, the lifespan of individuals, but measured instead by generations and the evermore of millennia. The air smelled of twilight. The stone bridge took him over the moat and into the green bowl-like space.

A hush dropped like a shroud, as if he was entering a room where secrets were being shared. Dan stood and listened, arms by his sides, fingers outstretched. The hum of expectation persisted, threaded through with birdsong, as he approached the ruined tower. Dan sat with his back against the flint wall, looking across the gentle arena of grass.

Stillness descended. Centuries ago, it would have been full of people. All that striving had gone, leaving behind these man-made structures that had been all but absorbed into the landscape. Reclaimed. Dan smiled a sad smile – he had come here to assess the castle's suitability as final resting place for Beth. He recalled glimpses of her laughing face. Beth's shriek when she almost slipped and fell in the moat. The rough flint on his back as she pushed him against the wall and kissed him.

Dan brushed a hand across his mouth and listened to the birds. Sun glinted in the canopy of trees. He swallowed, preparing himself, unsure what to say until the words formed.

'Is this where you'd like to be?'

No answer, no revelation. Dan sat there quietly as time breathed slower and slower. A deer came over the top of the overgrown battlements. It picked its way down the bank and across the grass, passing within a metre of him. Then it climbed the opposite side and disappeared. Dan pressed both palms to the ground and closed his eyes. Birdsong surrounded him like a halo.

Yes, this was it.

On the drive back to Summerlands, he tried to hang on to the peacefulness of that place, the sense that it was the right home for Beth. Like the castle walls, she too would return to the land and be reclaimed. Dan made himself dwell on this thought, but circling around it, in the moat, dark and glistening, amphibian, were questions that still remained. What took her to Magdalen Street? Beth had stepped off the pavement, oblivious to the oncoming vehicle.

What sense of purpose was so overwhelming that it blinded and deafened her?

Chapter 23

Next morning, Dan texted Cassie. *I have information on the solar farm victim. It's up to you if you're interested. Book an interview room.*

His phone rang moments later, Cassie's name on the screen. He let it go to voicemail, then listened to her message.

'Hi Dan, it's me.'

Cassie sounded weary, like she did not want to make this call. He had become a burden.

'Look,' she said, as her voice continued to play from his phone, 'I'm really sorry about the other day. My hands were tied. Walsh was going to stick me with a reprimand if I let our *potentially problematic friendship* get in the way. I kid you not. Those were her actual words.' Cassie gave an awkward laugh that seemed even more false on voicemail. 'She was having fits over what a smart-arse lawyer would do when they learned a former officer was interfering in the case. I mean that's absolutely not what you were doing. I know you're trying to help. It's just the optics? If you're wanting to speak to me about the icehouse, there's no point us meeting. That line of enquiry is dead. Kaput. But if you have any other information, I'm all ears. Especially if you whisper *green energy*. And yeah, you're right. Best make it official. Would eleven at Bethel Street suit? Bye, Dan. Hope you're okay. Sorry things have been a bit shit, lately.'

Frustrated, Dan wished he had chosen a different route. Already late reaching Norwich, he was now caught up in roadworks near the Market Place, with a three-way traffic signal. The car was hot, and he opened the windows, waiting for the lights to change. Music was coming from his left. Dan peered in that direction and saw a young woman with a guitar, busking. Then his heart slipped a beat. Jay Olsen. She was standing in the shade, next to a boarded-up shop. Playing an acoustic guitar and singing a song, a folk tune. T-shirt and cut-off jeans. Flip-flops.

Dan watched from afar. The way she tilted her face as she sang, and how her fingers made the notes like it was second nature. People walked past on the pavement – someone dropped coins into a cardboard box. Jay nodded in thanks and smiled, still singing. The smile remained on her lips, and now she began a different song, with a faster tempo, and Dan could see the pleasure it gave her. What was that like? The radiance of pleasure, woven into the music, the lilt of her voice.

The lights changed but Dan had no desire to leave. In his limbs, he felt the inertia of longing. The driver behind beeped his horn. Dan shook his head and tried to get the Volvo into gear. Jay had stopped singing and was now talking to someone. A man with fair hair. She was smiling at him, chatting. Their words were not audible but Dan heard laughter.

The driver behind gave an insistent blast of the horn. Jay looked over, frowning. Dan pressed the pedals, and his car lurched forward. When he checked again, Jay had the guitar on her back and was walking away with the fair-haired man. Just a friend, Dan decided. And why should it matter? He was not seeking a relationship.

But in that moment Dan registered how trapped he was. In his car, driving everywhere, taking people to different places but his own body going nowhere, completely stuck. And he registered how free Jay was. The freedom she put into singing, playing her guitar, but not trapped by the music, able to move off, do other things, meet a friend by chance, change her plans, see where they took her. Not circling the same well-trodden paths and roads, day after day after day, time glued into a solid lump of resin.

In the Forum car park, Dan sat for a while composing himself, setting aside the feelings stirred by Jay. Not his to receive.

The heaviness descended once more, the inner deadness that protected him from hurt. Not all hurts, but it lessened the impact. Dan locked the car and walked to the police station. Cassie was waiting in the lobby, but he did not return her smile. As he followed her along a corridor, Dan was aware of glances from other officers, the gap they left when skirting past. It seemed everyone now knew about his 'interference' in the enquiry.

'So,' Cassie said, once they were seated, 'what brings you here?'

An open question was standard procedure. And she was using it on *him*.

'Let's make this quick,' Dan said. 'I wouldn't want to waste police time.'

She gave him a look. 'Ha, ha, very funny.'

'Green energy? Seriously, is that your only lead?'

'Forgive me,' she said, her tone caustic. 'I must have been in a sharing mood when I left that message.'

'This is nothing to do with environmental activism.'

Cassie shook her head. 'I can't talk about the case.'

'Have you identified the victim?'

'Are you deaf? I cannot talk about the case.'

'Fine. Have it your way.' Dan stood up.

'Feel free to have a hissy fit and storm off. I apologised on the phone and I can apologise again if you're not bored of hearing me. But the fact remains that my reputation was on the line. Not yours. *Mine.*'

Dan breathed out heavily, then sat down.

'Don't keep a girl waiting, Danny Boy. What's this pet theory you're bursting to tell me?' Cassie was tapping her pen on a notebook, staring at him with a half-smile on her face. And for the first time Dan understood what else he had thrown away when he left.

'I miss this,' he said. 'I miss working with—'

'Don't. Stop right there.' The smile was gone. 'I'm not in the mood for a heart-to-heart. Save it for one of our Wednesday drinks,' Cassie said with a sneer.

Dan frowned. Then he told her about Ryan Taylor, beginning with when he realised the victim seemed familiar because he used to see him delivering papers in Attleborough. Cassie took notes throughout his account. She did not look at him or interrupt with questions.

'That's pretty much it,' Dan said, once he had finished relaying the information from the couple living at the chalet compound, including details of the stud farm where Ryan had worked. There was no point mentioning the possible link to the 'vagrant' John Strang. Cassie had already said the police were not interested. Nor did Dan intend to tell her about Felix, as that was a private matter between him and Mrs Faulkner.

Cassie's silence made him nervous. 'Well?' he said. 'Any of that useful?'

Still no response.

'Maybe you're right,' Dan said. 'Maybe this Ryan Taylor had dealings with a group campaigning about solar farms. But that's not the impression I got. He didn't seem the type.'

Cassie closed her notebook, lined the pen up next to it. Then she leaned back in the chair and crossed her arms. 'Quite the amateur sleuth, aren't you?' She was smiling but it was not a friendly smile. 'With people like you around, the rest of us should just jack it in.'

'I was trying to help.'

'Like you did with the icehouse? What a jammie bit of info that was. Didn't backfire on me at all. Really helped with progress on the case. And now you come forward with the identity of the vic? *Possible* identity. Let's not get carried away here.'

'So you're not going to bother following this up?'

'Did I say that? Did you hear me say that?'

Dan shook his head.

'I can't touch this,' she said. 'In fact, I should have asked Sullivan to speak to you. Only I didn't want her scratching your eyes out. Something about you being a poster boy for male privilege. She really didn't warm to you.' Cassie laughed. Not sharing the joke with him but with her new partner. 'I'll get Sullivan to look into this. Don't worry, she's an excellent officer. Very professional. She won't let personal animosity get in the way.'

'I didn't ask to be involved, Cass. You're the one who rang me, wanting to show me the body.'

'Oh and don't I regret it. We're trying to build a case here. If Ryan Taylor is our stiff and this gets to court, how d'you think it's going to look? Your DNA is all over the icehouse and it's also you that points us toward the identity of the vic?'

'Thought you said the icehouse had no connection to the case. That it was a dead end.'

Cassie frowned. 'If we are able to apprehend the murderer, the defence will use you to run interference on the evidence. To cast doubt in the minds of the jury. They'll claim you're a person of interest, a possible suspect, and we didn't investigate you properly because you're a former officer.'

He thrust his wrists toward her. 'Cuff me. I've nothing to hide.'

'Stupid twat. When did you get to be such a drama queen?' The words seemed like banter but Cassie looked angry. 'Right,' she said, standing up. 'Back in a minute.'

The door banged shut.

Dan was on the wrong side of the wrong table in the wrong room. His life had flipped. Tails not heads. Everything went wrong when Beth died. Police had felt like family. The room began to shrink, walls pressing in, the floor thrusting upward, tipping him off the chair. He slammed his hands onto the table.

Cassie opened the door, stared at him. 'What the hell? You look like a mental case.'

Dan blew out a breath. 'I'm fine.'

'I'd offer you something from the vending machine,' she said, 'only I can't be arsed.'

He smiled. That was probably the one truly 'Cassie' thing she had said so far.

She sat at the table with an iPad, finger flicking at the screen. 'Okay. You're going to give a brief statement which I will type into here and read out to you.'

'I know the mechanics, Cass.'

She glared at him. 'Which I will type into here and read out to you. Is that clear, Mr Hennessy?'

'Sure.'

'In his statement,' she said, her fingers typing while she spoke, 'the subject Daniel Hennessy recounts that he saw the e-fit reconstruction of the victim released to the media, and realised the face was familiar. Today, he came into the station as it occurred to him that the victim could be a male he had occasionally seen delivering newspapers in Attleborough. Hennessy had observed him on Hargham Road as he has a client he collects from that location in his current employment as licensed PHV driver.' Cassie stopped typing, looked up and met his gaze. 'That's where your statement ends. There will be no mention of Ryan Taylor's name or the amateur investigation you carried out. Ringing the distributor, the trip to the newsagents, your visit to Valhalla. You then conducting a stakeout and tailing two residents and paying them for information on this Taylor's movements. None of that goes in the statement. Not a word. Understood?'

Dan nodded. Thought about repeating that he was trying to help, but it would only make matters worse.

'Have you told anyone else what you've been up to?' Cassie said.

There was Hari, but Dan had not mentioned any names or details when he returned the Skoda. 'Nobody knows,' he said.

'I'll pass your statement to Sullivan. She'll take it from there.'

'But you'll be sure and tell her the rest? That the woman's called Tina and she's—'

'STOP.'

Dan flinched.

'Stop,' Cassie repeated in a whisper. 'You're not Norfolk Constabulary. You're not a DI. You're a civilian, Dan. You don't get to stick your oar in and tell me how to conduct a murder enquiry. You're missing all this? You want back in? Well, boo-hoo. You left, Dan. Nobody kicked you out. You had a great job and it was your decision to quit. Nobody made you do it. You were offered support. Grief counselling. Compassionate leave. It was a tragedy what happened to Beth. Beyond awful. And we, everybody here' – she gestured at the walls, people in the surrounding offices – 'did their best to help you. But you didn't want our help. You decided to go it alone. Yeah, and you're clearly making a bang-up job of that. Sleeping in an underground cavern like some weird dosser and chasing all over the place screwing up our investigation. I mean, the state of you. Have you looked in a mirror lately? You're a mess. I don't recognise you anymore. You've become one of those sad losers causing a public nuisance. The ones where you arrive at the scene and you know the moment you clap eyes on them that this is going to be a job for social services.' She reached her hand across the table.

'Correction,' he said, standing up. Surprised at the steadiness in his voice and legs, but not able to meet her gaze. 'You said everyone tried to help. Not true. I never had you down as a bullshitter, Cass. I thought you were different. Turns out you're just like the rest of them. *Fake.*'

Dan saw her hand retreat. The table shone, a vast expanse separating them. Cassie did not say a word. He could see her on the edge of his vision and it was like she was miles off and getting further away with each rapid beat of his heart. And Dan knew he would remember this moment. But even though this was not how he wanted to leave things with Cassie, he still could not pull back from the brink. Could not save himself from his full-time commitment to bloody mindedness and rash acts. He could not save the friendship or ward off the regret that was coursing through him.

Dan turned toward the door. 'I'll see myself out.'

For the second time, Dan was on a wall outside a station. Déjà vu. Already seen, but it was never just about seeing. It was about repeating the haptic, a body echo, finding yourself inside a moment you had lived before, stored forgotten in the memory, only to be resuscitated elsewhere. The angle of his knees as he sat on the wall, the roughness of the stone beneath his palms, the smell of car exhaust, and the soured taste in his mouth of a situation that had gone badly wrong. Three days ago, the interview with Sullivan. Today, his 'breakup' with Cassie. Dan wondered if a Jameson's would help, and he glanced right, recalling a pub along the street.

That was when he spotted Lomax, walking toward him, in a leather jacket and jeans. Lomax appeared not to notice Dan. Too busy grinning at his phone. Had Cassie texted him? Making some joke about what a jerk Dan was.

As Lomax drew near, Dan said, 'Look what the cat dragged in.' The best he could manage.

'Here to screw up another murder enquiry?' Lomax was laughing.

Dan stood up and the man backed away.

'Killed anyone recently?' Dan said. 'Any more innocent bystanders?'

Lomax clenched his mouth. He almost seemed upset.

'Is that genuine emotion?' Dan said. 'Maybe one day you'll get to be a real human being.'

'Fuck you,' Lomax muttered.

Dan scowled, unused to his own behaviour, the viciousness that was spawned by this bastard.

Lomax pressed a hand to his eyes, then blinked.

'Wow,' Dan said. 'Actual tears. You really are making progress. Cassie giving you lessons?'

'You know about me and her.'

'Of course I know. I'm a detective. Is this some sort of game to you? Not enough for you to murder my fiancee, you have to bang my best friend too?' Dan felt sick. Appalled at the words coming out of his own mouth.

'It's not like that. She's been helping me. I needed to make amends.'

Dan snorted. 'Is Cass your therapist too?'

'Yeah, well, I couldn't exactly speak to you, could I? D'you think I don't relive it every single day? Did it never occur to you that I had to get over it too? She stepped into the road. She didn't even look. We had the lights and siren going but she just ran in front of us like we weren't even there. You think that's easy to live with?'

Dan's jaw was rigid. He would never give that man forgiveness.

'Cassie was the only one who understood,' Lomax said. 'Me and her love each other.'

'Seriously?' Dan laughed in his face. 'You barely know her.'

'I know a lot of things you don't know.'

'Like what? Tell me all these things I don't know.'

'I know you're a crap friend who has no idea what she's done for you.'

What did he mean? Dan had thanked Cassie repeatedly for supporting him.

He glared at Lomax. 'You know nothing about me and Cass.'

'Always so superior.' Lomax gave a nasty laugh. 'Bragging about your perfect life and sneering at the oiks in uniform. Don't think I didn't notice. You and your *precious* liberal values. Is Cassie your token—'

Dan swung a fist at Lomax, but the man grabbed it and twisted Dan's arm behind his back.

'Bit out of shape, aren't you?' Lomax said, shoving him away.

Stumbling, Dan tried to stay on his feet.

'Your beautiful friendship,' Lomax said. 'Christ am I tired of hearing about it. About you and your endless troubles. *Poor Dan this, poor Dan that*. Quite the dampener on a decent stiffie. And while you cry on Cassie's shoulder and bleat about the terrible loss you suffered to your perfect life, you have no idea what she did for you.'

'Cassie's my friend. Friends care for each other, that's what they do.'

'Not a clue, have you?' Lomax said.

'She helped me. I'd do the same for her.'

'Cover up evidence? You'd do that for Cassie? Put your career on the line? Risk prosecution?'

'What are you talking about?' Dan said. 'The solar-farm murder?'

Lomax gave him a sly look. 'Try closer to home.'

'I don't understand.'

'You never did.'

Dan stared at him. 'Is this about Beth?'

'I'm going to tell you something that Cassie won't say to you, not in a million years. Because I'm sick of you treating her like shit. Sick of you taking advantage of her, when you've no idea what she did to protect you. Beth Davenport had two phones on her that day.'

'What are you talking about?'

'Cassie was one of the first on the scene. She ever tell you that?'

Dan shook his head. His mouth was too dry to speak.

'Cassie didn't want you knowing that your perfect fiancee was keeping secrets.'

The street seemed to judder beneath him. Dan sat on the wall, his mind reeling. He had never seen Beth with a second phone. The only one returned to him had been her Galaxy. 'Maybe,' he stammered, 'maybe it was for work.'

Lomax gave a dirty laugh. 'Let's just say Cassie had a little look. For confirmation purposes. Seems your fiancee was sending cosy messages to an old flame.'

He felt a hand on his shoulder.

'Sorry, mate,' Lomax said.

Dan thrust the hand away, then stood up. 'Screw you,' he said quietly.

Lomax laughed. 'The truth hurts like a bitch. Like a real bitch.'

Dan walked away. He could hear Lomax behind, yelling, 'Cassie put her neck on the line for you. Don't you ever forget that.'

Chapter 24

'You okay, love?'

Dan tried to focus. A woman was speaking, and her face loomed toward him.

'You seem a bit lost,' she said.

He glanced round, unsure how he had ended up here. Chapelfield Shopping Centre. Or Castle Mall. They were all the same.

'Careful,' she said. 'You might fall.'

He had fallen. Was still falling.

'Escalators are nasty,' she said. Like she was talking to a child.

Dan blinked at the metal treads that slid down and away. People pushed past, shunting him with bags of shopping.

'Come on, love,' she said. 'Why don't we go find a seat.'

She steered him to a bench and sat next to him.

'Is there someone I can contact?' she said, getting out a phone.

Dan stared at it then looked away. 'I'm fine.'

'You sure you aren't here with someone? Did you wander off – is that what happened? Why don't I call security.'

'I'm not... Don't call security. I just... I heard some bad news. That's all.'

'I'm sorry,' she said.

'I'll be okay in a minute.'

The woman was peering at him closely. 'I know you,' she said. 'I've got a really good memory for faces. My husband is always saying that. Have we met before?'

Dan had encountered so many people when he was in the police. He hoped this was not going to be a long conversation about some case he could barely recall.

'Don't let me keep you,' he said.

The woman frowned, still scrutinising him. 'You need help.'

'I'm not a suicide risk, if that's what you're thinking.'

'I couldn't forgive myself if you came to any harm.'

'I assure you, I'm not in danger.'

'Wait,' she said, her voice triumphant, 'you're a taxi driver. You picked me up from the station. I knew I knew your face. What sort of bad news? Did you lose your job?'

'Nothing like that. Look, I'm fine. You can go now.'

'I'm not leaving until you call a friend. You're in no fit state.'

'Says who?' Dan glared at her.

'Says someone who's seen the consequences.' There were tears in her eyes.

'I'm sorry,' he said. 'I shouldn't have…'

'About this number. I'm happy to speak to them if that would be easier.'

Dan still had Beth as the ICE on his phone. In Case of Emergency. He did not change it after she died. The emergency had happened. She had been his ICE and he had been hers. In the contacts list on her Galaxy. The one phone he knew about.

The woman patted his hand. 'Tell me a friend's number and I'll give them a call.'

Dan thought of Cassie. 'No, it's—I'm just going to sit here.'

'Me too, if that's alright.'

His eyes drifted across the people milling about the shopping centre. Chapelfield – he recognised the wide expanse of the first-floor walkway. How did he end up here? The Volvo must still be in the Forum car park. He searched his pockets for the ticket.

'Can I pass you a tissue?' the woman said.

Dan shook his head.

You seem a bit lost. He did not want to be found.

After a while, the woman went to stand by the balustrade. Dan watched her get out a phone and make a call. Maybe to her husband, explaining why she was late. *A strange man was stuck at the top of an escalator.*

The woman walked back. By the look on her face, it was clear she had reached a decision. Dan hoped she would offer her excuses and leave. Instead, she sat next to him again.

'I'm not going to do anything stupid,' he said.

The woman did not speak. Her hands were clasped in her lap. Chapelfield was getting busier, time passing, fast or slow – Dan failed to differentiate.

Someone stopped in front of him, he could see their shoes. Black Vans with a white rubber edge. It was Hari.

'Here to fetch me?' Dan said, without looking up. 'I don't remember ordering a cab.'

'This lady thought you might need company. I told her being a sad loser was part of your MO but she insisted I come.'

Dan saw the feet step away and he heard Hari speaking to the woman in a softer voice, saying, 'Thanks very much for calling. I'll make sure he's okay. How you getting home?'

There was a murmured reply, then Hari said, 'Ring the switchboard for a taxi. Tell them I said no charge.'

The conversation continued in whispers that Dan could not hear above the noise of the shopping centre. Then the woman stood in front of him and said, 'Take care of yourself, Dan. I'll be phoning Hari later to see how you're doing. I'm Susan, by the way.'

'I should have asked. Goodbye, Susan. Thank you for trying to help.'

Dan watched her walk away.

'Pub?' Hari said.

'Home,' Dan said.

'That shithole of a caravan? Hardly a cure for suicidal thoughts.'

'Susan got the wrong idea.'

'Sure about that?'

'I'm fine,' Dan said, 'and I don't need a lift. My car's at the Forum.'

Hari insisted on coming back to Summerlands. They drove in separate vehicles, Hari glued to his tail-lights. Once they were inside the caravan, Dan made coffee and attempted to act normal.

'Instant?' Hari said, peering into his mug. 'No wonder you're depressed.'

'I appreciate what you're trying to do, but I really am fine. That woman caught me at a bad moment. I had some things on my mind, that's all.'

Hari shook his head. 'Kes calls it my defence mechanism. He doesn't like it either.'

'Like what?' Dan said.

'He says I make jokes in order to avoid the difficult stuff. Do you want to talk? I *am* here for you, mate. You do know that, don't you?'

'I'm okay, Hari. You came for me. You've even drunk a mouthful of my coffee. I'll give you a call later, yeah?'

Hari quietly shut the caravan door, like someone leaving a sick room, then footsteps crunched across the gravel. Dan finished his coffee and washed both mugs at the sink. There were questions pulsing in his head, but he had days and weeks and years to answer them. Where was the rush? The answers would not change what happened, they would only make the present even harder to bear.

He texted Hari. *Thanks. I owe you.*

Five minutes later, a reply came. *You can't afford me.*

Dan sent an emoji of a crying laughing face.

He and Hari were not good at talking about feelings.

Christ.

Feelings. He shook his head. Sometimes feelings were just too much.

Beth's secret phone and what was on it – he refused to go there. Dan fetched the case file for Felix Faulkner. Anything to occupy his mind before he fell apart. His eyes barely focused as he turned page after page, but then he stopped. Went back to the beginning. Stared at the post-it note DI Drummond had left inside the cover. *Mistakes were made in the first two hours.*

Dan scanned his own summary of the investigation. Drummond had been thorough, persistent. And he had kept in touch with Mrs Faulkner, year after year. Always hoping to find her son. But Drummond clearly had concerns about a case where the primary witnesses were aged eight and nine. There were post-it notes stuck to the children's statements. Jack had 'an active imagination'. Emily was 'impressionable'. Yes, Drummond harboured misgivings.

But a crucial piece of evidence in support of the abduction theory had been provided by Lydia Armstrong. That trip to the toilet when she glimpsed 'a dark shape' through the frosted glass. Dan recalled his own visit to Chapel House, and the narrow window which overlooked the courtyard. According to Lydia's statement, the figure had moved quickly past this window, in the direction of the garden. She had thought it was her son, who was wearing a navy T-shirt that day. Later it occurred to her that the person was too tall to have been Jack.

Drummond and his team reached the conclusion that this had been the intruder. Dan frowned. Lydia's testimony seemed to corroborate what the children said. But all she saw was 'a dark shape'. Nobody else witnessed the intruder. The house-to-house turned up no leads or sightings. The outskirts of rural towns had frequent lulls where the streets were empty. Only a few minutes were needed for someone to walk away with Felix. The police were never able to establish how the abductor left Beccles. By car? Or was it a local person, who disappeared back into their own home. So many unanswered questions.

For a sickening moment, thoughts about Beth and the secret phone reared up again, but Dan blinked hard. Forced himself to continue his analysis of the Faulkner case.

Somebody entered the courtyard, possibly to commit a robbery, which was his current theory. A period of ten to fifteen minutes elapsed between Lydia seeing a figure through the toilet window, and the children reporting the abduction. During that time, the intruder waited by the corner of the house. Jack and Emily were down the garden, when they witnessed a man take Felix from the pram and run toward the courtyard. He then exited onto the lane.

Dan tapped the table. Why did no one summon the Dog Unit? A police dog would have indicated which way the abductor went with Felix. A baby blanket could have supplied the necessary scent. Was this one of the 'mistakes' which troubled DI Drummond? But the wording of his note was vague. Perhaps Drummond was afraid to admit he did something wrong, reluctant to acknowledge, even in a private note, that he should have initiated a, b, or c, maybe ordered a search of x, y, or z.

Instead, Drummond had written *Mistakes were made in the first two hours*.

Drummond had tried his best. He never gave up on Felix. But vital evidence had been missed in those early stages. Dan was convinced this was to do with the Dog Unit. He shook his head. No, not Drummond's error, someone else's. Drummond had wanted to bring in a dog handler, but his request had been blocked by a senior officer. Drummond was loyal to the service, and would not point a finger at the person responsible. *Mistakes were made*.

Dan stared at the case file. This quest was the only thing keeping him going. His thoughts went to Mrs Faulkner, mourning her lost son. It had been a week and a half since that conversation in her living room. He could still hear the low timbre of her voice, feel the warmth of the setting sun radiating from the west wall, smell the floral fragrance of an air freshener. His senses had conspired to weave that evening into the strands of his being.

He had gone to Beccles, met Catherine Nash, spoken to Lydia Armstrong, encountered the witness, Jay's father. Dan had also gathered a few details about John Strang and Ryan Taylor. But no tangible progress had been made, nothing that could be declared with any certainty. What of the intangible? Every time he examined Felix's disappearance, Dan was circled by 'things' on the edge of his vision, murky and indistinct.

Pieces of the past that had acquired corporeality. Clots of emotion that remained undissolved.

Being police had meant focusing on the verifiable, the empirical. Freed of those constraints, his mind had other methods, which Dan could barely understand. But he was certain that the truth about Felix was almost in reach. And that Strang and Ryan were part of it. Eyes shut, he tried to feel the lumps and contours that were circling him even now. Something brushed past him and was gone.

This was insane. He was really losing it this time. *You look a bit lost*, the woman had said. He thrust the file in a drawer, drank some water. What did people do with their days? How did they fill the ceaseless hours? Working, eating, sleeping. Dan had no real job, no appetite, no capacity for sleep.

He groaned aloud, mired in self-loathing. And with it came a vision of Lomax, his abject hatred for the man. Desperate to wash off their encounter, Dan set the shower to a vicious temperature. He stayed in there for ten minutes, then dried himself with a towel, banging his elbows on the cubicle walls.

Dressed in a clean shirt and navy trousers, Dan grabbed his keys, headed for the parking area. He programmed the satnav, no idea what to do once he got there. But anything had to be better than here.

Chapter 25

Dan's destination was north of the A11, but the dual carriageway made a barrier in the landscape, with few crossing points. He switchbacked east to an underpass, then west. Tina, the woman in the Lidl car park, had talked of Ryan Taylor working at a stud farm near Elme Green – that had to mean Holmewood Stud. Dan was approaching the estate when the road went over an old red-brick bridge.

A sudden memory came to him, and he pulled into a lay-by, then walked to the bridge. This was the River Ling. Dan stared at it, frowning. Two decades of droughts and rising temperatures had reduced it to a small stream. But back when he was in the Scouts, there had been enough water for kayaking. During a weekend camping, they had explored the Ling, a tributary of the River Thet. The expedition proved too much for the younger Scouts, and after a few hours they split up, half the group returning to base. The rest of them carried on, the river passing through remote fields and woods, away from footpaths or habitation.

Dan leaned on the brick parapet and peered west, recalling that journey. They saw no other people until they reached the grounds of Holmewood Stud. The Scout leader warned them, at an earlier stop, that they would not be welcome, but that the law allowed them to travel on the river through private land – provided they did not set foot on the bank. 'Your parents won't thank me for returning you along with a criminal conviction for trespass.' Her words made an impression on Dan. He was aged fourteen and adolescent cynicism had yet to take full hold.

The trip through the estate also made an impression. It was all he could recollect of that weekend. There had been an archway of barbed wire across the Ling, marking the boundary, and cameras must have monitored this area because within minutes two men appeared on opposite sides of the water. They did not speak, not a word. But Dan could remember an intense feeling of being watched, and how clumsy the paddle became in his hands, the certainty he would capsize.

The two men strode along the banks, keeping pace with the kayaks. The man on the right was tall. He stayed by the lead kayak. The man on the left was carrying a large stick, like a shepherd's crook. He was at the back, near Dan. The Scout leader tried talking to the men, but they did not respond, and after a while she gave up. It had been very quiet on the river, just the paddles slipping into the water, but every so often the man next to Dan thrashed at the undergrowth, beating it with his stick. The noise was menacing. The behaviour of the men was clearly intended as a threat. Looking back on it now, he was struck by how unnecessary it had been to intimidate a group of teenage Scouts and their young leader.

The kayak trip through the estate lasted about thirty minutes though it felt like several hours. Trees grew by the river and beyond them Dan had seen fields. The area to the south had the type of white-painted fencing that he knew was associated with racehorses. No horses visible that day, just green grass and sandy tracks. The silence of the men and the emptiness of the landscape became oppressive. 'Nearly there,' the Scout leader called at one point. 'You're doing great.' Dan had been gripped by the idea that they could vanish and no one would ever know. When they reached another barbed-wire arch across the water, the two men stopped and the taller one said, 'Don't try that again.'

It was odd that only now was Dan remembering the event because it affected him deeply at the time. Everyone in the group found it frightening. The Scout leader had seemed the same age as his parents, but she was probably just nineteen or twenty. She kept her cool during what had been a deliberately menacing situation. The men on the riverbank were bullies. Dan had always hated bullies. Maybe this was why he ended up in the police. Did Holmewood still employ people like that?

The world had become increasingly obsessed with security in the intervening years.

He got back in his Volvo and headed for the entrance to the estate. No one stopped him at the gates but there was CCTV. The driveway passed through woods, then a metal bridge over the Ling, after which the view opened out. As Dan drove between well-maintained paddocks, glimpses of horses, the stately profiles of mature trees, it felt like Surrey or Middlesex. This was not the make-do-and-mend landscape of the Brecks. This was a place with money, irrigating the green pastures in the height of summer, and paying for the staff numbers it took to achieve manicured perfection. Woods and high fencing shielded Holmewood Stud from casual observers on the public highway. Only on entering did the wealth became apparent. As an adolescent in a kayak, he had been oblivious to the economics that were so clear to him now. The type of privilege that did not flaunt, that quietly accumulated. There were young oak trees lining the long driveway, an investment in a future that would still be secure in a hundred years' time.

At a fork, Dan followed the sign for the stables. Ahead was a Victorian red-brick building with an archway and clock tower, but the arrow directed him past this and into a large courtyard at the rear. Modern stables, cream walls and slate roofs, surrounded him on three sides, and to his left was the back of the original brick building. Dan parked and turned off the engine. There were about forty stalls and a dozen staff, mostly young men and women. They were busy mucking out the stalls, sweeping the courtyard. No one glanced in his direction, just a momentary pause to their movements when he stepped out of the car.

Dan could see the heads of fifteen or so horses framed in the stable doors, and out in the courtyard two were being groomed, one russet coloured, the other black. Along the quiet roads of Norfolk, he was used to people on horseback, but as Dan eyed the creatures standing in the yard he was reminded of the sheer size of thoroughbreds. They were like deities, submitting to the rituals of the staff. The only sounds he could hear were horses whinnying and the rough rasp of a broom sweeping the courtyard. Nobody spoke as they went about their duties and Dan felt oddly reluctant to interrupt that silence. He recalled the thugs on the riverbank who had voiced their threat without any need for words.

An older man came out of one of the stalls. He looked at Dan, a professional hardness to his gaze. Then he put two fingers to his mouth and whistled. The noise was so piercing, Dan flinched. No reaction from the stable hands, who carried on with their tasks. The man cast a critical eye at what they were doing, then returned to the stall. Silence descended once more, but Dan noticed it was not in fact silent. There was a continuous drone from the A11, south of the estate. Holmewood used wealth as a barricade, but no money could insulate it from the ever-present hum of traffic, which pushed its way past trees and buildings, infiltrating the landscape.

'How can I help?' a voice called.

He spun round. A woman was walking toward him, through the archway from the old stable block. She was in her early forties and wearing black jodhpurs and a short-sleeved shirt, white linen, neatly pressed – like she had stepped from the pages of *Horse & Hound*. But as she drew near, Dan noticed an unusual silver necklace, ultra-modern and angular, and there was a tattoo on her right forearm, a long line of illegible script.

Her smile faded. 'I don't believe we have an appointment.'

Dan gestured at their surroundings. 'Terrific set-up you have. I'd heard good things, but this is, well...'

'Thank you,' she said. 'Who are you here to see? If you don't mind giving me a lift, I can direct you to the office. What's your name? I'll tell them you're on your way.'

'Are you hiring at the moment?'

The woman frowned. 'You're looking for work?'

'I'm used to being around horses.'

'We're fully staffed. And to be frank, we don't make a habit of employing people who walk in off the street. So to speak. This is a stud farm.' She scrutinised him. 'Different, perhaps, to the sorts of stables you may have been at before? I'll ask one of the lads to show you the way back to the main road. The estate is quite large. It's easy to get lost.'

'But I was told you do cash in hand.'

'By whom? Who said that?'

'Ryan. My mate Ryan Taylor.' Dan watched her face, but the name seemed to mean nothing. 'He told me you put the word out extra staff were needed. On a day rate.'

'Casual hiring has never been our policy. I can't vouch for other stables, so maybe your friend was referring to one of them.'

'No, he definitely said Holmewood Stud did cash in hand.'

The older man came out of the stall opposite and went to inspect the russet horse.

'Tony,' the woman called. 'Can I have a word?'

Dan had detected a precision in her speech that sounded studied, like she was faking an upper-class accent. But her pronunciation of the man's name suggested a different reason.

'Where are you from?' Dan said.

'And this is relevant how?'

'Your accent is very good.'

'Ah, the English,' she said. 'So skilled in the dark arts of condescension.'

'I meant it as a compliment.'

'Sure, sure.'

Tony was still keeping them waiting.

'I'm from Bremen,' she said.

Dan liked that she named a city rather than Germany.

'I'm local,' he said. 'Norfolk born and bred.'

'Lucky you.' Her tone was ironic. 'The land of big skies and recalcitrant workers.' She took a deep breath and yelled, 'Tony. Now.'

'Must be hard,' Dan said, 'owning a stud farm.'

She laughed. 'The board own it, not me. I oversee the business. Tony Foster does the day-to-day.'

'But I guess you must know everyone who works here,' Dan said. 'It's odd you've not met Ryan Taylor.'

Again, she appeared oblivious.

Tony Foster approached them across the yard. 'Problem, Mrs Schneider?'

Dan saw the woman bristle slightly.

'This gentleman,' she said, 'is looking for work. He seems to have heard we hire casual labour.'

'Not possible,' Foster said. 'It's not company policy, Mrs Schneider. You know that better than me.'

She fingered the angular silver necklace.

Dan decided to exploit the tension. 'Sorry,' he said, 'I didn't mean to cause an argument.'

'You misunderstand,' she said. 'There is no argument.'

Tony Foster was staring at him. 'Who told you there was work available?'

Dan was reminded of those thugs on the riverbank, twenty years ago. Foster was a bully. It explained the silence that hung over everyone at the stables. A dozen or so young men and women and nobody chatting or sharing a joke.

'Hi,' Dan said with a smile. 'Good to finally meet you, Tony. My mate talks about you all the time. My mate Ryan Taylor.'

If there was a reaction, it was very subtle. Mrs Schneider had noticed, as she was now frowning at Foster. 'You know this Ryan Taylor?'

'Never heard of him,' he said.

'This gentleman seems to believe otherwise.' She eyed Dan. 'What did you say your name was?'

'Michael Hughes.' The alias tripped off his tongue. 'Like I said, I don't want to cause an argument. Ryan definitely knows you, Tony. But lots of folk work here, must be hard to remember them all. He's thin, about five ten. Fair hair. None of that ring any bells?'

Foster turned to Mrs Schneider. 'Mr Hughes is clearly confused. I think it would be best if he leaves. We have never employed a Ryan Taylor.'

'Maybe,' Dan said, glancing round the yard, 'some of the others know him? You're starting to make me feel like I'm going mad.' He laughed. 'I swear, Mrs Schneider, that Ryan has worked here.'

'When exactly?'

'Earlier in the summer.'

'June?' she said.

Dan nodded, sensing he was onto something.

Mrs Schneider looked at Foster, repeating, 'June. A busy month.'

'To be in Italy, certainly,' he said. 'But we were adequately staffed.'

'Yeah,' Dan said, 'Ryan told me the place was humming. And that the overtime was double pay. He got the job through another mate of his. Someone he was at school with? They both went to Old Buckenham. Or was it Diss. One of the local high schools. Anyway, this bloke works here too.'

'Name?' Foster said.

Dan shrugged. 'Don't know. Not met him.'

'Tony,' Mrs Schneider said. 'I think we need answers.'

The man slowly tapped his fist against his jaw. Then he turned, saying, 'Emma. Is Neil Witton still in hydrotherapy?'

A young woman nodded.

'Fetch him.'

Neil Witton joined them a few minutes later. He had a jockey's physique. Clean-shaven, with short black hair. Dan put him at late thirties, but he had the weathered face of an athlete and could have been younger.

'Yes, guv?' Witton's full attention was on Foster, ignoring Mrs Schneider. The word *guv* was so anachronistic that Dan almost laughed.

Foster said, 'This is Michael Hughes.'

Witton looked at Dan, then back at Foster.

'Mr Hughes,' Foster continued, 'is very good at telling stories. He claims to have a friend who worked here. Ryan Taylor. That name mean anything to you?'

Witton shook his head. 'Never heard of him.'

'Are you sure about that?' Mrs Schneider said. 'Mr Hughes is convinced his friend was taken on in June. While I was away.'

'Paid in cash,' Dan said.

'He's wrong,' Witton said. 'We don't employ casual labour. Never have and never will. Company policy, Mrs Schneider.'

Chapter 26

Jay found an ancient tissue in the pocket of her dressing gown. She withdrew her hand then tightened the belt. The cottage was silent. She crept down the stair, holding the balustrade, her bare legs stirring the darkness. Outside the dining room she listened for a minute to her father's whispered snores.

The kitchen no longer felt odd, as she had grown accustomed to the absence of cupboard doors. Jay poured milk into her tea. At home she would have carried this onto her balcony, to measure the night sky, before her gaze sought out the bright threads and grids below, the nocturnal glitter of the city that lapped against the base of her tower block.

Jay took a sip of tea, then she switched off the light and stood at the window. The back garden was black, indistinct, merging upward into the outlines of trees, which framed a ragged segment of sky, scattered densely with stars. She had been woken by a dream, the feel of him still with her. Ruben. The rasp of his hair, dragging on her lips. There would be no second chances. Jay had known this all along but had chosen to deceive herself. In the unlit kitchen, the adult realisation was clearly seen. Her time in the band was finished. Jay could blame the vodka, but in the end it was her fault.

Her actions. Her words. Or rather, the failure of words. Ruben was always saying, 'I love you,' and yet Jay could never bring herself to say it back. *I love you* tasted wrong in her mouth, too ordinary and over-used for how she felt about him. Jay had always expressed herself through actions – a fun way to live, exhilarating and unpredictable, not to stop and articulate, but just do and be. Until she drank too much and slept with Theo.

No undoing it. Jay could not unbetray Ruben, or repair the damage.

A white handkerchief was being offered. She blinked, surprised to find her father at her side.

'Something upset you?' he said.

'I'm fine.' Jay dabbed at her eyes then returned the handkerchief. 'Actually I'm not fine. I made a huge mistake and now I'm living with the consequences.'

'Life's hard,' he said.

A hackneyed phrase, but when spoken by her father, the two of them staring at the dark garden, the place where he was patiently burying the sad remains of all those animals, Jay felt the truth of it so painfully.

'Can I have a hug?' she said.

The caravan smelled of bacon and Calor gas. Dan had woken at 2.43 a.m. with a gnawing emptiness, but it was not hunger. Unable to eat, he pushed the plate away, aware that the bad thoughts were returning, those with no fixed abode, always circling at a distance. Not now. Please. A few deep breaths, then he fetched paper and pencil and wrote *Holmewood Stud*. Pressing hard, Dan underlined the words three times – think, think, think, but not about Beth. He set his mind to analysing the visit, sifting his impressions and observations. There had been a strange tension at Holmewood. Breeding pedigree horses was a niche market catering to the super rich, when owning a Bugatti was no longer enough. Why not pay for a racehorse to be made, engineer its exact lineage? Dan could see why Holmewood might be wary of casual labour. The stud farm would want to employ trusted staff and avoid potential risks. They had a reputation to maintain. Racehorses were international big business.

During Dan's visit there had been a sense of Mrs Schneider and Tony Foster putting on a performance, one that was familiar, tedious even. Painful for her and less so for Foster. The man was a bully. Verbal but maybe physical too. There could be an accusation of assault buried in his past, but Dan had no access to the PNC. Foster clearly objected to Mrs Schneider interfering in how he managed the stables. His animosity was shared by sidekick Neil Witton. It was him who oversaw Dan's departure. Witton had collected a quad bike and Dan was 'requested' to follow in his car, on a route that passed semi-agricultural, semi-medical buildings. The quad bike was open topped, and the man drove as if riding a horse at a gallop, his arms braced on the handlebars.

After five minutes, they had reached a long drive lined with mature trees, leading to a gatehouse. Witton took him as far as the exit. Dan eased the Volvo forward in first gear, as the electric gates slowly opened. In his rear-view mirror he could see that Witton had left the driveway and was taking a cross-country route back to the stables. The quad bike was traversing the paddock at high speed. The ground looked flat but there were hidden dips that caused the vehicle to lurch and buck. Witton kept a firm grip throughout. Another performance, put on for Dan's benefit.

He stared at the congealed bacon on his plate, then checked the time on his phone. 03:56 Sunday 17 July. The minutes, the hours, the months, crawling past each other, dragging him in their wake. July would soon be November. The anniversary. And he found himself crying. Again. About loss, about love, about everything. Welling up inside, the savage emotion of it all, overwhelming. Dan swiped a hand across his face. What was he meant to do with his feelings now that Beth was no longer here?

What was he meant to do? His chest felt tight, short of breath. Dan stood up, and made his way to the door. From there he stared at the vastness of the sky, the pin prickings of the stars. Dan thought about the generations upon generations of people, millennia, aeons, all those beings who had loved and grieved, and how their feelings could not die. All that love and grief travelling forever through the cold expanses of the universe.

He had trusted Beth. Never once doubted her. And yet she had a second phone. He had trusted Cassie too. And yet she did not tell him about this secret phone or say a word about her relationship with Lomax. Dan looked at the dark sky, heard the siren calls of love and grief, felt the grip of Beth on his heart, clenching. He collapsed onto the steps.

'You alright, mate?' a voice said.

Dan glanced up. It was a resident from one of the caravans.

'Yeah,' Dan said, the word failing in his throat. 'Just dizzy, that's all.'

'Take care,' the man said, walking away.

After a minute, Dan went inside and texted Cassie. *I know about the phone*. That was all the message had to say. She was a DI now. She did not need him to join the dots.

His eyes opened. Dan was lying on the bed with both shoes on. In his caravan, not the icehouse – something to be thankful for. The bedroom was dark, but through the doorway he saw morning light glowing on the curtains next to the seating area. A black shape moved across the brightness, from one side to the other. There and then not there, followed by the quiet sound of scraping metal. The door latch? His heart was racing.

Dan sat up quickly, room spinning, and stumbled through, forgot to duck, banged his head. Rubbing his forehead, he peered into the tiny bathroom, needing the certainty he was alone. Dan listened to the silence, broken only by the scratching of a tree branch on the roof. He opened the door and looked across the site. No movement, no sign of anyone fleeing. It was early, around six. The distinct feeling remained that he had not imagined this. There had been an intruder. What did they want from him?

The caravan was not locked. Dan never locked it because there was nothing to steal. He glanced round, checked a few cupboards and drawers, the contents undisturbed. His wallet was still in his trousers. His phone was next to the bed. There was a message from Hari. *Forgotten you were meant to text last night?? I'm worried. If I don't hear soon, you're getting a wakeup call involving a bucket of water.* The message had come at 6.03 a.m. Five minutes ago. Was that what woke him? Dan texted Hari, saying *All good*.

Three dots pulsed on the screen, then a reply. *Glad you haven't topped yourself. Are you up to doing a collect from Stansted? Sheila's just balled and my hubby will kill me if I miss our daughter's ballet show*. Hari did everything at speed, not always weighing his word choice or checking the substitutions by predictive text. Dan smiled at the misspelling of what was probably meant to be bailed. He sent Hari a thumbs-up and moments later the details came, a passenger on a flight from Paris.

Dan boiled the kettle, listening to its slow crescendo. Hari's messages had distracted him, but now his thoughts were back on the intruder. His gaze strayed across the floor. There was mud on the carpet, under the table. But not where Dan usually sat. He knelt and picked up the dirt, crumbling it between his fingers. Leaf mould? Someone had sat here while he slept in the next room. This person may have watched Dan dreaming. It felt disturbingly intimate. Nobody got to share his bed or see him sleeping these days. Yet a stranger had entered his caravan. Dan recalled the flicker of dark as it passed across the brightness of the window and the glistening surface of his eyes. A solid shadow that was human shaped. Male or female? It had happened too fast. The edges of the darkness had been ill defined.

The sense of that shadow remained as he drove to Stansted. The legacy of something not quite seen. Nearing the airport, the dispatcher notified Dan the passenger's flight would be forty-five minutes late. He headed for one of the holding areas and parked the Volvo. His phone rang, startling him. The name on the screen was Jay Olsen.

'Hi,' she said.

'Hi there.' His heart felt giddy.

'Maybe I should have rung sooner. But I didn't know... what to say?'

'I'm glad you called.'

'It's about my dad.'

'Ah.' Dan swallowed his disappointment. 'He okay?'

'Yeah. Mostly. I wanted to tell you, it's just I wasn't sure what to make of it. But I'm trying to face up to stuff. You know?'

'Yeah. I know the feeling.'

Jay then told him that her father had remembered a particular detail from the day of Felix's disappearance. It seemed the two children, Jack and Emily, had been playing a game. Dan recalled Peter Olsen's original statement. In it, the children were described as having a picnic by the river. Now, according to Jay, her father saw them playing a game involving tea towels.

Dan frowned. 'What sort of game?'

She left a long pause, before saying, 'I think they may have been running around with tea towels on their heads. Look, you've met my father. He's not very vocal and what he does say isn't always the answer you expect. He didn't tell me about the tea towels. He acted it out. As in, he ran about the kitchen holding a tea towel above his head. Then he wrapped it around his face. And put his hands together like he was praying. Which makes no sense as Dad's not religious. I didn't ring you straightaway because... I mean, I thought he might have gone properly *crazy*.'

Jay explained that the memory seemed to exhaust her father. Later, several times from the sound of it, she had questioned him and was now certain this was a genuine recollection of what he witnessed Jack and Emily doing. Running about with tea towels. And then praying.

'I've got to go,' she said.

'Thanks. Thanks for phoning me. And for sharing all this. I, eh... I really appreciate it.'

The call ended. Dan stared at the screen. There was no mention of 'a game' in Olsen's statement from 2001. Why should Dan believe this new version of events? Summoned two decades later by a man possibly suffering from dementia.

Children running about with tea towels and wrapping them around their faces. It was the oddness of the memory, the specificity of its strangeness, that rang true for Dan. This was not some idealised notion of the sorts of games children played, like hide and seek or throwing balls. The tea-towel game sounded real, authentic, one of those involved rituals which children enacted in a private world the adults could never enter or understand.

Dan did not doubt the memory, but Peter Olsen may have been recalling different children on a different day. Confusing them with the boy and girl from that July afternoon in Beccles. And even if it was Jack and Emily he saw playing their game, did it change anything?

His Stansted passenger was ready to be collected. After delivering the man to an address in Mundford, Dan headed for Summerlands. His route skirted Holmewood and he found himself thinking about Mrs Schneider. It was clear that Tony Foster and Neil Witton made sure to humiliate her daily. There would be nothing she could put into a formal complaint – they were clever enough to avoid that. What else were Foster and Witton capable of? Dan was in no doubt that Ryan Taylor was employed as a casual hire in June, while Mrs Schneider was absent. Because they were short-handed that month. And because Foster was not going to be told by Mrs Schneider what was or was not permitted. The staff at the stables had mostly been in their early twenties. Foster looked about fifty, so that left Witton as the only one in the right age bracket to have been at school with Ryan. This was speculation, though, as during his one brief visit, Dan would not have seen everybody that worked there.

When he stepped inside the caravan, Dan's gaze went straight to the vacant seat at the table. He had forgotten this morning's intruder, and it shocked him anew. Dan sat where the person had been sitting, then placed his arms on the table. Trying to get a sense of who it had been. John Strang? He looked around the interior, seeing it with someone else's eyes.

Dishes piled in the sink. A jumble of shoes near the door, jackets and coats draped over two hooks. Ply veneer on the cupboards. Lace curtains, yellowing at the edges. He heard a tree branch scrape across the metal roof. Dan peered through to the bedroom. From this position there was a slant view of the end of the bed. Only Dan's feet would have been visible. Unless the intruder crept nearer and watched him from the corridor.

'What do you want?' Dan said, a thrum of fear in his veins. Had the person intended to hurt him? He stumbled through to the bedroom and yanked open the wardrobe door. Beth was still there. The canister of ashes stood quietly in the shadows. 'Soon,' he murmured.

Dan returned to the living area and glanced again at the garments hanging by the entrance. A scarf had slipped to the floor. During the night or several days ago? Dan did not pay much heed to what he wore, but back as a DI there had been a requirement to dress smartly. Over the years, he bought new jackets and coats but never bothered throwing out the old ones. Beth had suggested getting rid of some in readiness for the move, but he had still been left with eight or so.

Picking up the scarf, Dan draped it over the hooks. Beth had been much more interested in curating their possessions, keeping a mental record of everything and where it was, in that cupboard or under the bed, or donated to charity. Dan had always paid less attention. Things could be taken from him, the absence not noted, unless one day he reached and it was gone.

Dan scanned the interior of the caravan. Items had been removed from here and left in the icehouse. Why had he not recognised his own belongings? When Dan first spotted the broken padlock, he went down for a look but saw nothing familiar. The morning Cassie came, he watched over her shoulder as she checked the contents. Again, none of them his. But it had been dark, with the search conducted by the alienating glare of a torch.

Then the CSIs returned next day and removed everything to the lab. What did they find to convince them Dan was the icehouse sleeper? A plate with his fingerprints, a blanket with his hair on it, or a coat with traces of his sweat. He had no hope of persuading the police that Strang took all of these from Dan's caravan.

His old colleagues thought he was a nut job. After Beth died, he became a figure to be pitied but also spurned. Even Cassie had disowned him.

Last night's intruder was welcome to visit whenever he wanted. Watch Dan while he slept, listen to his nightmares, sit at his table in the dawn light. Steal his belongings.

Dan did not care. No harm could be done. He had lost all that was precious in his life.

Almost all.

Chapter 27

Dan showered and dressed for the occasion. Taking his time. He put on a clean shirt and tie, then rubbed a cloth over the leather of his black shoes. Taking care. He checked his appearance in the mirror, noticing he had lost weight. His face had a gaunt look. Dan swept the hair back from his brow. Beth would have told him he needed a haircut. Voiced with a smile, offering a 'Beth special' if he was too busy to get to a barber's. Dan could still feel the tentative care in her fingers as she trimmed the hair behind his ears, fearful of cutting him. Her breath travelling across his cheek as she leaned in for a kiss.

He opened the wardrobe and picked up the canister of ashes, hugging her to his chest.

'Ah, Bethie,' he whispered.

Dan laid her gently in the car. On the journey to Flaxton he spoke about the first time they met, and he could hear his voice smiling. Dan had been in the York Tavern. An old school friend cancelled last minute, and he decided to have a Guinness before heading home. *I spotted you straightaway*. Beth was sitting at the back, watching the door. *You were waiting for someone, and I felt sorry it wasn't me*. Dan was finishing his pint when Beth came over, saying, 'Seems I've been stood up.' *And I said, me too*. She then gestured to her phone. 'Would you like to be my "Marc with a c"? I'll buy you a drink.' *I couldn't believe my luck*. Dan and Beth talked and laughed all evening. On the street outside, she kissed him. He had known this was the beginning of something that would last.

Blinking back the tears, Dan parked near Flaxton Castle. He sat for a while, waiting for the shadows to lengthen. With his hand resting on the canister, he told Beth that it would last. *I'm holding on to our love. I'm not letting you go*. Dan got out of the car and stared up at the sky, seeing the first faint glimmer of the evening star. One day, when he was no longer able to bind her, when he himself was dead and gone, she might travel into the cold void, join all the love and grief that was slowly filling up the vastness. Until then he would keep Beth here.

She felt heavy in his arms as he carried her to the quiet circle of the castle ruins. She felt light in his fingers as he dipped them into her soft ashes. Beth fell between the blades of grass. She nestled on the moss. She brushed grey pollen on the dandelions.

The canister was nearly empty. Dan climbed over the rim of the ruins and down into the moat, darkness thickening under the trees. He crouched in the moat. Black mud clung to his funeral shoes. Dan laid the canister in the trickle of water, letting the wetness roll around inside as he sang a tune that came to him from somewhere, maybe a lullaby, but it did soothe. And somehow he managed to release the last of her, laying his hands in the water too, until she was gone.

Beth had become part of the land. He listened for the frogs, remembering when he and Beth had danced laughingly across the moat, trying not to step on the tide of glistening creatures. Dan tilted his head, thought he heard something, but it was just the quiet tremble of air brushing the treetops.

He left the canister in the moat with the lid off.

When Dan got back to the caravan, he sent a text to Cassie. *You're wrong about Beth.*

The mud had dried on his shoes. He put them in a bin bag, then shrugged off the black suit, bundled it on top, and left the bag by the door. The shirt and tie had been gifts from Beth. He hung these in the wardrobe, then changed into jeans and T-shirt. His stomach felt hollow. It was night and he had the prospect of all those sleepless hours. Dan pulled on a dark sweater.

The path was firm underfoot, weeks of no rain, the earth cracked and fissured. An almost full moon shone on the fields, turning them pale grey. Trees made blots of indistinctness against a navy-blue sky, and then ahead of him was the wooded mound of the icehouse. Dan undid the padlock on the door, using the code.

Dampness brushed his face. 'Hello? Anybody there?'

No response. He slowly descended the stair, then aimed his phone torch into the cellars. The place was empty, silent. Nothing had changed since his visit, five days ago, when Thomas mended the lock. Dan stared at the water in the stone trough, black, motionless, gleaming in the torchlight. He dipped his hand in, sent ripples across the oily meniscus and watched them die away. Then he climbed the stair, locked the door, and set off. Staying next to hedgerows, the moonlight enough to see by.

Ten minutes later, Dan reached the embankment of the reservoir. Near the top, he lay on the grass and eased himself forward, the water coming into view. The surface looked solid. In the centre was the metal gantry, like the arm of a crane. His gaze went skyward to the ghostly transit of an owl. The bird dropped to the ground near the church ruins, then took off.

All was quiet once more. Dan weighed up whether to head for the woods, where Strang seemed to have a second camp. The man knew something about Ryan Taylor's murder, but there were other troubling connections. Dan recalled the moment when he opened the lid of that ugly footstool, exposing the carefully folded items. The knitted jacket, the little bootees. He shivered. They were twisted up with a fetid emotion that even now made his throat feel tight. Baby clothes should be happy but those garments were so sad. A sadness that wanted to suffocate.

Lost children. Missing babies. The mirroring of Mrs Faulkner's painful history.

Dan had spent all his life in a world where the constituents could be explained. A place where reason prevailed. Until reason abandoned him and Beth. She died. And Dan was left with an existence where the parts could not be reassembled, where he could no longer trust the workings of his mind, and the only truths that felt true were the decisions his body made.

And in that moment, Dan heard a loud inhalation of air, as if the world had drawn breath, and he panted, dizzied by the thought of all that oxygen. A figure was crawling out of the water and up the metal tower. A slick creature with wet limbs, clasping at the struts, heaving itself upward. A man. Black clothing. Strang? From this distance, in the dim light, Dan could not be sure. The figure was now lying on the horizontal gantry, lungs fighting for air. Then he rolled off and plunged back in. Dan blinked.

Gone, swallowed by the water, the only trace being the rings of disturbance that travelled across the surface, then washed against the black rubber material on the shore. The ripples died away. Dan could feel panic thudding in his chest. The person was still down there. Searching for something? Dan was panting, his own oxygen depleting. Eyes checking the margins of the reservoir, the gantry, again and again. No one could last that long – they would drown. He pulled off his shoes and sweater, left his phone, and slid down the slope.

Once more, he heard that desperate noise of indrawn breath. Dan stopped at the edge, his legs submerged. Across from him, the man was half out of the water, clinging to the metal structure. He had his back to Dan and seemed unaware of being observed. Minutes passed, measured by laboured breathing. Dan was afraid to speak. A gust of wind pushed at the water, and shards of moonlight made a rapid scurry over the surface. The figure climbed the metal tower, grunting with every heave of his body. He lay on the gantry, peering up at the night sky.

Dan shivered. The reservoir was cold, chilling his blood.

The man turned onto his side. The glistening eyes were open and he had seen Dan.

They stared at each other. Kept apart by distance, darkness, water.

'Are you John Strang?' Dan called. Uncertain. 'I'm looking for John Strang.'

No response.

'You're not in any trouble,' Dan said. 'But I think you saw something. I think you witnessed the murder at the solar farm.'

Again, no response. Just the blank face watching him from far away.

'Is that why you've been hiding?' Dan said. 'At the icehouse and in the woods. Swimming at night, it's dangerous.'

Strang seemed in a trance. Behind him the black sky was a vast void.

'My name is Dan. Dan Hennessy. I'm the one bringing you food. Please talk to me. I want to help.'

A sharp gust blew across the reservoir, whistling through the gantry.

'You didn't kill him,' Dan said. 'You just saw what happened. I can explain it wasn't you.'

The man covered his face with his hands. Sobbing.

'I'm sorry,' Dan said. 'But once the truth is out, you'll be safe, I promise. You just have to tell everyone what really happened.'

Both hands slid from Strang's face, revealing a mouth that gaped in a smile. Dan felt it like a punch in the gut. The man had been laughing not weeping. Dan recoiled, as if he was staring into madness. He scrabbled further up the bank, but could not take his eyes off Strang, the black hole that was his mouth now venting an awful noise, a keening wail, part laughter, part pain, pressing on Dan, squeezing his skull.

'Stop,' Dan yelled. 'Please stop.'

Strang went silent. Closed his mouth.

Dan tried again. 'I can fix everything and make it better.' Like the man was a child. 'You just need to trust me.'

Dark eyes scanning him, across the cold hard water.

Dan was at a loss. Should he swim to the gantry?

'John,' he said. 'Do you mind if I call you John?'

Blank face.

'The big thing you need to realise, John, is you're not alone.'

Strang jerked in a spasm, then he fell off the far side of the gantry.

Dan gasped.

The man's body hit the water in a loud splash, hidden by the metal tower. Dan waited, one minute, two minutes, ears straining to hear Strang surfacing for air. At three minutes, Dan leapt up and started running round the reservoir, slipping, sliding. The gantry obscured his view, he could not locate Strang. Dan launched himself into the water. Hampered by clothing and heavy limbs, he swam on a tangent to the structure, wanting to see past.

'John,' he called, then he choked on a mouthful of water, sending panic into his lungs.

No sign of him on the other side. Dan aimed for the metal tower, intending to dive down and rescue Strang. Then a shape registered on the edge of his vision.

It was Strang, crawling onto the far bank, about thirty metres away. Dan swam toward him, but the distance seemed to grow, as if currents were dragging him off. He adjusted his course, still desperate to reach Strang, who was staggering up the slope.

'Wait,' he said, swallowing water.

Dan was ten metres away when he saw Strang look to the left. Poised and alert. Listening for something?

'Don't go,' Dan called, almost at the shore.

The man was above him now. Next moment Strang vanished over the rim. Running.

After a last push through the water, Dan stumbled out and headed up the bank. His eyes swept the land between here and the woods, where Strang had his second camp. Straining to see a figure, maybe near that hedgerow, or by those Scots pines. Nothing moved. Dan looked in the other direction, checking the fields. It was then that he heard the noise. Like an animal cry. Strang? Dan flinched, recalling the inhuman sound of the man's laughter. But this noise seemed different. Triumphant, like a war cry. Louder now, rising from below.

In the foreground was a clump of trees, obstructing his view of the land beyond. Then a figure burst forth, running through a wheatfield. It had to be Strang. He was whooping and hollering. Hunting a deer? Then a second figure appeared. A man chasing Strang. But it was Strang issuing the war cry, luring him on. The scene was primitive, reeking of bloodshed.

Dan raced down the slope, leapt the fence, and set off in a direction to intercept Strang. His bare feet thrashed at the rough wheat, all the while his eyes scanning to the left. There was a hedgerow between here and the next field, but it did not make a solid line, and Dan peered through the gaps. From the reservoir, he had been able to look down on what was happening. But from knee deep in wheat, his perspective was flattened and the field beyond was a pale stripe. Briefly, to his left, a dark shape passed across a gap in the hedgerow.

The soles of his feet were stinging but Dan kept going. The whooping was somewhere to the right. He veered in that direction, concerned he would miss his target. Who was Dan hoping to catch? Those bloodthirsty cries were coming from Strang, and his pursuer seemed the one in danger. But Dan forced himself to recall what he saw when Cassie unzipped the body bag and showed him Ryan Taylor. The condition of the face and head. The extreme trauma.

Ryan's murderer was the one to be feared. He was now hunting Strang, trying to kill the only witness. Dan reached the corner and vaulted a gate. The men were on his right, running next to a hedgerow, twenty metres apart, with Strang in the lead. Dan cut across the field toward them. He could feel himself tiring, and he forced his legs to go faster, ignoring the pain in his lungs and muscles, the gashes on his feet, from sharp flints.

Up ahead was a stretch of woodland. Strang disappeared among the trees, followed moments later by the other man. Dan aimed for the same entry point and ran into the woods, slowing when he realised how dark it was, the dense canopy blocking all light. He stopped, eyes blinking, trying to quell his breath as he listened for any clue to where the two men were.

Silence for half a minute, no calls or sounds of people running, then he heard the crack of broken branches. Loud, like the crack of bullets, but with a slight echo. Near or far, impossible to tell, but it had come from the left. Dan lurched in that direction, struggling to see, everything in shades of indistinguishable black. Hands in front, he was steering between trees, touching one as he passed, its bark smooth. Heart thudding in his ears, his chest panting. Adrenalin coursed through him, and riding with it was the fear that something awful was about to happen.

'*Stop*,' he shouted. 'Don't do it.'

Dan had no idea who he was yelling at – Strang? Or was he yelling at the future? Its overwhelming inevitability. Dan fell to the ground, beneath the crushing weight of his own powerless incapacity to stop anything from happening. His own ill-matched fight against fate and what it did to Beth. Every step she took in her life another step on the path that led her to run into the road that day. Neither of them knew what was up ahead, the dark hole into which they would both fall at the appointed hour. Beth to her death. Him to an existence that did not feel like life.

And as Dan lay prostrate on the forest floor, he heard again the crack of branches, beating against each other, like clapping hands. Applauding and celebrating his defeat, his inability to save Beth, his failure to divert her from that journey toward death. All it would have taken was one sideways step, an extra cup of coffee that morning at breakfast, or a longer kiss as she went out the front door, not the brief brush of his lips on her cheek, and a hug he released too soon. If only he had held on longer. If only he had stopped her going out the door at 8.57 a.m.

His heart heaved and he knew these thoughts would kill him. Dan knew he could not control the spinning and ricocheting chaos of events that marked the forward roll and unravel and terror of the future. Its uncontainability, its utter disregard for the tiny machinations of human desire. The future crushed them all. Maybe Beth had sidestepped a thousand deaths in her thirty-seven years before she ran in front of that vehicle. How could that thought be a comfort? He should have saved her. He was *meant* to save her.

Dan heard someone shouting, and the sudden circumstance of why he was here rushed back into him. He dragged himself off the ground and stood up, swaying. Black everywhere, no glimmers of light. Stabs of pain in his feet, Dan stumbled toward the noise, arms sweeping side to side, empty air, then a tree, adjusting his route. More shouting. Was he getting any nearer? Darkness smothering his senses, Dan had no clue how far his footsteps were taking him.

'Where are you?' he called.

'Here,' cried a voice. 'Hurry. I need your help.'

'John?'

'Over here,' the sound distorted by the unseen woods.

Relying on instinct, Dan aimed for where Strang seemed to be, homing in on his voice, Strang repeating, '*Help me, help me.*'

Dan stepped into nothingness.

Sliding, thumping, spinning, something gashed his face, then a twisting of his ankle as it was trapped then released. Arms flailing wildly, his hands tried to grab, but he was plunging into the abyss. And yet – with the calm precision the mind still achieved in the midst of disaster – Dan found himself thinking about the medieval maps of an earth conceived as flat, and the horror of what would happen if you fell off the edge.

Then his back slammed into hardness and he gasped, as pain shot up his spine and down to his feet. Reeling, his inner gyroscope spinning. A tree, it must have been a tree, had stopped his descent. Dan rolled onto his stomach. No broken bones, but the throb of bruising and a stinging cut on his cheek.

Footsteps rushed toward him through the dark. And Dan knew this person intended to kill him. He tried to run but was grabbed from behind. The man threw him back down with a grunt. Dan instantly assessed his opponent was smaller, lighter. Fists ready, Dan leapt up, his body braced. He could see nothing, hear nothing. No sound of his opponent's breathing, just blind silence. A punch landed on his kidneys and Dan flew forward.

As he writhed on the ground, someone said, '*You.*'

Then the click of metal. A gun?

Dan scrambled away, rising to his feet, when something hard struck his skull.

Consciousness wavered, became fluid, and he slid downward.

A voice yelled, '*No.*'

He heard a scream of rage, the sound of a violent tussle, and his mind crept away. Dan had no certainty if it was him fighting or whether he was lying on the ground or maybe he was both, but his brain was shutting down and he felt bathed by peacefulness. Whoever was fighting that fight, him or someone else, it no longer mattered, because although his body was here, his being was taking a long and blissful glide into—

Chapter 28

Waking began. Dan barely knew who or what he was. All he registered was the bird sweetly unravelling its tune in his head, and he felt he might be that song, so light and airy, so beautiful, other songs weaving in and through him, an insistent joy to this floating, swooping way of being. No boundaries, just freedom. Then his eyes opened.

He lay for a while, cradled on the ground, looking into the tiny cave made by the curl of a dead leaf, inches from his face. A woodlouse appeared from the depths and crawled toward his eye, negotiating clumps of soil and rotting vegetation, the creature tilting onto its side to bypass these obstacles. Unhurried but relentless in its progress. Next in its way was the husk of a beech nut, but the woodlouse was tipped onto its back. Dan watched the myriad legs, smaller than his own eyelashes, waving in the air as the creature arched its ribbed carapace and tried to right itself.

An instruction went from Dan's brain, telling his arm to move. The delay was palpable, and when the limb did consent, it felt stiff, like a splintered branch. His hand wavered into view. Dan held his breath, aimed a finger toward its target. He flipped the woodlouse over. Brief pause, then the creature continued its journey, disappearing under shredded mulch to the left of his vision.

Dan sat up slowly, gauging the throb of pain in different quarters of his body. He peered round. No one here. It was morning. Early, judging by the volume of birdsong. He was at the bottom of a large pit, the shape of an upturned dome. Above him, crowding the circular rim, were trees, the verticality of their trunks almost frightening when seen from below. A few trees grew on the slopes, but down here was like a sunken clearing, with a single beech tree that reached its etiolated limbs toward the canopy high above. Dan realised he was in a pingo, a legacy of the last ice age, when permafrost generated a mound of frozen water, trapped like a blister in the soil's skin. Pushing upward and pressing down, then melting away with the retreat of glaciation.

The void memory of that ice was still here, hollowed into the terrain. As Dan sat beneath its absent weight and ferocious cold, a message came to him from the ancient past, but in a language he had no hope of understanding. Dan breathed in deeply, noting again the ache in his lower back. Stray moments were returning of the night before. There had been a fight. Strange whooping. A shape skimming across a field. Water in his throat and lungs. Gradually he pieced together the events and the order in which they happened. Vaguely aware that he had suffered a concussion.

Dan ran a careful hand through his hair, finding a bump. Sore to touch. Then he noticed the blanket, covering his legs and torso. How did it get here? These were the blankets used at Summerlands. Dan frowned, thoughts fleeing any attempt at explanation. He pushed the blanket aside, saw the state of his feet. Dirt and dried blood, cuts and splinters.

Next, he began the process of standing up. Stopped partway, arms braced against his thighs, surprised by the discovery, unjustifiably new, that he was tall. Another minute and Dan managed to straighten up. Swaying slightly, he glanced at the shafts of low morning sun slipping through the trees higher up. Down here the shadows of the night still lingered. A dull pain in his head, the soles of his feet hurting, Dan limped across the bottom of the hollow. Easing his bruised muscles, rubbing his back. That was where he tumbled down the slope. Slide marks in the soft soil, and the tree stump which halted his descent.

Dan had a sudden memory of footsteps running at him in the pitch black, and him being grabbed by the shoulders and thrown down. The recollection was so visceral, he felt alarm coursing through his body. Nearby were churned up leaves and scuffed earth. Dan took his mind to the moment when he passed out, trying to recall the final details gathered by his senses before he lost consciousness. There had been a fight. The shouting and sounds of a violent struggle had continued after he was immobile on the forest floor.

Strang saved his life.

Someone had tried to kill Dan, and Strang intervened – it was him who yelled *No.*

The man who chased Strang into the woods must have switched his attention to Dan. Luring him into this pit, by pretending to be Strang. He had pleaded for help, calling from the far side, knowing that the ground was about to disappear beneath Dan's feet.

Strang had come back to rescue him. Had fought off the killer. Strang then fetched a blanket and placed it over Dan. But what happened to their attacker? Dan checked the area for blood. The sun was rising higher with every minute, dissolving the shadows. He crouched down, picked up an opalescent shard of glass, and put it in his pocket. Evidence supporting his theory. The man had worn night-vision goggles, making it easy to find him in the dark.

Dan went over to the blanket, considered taking it back to Summerlands. Instead, he folded the blanket and left it on the ground, for Strang.

It took several minutes to climb the slope. His limbs ached and his balance felt skew. Reaching the top, Dan grabbed a tree trunk to steady himself. On the far side of the pingo, something moved. A sudden flitting between trees.

'Who's there?' he called.

No reply.

A deer. Or Strang watching over him.

Dan breathed a quiet thank you, then he limped toward the reservoir. His body was on alert as a second attack seemed likely. He made his way round to where he had left his belongings. Wincing, Dan bathed his feet, aware of contaminating the public water supply with blood. Then he remembered – this basin was for irrigating crops. Dan eased on socks and shoes, fetched his sweater and phone. On the way back, he remained vigilant. Dan had become a target as well as Strang. Both were a threat to the man who murdered Ryan Taylor.

Once inside, Dan locked the caravan door. He swallowed two paracetamol and two ibuprofen, along with a pint of water. Then he had a coffee followed by a long hot shower, the cuts to his feet stinging. Dan towelled himself dry. A wound on his left foot kept bleeding, so he applied a plaster. Standing before the mirror, he examined the discolouration where he had been bruised by his fall. Staring at his naked body, Dan thought about Beth. He got dressed, then sent a text to Cassie. *I will collect the phone from Wymondham at 5 p.m. today.*

Cassie was wrong. Beth had been faithful to him just as he had been faithful to her. But he needed to know why she was on Magdalen Street. The messages on her second phone could hold the answer. For a moment he was taken back to last night, the desperate way Strang plunged into the reservoir, as if searching for something in the black depths.

Dan was desperate too. But did it really matter if Beth had been seeing someone else? If she was on Magdalen Street because she was meeting another man? None of this mattered in the end. Nothing could undo her death, or alleviate his emptiness.

Jay attached her wet clothes to the washing line with plastic pegs. This part of the back garden was overshadowed by conifers, but the warm breeze would dry everything soon enough. She returned to the cottage and checked the living room. The curtains were shut, but bright sunlight was visible round the edges. Her father was watching a nature programme on the vast screen, with the sound off. After a few minutes he sank deeper into the chair, rearranging his bony frame. Jay tiptoed away, and went into the front garden.

The sky seemed as radiant as the TV, the blue almost fluorescent. She stood next to the porch, eyes blinking. Unlike the lawn at the back, the land here had always been left to its own devices. A meadow of sorts, but yellow and parched, with a track leading to the garage. Near the front door there was a small circle of paving, a metal table and two chairs. They were replica cast iron, and the dark paint had faded to pale green. The cottage faced due south and this spot was a sun trap. Jay could not recall it ever being used.

The furniture was entangled with ivy. Jay fetched secateurs along with a bucket of water and a scrubbing brush. Half an hour later, the table and chairs had been rescued from the undergrowth and the damp metal gleamed. Then she looked up a recipe on her phone and made a batch of scones, ten of them, which she slid into the oven on a rusty tray that had escaped her father's cull in the kitchen. Jay never did any baking in London and the domesticity felt almost comical. By the time the scones were ready, the garden furniture was dry. Her father was persuaded to join her on the small patio.

'This is nice, isn't it?' she said.

He had disrupted the pattern of her Norfolk trips – of her childhood and teenage years – by stripping the cottage of comforts, and interring roadkill. Jay hoped to introduce a more positive change, a morning coffee ritual in the sunshine. *Yes, we don't have to behave as we've always done, we can explore different ways of living here.* But as soon as her father lowered himself awkwardly onto the metal chair, she realised this was not going to work. Nothing Jay did could compete with his own quiet revolution in the back garden.

His scone was nearly finished.

'Was it okay?' she said. 'I put some raisins in.'

'Better than shop-bought,' her father said. Moments later, he went indoors.

With a sigh, Jay looked at her hands. Remembering that time in her early teens, maybe her emo phase, when she decided to 'revamp' her bedroom. The wardrobe, bookshelves and bedside table had belonged to a set chosen when she was at primary school. They were white, with pink roses decorating the edges. Aged fourteen or so, Jay declared war on those roses.

It had taken an adolescent week of evenings and Kiss FM to scrape off the floral transfers. Jay could still see her black-painted fingernails as she picked away at the garlands, flecking the carpet with curls of pink and green. Not all the transfers came off easily. When her father noticed Jay's painstaking act of vandalism, the scratches on the chipboard, his response was, 'I've got some gloss paint if you want. Up to you, Jacqueline.'

He did not pass judgement on what she did. Who she was. Glancing at the garage, Jay recalled the 50cc she owned at sixteen. The image was clear, of the blue moped with learner plates, bought second-hand using money from her job on the chip van. No need for her father's permission so Jay never asked. But she knew, even at the time, that he was worried. It was her father who paid for the proper helmet, the gloves and boots, the jacket and trousers with built-in protection.

He had always been there for her. Adapting his parenting to who she was. Who Colin was. Not always getting it right. Often clumsy, misguided, but making the effort.

Jay stacked up the dishes and went inside.

Dan was limping to the shop when Mrs Faulkner approached him across the gravel. He had not seen her all week. Samantha had been at the reception desk every time he called by.

'According to you,' Mrs Faulkner said, 'my convenience store is a rip-off.'

'I never said that.'

'Samantha seems to think you did.'

'I told her you had a captive market. She may have felt the need to rephrase that.'

Mrs Faulkner laughed. 'You're quite funny, you know, for a depressive.'

'Free for a chat?' Dan said. Food could wait.

'We'll use the lounge.'

As Dan followed Mrs Faulkner to the bungalow, he noticed she was moving differently, as if her muscles ached. He too was finding it difficult. Pills had alleviated some of the pain but his feet were still tender.

She gestured for him to sit down, then lowered herself carefully onto a chair.

Dan glanced at the mantlepiece. Definitely two ceramic figures last time he was here. Now there was only one. 'I've been meaning to—'

'The disarray has got to end,' Mrs Faulkner said.

He blinked. Felt a throb behind his eyes.

'You need a haircut, Daniel. And how did that happen?'

Mrs Faulkner was staring at the side of his face, and Dan remembered the scratch he got from falling into the pingo.

He shifted in his chair. 'I made the mistake of going for a walk before bed.'

'Were you attacked by the local wildlife?'

'Something like that.'

'A decent haircut will make you look less like a Friday-night drunk.'

Dan considered whether to take offence. But he and Mrs Faulkner did not waste time on niceties.

'I'll book one today,' he said.

'You're representing me and I'd like you to look the part. As a mark of respect.'

Dan stared at her. This whole conversation was about Felix, though she would never say as much. 'Of course,' he said. 'Apologies. I promise to smarten myself up.'

'You understand.'

'I do.'

Mrs Faulkner smiled a sad smile. Her right forearm was resting in her lap, the palm upturned. As if cradling a baby.

Dan swallowed. *He was my son. My beautiful son.* The air grew heavy in the room. His gaze went to the mantlepiece, the blue ceramic of a mother in a long dress, arms reaching toward empty space.

'Sorry,' Mrs Faulkner said. 'I believe you were wanting a chat?'

He hesitated. A rank smell rose from his body. Sorrow always made his heart race. To be a childless mother, part of a whole that was torn apart. His own lopsided life now that Beth was gone. Dan looked out the window at the blank sky. He had come to ask about the small ceramic of a child, and why it was missing. He shook his head, unable to go there.

'I seem to have...' Dan searched for something to say. 'That's right, it was just to let you know the police are no longer interested in the icehouse. They don't believe there's any connection to the murder at the solar farm.'

On the way out, Mrs Faulkner said, 'Given you're here, you can make yourself useful.' She opened a cupboard and pointed to a box. 'Could you carry that to the kitchen, please.'

He expected the box to be heavy, but it weighed very little. Dan was not sure why she had asked him to do this. Then he remembered how stiff her movements had seemed, walking to the bungalow, and her story the other day about a hospital trip. Was Mrs Faulkner undergoing some type of treatment?

In the shop, it took Dan five minutes to decide which bread to buy. How many eggs. Six or twelve. Six. Making scrambled eggs also proved a challenge. He carried his plate and mug to the table, then eased himself onto the bench. As he forked food into his mouth, his mind drifted. Dan was not thinking about anything, but there was a sense of thoughts forming below the surface.

Once the meal was finished, he wiped the table, then got out OS 144 and spread it across the worn Formica. As his hands flattened the creases in the map, his gaze explored the terrain, picking out all the places that had figured in his journeys. There was the Candlesham road and the small blue caravan symbol for Summerlands. Above to the left was the icehouse, with its radiating pattern of small black dashes. His eyes travelled in search of the ruins of St Cecilia's. On finding *Church*, written in gothic script, Dan worked out where the reservoir must be, then back down and along to the solar farm. Neither appeared on his OS, which was a few years old.

An online map would provide current information, but he needed the tactility of paper beneath his fingers. Further up the map was Mettlesham and the road past Valhalla. That wavering blue filament was the River Ling, flowing south-east, through hatched areas of green woodland and the white blankness of fields. The thick diagonal green line was the A11. Not many routes across it, but Dan knew – having glimpsed this from the dual carriageway – there was a small tunnel that passed underneath. He peered closer, identifying its location. The tunnel served a narrow farm track on private land, linking fields on the north and south sides. His finger then traced the inky black of the trainline, looking for lesser-known crossing points.

The phone buzzed. His Volvo was booked for a service and that was Hari texting a reminder. *Jem doing me big fat favour opening Sunday*. Dan folded up the map, tapped it against his hand, and slid it into a drawer. Then he swallowed more painkillers.

While his car was with the mechanic, Dan took a bus into the centre of Norwich. At the Millennium Library, he asked for back copies of the *Anglia Herald* and was told how to access these via the computer terminals. He logged on and checked BBC News first. The hottest temperatures on record were being predicted for the next few days. Dan clicked through to the regional news. Police had issued a statement yesterday confirming that enquiries were ongoing into the murder at the solar farm in Norfolk. 'Second or third week of June' was still the estimated date for when the male was killed. There was no mention of the death being related to campaigning about green energy. Walsh had decided not to share this with the media. Nor had police identified the victim. Dan was an unreliable source.

He opened the online directory for the *Anglia Herald* and scrolled through back copies of the paper. Skimming headlines, until several articles caught his eye. In June, around the time of the murder, there were reports of vandalism to solar farms, paint sprayed on the panels, and in some instances the transformers and substations had been set alight with petrol. Environmental activism, but *against* rather than in favour of renewable energy.

Journalists had interviewed people living in the vicinity of these incidents. Nobody went so far as to condone the damage done, but there was clearly a lot of ill feeling. Dan then read an article published in May – before the vandalism began – about a solar farm near Thraston. It was at the planning stage and South Norfolk District Council had no objections. The villagers and parish councillors, however, were worried about its impact on the local area. There was already a large solar farm next to the main approach to Thraston, on the left-hand side. The new facility would be on the right-hand side, resulting in a combined area of 120 acres.

Access to the village would be along 'a corridor of glass' according to an unnamed resident. Another was quoted as saying, 'Nobody on the council is listening to us. We feel swamped.' Dan had assumed there was a coordinated UK policy for solar farms. The aim being to distribute them on separate sites so that the traditional image of countryside – crops and livestock – could be maintained. It appeared from this article there was no such directive, the result being 'the wholescale destruction of our land'. A resident claimed that much of the output of this 'mega solar farm' was intended for London. Norfolk was being ruined for the sake of 'outsiders'.

The May article highlighted the reasons behind local attitudes to solar farms. A growing hostility that, in the weeks which followed, seemed to prompt direct action. Dan scrolled forward to the latest edition of the *Anglia Herald*. The headline was 'New Lead in Solar Farm Murder'. The article was connecting the death to the recent vandalism, though there had been nothing about this on the BBC. Maybe someone on the enquiry team had leaked information to the local press. Several scenarios were suggested by the *Herald*. That the victim was killed when he stumbled upon a group breaking into the solar farm. Or the victim was one of the protesters and there had been a disagreement.

Dan drummed his fingers on the table. The body being left at a solar farm seemed a significant 'clue' that the murder was linked to anti-environmental activism. A plausible theory for police and the media to pursue. But it was a big step to go from spraying paint on solar panels, to beating a man to death and chopping off his hands.

Chapter 29

After picking up his Volvo from the mechanics, Dan drove to Wymondham HQ. He was early. An hour to wait before he was due to collect Beth's phone. He parked in one of the visitor places and thought about his six years working out of this station. Over there, by the cherry trees, was where he used to leave his vehicle. As he looked at the trees, Dan could sense an earlier echo of himself, getting out of the Renault he owned back then. In the unfolding of his life, he had held on to the present moment and moved forward, keeping pace with time. But along the way he had left imprints. These Dan had noticed before, finding residues still snagged in a location. Never a significant episode, always something mundane, like getting out of his car at HQ.

He felt sorry for the younger him, walking across the tarmac with no idea of what lay ahead. Dan looked round, wondering if he would now see Beth, but this was not one of her haunts. A few weeks ago, he caught sight of her at the Friday market in Wymondham. Beth was weaving through the crowds, in a hurry. Searching for Dan? He hoped she found him, some spectral trace he had left in the places where they used to go.

It did not matter what was on the phone, waiting for him on the other side of those doors. Dan could collect it and throw it in a bin. He could collect it and examine the contents. Nothing on there would alter what happened. But the detective in him still wanted answers.

A vehicle pulled up and a woman got out, just as another two cars arrived. The shift change. A few people headed toward the entrance, chatting, and Dan recognised some of the faces. Which of them, he wondered, was deployed on the solar-farm murder? Cassie and Sullivan of course. Maybe Davidson, who had swept past in his white Land Rover Discovery. The man did his usual lazy parking, tight against the driver's door of the neighbouring vehicle. Seven months had not made him any less of a wanker.

Dan glanced at the second floor where MIT were based. They were focusing their efforts on the recent vandalism at solar farms. All that time wasted on determining if the perpetrators had links to the murder victim. Nobody had come forward saying their friend or relative was missing. Nobody had recognised the e-fit. His information about Ryan Taylor was being ignored. Dan had crossed into a lunatic place where people talked to each other over the cold wet surface of a reservoir. Where people went night walking and lived in woods and slept in icehouses. Where people hunted each other like animals. Dan had brought his knowledge back from that nocturnal world. Who in their right mind would believe him?

Jay lay on the grass, the warm ground beneath her, the bright sky above. In a nearby tree, a thrush performed its repertoire, each small melody repeating three times. Jay closed her eyes. In the past few days, she had thought about phoning her brother. There were updates to be given. The burial of the muntjac. The visit to Beccles. The strange scene in the kitchen, and what she then told the detective. Colin would want to know all this, but how would he react? Her brother was inflexible. Barricaded behind his wife, two children and a regular income. Jay pictured the efficiency with which their father could be removed from his life and 'placed' in a care home. The verb said it all, consigning him to the role of inanimate object. A time might come when that move was unavoidable. But not yet.

Her and Colin had always seen things differently. Jay was reminded of the Renaissance paintings that used optical tricks. Shift your position and a piece of fabric became a skull, memento mori. She had never shared Colin's perspective, his forensic 'voice of reason'. Her choice was velvet not bone. Jay would not let Colin diminish their world.

If her father was changing, she could try to change with him. He had always been there for her. Even when she went to places he did not want to go.

It was her turn now, to follow him. Memories were emerging about the baby's disappearance – was there more to come? The prospect no longer frightened her, and Jay felt strangely calm. He was her father, she was his daughter. She would stick with him.

It's the right thing to do.

Jay peered up at the beech tree, searching for the song thrush.

No air in the car. Dan tried to slow his heart rate and pay attention to the road. He gnawed his cheek, tasting blood. There had been no sign of Cassie at Wymondham – just her handwriting on the padded envelope, which had been left at the front desk. He would look at the phone once he got back to the caravan. That was what Dan told himself as he drove south, but via the wrong route.

After twenty minutes, somewhere near Quidenham, fields either side, he stopped on the verge and tore open the envelope. Inside was a black Nokia, a basic model designed for calls and texts. Dan swallowed. No, he had never seen this in Beth's possession. A second phone was not something he would have forgotten. He switched it on. The battery was charged.

Dan studied the messages, going backward in time as he read them one by one. At the end he turned the Nokia off and put it back in the envelope. Then he stared across the wheatfield on his left. In the middle was a giant green drum, around which was coiled a hose for irrigating crops. The drum had been pulled by a tractor, then abandoned in the field. Dan wondered about the stasis now attached to this object. No longer needed for watering as the crop was ripe. And so it sat there in the quiet limbo of its current lack of usefulness.

He wanted to get out of his car. He wanted to walk through the wheatfield. He wanted to climb onto that drum, slip between the coils and wrap himself around the spindle. It would be dark and green and cool in there. He would be tightly bound. He would not have to think. He would not have to be. Just exist. Like that giant green drum. No questions asked of it. Just a thing, an object. Allowed to pass, unremarked, through time, to become obsolete and gently decay. No emotion.

Just peace with no beginning or end.

When Dan got back to Summerlands, Cassie was waiting on the steps of his caravan.

'We need to talk,' she said.

'Is that so?' he said with a sneer. 'I've just come from Wymondham. Why didn't you book an interview room?'

'Stop being a dickhead.'

They were being watched by a couple sat in deckchairs. Dan glared at them.

When had anger become so easy?

He blew out a breath and frowned at Cassie. 'Got water in the fridge. Up to you.'

She followed him inside and slid in next to the table. Dan filled two glasses and sat opposite, not meeting her gaze. Neither of them spoke. The caravan was hot. His back ached and his head throbbed. Dan reached for the blister packs, fingers pushing out pills, the noise of it too loud. He swallowed them down.

'Bad night?' she said, raising an eyebrow.

He ignored her.

'I thought we were bigger than this,' Cassie said. 'I thought you would put up more of a fight.'

Dan did not speak. Her words had been ambiguous, but he knew she was referring to their friendship. After a while he said, 'I'd like you to leave.'

'I'd like you to behave like a human being.'

Silence again. He took a long gulp of water and placed the glass carefully on the table. Another minute ticked by, then he said, 'I don't want to talk about the phone.'

Cassie shrugged. 'That's not why I'm here.'

'Please go,' he said.

'I was trying to protect you.'

Dan studied the green and brown fabric of the banquette. The pattern was based on foliage. He recalled the woodlouse that crawled from under a leaf. This morning? Or another century. His hand stroked the fabric. The fibres were synthetic and had become shiny in places, through wear. He thought about all the other conversations which had happened around this table. From *I love you* to *Where shall we go tomorrow?* to *Pass the ketchup* to *Why would I have a problem with your mother?* to *I was thinking Banham Zoo.*

He looked up and met Cassie's gaze. 'You kept me in the dark for seven months.'

'You didn't need to know that your dead and beloved fiancée had been two-timing you. Shagging an old boyfriend.'

Dan scowled. 'You have no idea what was on that phone.'

'I saw enough to know it would hurt you.'

He recalled what it had been like working with Cassie. The way she used to fixate on one interpretation.

'You never liked Beth,' he said.

'I thought she was a bit on the dull side. That's not the same as not liking her. Have you got any food?'

Dan laughed, despite himself.

'What?' she said. 'I'm starving.'

'You're unbelievable. You're so annoying it's making my skin itch. Did I ever tell you that? Did I ever say there were times when I hated you, because you were always so sure of yourself? So convinced you were right about *every single thing*.'

'Now we're getting somewhere,' Cassie said, rubbing her hands together. 'Mr Nice Guy confessing he used to hate me sometimes. I used to hate how polite you were. I knew I was annoying you. I was doing it on purpose. Trying to press your buttons. And you still kept on being reasonable, seeing things from every conceivable angle. Finding excuses for people the whole time, refusing to admit that some folk are just shits from the get-go. I mean we've all got difficult lives, but that's not a free ticket to rape and murder and steal. Like it's the only outlet? Give me a break.'

Cassie was breathing hard. Avoiding his gaze. He fetched a packet of chocolate digestives from the cupboard, then sat down again.

'Own brand,' she said, with a dismissive shake of her head.

Dan watched her eat three biscuits with the detached efficiency she applied to all acts of consumption. Egg noodles. Jerk chicken. Burgers. Biryani. Eaten in their vehicle while they were on a long shift. Never anything spilled. Never seeming to gobble her food, and yet it always disappeared before he had barely started.

Cassie flashed him a look. 'When are you going to quit this experiment in how to screw up your life?'

'This *is* my life. This is how it is.'

She frowned. 'You had a good job.'

'Had. Past tense.'

'Is the friendship over too?' she said.

Her vulnerability was palpable in the small space. Dan turned away, unable to respond.

Cassie stood up and he felt thankful she was leaving. Instead, she refilled her glass and sat down again.

'Just so you know,' she said, 'that was a moment when I really needed *Mr Nice Guy*.'

He stared at the lace curtains. Beth would have hated every detail of this caravan. 'Lace is for underwear,' she said to him once. Had he moved to Summerlands because her ghost would not follow him here – was he hiding from her?

'By the way,' Cassie said, 'you were correct about the identity of the vic.'

Dan studied his left hand. At some point, today or yesterday, he had put Beth's engagement ring onto his little finger.

'Don't tell me, is that her—*Jesus*, Dan, I swear I'm going to shoot you in the leg and lock you in a room with a therapist. This can't go on, you hear? Stop torturing yourself.'

He glared at her. 'Why didn't you tell me about Lomax?'

'Because it's no big deal. *He*'s no big deal. I mean, you've spoken to the guy. Do you think I'm in it for the chat? We do it maybe once a week. Neither of us is suited to a proper relationship. Can you imagine me saying to him, *It's your turn to take out the bin, babes?* I can't do that shit. I did it briefly with Archie's dad and it nearly killed me. The mundanity of it. How can there be passion when you've just had to arrange a service for the boiler, and by the way could you stop leaving potato peelings in the stupid little grate thing in the sink? I mean, who wants sex after that? I like owning a house and making a home for Archie. I love being a mum. I don't need some guy messing it up. Maybe Lomax is secretly nursing dreams of a rosy future for the two of us. But I tell him all the time he's my Tuesday bootycall and he never complains.'

'When did it start?'

Cassie snorted. 'Really? How pervie are you?'

'You know that's not why I asked.'

'A couple of weeks before Beth died.'

'*He killed her*,' Dan said, his fists clenched.

'Which is exactly why I couldn't tell you. Because I knew you'd make it part of some totally demented theory. I mean you're doing it now, I can see it in your eyes.'

'No, I'm not. I'm thinking you should have told me.'

'I didn't want you getting hurt. I didn't want to add to what you were already dealing with. Because I'm your friend, for Christ's sake.'

All these things Cassie had done to protect him and yet he was furious with her. Dan pressed his hands to the table, thinking about the Nokia phone. What he had learned about Beth. The secrets she had kept from him.

There was a knock at the door. Dan looked up, startled.

'That'll be the pizza guy,' Cassie said. 'I knew you'd have bugger all to eat in this dump.'

She went to take charge of the delivery, exchanging a few words with the person outside, then the door was closed and she placed two Dominos boxes on the table.

'I got you a Veggie Supreme,' she said. 'Wasn't sure if you'd given up meat as part of the whole reassessing-your-life-goals routine.'

Cassie pulled the top box toward herself and opened the lid. He could smell pepperoni.

'I'm happy to do swapsies,' she said, 'if you fancy some spicy sausage.' She laughed what he recognised as her dirty laugh.

Dan ignored this and focused on the food.

Cassie finished hers first, saying, 'Should have got family size.'

'Here,' he said, pushing the veggie pizza across. 'You paid for it.'

'Nah,' Cassie said. Then the afterglow of eating left her face and she looked sad. 'I doubt you remember, but it was my turn. I'm talking about the last shift we did, the two of us. Before... before everything happened. We stopped at that burger van on the Thetford bypass and you paid. They put onions in yours even though you'd asked them not to. We ate in the car. You scraped off the onions and wrapped them in a paper napkin. But when we were leaving you still lowered your window and told the woman that the burger was *Delicious, thank you*. I ripped the shit out of you for that. *Obvs*.'

Dan stared at his lap. 'I don't remember any of that.'

'It was my turn. You left and it was still my turn. To buy the scran.'

'I despise that word,' he said. 'You're from London not Manchester.'

'You're getting good at this.'

'At what?' he said.

'At being a total dickhead.'

'Cass, I'm not sure who I am anymore. I don't know who that guy was who scraped onions off a burger. He doesn't feel part of me. I mean it's the same body it's always been. But I'm no longer sure it's me inside.'

Cassie reached across and squeezed his hand.

Dan blinked. 'You've always been so certain,' he said. 'Of who you are.'

'You think too much,' she said, giving his hand another squeeze. 'It's the curse of your middle-class upbringing. You intellectualise every issue to death. Analyse it with your giant brain and weigh up all the variables from every conceivable angle. Only there aren't answers to every problem. Or at least not the sort you can arrive at with this.' She tapped her head. 'You can't *solve* Beth's death. Do you get what I'm saying? There is no answer to why she died and there never will be.'

Cassie sat back. The sun had crept round and was now shining through the lace curtains. Dan was transfixed by the elaborate patterns that were etched across her face, following the curves of her cheek.

She frowned. 'Did you catch what I said earlier?'

As she spoke, Dan stared at the bright swirls of evening sun that eddied and danced on her face. Words were coming out of her mouth, from inside that skin, beneath the presence and absence of light. Cassie could not know and nor could he explain how it seemed to transfigure her.

'Dan. Earth to Dan.'

'Sorry. What?'

Cassie had moved, the light no longer on her.

'You were right,' she said, 'about the vic being Ryan Taylor.'

'You should have listened to me sooner.'

'But we can't find anything linking him to the recent vandalism at solar farms.'

Dan shrugged. 'There's a surprise.'

'My shift finished an hour ago. I'm now at liberty to hear whatever crackpot theories you have about the murder.'

'In need of a laugh? Something to liven up the locker-room gossip?'

Cassie blinked, then her features became a barrier. Dan recognised this as her interview face.

The two of them sat saying nothing. After a few minutes she spoke. 'You never used to be so bitter.'

'Are you here because you're trying to mend our friendship? Or because you think I might know who the killer is?'

'If I said both would you kick me out?'

Dan glanced away, shaking his head.

'Thanks,' she said.

But his response was not directed at her, it had been exasperation with himself. Dan would have done the same as Cassie when he was a DI. Trade everyone and everything for the sake of answers. And now he had become the person she was prepared to sacrifice. This was what happened when you left the police.

You became a commodity, useful to an investigation and nothing more.

You became an outsider, who could remember too well what it felt like to be on the inside.

His grief had never just been about Beth, and he hated himself for that.

'So?' Cassie said. 'Are you going to tell me who murdered Ryan Taylor? Or do I have to beg? *Please, Danny Boy, you're the best, we really need your help.*'

His jaw was tight.

'Annoying you again, am I? Good,' she said. 'You're a whole lot more bearable when you're angry than when you're wallowing in self-pity.'

Cassie stood up and put the kettle on. 'Got any tea?'

Dan unclamped his mouth. 'Some in the cupboard. Left by the previous residents.'

'Coffee it is, then.'

'There's no milk.'

'Tell me something new.'

Dan watched her make two black coffees.

Here,' she said, placing a mug in front of him.

Cassie sat down, drank some. 'Yuck. This better be worth it. You better have something juicy to tell me.'

'You're relentless,' he said grimly.

'You should try me in bed. Stop. Forget I said that. Double yuck.'

'Ta very much.'

'Ours is a thing of beauty. A friendship with no bump and grind. I bought you a pizza and made you a foul coffee. Now you get to tell me what you know about the murder.'

The patterns that had been so sharply drawn on Cassie's face had shifted to the table. Evening sun slid across the top of his coffee. Dan studied the light as it bounced through the tiny particles of steam that rose from the circle of black liquid.

'The vagrant sleeping at the icehouse,' Dan said. 'It wasn't me.'

'So who was it?'

'John Strang. The guy I told you about, who disappeared from Summerlands owing rent.'

She nodded. 'With the messy caravan. What about him?'

'Strang witnessed Ryan's murder.'

Cassie frowned. 'You know this for a fact?'

'I don't have to, I'm not police.'

'Fair point.'

Dan fetched a teaspoon, stirred his coffee to cool it down. 'Strang took something from here. From my caravan. A coat, I think. Maybe a jacket? That's why you found my DNA at the icehouse. But instead of considering the alternatives, you all decided I'd been trying to derail the investigation.'

'The evidence was pretty damning,' she said. 'There was a mug with your fingerprints and saliva. A black hoodie. A T-shirt. A sort of parka thing. Your hair was all over the clothes. Oh, and a pair of your shoes. Trainers, with cracked soles.'

Strang had been in and out of his caravan – stepping into his belongings.

'And you found traces of no one else?' Dan said.

Cassie looked uncomfortable. 'Well, yeah. There was other clothing. Three DNA profiles, but yours was the only match. The mug kind of sealed the deal. A red one, like this.' She raised her mug of coffee.

'Somebody steals stuff from my caravan. And yet I'm the one accused of putting myself front and centre of a murder enquiry? How desperate do you think I am?'

'Honest answer? A lot of your behaviour has been nuts since... well, since after Beth.'

'You should leave now. You already don't believe me.'

'I'm not on duty, Dan. I've arranged a babysitter. All you'll be doing is wasting *my* time not police time. If I decide it's a total bust then you might owe me the twenty quid for Gemma. You can pay it back in pints next Wednesday. Obviously, I need to speak to Strang. Do you know where to find him, is he still around?'

'I'm going for a walk,' Dan said.

Chapter 30

Dan and Cassie headed along the path, accompanied by a loud silence. He was furious at the things she had done, all those lies, month after month, the number of times she had deceived Dan in order to keep him in the dark. Lomax. Beth's phone. It made him feel an idiot, embarrassed by his own credulity. Fields, hedges, flint, mud, wheat, birds, evening light, they clamoured for his attention but Dan ignored them. His body knew the route. Cassie was next to him saying nothing as they continued north. He noticed his feet were less sore. Moving more freely, he noticed some of the emotion had lessened too.

'You seem pretty familiar with the area,' Cassie said after a bit.

'Keeps me busy,' Dan said, not looking at her. Just walking.

'I want to be sure I've understood. John Strang, your misper from the caravan site, has been sleeping at the icehouse. He went into hiding after witnessing the murder of Ryan Taylor – because he was too frightened to tell anyone?'

'Something like that,' Dan said. 'Though I think what he may have seen was Ryan's body being dumped.'

'The killer is aware John Strang can identify him.'

'Yes. He's been hunting for Strang. Last night he almost caught him.'

Dan gave Cassie a summary of what happened, omitting his own assault and injuries. In this version, Strang had been washing himself at the reservoir, not plunging in repeatedly and nearly drowning. Nor did Dan tell her that when Strang was being chased, it was like he was the one in charge. Why keep quiet about these details? He did not really know, other than a sense that he and Cassie were on different sides. Nor would he say anything about Mrs Faulkner's son. The more information Dan gave the police, the more they would distort it.

'Wait,' Cassie said, fetching her phone from a pocket. 'It's Gemma. I better take this.' Walking off a few paces, she answered the call, speaking quietly, her back toward him.

It could be Gemma or it could be Lomax. Dan did not want to know. He still had to deal with suspicion on a personal level, but at least he was no longer committed to it as a professional duty. Dan continued on the path until he was out of earshot, then he stared across the land, waiting for Cassie to finish. The distant sound of an engine came from somewhere in the east. A vehicle on one of the roads, or possibly a combine harvester in a faraway field.

Something touched his arm and he span round, fists clenched.

'Christ,' Cassie said. 'Why are you so jumpy?'

Dan blinked.

'What's this about?' she said. 'Anything to do with that cut on your cheek?'

He looked at her, wondering whether to say more about last night.

But then she laughed. 'You kidding me? A punch-up down the boozer? I hope no one presses charges.'

Annoyed, he started walking. Cassie seemed to think 'antisocial behaviour' was his new thing now that he was public not police.

She caught up, saying, 'Why hasn't Strang left the area? Why stick around when the killer is trying to finish him off?'

Dan gave a shrug.

'You've formed a connection with this Strang,' Cassie said.

'Sort of.'

'Reckon you can persuade him to come forward as a witness?'

'Our best chance of talking to him is at the reservoir,' Dan said, pointing up the slope. 'I'll sit where he can see me. But if you keep below the ridge, you can watch from there.'

They took up position. Dan tried to let his mind go blank, but he could sense Cassie behind him. His eyes focused on the water, the ripples that were the only trace of a breeze he barely felt.

'When does Strang tend to come here?' Cassie said quietly.

'You'll have to be patient.'

'What about the killer? I assume he's still hoping to get his hands on Strang.'

'It's not dark yet. We're okay for now.'

'You sure about all this?'

'You can go,' Dan said. 'There's no guarantee my theory's any better than the SIO's.'

'Where's the wood Strang's sleeping in?'

'On the other side.'

'If we sit there' – she pointed across the reservoir – 'we'll have more chance.'

'It might scare him off.'

Cassie laughed. 'As the DI, I decide.'

Dan followed her as she stepped over the granite rocks and went down to the water. They walked round on the exposed rubber lining. No view of fields or distant countryside, which lay beyond the stark horizontals of the grass rim, just above eyeline. As he and Cassie turned along the east shore, the tower of St Cecilia's reared up, a ragged outline of flint, its broken belfry engulfed in ivy. On reaching the corner, they ascended the slope. Aware his silhouette was exposed, Dan dropped to his knees.

Cassie crouched next to him, saying, 'Why are you so tense? Is Strang likely to lash out?'

Dan did not reply. The sky had become a strange blue that no longer seemed like air, the colour had a thickness and weight. As if he was staring up from the depths of a warm sea, and the pale moon was a sun seen from beneath the surface.

Then he heard the faint throb of an engine. The same one as earlier? Not many roads nearby. Dan scanned the terrain, looking for the source of the noise.

'Shit,' he said, leaping to his feet. He ran down the grass embankment and vaulted the fence, Cassie behind him, yelling, 'What the hell?'

No time to explain, Dan was running through the wheat. He had spotted a quad bike hauling something by a rope. A body, which bounced and twisted as it was pulled across the ground. There was now a line of trees between him and the vehicle. Dan could no longer see what was being dragged, but he spied two people on the quad bike. The man from last night had brought back-up. And this time Strang had been captured. It had to be him on the end of that rope. Still alive? Or were they taking away his body.

Dan raced across the field. His only hope was to catch them near that gate, but they could change direction, and the quad bike was moving at speed.

There was a yell of surprise. The vehicle halted and two figures jumped down.

'Over here,' Dan called. He needed to get them away from Strang.

The two men ran toward Dan. He set off at a sprint, drawing them on. He glanced round, trying to locate Cassie. She was thirty metres to his left.

'Stop,' she shouted. 'Police.'

The men split up, one of them veering away.

Dan turned on his heels and charged at the man behind him. Recognised the face instantly. Neil Witton from the stud farm. Witton had killed Ryan Taylor – Dan was certain – and dumped his remains at the solar farm to divert suspicion.

Witton had his fists ready, but Dan twisted at the last second and shoulder barged him, sending the man flying to the ground. Two sharp punches to Witton's head were enough to knock him out. Dan leapt up and looked for Cassie. He should have warned her. He should have said more about the dangers.

The field was eerily empty. No sign of Cassie or Witton's accomplice. He glanced at where the quad bike was parked, beyond the line of trees, its engine on. Were they over there?

Then he heard shouts from the other direction. Dan ran, aiming for the noise. It was coming from a clump of trees, which made an island in the vast field. He found Cassie on the far side. She was limping toward him, clutching her arm, yelling at herself now, 'Damn, damn, damn.'

'You okay?' he said.

'You *knew* this would happen.' She glared at him.

'It's early. I thought we'd be safe. One of them's—I managed to knock him out.'

'Where is he?'

'This way,' Dan said, heading along the path he had trodden through the wheat.

The man was still unconscious. Cassie checked his breathing.

'Neil Witton,' Dan said. 'Him and Ryan Taylor were at school together. Witton works at Holmewood Stud. Remember me saying they hired Ryan? He must have seen or done something that got him killed.'

'*Satisfied?*' Cassie said.

'How d'you mean?'

'Solving the case all on your own? Making the police look like morons?'

He frowned. 'That's not... I need to find Strang.'

Cassie did not reply, and he left her securing Witton's wrists with a belt.

Dan ran toward the quad bike. No one there, just an empty rope. He turned the engine off, then shouted, 'John. Can you hear me?'

Silence. The rope was frayed. Either worn through or cut with a blunt knife.

'It's me. Dan,' he called. 'From the reservoir.'

No response, just wind stirring the trees. He thought about the cross-country route from Holmewood Stud, the one his mind suspected from the map.

'You okay? Speak to me.'

Holmewood was north of the A11, but a tunnel for farm vehicles went under the dual carriageway. Leading to fields on the south side, then woodland, and an unsupervised level crossing over the trainline, with manual gates.

'John?' Dan ran along, scanning right and left. 'Answer me, please.'

For most of its journey, the quad bike would have been on forestry or agricultural land. The secret route Witton used when dumping Ryan's body at the solar farm. Being used again tonight, but this time for John Strang.

'Where are you? Are you hurt?'

Dan strained to see, hearing his panting breath, his pounding feet as he zigzagged this way and that, searching. Shapes and shadows, clefts and hummocks, but no human form. The light was beginning to darken, the strange blueness to the sky becoming more opaque. Dan stopped. Cassie would be wondering where he was. Walking back, he saw her on the phone. The call ended.

'They'll be here in ten minutes,' she said, scowling. 'Ambulance too.'

Cassie had put Witton into the recovery position. Still unconscious.

'No sign of John Strang,' he said. 'I think the rope broke. He was being dragged behind the quad bike.'

'What is this, the Middle Ages? *Jesus*. I *hate* the countryside.'

'I should probably stay,' Dan said. 'Until they get here.'

'What – were you hoping to run away? Pretend this never happened? Yeah, right. Witton saw you. Even with a concussion he's likely to remember. Christ.'

'I'm sorry. I should have said more. Earlier.'

Cassie glared at him. 'I won't forgive you for this.'

'I know.'

'You'll get to play your grieving nutter card and I'll have to live with a permanent stain on my record. There isn't any conceivable angle from which this can be viewed as professional conduct.'

'You caught the man who murdered Ryan Taylor.'

'It's only your pet theory that Neil Witton's the killer. Who knows if forensics will support this? And even if it does turn out to be him, let's not forget I apprehended the man when off-duty and without calling for backup. Accompanied by a disgraced former officer who managed to assault Witton while I was allowing the other perp to escape. It's a shit sandwich, whichever way you try and chew on it.'

Dan did not speak.

Cassie shook her head. 'You're a walking disaster area. Everyone said I should steer clear of you. Why didn't I bloody listen? You messed this up from the start and now you've dragged me into it too.' She was almost spitting. 'You might have nothing to lose but I do.'

'I'm worried about Strang,' he said.

'You've no idea what it's cost me to get to where I am. Not a clue. You're supposed to be my pal, yeah? But you've screwed me over and ruined my reputation. Because hey, reputation means bugger all to you, so why should I care about mine?'

He tried to touch her shoulder, but she thrust him away.

'I know how difficult—' Dan swallowed his words. How could he presume to know what it was like for Cassie? But he did know she had every right to be angry. 'Me saying sorry won't change anything. But I am sorry.'

Cassie was breathing hard.

After a moment, he said, 'Strang could be injured. Possibly dead. I need to keep—'

'Don't you dare. I'm telling you this as a DI not as your so-called *friend*. You're staying here. You're a witness in a murder enquiry. You're not the freelance fucking cavalry.'

'He could be seriously hurt,' Dan said.

'Do I look like a give a shit right now? Do I?'

'But—'

'You move one inch and I'll charge you with obstruction.'

Chapter 31

At Wymondham, Dan was shown to a cell and told they would be back for him later. The door was left open. The blue vinyl mattress smelled of antibacterial wipes. Dan lay there, worrying if Strang was alive, if he had been found. His mind replayed the statement he gave DC Sullivan.

John Strang was a resident at Summerlands Holiday Park. It is my belief that he either saw the murder of Ryan Taylor or he saw the body being disposed of at the solar farm. Strang then went into hiding and was living in a ruined icehouse as well as the local woods. The murder suspect has been searching for him ever since.

'I wanted to persuade Strang to come forward as a witness. DI Fisher accompanied me as she was concerned for my welfare. She has given me a great deal of support following the death of my fiancee. It was extremely fortunate that DI Fisher was with me when the attack happened.'

The less said, the less unbelievable it all seemed. Dan had tried to minimise the damage to Cassie. He turned over on the mattress, his clothes and skin brushing against the vinyl, the sound amplified in the small space.

The ambulance crew had spent ten minutes treating Neil Witton, before lifting him onto a stretcher. Dan had watched from a distance. The man had regained consciousness, and he gave Dan a vicious look. Then he was taken away, handcuffed to the stretcher and accompanied by Cassie. The ambulance had driven off, with her and Witton.

Dan knew she was angry. Pointedly ignoring him at the scene, and no attempt to speak to him here at HQ. He hunched his shoulders. Tiled walls robbed any heat and the air-conditioning made it even colder. No chance of sleep, but then he woke to the sound of someone saying, 'Rise and shine.'

The young recruit had a sarcastic smile on his face. Dan recognised the how-the-mighty-have-fallen attitude meted out to local celebrities who wound up in custody. Dan was not famous, but he had acquired notoriety. Maybe he should leave Norfolk – Cassie would be relieved to see him go. The house was on the market, Dan had no proper job, and there was nothing keeping him here.

Except for Beth.

Once again, he found himself thinking about John Strang. The man knew a killer was hunting for him. And yet he remained in the area, putting his life at risk. Why?

Someone tugged his arm.

'Sorry,' Dan said, glancing at the freshly shaved face.

'I was asking,' the PC said, enunciating each word, 'if you wanted a coffee.'

'Thanks. Black, no sugar. And I'm due a meal from the canteen. A bacon roll will ensure I'm in a fit state.'

Dan was taken to one of the interview suites. The PC returned with the food and coffee, which he almost threw onto the table, and then Dan was left alone. Once he had finished eating, Sullivan entered the room. Maybe she had been watching through the one-way mirror.

Sullivan took a seat opposite. Dan sensed a change in her manner. Earlier, when questioning him at the scene, she had seemed excited that the investigation had reached such a dramatic climax. Now, eight hours later, Sullivan was regarding him with the suspicion and mistrust that tainted their first encounter at Earlham Road.

'Will you be taping this?' he said.

'You aren't under caution or facing charges. This interview is intended to clarify the events of last night. I'll then ask you to add to your statement. Is all of that clear, Mr Hennessy?'

'Crystal,' he said. 'Seeing as it isn't being taped – tell me, is Cassie okay?'

Sullivan had her back to the one-way mirror. She met Dan's gaze then flicked her eyes to the left, mouthing what could have been *stop*.

They were being observed. Sullivan was trying to protect Cassie. Prevent Dan's 'potentially problematic friendship' from doing further harm to DI Fisher. Dan decided he might like Sullivan after all.

'Have you found Strang?' he said.

Sullivan sneered, and they were back on opposite sides.

'No sign of this John Strang,' she said. 'Your mystery man who's supposedly hiding in the woods. The search is still underway, but the big question is whether they'll find him or the carcass of a deer. According to Neil Witton, the person whose skull you nearly fractured, him and a friend were poaching. Collecting game from illegal traps. Naturally they were not pleased to encounter anyone, let alone a police officer. Hence why they reacted the way they did. Witton claims he wasn't thinking straight. He's now full of remorse for his actions. He has yet to name his accomplice. The concussion you gave him has caused partial loss of memory. According to his solicitor.'

Dan smiled and shook his head. There was no point in saying another word. Maybe Strang would be found alive. Maybe Neil Witton's DNA would connect him to the murder of Ryan Taylor. It was beyond his powers to turn this around.

'You've already got my statement,' Dan said. 'I have nothing further to add.'

Sullivan frowned. 'But you've not heard my questions yet.'

'I have nothing further to add.'

Shielding his eyes from the sunlight, Dan headed for his Volvo. Thankful that last night he was allowed to drive himself to Wymondham. The dashboard clock said 11.06. He checked his phone. Monday. A message had come from Hari, saying Mrs Bailey had moved her visit to Thursday, which was just as well. Dan could not have managed his 10 a.m. pickup from

Hargham Road. The place where he saw Ryan Taylor delivering papers, all those weeks ago. A dead man nobody seemed to miss. Dan would attend the funeral. Everyone deserved to be mourned, even by a stranger.

Returning via Flaxton, he stopped near the castle ruins. Dan wanted to speak to Beth, but not now, as any conversation would be clouded by what he read on the Nokia. She had not been having an affair with an old boyfriend – Cassie was wrong. But Beth had been keeping a secret. Dan needed to think it through. He was not yet ready to face what that secret said about the two of them. What it revealed about him.

The beat of his heart felt slow and heavy. He started the car and drove to the area of last night's incident. Dan parked on the verge and lowered his window, blinking at the glare that bounced off the scorched earth. No signs of activity in the far distance. The search for John Strang had been called off. If a dead or injured man had been found, then vehicles and CSIs would be there, but the fields were empty.

Nor could Dan see the quad bike. Impounded? Or staff from Holmewood had come to claim it. Mrs Schneider would erect a wall between the stud farm and Neil Witton. Poaching might be her current concern, but Witton would be charged with the murder of Ryan Taylor back in June. Provided the police bothered to investigate. Dan squeezed the steering wheel.

What could happen at a stables to get someone killed – race fixing? Or did Ryan's death stem from a more primitive motive? Love. Hate. Jealousy. Neil Witton had been angry. Incensed enough to bludgeon Ryan, his former classmate, and take an axe to the body.

Dan wondered who was with Witton last night. His boss Tony Foster? Events at Holmewood had led to Ryan Taylor's murder and the attempted murder of John Strang. Dan was certain Foster made the key decisions. Who to kill. How to cover it up.

But John Strang had outwitted them all. He managed to escape Witton and Foster. The rope broke or Strang cut through it. He had also evaded the police, who were not even trying to find him. According to Dan's former colleagues, Strang was a product of Hennessy's imagination.

He scanned the fields, east to west. Yes, Strang was still out there. Something or someone was keeping him here. The man could not, would not, leave.

Mirages shimmered like black pools on the road, as Dan continued toward Summerlands. The inside of his caravan was sweltering. He drank a pint of water, made a stack of cheese sandwiches, ate some and wrapped the rest in foil. Then he headed for the barn, to fetch the items from Strang's caravan. Only two weeks since Dan emptied the place. It felt like last year. He peered into the bag, chest constricting at the sight of the soft knitted cardigan and bootees, the tiny hat. His thoughts went to Mrs Faulkner. Missing children. Babies who were mourned and never found.

Dan wanted to prove to Strang that he did care. His best way of doing that was to return the baby clothes. The man might talk to him then. Reveal his secrets. Dan set off for the woods, hoping to catch him there. Mad ideas were firing in his head as the sun beat down from above.

Was Strang in fact Felix? But Felix would be twenty-one. Strang was older.

Was Strang the abductor? Or was his baby taken by the same person who took Felix? That made no sense. Surely Strang would have spoken to Mrs Faulkner about this, but they barely had any dealings. She talked of him deliberately avoiding her.

Frowning, Dan strode along the path. The ground was baked hard, and the soles of his feet hurt, still sore from the other night. Glancing up, he saw the edge of the woods, a dark green barrier, fending off the heat. Dan left the food parcel and baby clothes in the usual spot. Then he entered the woods and called Strang's name. Telling the man he was still in danger. One of his attackers was in custody, the other had escaped and would be looking for him. Dan wanted to mention the baby clothes, but the trees stood mute, and the words died in his throat.

The walk back made him sweat, T-shirt sticking to his skin. On Primrose Drive, Dan saw Mrs Faulkner talking to a resident. The discussion ended and she continued down the gravel track. Slightly stooped, like she was in pain.

'Everything okay?' he said.

Mrs Faulkner stopped in the shade of the laundry room. 'Some people are never happy.'

Dan did not respond.

'The weapon they try and wield,' she said, 'is that they'll post a bad review. My 4.65 rating is unlikely to do a nosedive due to him complaining there's no air conditioner and he was too hot to sleep.' Mrs Faulkner winced. 'Thankfully I'm due another dose of codeine.'

'Are you...? If it's a health issue, I don't mean to pry.'

'I had a mastectomy last week.'

'Sorry,' he said, blinking. 'I didn't realise. I hope the operation went well.'

'They say I'm one of the lucky ones. That they caught it in time and I should make a full recovery. I tried not to laugh in their faces.'

Dan stared at his feet. 'Are you telling me this never ends?'

'A loss is always a loss. What did you expect?'

'That it might become easier to bear.'

'Good luck, I really mean it. Some people manage to recover. The alternative – not getting over it – is hard. But that implies an element of choice.' She shook her head. 'Grief doesn't let you choose.'

'You don't know for sure Felix is dead.'

'Oh, Daniel, if only. If only that were true. What I would give for that. For my son to still be alive.'

He felt the longing radiate from her skin, like a conflagration. Then Mrs Faulkner stiffened, as if extinguishing the fire.

'But you still have hope,' he said.

'Hope.' She swallowed. 'The only hope left is that something will make a difference. Bring me some relief. I keep telling myself it must be because Felix is not at peace. And maybe there's something that needs to be settled first.'

Dan thought about Beth. Was she happy now he knew her secret?

'The endless search for a moment's relief.' Mrs Faulkner sighed. 'It's exhausting.'

He could feel himself swaying as her words continued to batter him.

'You invent things that will *help*,' she said. 'You erect a marble memorial with his name on it. There was no grave, no burial, but his passing did happen. And Felix needs somewhere to be. Somewhere that's *his* in a world that made him leave too soon. You keep coming up with new ideas. If I do this, we'll both be at peace. None of it makes a difference. Nothing can.'

Dan brushed a tear from his face.

'Forgive me,' Mrs Faulkner said. 'I think I've reached the stage in life where I'm tired of saying the answers other people want to hear. Perhaps I need a lie-down as well as some pills.'

He watched her slowly walk away, toward her bungalow.

Jay was crouched next to her father. He was seated on a canvas chair in front of the garage, both of them peering at the Haynes manual in his lap. To their left, oily parts were arranged on a blue tarpaulin. Today's temperature was predicted to reach forty degrees, but there was shade here, beneath the trees. It had seemed a good idea to service the Virago. Her father was confident they could manage.

'See?' he said, pointing at the diagram. 'That comes off next.'

Her phone rang and she glanced at the screen.

'Maybe it's work,' her father said.

Jay frowned. The ID on the screen was Detective Dan.

'I'll clean the air filter,' her father said, heading inside the garage.

She stood up, answering the phone with a 'Yup.'

'Hi, it's Dan here. Dan Hennessy?'

'Look,' she said, 'can I call you back?'

'This won't take long.'

Jay peered through the open door of the garage. Her father was next to the workbench.

The detective was speaking again, saying, 'Please? A few minutes, that's all.'

'I'm in the middle of something,' she said, assessing the array of components that surrounded her. Metal parts, with bulges, shafts, teeth, polished planes, fins, deliberately shaped but incomprehensible. The logic had all been in her head of how the pieces related, but it seemed to vanish when she saw the detective's name on her screen. She nudged a chrome capping with her toe. Further apologies were issuing from the phone, then he mentioned something about the children.

Jay squinted at the sun. 'Did you say *eating*?'

'Maybe. Look, I'm still hoping to get to the bottom of what happened. So the baby's mother can... Sorry, I've caught you at a bad time.'

Jay left a silence.

The detective cleared his throat. 'I was thinking again about what your father told the police. In his original statement. He described the boy and girl as having a picnic. I don't suppose he's said anything to you about a picnic? I was trying to link that to the business with the tea towels.'

'I'd have rung you,' she said, 'if there was anything new to report.'

'Apologies, I just thought you might have been able to...'

His voice tailed off.

Jay knelt and peered at the Haynes manual. What was this phonecall really about? Detective Dan seemed at a loss.

'Bye,' she said, cutting the connection.

Chapter 32

Dan shook his head. Took a deep breath, but the air in the caravan was hot and stale. His conversation with Jay had been excruciating. Had he forgotten how to talk to people? Always wanting something from them. Answers to questions. Acting like police, even in his personal life. And in that hateful moment, unfurling, Dan recalled the secret, hidden on Beth's phone – the news she chose not to share. That she had managed to find her birth father. They had been messaging each other for months. Beth had met up with him three weeks before she died.

There was sweat on his palms. Dan rubbed them dry and stared out the window. He always thought of himself as a forgiving person. Full of understanding and compassion. He had been 'one of the good guys' in the police. They called him the social worker. And yet Beth had seen a different Dan, someone who made judgements and divided the world into innocence and guilt.

I'm waiting for the right moment to tell him, one of her texts said. *Dan's so lovely and I'm sure you and him will get along great. But his job means he's always being exposed to the worst in people. He doesn't always realise it's possible to do a bad thing but not be a bad person. I want him to see the good in you! Which he will. Lots love B xxxx*

Her birth father had been living in Durham for the past five years. Prior to that, the man had been in prison. Piecing together references in the messages, it appeared he had served an eleven-year sentence for GBH. His name was Paul Harbison. Beth was the one to initiate contact.

Dan had a sudden recollection of the argument he had with Beth, in the pub garden in Spooner Row. What he said to her that evening about tracing her birth parents. *They clearly didn't want to be a part of your life, so why bother? It will only upset you.* Dan had always liked home to be a calm place. Somewhere to retreat to after a day dealing with 'the worst in people'. Beth's long-lost father would have upset the balance. And then the ex-father turned out to be an ex-con. No wonder she never said anything.

On the day Beth died, she was not on her way to meet the man. She had been on Magdalen Street for some other reason. Paul Harbison was three hundred miles away when it happened. Beth's secret was not the cause of her death. But a different truth now weighed on Dan, cold and unpleasant. Although he had hoped to support Beth in every aspect of her life, she had not felt able to speak to him about this. Beth was waiting for the right moment, but it never came.

Dan stared at his left hand, the grief hand, Mrs Faulkner's voice in his head. *A loss is always a loss. What did you expect?*

'I'm sorry, Beth,' he said. 'I'm so sorry I made it difficult for you to talk about your dad. That was my fault. All mine.'

In saying it out loud, Dan felt the beginnings of relief. Given the chance, she would have told him. And he would have been okay with the news. Better than okay, because he was doing it for Beth. Dan would have done the right thing. He had always tried to do the right thing – knowing this gave him comfort.

Then his thoughts turned to Mrs Faulkner. How for her, there was no release. *None of it makes a difference. Nothing can.* For twenty-one years, nobody had been able to say what happened to Felix. Dan hauled himself off the seat, tiredness catching up with him after last night. He fetched a jug of water from the fridge, reached down a jar of instant. Made himself a chilled coffee.

It had been an act of desperation to ring Jay. But why had Olsen referred to 'a picnic' in his statement – was this the fault of the officer who interviewed him? The story had been shaped into something that made more sense than a game involving tea towels. Which the children wrapped round their faces. Praying. Dan was reminded of the nativity play at his primary school.

He was Joseph. His costume had been a dressing gown and a tea towel, tied to his head with a length of shiny braid. A girl in his class was Mary. A balloon under her dress, which was removed between scenes and a doll brought on stage. A plastic baby Jesus.

Jack and Emily had been playing with tea towels on their heads. Was Felix 'borrowed' to make a nativity game more real? But it was summer not Christmas.

Dan stood by the sink and stirred his coffee, watching the black liquid swirl around his spoon. The river. Significant not incidental. Jack and Emily were playing by the water, but this was not the first time. Dan knew, from their statements, that Lydia and Catherine spent many afternoons together, leaving the children free to roam the outdoors. And, of course, Jack and Emily were drawn to the river as that was forbidden. But on this particular Wednesday there was a crucial difference. Alice Faulkner had been a guest, and for much of the afternoon her baby son was asleep on the terrace, supposedly being watched by Lydia.

His phone beeped. Jay had sent a voicemail. Dan stared at the notification, nervous of what she might say – that he was a nuisance and to stop calling? He pressed the arrow to play her message.

'Okay, so... Maybe I should start by saying *Hi, it's Jay here*. And I would like to help if I can. Because I know all you're trying to do is help the woman who lost her baby. So I had another go at talking to my father. I told him what you said about the boy and girl having a picnic. I mean he hasn't mentioned a picnic when we've talked about this before. So I told him that apparently he said to the police he saw the children having a picnic that day. And I asked, could he remember anything more. And he said *Lunch was in the water* –

Dan heard her pause.

– 'so I'm thinking, *typical Dad*. Another of his cryptic utterances. Anyway, I asked what he meant. I mean you never know with him. And he said he saw a picnic basket in the reeds. In the marshy bit at the edge of the river. I don't know if any of this is useful, but you said—well, you wanted to know... Maybe this was all in his witness statement and is nothing new. But I thought I'd better call you in case. I'm going to go now' – her voice pulled away, as if she had lowered the phone – 'me and Dad are in the middle of a big project. Bye, then.'

Frowning, Dan locked onto something Jay had just said, *basket in the reeds*. The sudden significance made his body jerk. *Moses in a basket*. Not the nativity – Jack and Emily had been playing a different bible game. Dan raced to assemble the pieces, the story learned in Sunday School. Exodus? The pharaoh gave orders to kill every Hebrew male baby. Moses was put in a basket by his mother, then hidden on the banks of the Nile.

Dan knew with a brutal clarity what happened to Mrs Faulkner's son.

Felix had been Moses that day. Left among the reeds while Jack and Emily got on with their game. The two of them running about as they pretended to flee the pharaoh. The baby had been forgotten, the wake of a boat then nudging the basket from the reeds, water seeping through the wickerwork. The basket now sinking below the surface, carried by slow drifts, bumping across the muddy floor of the inlet, and out into the main thrust of the river.

Felix Faulkner drowned. Dan sat down, his mouth trembling.

DI Drummond had not suspected Jack and Emily of being involved, but he had known the Waveney posed a danger. Police conducted a search of the banks, and divers were deployed. Dan had seen reports on file confirming that the weirs and sluice gates were checked. The baby was so small, hard to find in a large mass of water that was constantly moving, tumbling that precious cargo in its currents, to be deposited many miles distant, and absorbed in the silty depths of the riverbed.

That afternoon, when Olsen saw Jack and Emily by the water, it was possible Felix was still alive. Dan gripped the table. The witness had no idea. Why would anyone think that a six-week-old baby was in that basket about to drown? Olsen glanced across, took in a few details of what the two children were doing – the tea-towel game, a picnic basket nestled in the reeds – all seemingly harmless, and he continued along the path.

Jack and Emily carried on playing. Then came the realisation that Felix had gone. The horror of it. No sign anywhere of the baby or basket. The two children hunting for Felix but finding vacant reeds and empty water. Their panicked desperation – how long did the search last before they ran up the garden and into the house? Claiming that a man stole Felix from his pram. Or did an adult invent this? When Lydia went to the downstairs toilet, she could have encountered Jack and Emily. And heard about the baby vanishing in the river. But instead of raising the alarm, Lydia coached them on the story about an intruder. Corroborating it with her own testimony of a dark figure passing the window.

Life has to go on, you know. I can't bring her baby back. Lydia had been wrong to think that hiding the truth would prevent further harm. Emily Nash died in her first year at university. A warm evening, she was sitting on the sill of a third-floor window. Dan had tracked down an article online, with details from the inquest. An accident, but he could read between the lines. Emily killed herself. And what about Jack? He too had been affected, though Lydia had avoided giving much away. *Poor boy took the divorce very badly.* But it was not the divorce that damaged him.

Dan stared out the window, as a further truth emerged, flushing his skin. *Him.* The same person. Jack Ingleby was John Strang. The man sleeping in the icehouse, hiding in the woods, swimming in the reservoir – it had been Jack all along. He had shed the childhood nickname and changed his surname. He had come looking for Mrs Faulkner, tracing her to the caravan park.

John Strang had stayed at Summerlands, wanting to make amends, not finding the right moment. Then in mid June, maybe on a late-night walk, Strang witnessed Neil Witton disposing of Ryan Taylor's body. A violent event that derailed an already disturbed mind. And even though Witton then began hunting for Strang – intent on killing him – Strang had remained in the area. Still hoping to approach Mrs Faulkner.

Dan's heart was beating fast, his body gripped by the certainty that, after all this time, he had found the answer. Jack and Emily with their 'innocent' decision that Felix could be part of the game. Whose idea? However it came about, they were branded with the guilt. Emily was dead. Jack was alive but suffering.

Mrs Faulkner needed to be told what they did that day. How she lost her son.

Dan shut the caravan door and set off toward reception. The hot air pressed on his skin, almost pushing him back. In the distance, he caught sight of her leaving the bungalow. Mrs Faulkner was making for the entrance to Summerlands. Dan followed, consumed by what he was about to tell her.

There was a man in a green polo shirt near the main gates. Mrs Faulkner was meeting a delivery. Shrubs had been unloaded from a flatbed truck, and she was pointing at a document. Dan waited, struggling to contain himself. He could not hear what was being said, but Mrs Faulkner was clearly annoyed. The man picked up the shrubs, loaded them into his truck, and drove off, tyres screeching.

A cloud of dust hung above the gravel, then drifted away. Mrs Faulkner glared at Dan. Her face was a mixture of pleasure and wrath. The sun honed her edges, metal not flesh. And in that moment Dan could not bring himself to do it. He could not summon the words to tell her what happened to Felix. He could not help her. He could not save her son. He could not make anything better.

None of it makes a difference. Nothing can.

But he could help Jack. He could help the boy who grew up to be John Strang. Dan took a last look at Mrs Faulkner, the fierceness of her closely guarded grief, and he turned away, heading for the woods.

Dan could feel intense sunlight on his back as he stared at the ground. The food was still there, the foil parcel undisturbed, but the plastic bag had gone. Proof that Strang was alive – he had taken the baby clothes. Dan smiled, certain that the man was grateful for their return. Certain too that he viewed Dan as an ally.

'John, are you there?'

The sky was hot and heavy. No creatures stirred, no birdsong. Moving from glare into green shadows, eyes blinking, Dan entered the woods. It was a few hours since he was last here. The temperature had risen, releasing fecund smells into the air trapped beneath the canopy. Dan glanced up, seeing the tightly entwined branches, lush with leaves. He called Strang's name but got no response. After a futile circuit of the trees, Dan aimed for the reservoir. He would check there next, then walk back to Summerlands via the icehouse. Strang might lie low for most of the day. More chance of finding him this evening.

His thoughts went to Mrs Faulkner. Dan could not hide from her forever. He had to tell her Felix was dead. He had to tell her that Jack wanted forgiveness. Mrs Faulkner was a fortress, unassailable. Dan cowered at the idea of speaking those words and having them rain down like broken arrows.

Ahead of him, the reservoir embankments were thrust into the landscape. Dan grasped the wooden post, and hauled himself over the fence, registering exhaustion. Legs heavy, he climbed the slope, the grass singed to an orange yellow. Punishing heat rose from the ground and fell from the sky, making him dizzy. On reaching the top, Dan looked at the water. How still it was. Not a breath stirred the surface. To the east he could see the ruined church tower. No sound of birds. No sounds of anything, not even the faint drone of a car on a distant road.

Dan glanced again at the reservoir. That was when he saw it, something floating. Like a black bin bag, about thirty metres from the edge. He ran down the slope and plunged in, arms and legs thrashing the cold water as he swam toward the shape in the middle. Dan knew, with a sick dread, it was Strang.

The man was face down, limbs and head drooping. Dan grabbed an arm, attempted to turn him, wrestling with the water. Strang's fish-like face swung upward, seeming to stare through closed eyelids, then he rolled onto his back.

Dan hooked a hand under the chin and swam for shore, moving backward through the water, Strang's body almost on top. He could barely think, so caught up in the struggle of this lopsided swim, the worry that Strang might sink them both, they were making no headway, dry land would never come, the next gulp of water would drown him. And pulsing through it all was the fear that he was too late, the man was dead.

His stabbing feet found the rubber lining of the reservoir and he dragged Strang out of the water. Dan tilted him to the side, a trickle emerging from slack lips. Then he began mouth to mouth resuscitation. When Dan first joined the police, he had decided not to keep a tally of how often this failed to bring the dead back to life. There had to be hope, each time. There had to be a chance.

Dan blew air into the cold mouth, the kiss of life, and he pumped his fists on the man's chest, one, two, three, four, and repeat. On and on. Racing through his head were the miracle stories of people who had been revived after being submerged for ten minutes or more, because the freezing water put their body into stasis, and more importantly their mind, the very slow beat of a chilled heart just enough to keep the brain from dying. The reservoir had been cold, he must not give up. Strang was still in there. A glimmer of the man was still alive.

How long did Dan continue? He had no idea. Five minutes. Ten. Until his own lungs were raw and the thought came to him that this act of resuscitation had become an abuse. The final degradation of a man who was dead. Strang had walked into the reservoir and he had swum to the depths and drowned himself. Dan recalled the stone trough in the icehouse, full of water. A flooded tomb. Strang had been preparing for death, readying himself over a period of weeks and months.

Dan fell on his side and sobbed. His muscles ached from the long effort of trying to revive Strang, all these signs in his own body an insistent reminder that he was alive and what lay next to him was not. For it all to end, for all the memories, all the years, all the breaths indrawn, all those blinks of the eye, all the sights and visions, all those tastes on the tongue, all the feel and touch in the fingers and skin, and the wealth of thoughts, the wonder of all those ideas, the profundity of what the mind was capable of, for that all to be gone. For it to end in the starving of breath underwater or the trauma of a skull cracking against a kerb. For it to narrow to a single moment between being Beth and being her dead body left behind. Dan could not bear it. He could not. Could not. Could not.

Numbed, Dan stood up. Aware of things that needed to be done. He picked up rocks from the reservoir edge – choosing the smaller ones – and carried them down to Strang. Shivering in wet clothes, Dan knelt on the black rubber, not feeling any warmth from the sun. As he pushed a rock into the man's pocket, his fingers met the sodden touch of something. Dan pulled it out. A tiny knitted cardigan, drenched in water.

There were five items in Strang's pockets. The contents of the bag Dan left by the woods, a few hours ago. He laid them on the ground next to the man's body. These were not what Felix was wearing when he died. Maybe Strang bought them from a charity shop and they became, in his mind, the real thing. Dan put them back in the pockets and lodged them there with rocks, scraping his knuckles on the granite. Strang had wanted these precious items. Unaware they were in the west barn, he had searched Dan's caravan. Dan then brought the baby clothes to the woods.

Strang found them. And drowned himself.

Please say it's not my fault. Dan whispered these words as he stroked Strang's arm. The sun's heat made him seem alive. Dan thought about the nine-year-old boy. Lydia left her stepson to suffer, rather than admit the truth. Was Catherine part of it? What did those women say to Jack and Emily. *You didn't mean it to happen, so let's all pretend it didn't. The baby's gone because a man took him. A scary man stole the baby.*

Dan pulled Strang gently toward the water and he walked into the reservoir, the body already sinking away from his grip, dragged down by the heavy rocks. Dan kept going until the water was at his neck and then he swam forth, kicking out with his legs, gulping at air, all the while maintaining a tight hold on the man's jacket. Then they were both underwater and Strang was leading him down into the comfort of nothingness.

How easy it would be to die. Dan felt an almost ecstasy at the proximity of his own death, the blessed relief of it all ending. He dived with Strang into the deeper depths, his lungs screaming at him but his limbs still making the descent, the water blackening now, his vision becoming indistinct, his body so cold he could no longer feel. His frozen fingers unclenched, releasing Strang. He watched him sink, grow murky, and then Dan turned and thrust for the surface, the blurry brightness far above.

Chapter 33

In the shower, Dan took a long time to rid himself of the reservoir smell. He dressed in sombre clothes and combed his hair.

Mrs Faulkner was behind the reception desk.

'We need to talk,' he said.

'Good to see you've smartened yourself up.' She laughed. 'You almost look half decent.'

Dan frowned. She seemed on edge.

'We may be a while,' he said. 'Perhaps Samantha can take over on reception.'

Mrs Faulkner straightened a pile of leaflets. 'Right. Of course. Whatever you say.'

He waited for her to make a brief phonecall.

'Let me,' Dan said, holding open the door as they headed outside. Aware she was still in pain, following her operation. The two of them walked to the bungalow in silence. Dan felt heavy, like he might crush the earth.

Mrs Faulkner showed him into the living room, saying, 'This weather is so dehydrating – I'll fetch some water.'

'Would you like me to?'

'No, no, have a seat. I can carry small items.'

Bright sunlight angled through the bay window. Dan sat down, glanced at the ceramic figure on the mantlepiece. A mother with no child. Stolen, gone, dead.

A minute later, Mrs Faulkner reappeared with two glasses. Kneeling with a certain awkwardness, she placed them on coasters on a low table. Then she shut the living room door and turned to face him. Dan felt the finality of what he was about to do. The killing of hope. The confirmation that Felix drowned, his remains long dispersed. A scattering of tiny bones on the riverbed.

'So, Daniel,' she said, sitting in the chair opposite, arranging herself carefully. 'What is it you wanted?'

'I'm afraid it's about your son.'

'Ah.' Mrs Faulkner closed her mouth, nodding slowly.

'I know what happened to him.'

Anger flashed in her eyes, then she looked away.

'You asked me to find out?' Dan said.

'I did.' An odd expression on her face. As if she was trying to appear grateful but had forgotten how.

'Do you... would you like me to tell you the results of my investigation?'

'Go ahead.'

He watched her tuck a strand of hair behind an ear. Fingers shaking.

'I can only imagine,' he said, 'how hard this must be for you. After so many years in the dark.'

Mrs Faulkner was staring at him intently. Hands clasped in her lap but feet pointing at the door. Forcing herself to stay and listen.

Dan said, 'I'm sorry. So very sorry.' He heard his voice describe the drowning of Felix Faulkner and subsequent coverup. It was the police officer in him, summoning and ordering the details. Not able to look at her face while he did so. Adding that his facts were mostly suppositions, although he felt certain, if further enquiries were made, his account would prove correct. Dan avoided telling Mrs Faulkner that the boy Jack had, as an adult, tracked her down. He wanted to establish the events of 2001 before he talked about John Strang.

'A tragic accident,' Dan said, sickened by the banality but also the accuracy of those words. 'I don't think the children meant to drown him. If the truth had come out, instead of all those lies about an abduction, then maybe...'

He stared at the glass of water. So thirsty but unable to touch it.

'Maybe what?' she said after a pause. It was like hearing a stone goddess.

'I was going to say maybe it would have been better for everyone concerned.'

Mrs Faulkner smiled, and again Dan had the impression she was an ancient deity that people had neglected to worship, and who was here to wreak the most terrible vengeance.

Then the realisation struck him. 'You already know all this, don't you?'

'Jack was wearing a plain navy T-shirt when I arrived that day. Later, after the police came, I noticed there was a pocket on the front. It was not the same T-shirt. But the trouble with being female is we get labelled as hysterical. The police didn't listen. They told me I was overwrought. In shock. They didn't trust a word I said. I began to doubt myself. It's hard. To be raised in a world where you are taught, from day one, to doubt yourself. Because the men *always* know best.'

Wet clothes that had to be changed. Did Jack put the wicker basket in the water? Or had he tried to save Felix. It was beyond knowing.

Mrs Faulkner seemed so defiant.

Dan gave her a long look, then shook his head. Sad and disappointed. She was human after all. 'He came to see you.'

'Who?'

'Please don't lie to me, Mrs Faulkner.'

'The curious thing is, I am unable to accept these explanations about Felix. They simply won't enter my body.'

'I'm sorry,' Dan said, 'I really am. But you need to—'

Mrs Faulkner thrust her palm toward him, a gesture that made her wince in pain. 'I decide what I *need* to do. Not you.'

'He was here, wasn't he. John Strang. *Jack.* He came to see you and confessed what he did.'

'I'm not a priest. And confession would hardly describe what he said to me.'

'He's dead,' Dan said. 'After he left here, he killed himself.'

Her hand came up, then she put it back in her lap.

'What did you say to him, Mrs Faulkner?'

Her mouth smiled. 'Nothing about suicide, that's for sure.'

She looked at the chair next to Dan. The conversation had happened in this room. Earlier, when he saw her leaving the bungalow, it must have been just after she spoke to Strang. Dan had missed him by a matter of minutes. Strang went off to kill himself and Mrs Faulkner had continued with her day. Rejecting a delivery of shrubs.

Dan wanted to weep.

Mrs Faulkner was peering at the walls, the ceiling. 'Do you know, I think I might redecorate.' Then her gaze landed again on the empty chair. 'He said *the happiest times in my life are underwater, holding my breath until my lungs burst*.'

She had put on a sing-song voice to imitate Strang, and it sickened Dan.

'That man,' she said, 'had the utter gall to claim he could talk to Felix in his head. *It's where the two of us get to be together*. He had no right to speak to my son. How dare he.'

'It was an accident,' Dan said quietly. 'They were just kids. Playing a game. They didn't think about the consequences. Children don't.'

Mrs Faulkner touched a trembling hand to her mouth.

Dan looked at her. 'What did you say to Strang?'

She blinked several times, then smiled. '*Jack* told me he was very sorry for what he did. And I told him what he'd been waiting to hear all these years. I said, *I forgive you*. There is nothing worse than forgiveness. It digs a deeper hole for the guilt.'

Dan flinched.

'Oh please,' Mrs Faulkner said. 'Spare me the holier-than-thou act.'

'He wasn't mentally stable. You pushed him over the edge.'

'I didn't want him dead,' she said. 'But I am happy he won't be speaking to Felix anymore.'

'The man needed help.'

'You tell me he killed my son. And yet you sit here and make excuses for him?'

'I should leave,' Dan said, standing up.

'Apparently,' Mrs Faulkner said, 'I have you to thank for him coming to see me. You left some baby clothes next to the woods?'

He staggered. Sat down again, heart racing.

Mrs Faulkner grimaced. *Jack* took it as a sign. That the day had finally *dawned* for him to speak to me. His bizarre language, like he was enacting a prophecy. He wanted to give me the clothes. As if those revolting items had anything to do with my beautiful son.'

She was staring at Dan with a fierceness that scorched his skin.

'Would you like to know,' she said, 'what I've learned today? *That my son is still alive.*'

'How?' Dan said, the word drying on his lips. 'How can you possibly think that?'

'Think?' Mrs Faulkner pressed a hand to her heart. Briefly, as if her torso was aflame. 'I *know* he's alive. That man, that twisted man, he showed me something I didn't realise was still there. And I felt it again, just now – like an electric shock – when you were telling me the same story about what happened. The game, the water, the basket, floating away in the current. Felix isn't dead.'

Dan swallowed, unable to speak.

'Don't you understand?' she said. '*He isn't dead*. For all these years I've been hanging onto a last thread of pathetic hope. Now I know why. Felix didn't drown that day. Don't you see, Daniel? He floated away.'

'It's not—' Dan shook his head.

Mrs Faulkner glared at him. 'It's you that's wrong. This is the reason I've not been able to find any peace. Felix is still out there. *He's alive*. I can feel it.'

'Alice,' he said. 'Please.'

'Give up on my son? Is that what you want me to do? Abandon him? Add my name to the long list of people who didn't care, who didn't do enough to find him? Who decided it was time to move on, get a new life, make a fresh start. Like none of it mattered, like Felix didn't matter, like he didn't happen, like I never gave birth. But he did happen. I had a son. I still have a son. I will never give up on Felix. Never, never, nev—' Her chest began to heave.

There was a clean handkerchief in Dan's pocket.

'Here,' he said, passing it to her.

'I know he's alive,' Mrs Faulkner said, her voice thick with tears.

Dan left the room, closing the door. He stood in the dark corridor. Struggling to breathe.

Chapter 34

Not in his own skin, Dan walked to the caravan. Across his vision, tangling with his surroundings, tripping him up, were Strang and Mrs Faulkner. Sad about him, angry at her. All her words, too many of them, trapped in his head, her fury and vengeance and lunatic hope, and then he thought about what that torrent of words did to a vulnerable man. Mrs Faulkner had pushed Strang over the edge, but Dan sent him there by returning the baby clothes. Groaning, fingernails biting into the flesh of his palms. Back when Dan joined the police, he made a declaration to 'faithfully discharge the duties of the Office of Constable'. Where was that person? His actions meant an unreported death, no coroner's inquest, no lawful burial.

Dan let himself into the caravan and lay on the floor. There had been no decision to abide by or break the law. He left John Strang in the reservoir because the man chose that ending. But it was the *wrong* ending. Everything about this was broken. His fist thumped the carpet. So angry at Mrs Faulkner for manipulating Strang. So angry at her for refusing to believe her son was dead. And along with his anger there was childish annoyance, like he was back at school. She had issued him a report card with F for failure. F for Felix, the child he had failed to find. The woman's ludicrous conviction that her son was still alive.

Crawling into bed, Dan pulled the pillow over his head. Angry. Sad. Annoyed. Sad. He slept, woke, felt sad. Drank water and replied to a worried text from Hari. Told him he was not dead and would return to work later in the week. Then Dan slept some more. Ate bread that tasted of mould, fell back into bed, pressing the pillow to his face.

Strang took his own life. Dan's fault. Mrs Faulkner's fault. He went over it again and again, the words spoken, the sequence of events. Mrs Faulkner had forgiven Strang as an act of vengeance. But Dan kept coming back to what she said before that point. Telling him what Strang told her – *the happiest times in my life are underwater, holding my breath until my lungs burst.* Did he kill himself? Or did Strang stay too long in the depths of the reservoir, talking to Felix until he drowned. An accident, not suicide.

Dan slept. Sweated. Stumbled to the sink, drank water, and climbed into bed. A convoluted dream. Then he woke, this time properly. Seeing the interior of the caravan with sudden clarity, the walls, his clothes on the floor, the closed curtains, daylight at the edges, noises from outside. Registering it as reality. His reality. No longer angry or annoyed, those had leached away, into the mattress, the feather pillow. But Dan was still sad. To listen and find it there, that ever-present background hum, was almost reassuring. *Yes, I'm back.*

The cupboards were bare. He walked to the shop on stiff legs, squinting at the bright sky, his stomach hollow. It was midafternoon on Wednesday 20th July. He had been out of commission for forty-eight hours. Samantha was on the till. When Dan was paying for the basket of supplies, she told him sweetly he should consider buying toothpaste. 'Your breath pongs.'

'Always a kind word,' he said, laughing.

On the way back, he caught sight of Mrs Faulkner in her garden. She was speaking to a woman in a paint-spattered boiler suit. It seemed the plans to redecorate were underway. John Strang's presence in her living room would be papered and painted over. As Dan passed by, Mrs Faulkner turned to smile at him. Hope radiated from her face, like she had opened a door and joy was shining forth. And Dan found himself smiling too. His anger at her had gone. What was left in its place? A sense of something unresolved, like they were in a holding pattern. The two of them circling a decision he was yet to know, or afraid to admit.

After eating cold beans straight from the tin, Dan stared at the drawer with mutinous eyes. Inside it was the police file.

Felix was gone. Why could she not accept that? And now her refusal had spread to Dan too, unravelling the conclusions he had reached about her son. It was cruel of Mrs Faulkner to do that to him. He had his own problems to deal with. His own loss.

Dan shed his clothes then stood under a hot shower. Water drummed his skin, all that stale sweat washing down the plughole. Then he cleaned his teeth for several minutes. Trimmed his beard. Drank another pint of water. While he was dressing, his phone beeped. A notification on the screen telling him Cassie had texted. With a wary finger, Dan opened the message, anticipating a tirade about him ruining her career.

See you 8.30 usual place. Hope you're surviving the heatwave x

Dan was first to arrive. The pub seemed unfamiliar, even though it was only a fortnight since he was last here. Their corner was now occupied by a large TV, showing highlights from an athletics competition. He carried two pints to a table by the far wall. At that moment Cassie came through the door, frowned at the TV, then headed his way.

'We may need to find a new venue,' she said.

He had assumed this would be a farewell drink, but Cassie was referring to future meet-ups.

'I can't bear,' she said, 'all that flickering on the edge of my vision. Get enough of it at work.'

'On the plus side, the sound's off. And there's aircon.'

'You seem different.' Cassie scrutinised him. 'And thanks for this.' She swallowed a mouthful of lager then put down the glass, nodding. 'Definitely less depressed.'

Dan laughed. 'I barely spoke.'

'Yeah, but it's the signals you're giving off. And here's some more news that'll bring a smile to your face. You were right about Neil Witton.'

'Was I?' Dan blinked, racing to catch up. He had forgotten Witton. How much had been said about John Strang? The last thing he needed was police dredging the reservoir.

Cassie gave him a quizzical look.

'Sorry,' he said, 'brain's a bit fuzzy. I've been ill the past few days.'

'Hope I'm not going to come away with some awful lurgy.'

'No, no, I'm fine now – you're safe.'

'Glad to hear it,' she said. 'Keep this info to yourself, but Neil Witton's DNA was found on the murder vic.'

'So it was him who killed Ryan Taylor.'

'They were part of a scam involving blackmarket jism at Holmewood Stud.'

Dan frowned. 'What, selling equine sperm?'

'Illegal wanks but very plausible paperwork. Made it seem like the owners of the horses got paid for the semen but then the funds were diverted elsewhere. Worth a shedload, apparently, if the stallion's won a few races.'

'Money,' he said, shaking his head. 'Maybe one day criminals will invent a new motive.'

'Not the sort of racket I'd want to get into, jacking off a horse.'

Dan laughed, still trying to emit the right signals. 'I'm sure there are procedures these days.'

'Whatever,' she said with a smile. 'Our vic Taylor may have been part of this from the start, given he and Witton were at school together. But I doubt it, as I mean the poor bastard was doing a paper round to make ends meet. The more likely scenario is that Taylor got wind of their activities and tried blackmailing them. Or he caught them at it and they killed him.'

'You said *they*. The other guy on the quad bike?'

'I have a fair idea who else is implicated,' she said, 'in the jiz scam and possibly the murder. But I better keep it under wraps for now.'

Cassie was police and Dan was not. Not anymore and never again.

'Of course,' he said. 'I appreciate you telling me what you have.'

'Call it a cack-handed thank you. I'm not sure we'd have found our way to Neil Witton if you hadn't taken me on that Norfolk-style safari.'

'I probably owe an apology to your footwear.'

Cassie laughed, then her expression changed.

'It's your round,' Dan said, 'if that's what you're eyeing me about.'

'That night, when you and me first saw the quad bike... Witton swears it was a deer. I never got a proper look, but you were nearer. Do you still believe there was someone's body on the end of that rope?'

'Must have been a deer.' Dan shrugged. 'I'm not getting much sleep at the moment. The caravan's like an oven.'

Cassie drained the last of her glass and put it down carefully. 'A search was conducted of the area. There was nothing in the reports about a deer carcass.'

'It probably rolled into a ditch,' he said. 'Who knows.'

'Did you ever find your wild man? Strang? The one sleeping at the icehouse?'

Dan looked away. 'It's been a difficult few weeks. Half the time I'm not sure what I was thinking. I mean there was definitely a John Strang who stayed at the caravan park, then bunked off owing a fortnight's rent. But whether he then started living in the woods...' Dan shrugged. 'All I can say for certain is, he's gone now.'

His glass had left a damp ring on the table. Dan placed a beer mat on top, soaking up the wetness. He hated deceiving Cassie. His words had been shaped to avoid outright lies, but this made it worse.

'After what you've been through,' she said, 'it's hardly surprising that, well, that things got a bit jumbled.'

'Yeah,' Dan said, meeting her gaze. 'Jumbled.' Cassie knew. Maybe not all of it, but she knew he was hiding something. And she was prepared to accept this.

'Another pint?' Cassie said, her bright tone signalling the topic was now closed.

'You trying to get me arrested?' Dan said with a laugh. 'I drove here, remember? Not all of us have friends in high places.'

'It's the low places where you want to be making pals. Let's just say I know a couple of newbies currently on patrol in an IRV. They're going to chauffeur me home at eleven. Then they'll be back here to collect you and your Volvo. And deliver you both to Shangri-La.'

'Summerlands,' Dan said. 'You know fine well what it's called.'

'I know it's a dump and the sooner you leave there the sooner...'

'The sooner I'll be able to move on with my life?'

'Something like that.'

'I'm fine, Cass. You need to quit worrying about me. I'm okay. I'm not great, but I'm okay. Better than I was.'

'Let's drink to small victories,' she said. 'You and me are going on a bender. And before you say anything, you can tell your inner school marm that yes, I will be ordering burger and chips to go with the next round, as I know what a lightweight you are when it comes to boozing on an empty stomach.'

Dan watched her cross toward the bar. Thankful he still had Cassie's friendship. That of all the losses, this was not one of them.

When Dan woke, it seemed he had been in the same position all night. For once, the sheets were not twisted round his limbs. He had a hangover, but it felt like harmless pain. Then he found himself recalling what Jay had said the other day. *I'm trying to face up to stuff.* He went through to the small kitchen with his phone. Brought up Cassie's name, set it to voicemail.

'Listen,' he said, flicking on the kettle, 'I meant to say last night that I'm okay with you seeing Lomax. I know I'm an entitled ass and you don't need my permission. But I wanted you to know I don't feel angry anymore. I'm trying to forgive him for what he did. For killing Beth. I really am trying. I still think he's a—' Dan put a hand on his chest, slowing his heart. 'It's a work in progress. Maybe I'll get there. Maybe I won't. But I wanted you to know that I am trying.' He pressed send.

Dan was finishing his coffee when a text came from Cassie. *I've had several goes and deleted them, because they were just crap ways of saying what I actually wanted to say, which is thank you. Thank you for trying and thanks for being my mate xxxC*

His mouth twitched. He had started the day with a positive act. He had let the stuff in his head spill out, sharing his inability to cope, his attempts to rectify. And it had been okay. When the smile came, it faltered, but it was there, and that meant something.

Dan left early for his 10 a.m. pickup in Attleborough, the usual time but a Thursday, because of the changed arrangements. He took the drive slowly, holding on to the precious calm inside. Another blue sky, bright sunlight, but less hostile. He parked the Volvo outside Mrs Bailey's. As he stared along the street, Dan tried to remember those stray glimpses of Ryan Taylor delivering papers. Dan had barely paid him any heed. Ryan only mattered after his murder. This was wrong. Dan could have smiled at Ryan when he passed the car on one of these occasions. A small acknowledgement of the man's existence.

The door on the pavement side opened and the car was filled with Mrs Bailey's voice. Dan headed to her son's care facility, while she talked about her morning so far, lost keys and her phone being out of charge.

Then Mrs Bailey broke off and said, 'I didn't want to put him there.'

Dan nodded, saying, 'Sometimes we don't have a choice.'

'Oscar's a gentle soul but he doesn't know his own strength. It's nice for him to have company his age. They do lots of activities. The staff are brilliant. He's so much happier, but I still feel guilty.'

Dan had been driving Mrs Bailey for six months now. To begin with there had been a plaster cast on her right wrist. She did not explain how it happened, but Dan had guessed the injury related to her son's recent move into residential care.

'I hope,' he said, waiting for the gates to open, 'that today's visit goes well. I'm glad your son's happy. That's a good thing.'

As Dan parked by the building she said, 'All this talk about me and I never asked about you. You look a bit tired. Everything okay?'

'I had a beer. Or two.'

Mrs Bailey laughed. 'Sounds like a great night.' She got out of the Volvo and approached the entrance. She seemed to brace herself before going inside.

Dan drove away, then paused for several minutes at the exit to the main road. Allowing himself to register that the pieces and patterns of his life had shifted. He flicked the indicator and turned right. Not left toward the house in Wymondham. Beth was no longer there, and the place did not belong to them anymore. The estate agent phoned yesterday to say someone had put in an offer and they were starting on the paperwork and how lucky he was to get a cash buyer not in a chain. The contract had yet to be signed, but as far as Dan was concerned the house was gone and that door was closed. Another of the losses.

He parked at the side of a field and checked his roster. No other bookings. Dan marked himself unavailable for the rest of the day, then he programmed the satnav for Beccles.

Sometimes we don't have a choice.

Chapter 35

Dan took his time on the path by the Waveney. The sky was fretted with small white clouds and there was shade among the trees. He walked back and forth, demanding his eyes absorb every detail. The way the water flowed, where the eddies were, the confluences, the areas of calm. He drew a diagram in his notebook, the river divided into sections and spread across five pages, with arrows showing the movement of the current. Dan was no artist, these were working sketches, a habit he had developed in the police service. To draw something required a different mode of looking. An intense seeing. An act that fed details into the subconscious, material to analyse, the mind so often secretive in its doings.

The boats were added, prow-shaped marks on the paper, alongside his pencil-lined bank. Each vessel assigned a number, and a list on another page, describing them. Photographs on his phone, also numbered. Methodical. A lot would have changed in twenty-one years, but Dan felt there was significance to be had from mapping the river and its contents. Somewhere in here were the features that had not changed, the messages still present in this fluid text. He knelt at the edge, dipped his hand in, closed his eyes. Thought about the particular words Mrs Faulkner had used.

The game, the water, the basket, floating away in the current. The basket floating away.

Next, Dan studied the other bank of the Waveney, a jumble of buildings, and he drew an approximation, filling their shapes with hatched lines to indicate solidity. Turning the pages as he walked along, his focus still on the far side, Dan added small boathouses and quays to his diagram, and any gaps in the straight embankments. Compiling photographs and videos. Then he returned to sit across from Chapel House. He examined the end of the garden, where it slid into the river. The brick walls created a square inlet, the water slowing. On a fresh sheet, he traced a plan of this at larger scale, with further details and scribbled comments, the location of the wooden jetty and the extent of the reeds. Dan strode to and fro, checking angles, reminded again how hidden that area was, the walls and brick pillars shielding it from passersby on the footpath but also the river.

Then he went back along the path, the Waveney flowing beside him at walking pace, both of them heading for the bridge. His observations were now of the places where debris gathered. This was less evident on the opposite side, water skimming past the vertical face of the embankments. But on Dan's side, at certain points the reeds and jetties made pockets at the edge of the river, watery cul-de-sacs full of sticks, petals, a plank, soft chunks of polystyrene, a plastic glove. When disturbed by the wake of a boat, these rose up and down in languid ripples. He took photographs, assigned each floating midden an identifying letter, and logged the positions on his map. Increased attention was paid to the stretch downriver from Chapel House, how the coalescing of detritus related to his arrows recording river flow, fast and slow. Dan considered the impact of the tide, which pulsed inland from the North Sea, changing the depths and contours.

And all the while, at intervals, boats passed him on the Waveney, heading upriver to Bungay, or wending toward the coast. At this time of the year, it was day trippers, holidaymakers, people who owned or hired an assortment of vessels, mostly motorised, some with cabins on top and sleeping accommodation. There was also traffic on the path, the occasional person with a dog. At one point, Dan looked up and saw a plastic bag floating past, down the centre of the river.

Then the time came to return to Summerlands. Sitting at the table in his caravan, only then did he admit what that trip to Beccles was about. Dan was allowing himself to believe the impossible. He leafed through his notebook, adding comments and question marks with a blue biro, circling areas. Then he glanced at the photos on his phone, the videos, reaching tentative conclusions. Dan got out OS 134, 144, 156 and spread them over the table, folding away the unwanted halves, flattening out the sections needed. Lining up edges, an awkward process, the map divisions slicing across the sinuous meander of the Waveney.

On his feet, looking down at the maps, Dan pinpointed the river's source in Redgrave and Lopham Fen, about fifteen minutes' drive from Summerlands. His finger travelled the Waveney's wavering blue length as it flowed through Diss, Mendham Marshes, the oxbow around Bungay. Then Geldeston Marshes, on through Beccles, skirting Oulton Broad and Lowestoft next. The water acquiring heft as it pushed past New Cut on the left – a canal leading to Reedham, the Yare, Norwich – the river ignoring this shortcut, intent instead on its own onward mission. Fattening into Breydon Water, like a bladder, and narrowing again for Great Yarmouth, where it headed south through the town, then swung past Gorleston lighthouse and out to the North Sea.

In the summer of 1999, Operation Hyacinth had put a stop to the transportation of drugs by boat. But Dan knew from experience that trafficking never really went away. The Waveney was an ideal conduit. Trade could have started up again the following year. Pulling the police file from the drawer, Dan turned to the section with statements by people who had been on the river the afternoon Felix disappeared. Checking the pages, knowing he had read something, a passing reference. Here it was. Steven Pryce, 62, owner of sailboat Belle Isle, when asked if he had seen anything unusual, reported a brief altercation that Wednesday near Geldeston Dyke with 'a pair of louts in a gin palace'. According to Pryce they were in their late teens. The male was at the helm of the cruiser. The female was in an inflatable dinghy, being towed behind. She had red hair and was 'sunbathing in a bikini'. Motorised boats were supposed to give way to sail. The cruiser cut across Pryce's sailboat, almost causing him to capsize. The witness had wanted it recorded in his statement that the youths were 'foreign' and 'high as kites'.

Dan swallowed. High as kites could signify drugs not alcohol. Foreign, what sort of foreign – how they spoke? Dan checked back through the reports. It seemed the male and female were never traced or identified. The incident had happened about three miles upriver from Chapel House at around 2.45 p.m. An inflatable dinghy would have placed the woman close to the surface of the water. Dan found himself recalling the pockets in the reeds, which he had seen only a few hours before, and how flotsam gathered there. He pictured again the plastic bag that had drifted past, in the middle of the river, air filling it like a balloon.

The game, the water, the basket, floating away in the current. An investigation relied on assumptions, on the interpretation of words, on names and labels, not all of them correct. Dan sent a text to Jay, asking if she would speak to her father. Find out if he could remember any details about 'the picnic basket'. Size and shape. Colour. What it was made of. Jay's reply came the following day. And as he stared at the description, Dan felt a tug on the thread of pathetic hope. Not broken. Still intact.

In between shifts for Hari, Dan spent hours online. Additional data on his phone package to supply the wifi on his laptop, multiple tabs open. His initial focus was on Operation Hyacinth, different news reports, unsure what he was looking for, but sensing this was the right direction. Dan established that the trafficking had been confined to Norfolk and Suffolk. But when business picked up again, after the lull in 1999, what if the network reached further? He jotted down everything he could remember from that conference in 2017 about Hanseatic criminality.

So much material to wade through, via lists of search terms, different cities and locations, date ranges, keeping a typed record of outcomes along with associated articles and website addresses. Dan ate meals with a fork, his other hand continuing to click on links, scrolling past maps, images, text, his eyes only seeing the bright rectangle of the screen, the rest of the caravan disappearing as darkness fell, his body evaporating too, and he was just a brain plugged into Google. On the occasions when he went to the shop or headed to his car, Mrs Faulkner seemed to sense that he wished to avoid her. The holding pattern meant they passed each other at distance, though never without Dan being aware.

On Friday 29th July he took time out for Ryan Taylor's funeral. Cassie had texted him the details. It was a simple ceremony in a crematorium, the first funeral he had attended since Beth's. Dan sat at the back, focused on his breathing. Up front there were five mourners, including the couple he had spoken to in the Lidl car park. When everyone filed out of the chapel at the end, the woman Tina looked at him and said a quiet thanks. That afternoon, Dan returned to his task, needing to block off the day's additional sorrow. He rechecked the OS maps, flicked through his notebook again, examined his drawings of the Waveney and the garden at Chapel House. Over the weekend, Dan reviewed the long document where he had listed his various online searches. He highlighted the possibilities in bold, put them in order of likelihood, but none of them were conclusive. All of them were wildly circumstantial.

Dan was on his way to the shop, Monday lunchtime, when Mrs Faulkner approached him. Voicing the silent message she had been broadcasting at him across the parched slopes and gravel paths of Summerlands, ever since that evening in her bungalow, a fortnight ago, when she told him her son was still alive.

'How's it going, Daniel?'

He could see her lips twitching with the urge say more. Hands like hooked claws, ready to grab his skull and shake it. She knew what Dan was up to. He had heeded her plea not to abandon Felix. The mutual knowledge almost palpable, a shared burden, unspoken, too painful to touch. After a minute he said, 'So far, nothing to report.'

Mrs Faulkner nodded, then walked away.

That evening Dan set off across the fields under a cloudless sky. Aware of the date, 1st August, new week, new month. A time of reckoning. At the door to the icehouse he stood for a while, thinking about the underground void. Then he made his way north, late sun slanting across his face. Dan sat on the dry grass and looked at the reservoir. Sensing himself on the brink of something but wanting to acknowledge where he had come from. Maybe he could find Felix. Maybe. On the other side of maybe, there was failure. A tremor disturbed the water, agitating the surface. Dan thought about John Strang. This was the man's tomb. Dan had tried to help him, but he did not do enough. And what he did do, was badly done. Giving him back the baby clothes, setting in motion his purposeful or accidental death.

A detective was meant to have all the answers. Dan failed. He did not save Strang. With a sigh, he knelt by the reservoir and immersed his hand. The chill meniscus circled his wrist. Words crowded his head, things he could say, apologies, explanations, and running through them all was Cassie's teasing accusation about his saviour complex. The what-might-have-beens did not matter anymore. Dan stroked his fingers slowly through the water. 'Rest in peace, John Strang.' Water shaping everything that had happened, pouring through the fissures and cracks, along the riverbeds, falling from the sky, seeping into the soil, and lying darkly underground, filling the stone sarcophagus in the icehouse. *Rest in peace*. As he lifted his hand from the reservoir, Dan felt a calmness spread through him. His own peace. His own acceptance of fallibility, the recognition that sometimes he lost his way. A lost detective could still help people. Not everyone but some. Some was better than none. Dan thought about Mrs Faulkner. Maybe he could. Maybe.

The tentative sense of resolve accompanied him to the caravan. Dan could do this if he did it now. His body felt briefly strong enough. From the depths of the wardrobe, he retrieved the thick plastic bag. Beth's belongings, her leavings. What she left behind the day she died. His hands reached into the bag and he spread the contents across the bed. Arranging them carefully, aware of his breathing. Her leather bag with the thin strap, her shoes, coat, scarf, jacket, blouse, skirt, underwear, tights. Patting and straightening, folding, making it neat. Dan had been through her things once before, the morning he came back from the morgue, his eyes barely seeing. He could remember ransacking the tangled pile of clothes, bra straps and sleeves and nylon legs all knotted together. His fingers had jammed into pockets and zipped pouches, but only finding old receipts, handfuls of coins, a few paracetamol, a comb, Beth's lipstick, wrenching at his heart, but nothing to explain what took her to Magdalen Street.

This time, the room bathed in twilight, Dan went through the items more slowly, in preparation. He did not want people walking about in the clothes Beth wore to her death. Dan would consign these to the sky, not a charity shop. But first the pockets had to be checked, all the compartments of her purse and handbag. A ritual and respectful examination, like a sacrament.

In the zipped end pocket of her bag, Dan found a small piece of fabric, heavy linen, the yellow of butter or sunlight. There was a strip of paper stapled to it, printed stationery for Upholstery Queen. He felt himself swaying as he read the address. Magdalen Street. Below this, Beth had written *Living room??*

Clutching the fabric in his hand, Dan fell onto her clothes, his face smothered in her belongings, her smell, and he cried great heaving sobs that pulled him apart. She had been choosing curtains for their new home. The last thing Beth did before she died, was done in hope.

In hope.

By the time his eyes were empty, it was dark outside. Dan gathered everything into the bag and sent a text to Thomas.

Then he walked to the workshop. The man seemed to know, from his face, that Dan did not want to explain. Thomas gave him the petrol can and box of matches, then left with a nod.

One by one, Dan laid the items into the galvanised bin, adding petrol as he went. He searched for something to say as he lit the match, but these were not her. They were not Beth. The flames reared up, engorged, and he put on the lid with its metal funnel. Watched the column of grey smoke rise into the charcoal sky. Dan tried to smile. He tried hard to smile. Beth had been dreaming of their new home when she died. She had been thinking happy thoughts. He would think them too, he would try to feel her happiness.

And then the words did come, all the unspokens that had been crowding his lips. As the fire burned, Dan told Beth he was glad she traced her father. He told her the house was sold. He told her she gave him strength every day. *Love you. Miss you.* Dan closed his eyes. When he opened them, the smoke had thinned, the fire was dying down. Ash and embers. As he walked away, Dan felt again that moment of balance, of wavering. Sensing himself on the brink of something.

The light was on at Mrs Faulkner's when he went past. And he thought about what hope meant for her. The possibility that was being kept alive by Dan's searches online. The chance of finding and holding on to a last thread of pathetic hope, stretching across the years, weaving through the water, along the Waveney, across the North Sea.

Three days later, Dan hit upon details of a drugs raid in Rotterdam. Conducted by officers of the Korps Nationale Politie on a large brick warehouse with boarded-up windows. 27th October 2001. A suspected cannabis farm in Hoogvliet, an area on the southern edge of the city, by the banks of the Oude Maas river. Dan pieced together information from Dutch websites accessed with translation software. Four people apprehended that night, but an exit via a cellar, connecting to the courtyard of a building at the rear, was missed in the preplanning of the operation. The entrance to this building was on a different street. CCTV, its footage grainy, had captured two people fleeing, possibly male and female, the latter clutching something.

A baby, in the early stages of hypothermia, was discovered next morning in the lobby of an apartment block. Male. Malnourished. Estimated at between four and six months old. When Dan first came upon this, he had stared at the screen for a full five minutes. His skin tingling. The child was thought to have been abandoned by the two fugitives. Formula milk and nappies were found at the warehouse. One of the four, detained during the raid, subsequently confirmed that a Dutch couple with a small baby had been living in the basement.

The man claimed not to know their names. But he said they were very young and the woman had red hair. In the following weeks repeated attempts, via appeals in the Dutch press and on TV, were made to trace the couple and reunite them with their baby. Then the trail went cold. As far as Dan could tell, the man and woman were never found. Nor was there further mention of the baby. If procedures matched those in the UK, the Dutch courts would have designated the child a ward of state. The result being he was taken into care.

Dan frowned, knowing he had reached a barrier. One that could not be breached, no matter how many hours he spent online. This could be Felix, but he had no way of verifying. Dan needed help. Not Cassie. They were back on good terms, but he had never spoken to her about Felix Faulkner. Cassie would insist on making it official, but Dan's investigation was private. The enquiries had to be discreet, a favour by someone with access to sealed records. He tried to recall the woman he met at the Hanseatic conference. What was her name? The delegate who slept in their spare room because of the hotel mix-up.

On the A140, near Tasburgh the following morning, two passengers in the rear, it came to him. *Ilse*. Ilse Timmerman. That afternoon, in the caravan, Dan went back online, searching various directories. Ilse appeared to be with the

Amsterdam division these days. He tracked down her work email, sent a message with his phone number, asking if she could call him. Not urgent, maybe this weekend if she had time. Dan had to make the request casual, nothing red-flagging it on the Politie server.

When Ilse Timmerman rang on Sunday, she was shocked to hear he had left the police service. 'What happened, Daniel? You were so passionate about your job.' He told her about Beth. Another shock. And then Dan explained why he had got in touch. She went silent.

'Ilse, I know this must seem like I'm trading on my tragedy in order to twist your arm into backchannelling something you don't want to do. You're perfectly at liberty to hang up right now. It's just there's someone I'm trying desperately to help. A friend. Who's been waiting twenty-one years to find out if her son is alive or dead.'

Another long pause, then she said, 'I'll see what I can do.'

Ilse came good on the favour. At 4.35 p.m. on Saturday 20th August, Dan was in the caravan when she rang with a name and address. Spelling each word. His hand shaking as he wrote them down. Then he checked the spelling, just to be sure. After the call ended, Dan folded the piece of paper and put it in a plain envelope. He felt lightheaded, trembling, ready to fly away. Needing to compose himself. A cold shower to bring him back to earth.

Thirty minutes later, Dan asked Mrs Faulkner if they could speak in private. The two of them walked to her bungalow, not uttering a word, the anticipation fizzing in the gap between them. He was acutely aware that what he was about to do could change everything for Mrs Faulkner. In the living room, Dan handed her the envelope, saying, 'This might be him. But I'm not making any promises. Only a DNA test can confirm it. Provided he agrees.'

Dan could not really remember what was said after that. The intensity of their exchange had been overwhelming. He managed to communicate the main points of his new version.

There had been a game on the riverbank involving Jack and Emily. But Felix was put into a coolbox not a wicker basket. An orange coolbox that stayed afloat. A cruiser went by, towing a dinghy. A male and female 'rescued' Felix. Took him across the North Sea to Rotterdam. Attempted to be parents for the next few months, after which he went into care. Dan was sparing with the details. Mrs Faulkner hugged him and laughed and cried, never letting go of the piece of paper, reading it again and again. At one point she pushed him to arm's length and peered into his face. *You believe me now, Daniel?*

When Dan left the bungalow, a burst of energy surged through him. He vaulted the garden gate, but landed awkwardly, the sky rushing away from him. Next moment Dan was flat on his back. Laughing so much his belly ached. Climbing to his feet, winded but elated. Walking through the dusk, he spotted the queue of people. The chip van visited Summerlands every Saturday in the holidays, but Dan felt it was there especially for him. Haddock and chips, extra sauce, damp paper smell. Sitting in his caravan, crunching the batter, dipping the chips in salt. And now he was full, relishing the sensation. Dan eyed his phone on the Formica table. Why not? He wiped his fingers on his thighs then picked it up. Scrolled through the contacts list. Jay answered after three rings.

'Hi, it's Dan here.'

'Mr Detective,' she said, teasing him.

'That's the one. Have you got a moment? I don't wish to disturb you if you're...'

'Now's fine.'

'I wanted to let you know,' he said, 'that I've finished my enquiries.'

There was silence on the other end. Then Jay said, 'Did you find out what happened to the baby?'

'Yes, I think so. It's not conclusive yet.'

'Did it help? The stuff my father remembered?'

'Very much so,' Dan said, gripping the phone.

'My father wasn't involved in any way. With the baby's disappearance.'

'No. He had nothing to do with it. I'm sorry for all the worry this has caused you. I didn't mean to...'

'I know Dad could never do such a thing. But the tea towels and the coolbox. They were important.'

'Yes, the children—'

'If the boy and girl had something to do with it, I don't want to know. Does that make me a coward?'

'Not in my book,' Dan said. 'But there's good news. Potentially. I think I may have found him.'

'What – Felix is alive?'

'Yes, if it's really him. I'm fairly certain it is.'

'Have you seen him?' Jay said.

'No, but I think I've located where he ended up.'

'Is he in a bad way?'

'I don't know yet,' Dan said. 'My hope is he's doing okay.'

'But you've found him.'

'Yes, I believe I have.'

'What are you, some kind of miracle worker?'

Dan heard her laughing. 'Not really,' he said, smiling at the phone. 'Just very persistent.'

'Will I be reading about this in the news?'

'I don't think so. The mother doesn't want police involved. Or the media.'

'I'm glad,' Jay said. 'I'm not sure my father could handle it. People think he's mad. I do too, often enough. But he just thinks differently. I'm super happy you've found Felix. And don't worry, I won't say anything to anyone. That's so cool, Dan. You did a great thing. Thanks for calling. I better—'

'Wait, sorry.' He was losing her.

'Yes?' she said.

'Now that my investigation's over, there's something I've been meaning to...'

It had been so long, Dan could not remember how to do this.

'I'm still here,' Jay said. 'You seemed to stop mid-sentence.'

His heart was pounding. 'If I phoned you some time and asked you for a drink, would that be something you might consider?'

'You mean like a date?'

'Yes, a date,' Dan said. 'I'd like that.'

Her silence made him wince, then she said, 'This is really awkward? I've just started seeing someone. We were at school together.'

'Oh, I'm sorry. I mean, I'm sorry for asking.'

'No worries,' Jay said. 'How were you to know? I'm glad you were able to solve your case. I'm glad the woman found her son. Goodbye, Detective Dan. Take care of yourself.'

The line went dead.

He laughed and shook his head. It was worth a try. His cheeks burned with embarrassment, but that was okay. Nothing fatal.

Pulling the curtain aside, Dan looked out the window. Thinking about the future. It was a new sensation, the idea of planning what he might do. He would stay at Summerlands for now. He would carry on working as a taxi driver. This was no different to the status quo, and yet he was making these decisions not letting them happen. That was a good thing. There were good things in this world. There was happy in between the sad.

Dan felt a thread of hope tugging at his heart.

Epilogue

In early October, Alice Faulkner travelled to the Netherlands to be reunited with her son. His name was Lars de Vries. He lived in Groningen and was a student at the university there. She and Lars had spoken on the phone several times. He had offered to do a video call, but Mrs Faulkner asked him to wait. She wanted to see him with her own eyes. Mrs Faulkner told Dan these things in giddy bursts. Saying how lovely Lars was, warm, curious, keen to meet, asking about her life, talking about his. She said his English was perfect and he had taught her a few words of Dutch.

Moeder. Zoon.

Dan drove Mrs Faulkner to the airport. She sat in the passenger seat, a friend not a customer. A friendship forged from grief and love, anointed by survival. They barely spoke on the way to Stansted. Dan had a sense of her stillness next to him, like a Sunday School child, hands folded in her lap. Eyes gazing ahead, through the windscreen.

When he pulled in at the drop-off zone, she said, 'I'm not sure I can manage this on my own. I feel strangely nervous. Come with me, Daniel, we can get you a last-minute flight. Please say you'll come.'

Dan looked at her with a huge smile. 'Mrs Faulkner. You are the strongest person I have ever met. Are you seriously asking me if I think you're going to manage this?'

Then the two of them burst out laughing, filling the car with pure joy.

'Besides,' Dan said, regaining his breath, 'you won't be on your own. You'll be with your son.'

'*Yes.*' Triumphant. 'Can you believe it? Lars, I have a son called Lars.'

Dan watched Mrs Faulkner walk away, across the busy pavement, through the crowds and queues. Her trajectory was unwavering, gilded by the early evening light.

Acknowledgements

I will be forever grateful to Story Machine for publishing my debut novel, and I am so lucky to have Elizabeth Lewis Williams as my brilliant and insightful editor. I would also like to thank Natty Peterkin for his beautiful and evocative cover design, and Sarah Bower for her excellent suggestions on an early draft of the novel. On its journey to publication, *The Lost Detective* has had many kind advocates, and I would like to thank all my readers and supporters, including Emma, Emma, Peter, Honor, Sally and Henry. My writing life has been enriched by the University of East Anglia and the School of Literature, Drama, and Creative Writing; I have been fortunate to meet and spend time with so many inspiring authors who have either taught or studied there. The writing community is very generous, and I really appreciate the authors who read digital proofs of my novel and kindly offered quotes for publication. Huge thanks also go to Caroline Ambrose and everyone involved in the Bath Novel Award; when *The Lost Detective* was shortlisted, this gave me the boost to keep going. I owe my gratitude to the Brecks too, where I have walked and explored and imagined the world contained in my novel. You will encounter places that are real in *The Lost Detective*, but you will also find places I invented, and which only exist here on these pages. There are so many words in a novel, and so many variations on those words, as one writes, and rewrites, and revises, and reshapes, and edits. None of this would have been possible without the love and support of my darling husband Martin and our wonderful children Toby, Eddie, Ethan, Imogen, and their lovely partners. I would like to end with an extra thank you to my husband. He has read this novel multiple times, discussed it on many a walk, and given me lots of fantastic advice and detailed comments, all of which have helped me refine and develop it. Throughout all this, Martin has never stopped being enthusiastic about *The Lost Detective* and he has been there for me, every step of the way!